DEAD RED HEART

Also edited by Russell B. Farr

DEAD RED HEART

AUSTRALIAN VAMPIRE TALES

EDITED BY
RUSSELL B. FARR

T꙳
ᵽ꙳ Ticonderoga
publications

for

Liz

— constantly putting life into my red heart

Dead Red Heart edited by Russell B. Farr

Published by Ticonderoga Publications

Designed and edited by Russell B. Farr
Typeset in Sabon and Bernhard Modern

A Cataloging-in-Publications entry for this title is available from the National Library of Australia.

ISBN   978–0–9807813–0–4 (hardcover)
       978–0–9807813–1–1 (trade paperback)
       978–1–921857–99–7 (ebook)

Ticonderoga Publications
PO Box 29 Greenwood
Western Australia 6924

www.ticonderogapublications.com

10 9 8 7 6 5 4 3 2 1

I'd like to thank all of the writers involved: Martin, Shona, Angela, Jeremy, Chris, Alan, Felicity, Yvonne, Patty, Manda, Marty, Zmon, Jodi, Jane, Joanna, Damon, Jen, Jay, Jason, Joanne, Sonia, Tracie, Pete, George, Kathryn, Ray, Helen, Donna, Jacob, Anne, Lisa, Penny, Devin, Chuck, Andrew, Lezli, Daniel, Carol, Kaaron. I never meant this book to be so big, but there were so many stories I couldn't say no to. Thanks for your patience, enthusiasm and I hope you've reinforced your bookshelves! Thanks also to the editors in whose footsteps I have been able to follow (and whose boots I am yet to fill): Peter McNamara, Jonathan Strahan, Ellen Datlow and Bill Congreve. And to those folk who probably always knew I'd one day edit a big book of vampire stories: Mel, Phil, Al, Jody, Steph, Kate and Liz.

Thanks also to those who inspire, nurture and support independent creativity and talent.

CONTENTS

DRACULA IN MIRRORSHADES

(AND ZINC CREAM)

Numerous travel writers have taken the time to document the natural challenges to be found in Australia. Firstly there are all the varieties of poisonous animals: snakes, spiders, fish and even jellyfish. There's the deserts that only the most intrepid chose to brave. There are the extremes of weather, I'm writing this in early autumn, where it has been over 32 degrees for as long as anyone can remember and rain is barely a memory. And I don't live in the exceptionally dry parts.

So what does a land like Australia have that would appeal to the average vampire? At first glimpse, not too much. The country is blessed by an abundance of sunshine, generations of European migrants have found soil that supports large crops of garlic, and outside of major population centres necks are few and far between. As the 33 stories to follow show, Australia is a large and diverse country, and as you would expect in a multicultural country, not all vampires are alike. Some have adapted to Australia's sun; other vampires are content to follow the traditions of their European heritage; and there is also an indigenous vampire-like being from some Australian Aboriginal legends. The last one excites me a lot—before I started this adventure I didn't know of the *Yarama'yhawho* (or little red man), and was driven into a research frenzy when this intriguing creature appeared in three stories.

I'm impressed by the Australianness captured in these stories. While each story is at its simplest, a bloody good tale writers have consciously or subconsciously used vampires to explore the real Australian culture and psyche. You won't find any fakery like shrimps on the barbie, Fosters-swilling or travelling in kangaroo pounches. Whether it's the bush, suburban sprawl, climate, iconic moments of history, multiculturalism, migration, environmentalism or the beach. Australia is a big, diverse island and it shows in these tales.

Welcome to the extremes of Australia's climate and geography: from urban tales in the Mediterranean-climed south, to the cyclone-prone city of Darwin; tropical rainforests of Queensland to the very cool temperate climate of Tasmania. And, of course, the hot, arid centre.

These stories run the length of Australia's past, present and future. From early colonial days, through the goldrushes and bushrangers; through the World Wars, into the present and beyond. For such a young/old country, Australia has a wonderfully vibrant history that some of these stories have tapped into. Ned Kelly appears twice; the Victorian gold rushes, convict fleets and Cyclone Tracy all provide fertile settings.

We can't forget Australia's cultural leanings, either. What could be more Aussie than a pie and sauce and vampires at the footy? Or nosferatu at the beach? Or the good old esky filled with . . . I'll let you discover that for yourself.

Some might find a few of these stories a little rough around the edges. If they were on the menu, rustic might be an apt description. To me these are fine examples of the rough and ready nature of the Aussie yarn: frank, earnest and engaging in a natural voice.

These tales seek, above all, to entertain. I think that vampire stories are one of those wonderful, guilty pleasures. I've heard it said that vampires are so last year, and that there's nothing new under the sun when it comes to telling their stories. Regardless of the this, it's plain to see that that we still love vampires! Dark and brooding, violent and cruel, insatiable femme fatales or victims of circumstance, there is something about them that we find irresistible.

This anthology amply illustrates that Australia possesses more fertile imaginations than fertile soil. Turn the page and you'll be transported into a series of incredible environments and situations— as the almost-never sung second verse of Australia's national anthem says, "For those who've come across the seas, we've boundless plains to share". The writers of the words that follow invite you to share in their boundless visions of vampires in the antipodes.

And as the lyrics would say in "Down Under" (the Little Red Men at Work version, of course): "dare to come to land down under, where blood is fresh and vampires plunder . . ."

RUSSELL B. FARR
MARCH 2011

DEAD RED HEART

THE TIDE

MARTIN LIVINGS WITH ALAN BAXTER, FELICITY DOWKER, PATTY JANSEN, DEVIN JEYATHURAI, CHUCK MCKENZIE, ANDREW J. MCKIERNAN, LEZLI ROBYN, DANIEL I. RUSSELL, CAROL RYLES AND KAARON WARREN

ILLEGAL REFUGEE BOAT EXPLODES OFF WA COAST, 27 KILLED.

Immigration officials and the Australian Navy have confirmed that a boat that exploded off the WA coast north of Broome yesterday was smuggling a number of asylum seekers.

The explosion occurred when Australian Navy officers opened the hold of the boat at approximately . . .

. . . two officers who had boarded the boat and all the asylum seekers were killed instantly, 27 in all. Another eight crew have been rushed to Darwin Hospital with second and third degree burns, including the captain of the boat, reportedly an Indonesian national. Investigations continue into causes for the explosion . . .

VAMPIRES!

Boatload of explosive bloodsuckers and more are already on their way!

In a stunning revelation, the Australian Federal Police and Immigration officials have confirmed that the boat that exploded off our coast three days ago was not booby-trapped, but was in fact carrying VAMPIRES to our shores.

The press conference held this morning confirmed what had already been a matter of some speculation on many radio talkback shows, including 2GB's breakfast show. The explosion occurred when Australian Navy officers opened the hold of the boat at approximately . . .

. . . occurred when officers opened the hold of the boat, allowing the sunlight to strike the hidden illegals. The vampires immediately burst into flames, causing nearby fuel canisters to explode, killing the two officers.

Officials have also confirmed that at least three more vessels are currently on their way from Indonesia, all of which bear the hallmarks of carrying more vampires. "Their holds are closed tight," reported one anonymous source who claims to have flown over them in his helicopter.

"BURN IN HELL"
ARCHBISHOP'S BLUNT MESSAGE FOR THE UNDEAD REFUGEES

Sydney's Archbishop, Frank Popper, has divided popular opinion with his recent outburst on the vampire immigration debacle. His polarising opinion comes on the back of recent revelations that a multi-faith committee is planning a large protest march, co-ordinated through all the capital cities, to demand vampire immigration be blocked immediately.

"Vampires are not welcome in Australia," the Archbishop declared yesterday. "They are abominations in God's eyes and should not be welcomed as citizens. These creatures are dead, defying God's order. They burn in sunlight and that's all the proof we need that God abhors them. Let them burn in Hell!"

Archbishop Popper's opinions are shared by a large number of Australia's religious leaders, it would appear . . .

. . . in record numbers.

Citizens in defence of vampires have derided the Archbishop's position. "If God abhors vampires so much, why did he create them? Didn't God create everything?" asked Tyrone Brown, president of the Give Vamps A Chance organisation. "Didn't Jesus die and then rise again? If anything, vampires are closer to Christ than the Archbishop from that point of view," he added. Brown defended vampires, claiming that they may be dead, but they're still people and deserve our respect and equality in society.

The Archbishop expressed outrage at people standing up for vampires. "They're a travesty!" he declared. "They are the spawn of Satan and anyone defending them is doing the Devil's work for him!"

"OUR UNLIVES ARE IN DANGER," VAMPIRE ILLEGALS CLAIM.

DARWIN—speaking from detention, one desperate vampire asylum seeker has claimed they face torture and "true death" in their homeland.

"The humans in our country, they despise us," the vampire, who asked to be identified only as Vlad, told this reporter. "They cling to the old ways, the old superstitions. Many thousands of us have been destroyed at their hands. It is simply not safe there for us."

The vampires have fled their homes in Eastern Europe, where their kind has existed for thousands of years. The first boats arrived off our shores over a month ago, when the infamous explosion caught both the Navy and Immigration officials by surprise . . .

. . . the wrath of anti-immigration groups.

"What we're saying is that, since the vampires are not technically human beings, and nor are they alive, that granting them asylum on the grounds of danger to their existence is simply ludicrous," one member told us.

"There are enough hardships already for decent, human Australians, without having to deal with these undead monsters."

These claims are being investigated by a new team of Immigration officials who have been put in charge of assessing the Romanian vampires claims for asylum.

MAYOR LAUNCHES LARGEST OUTDOOR SUNPROOFED AREA IN THE SOUTHERN HEMISPHERE

To a large crowd of human and vampire listeners, Mayor Tom Carelli yesterday introduced designer Genie Marlo as the person who brought change to Kangaroo Island. Ms Marlo gave the following speech:

"When I first came to Kangaroo Island, I expected a pleasant walk from my hotel to Vivonne Bay. For the most part it was lovely. However, my feet quickly became crusted with a grey powder. There was a slight greasiness about the dust and was about to bring a finger to mouth to taste it when I heard a scream.

I was being watched by a group of children and it was one of the older girls who'd screamed.

"Don't eat them!" she said.

"Them? Whatever do you mean?" But they scattered.

You all know what I'm talking about. I'm talking about the time some misguided Pied Piper led the younger vampires out into the sun and they disintegrated into sad piles on the ground.

They are calling him the Pied Piper, but truly he is a killer. I was inspired by this to make 'outside' safe for our vampire friends.

And I have done so.

It was your collective guilt which allowed us to do this sunproofing. I think that's a good thing. And so do they.

The sunproofing of the island is now complete. Some may say too little too late, but at least we have done something.

Well may we return to dust, but not before our appointed hour."

Ms Marlo's speech ended abruptly at this point and there is no record of further words.

In other news, this paper, previously known as the *Kangaroo Island Daily Bulletin*, will now be known as the *Nightly News*.

"INHUMAN, UNCLEAN DEMONS" RELIGIOUS BACKLASH AGAINST
THE INCREASING VAMPIRE POPULATION

God's Shining Sun, the multi-faith committee against growing vampire immigration, has stepped up its campaign. Imam Agri Hilaly and Rabbi Seth Goldstein have spoken out today about the "inhuman, unclean demons" and the toll they're taking on modern society.

"We don't agree on everything," Hilaly said yesterday, "but we most certainly agree on this."

"It's unacceptable that the government is moving to grant rights to vampires equal to the living," Goldstein said. "Vampires are dead, they feed on the blood of the living and have no place in modern society. We should not have to stand for these politically correct panderings to these atrocities in God's eyes. It's a ridiculous state of affairs . . .

. . . together."

Police are calling for calm and a peaceful march on Sunday, when tens of thousands are expected to gather in every capital city to march against vampire rights. Sydney's Mayor has called the response "unprecedented". She added, "We've never seen anything like this before, which is to be expected when so many disparate groups join forces in a common cause."

Ethicist Solomon Grady said, "It's a real shame that the first time we see anything even resembling an interfaith agreement, it's hate that makes it happen. Vampires are certainly a challenging group for people to integrate into their daily lives, but calling for their eradication is akin to the Holocaust or years of African slavery. Humanity will look back on this period of history with shame and embarrassment."

When told of Grady's words, Rabbi Goldstein said, "This atheist seems to be missing the point. If something isn't done about this unholy epidemic now, there won't be any humanity left to look back!"

BLOOD-SUCKING FREAKS!

Dear Editor,

I'm sick and tired of all these people trying to defend the rights of vampires. These things are not people. They're walking corpses, an abomination to nature, and have no rights. Would we grant human rights to a dead body in the ground? Of course not. So why should we consider rights for dead bodies above ground?

These bloodsucking freaks are nothing but a parasite. We don't stand for malaria and do all we can to eradicate it. We wiped out smallpox. The same needs to be done for vampires. Instead of liberal latte-sippers whining on about vampire rights, we should all be reading them the last rites. Take up your cross and holy water, open your house to sunlight, buy UV lamps for protection at night, or this latest scourge will claim your life too.

—NAME WITHHELD

(This is not the view of this paper or its staff and we would like to remind readers that killing vampires is still considered murder under current law—Editor)

AUSSIE JOBS DRAINED BY VAMPS: REPORT

Almost all the new jobs created in Australia in the last three years have gone to vampire workers, official figures released today show.

Of the 600 thousand jobs created since 2007, the vast majority went to the fanged.

At the same time the number of unfanged workers in employment fell by 62,000.

Pressure group Nightwatch, which closely analysed Government data said nearly half a million jobs went to the living dead. This goes against existing predictions.

Nightwatch chairman Anthony V. Helsing said: "From a national point of view this means that the undead/living population ratio is moving into balance as we have been predicting, but from the point of view of Aussie workers, the damage has already been done."

The figures are further evidence of the changing demographics within Australian society, and some claim that we are on the road to ruin.

At a time when jobs of almost all kinds are at a premium, this is a blow that the Aussie workforce cannot afford. Government predictions did include rising vamployment, particularly for after-hours jobs, but the magnitude of the shift is still surprising.

Labour minister Daniel Grieves said "This comes as somewhat of a shock—we were aware that some jobs were uniquely suited to our vamp constituents, but we didn't realise that they were taking waking jobs, too."

There is also growing civic dissatisfaction with the number of vamps working in night-time or after-hours jobs.

"I can't buy petrol after 5pm or go to the 24-hour supermarket without coming face to face with one of those toothy bastards," said Ms Ellen Christofori. "An old woman like me can't be expected to deal with them. They're scary, and I can't understand what they're saying—it's the fangs, you know."

VAMPIRE LUCY BRAND TO BE GRANTED CITIZENSHIP

Vampire immigrant Lucy Brand will officially be granted Australian citizenship today in the wake of vigorous opposition from both God's Shining Sun and the newer Live Nation Party.

The British-born vampire will be sworn in during a special midnight conferral ceremony.

Orphaned in London after her human parents were transported to Australia for thievery, Brand was turned vampire at the age of ten in 1790.

"My citizenship is a dream come true," she said from her basement dayroom.

"At last I can reconnect with so many of my parents' descendants."

Brand has insisted that her ties with the country run deeper than those of most living Australians.

Brand's lawyers, who used DNA tests to confirm her family ties with at least five thousand living Australians, see this as a major coup for vampire refugees. "Like it or not, many of us are their living descendants.

"Vampires should not be discriminated against, regardless of their skin temperature or dietary preferences."

Live Nation Party Leader, Tonya Cookson, defended her stance by saying, "This is not about bloodlines, it's about blood. If we didn't have vampires, we would not be wasting money on promoting anaemia awareness and fang hygiene. We would not have to scrap daylight saving."

Cookson refuses to submit to DNA testing.

KILLING HUMANS? FINE!
VAMPIRE TOURISM GUIDE CONDONES MURDER.

An instructional guide allegedly sent to its members by the Friendly Australian Nosferatian Group, or FANG, for acclimating Vampires, has been unearthed yesterday by a scared, newly-turned vampire, "Alice" [true name withheld]. Its alarming contents raise further concerns as to the validity of vampires' claims that they have evolved past the need to indulge in their predatory instincts, and begs us to ask the question: Are we truly safe?

Readers can make up their own minds.

VAMPIRE SURVIVAL IN THE AUSTRALIAN OUTBACK: 5 BASIC TIPS

First of all, the surest way to survive the Outback is to not go there at all. Why do you think 85% of humans live along the coastline in Australia?

Think about it.

However, for those of our ranks who find it necessary to traverse the red heart of Australia, here are five key points to remember:

1. Travel by moonlight. It's easy to get lost in the desert, even with our excellent night vision. There are no night-time predators that are a threat to us. I know you've heard the stories of Weredingos, but these are just silly myths designed to frighten you, as are Dropbears. Use the moon to see clearly.

2. Daytime Burials. During the daylight hours bury yourself in the outback soil. Yes, it's a crude method of sleep we grew out of over an eon ago, but the soil insulates against the searing heat of the day, and studies have also discovered the high concentration of iron is great for moisturising our complexion.

3. Stay cool. Do not sit around evening fires with humans, toasting marshmallows and swapping undead stories, just to fit in. You hate fire. And fire loves you.

4. Hands off snakey. Aussie snakes are NOT akin to Vampires, despite their impressive looking fangs and elegance in motion. You should avoid your fascination for them at all costs. Contrary to propaganda, they would not make a suitable pet. Cold-blooded animals and the undead simply do not mix. Even though the most poisonous of them all can't kill a vampire, they can make you seriously ill. Stick to arachnids. They are easier to transport, and take minimal care.

5. Provisions. In case, for some unforeseen reason, you ARE exposed to the harsh elements of desert life, it always pays to have at least one human travel companion with you during all forays into the Outback.

In instances of severe dehydration and heat stroke the active enzymes in fresh blood could be a lifesaver. However, we severely caution against the urge to drain all available blood—no matter how fevered and thirsty you are. The humans seem to frown upon that, and it could affect public relations. (Point in reference: the Sahara Desert Bloodbath. It took us several years to clear up that little misunderstanding.)

If a complete draining cannot be avoided, the Outback is full of places where a body can be buried and never see the light of day again. Please use common sense, and your vampiric-honed skills, to bury any used vessel as far away from human outposts or public roads as possible, eradicating all traces of human DNA above ground to avoid detection.

Feel free to contact FANG. if you have any questions or are seeking further advice.

A spokesperson for FANG has denied the instructional guide originated from their office, although "Alice" reports that it was a part of her Welcome Pack when she became a member. Further investigation will be conducted before the validity of her claim can be proven, as Alice's mental state is considerably unstable due to the recent nature of her turning. We will update our readers when more evidence comes to hand.

VAMPIRES FIGHT OVER PERTH'S 'EASY STREET'

Violence erupted in Perth last night as tensions between vampire gangs broke out once more.

Already known for its 'lively nightlife', the suburb of Northbridge has seen its fair share of spilled blood. Conflicts between police and drinkers have forced the licensing laws to be reviewed for the second time this year.

However, last night saw police tackling a potentially greater threat; that of the rising vampire population residing in Western Australia.

"People don't realise," said Sergeant Hartnett of Perth Police. "The vampire gangs call Northbridge 'easy street' or 'the meat market' because of the easy kills, and this makes it a prize territory for the gangs. The message is not getting through: If you're out for a drink, stay in a group and stay in a UV lighted area."

Revellers enjoyed last night's clash, dancing in the plumes of garlic tear gas and forming rudimentary crucifixes with empty bottles, which were later used in brawls.

"I didn't even see any vampires," said one drunken partygoer.

While the vampire gangs are seen as a threat, alcohol related incidents still outnumber neck assaults. Some people have even suggested the vampirism can "balance the problem".

NIGHT SHIFT
VAMPIRES CLAIM AFTER-HOURS JOBS

We have all met the pale-faced, dead-eyed chap who works the night-shift at your local 24 hour convenience store. He stands, wan and corpse-like behind the counter, serving out red slushies and cigarettes. And, as he tells you the price, his breath rushes over you like something that died a week or two ago.

Well, that poor university student might soon be out of a job as the new wave of Vampire immigrants offer to work later for less. Union bosses and some politicians argue that Vampires are taking the jobs of low income earners and students struggling to meet HECS debts and deal with rising living costs.

But, it is not only at the 7-Eleven and the late night McDonalds drive-thru that you can expect to see these hard working fanged-foreigners. Vampires are also happy to take the jobs nobody else wants. Bus drivers on midnight routes, selling grog at all-night liquor stores, taxi-drivers, and even answering phones at non-outsourced call centres. Surely, that has to be good for the economy and for employment figures no matter who is behind the wheel or the till?

Not according to worker's rights groups and the plague of talk-back DJs currently stirring up a storm on the airwaves. According to them, Vampires are not yet entitled to full worker's rights and nor are they covered by WorkCover laws. Meanwhile the politicians argue ad nauseam over definitions and refuse to offer a clarification on the laws, leaving many already employed Vampires in a limbo of uncertainty.

RED CROSS URGENT DONATION CALL
NEW NATIONAL "FOOD BANK" ANNOUNCEMENT

Although the scientific evidence for Human to Vampire disease transmission is still not definitive, the Australian Red Cross are acting quickly to stop a possible epidemic of diseases among our new immigrant population.

Their announcement today of a new, nationwide 'Food Bank' initiative is the first step in an effort to stem what they see as an inevitable disaster for the health of the nation's newest immigrants.

"Our Blood Banks across Australia, and especially those in major city centres, will be gearing up to supply fresh food-grade blood to registered vampires on a rationed basis.

"At first there will be a small charge but we hope that future health initiatives by the Federal Government will assist in subsidising these costs," a spokesperson announced today at a press conference.

"The science is still open to peer-review, but preliminary results show a strong possibility that some diseases—especially those of a sexually transmissible nature—can almost certainly pass from human to vampire and back again. There is already a growing trade within the sex industry to offer blood-letting as a new service, and this is a very high-risk area. By making clean, food-grade blood available at a very low cost, we hope to stem a possible epidemic of these diseases among both populations."

The announcement, and the Red Cross's call for urgent donations to help start the project, have been met with much protest. Lobby groups say the organisation is forgetting its main role of saving human lives, and that vampires do not count as 'lives' nor do they count as 'human'.

The Red Cross spokesperson countered, saying, "We have a strong responsibility to remain impartial and neutral in regards to nationality, race, religion and political beliefs. The actions we take remain focused on the health of the nation and, in these changing times, we have to become more than just a humanitarian organisation."

SUBURB OF THE NIGHT

Our reporter, Ed Garrett, ventures into the neighbourhood that few humans have dared to enter, and finds that, perhaps surprisingly, the residents are more human than not.

At first glance, Harker Road looks much the same as any other Melbourne suburban street; houses, mailboxes, a nice park with a playground at one end, a corner shop.

But then, when you look again, you notice the little differences. There are no open windows here; all entrances to the houses are sealed tight against the day. And when I arrived on Harker Road, at around six in the evening, the sun not yet below the horizon, there was barely a soul around. The park is empty, the playground unused.

So I sat and waited for this new and unique neighbourhood to awaken.

Once the sun went down, one by one, windows were unsealed, doors opened, and Melbourne's vampire community, for want of a better word, comes to life. Within half an hour of sunset, I saw these residents gathering their mail, heading off to their night jobs, even playing the park. There was an odd age demographic here; vampires reproduce by "turning" a willing human, so the age of a vampire is not readily apparent by their physical appearance. But if the appearance of the family unit is somewhat different to what we're familiar with, their activities and behaviour towards one another is, quite frankly, entirely human.

"Mind the traffic," a young-looking woman called out to another vampire of similar appearance, and the note of motherly concern in her accented voice . . .

... is simply another neighbourhood in what is already a culturally diverse city. The residents of Harker Road might sleep during the day and only come out at night, but that doesn't make them much different to many human shift workers or party animals. The vampires survive on different food to us, yes, a food that we might find revolting, but the market for pig's blood has boosted the city's butchering trade, and really, this dietary requirement is not that much more exotic than halal or kosher foods. In short, Harker Road represents a more tolerant approach to human/vampire relations, one that, for now, is surprisingly successful.

PERSONALS

Mature woman seeks vampire, age 20–500, for sexual experimentation. Don't worry, I won't bite, but I certainly hope you will!
    Box 2715

Man, 40s, seeking a beautiful young-looking vampiress to show me the world of darkness! If you like me, please turn me, and I'll be yours forever. Non-smoker.
    Box 6243

Vampire, 800, seeks young men for sensual feeding. Will pay handsomely to be your sugar glider!
    Box 1903

VAMPIRE ACTIVIST NAMED AUSTRALIAN OF THE YEAR

CANBERRA—The Australia Day Council has named the well-known and liked vampire activist Viktor Albescu as Australian of the Year.

It is the first time that this honour has befallen a vampire, and was given in recognition of Albescu's many contributions both to local community safety programs and the cause of vampire rights in this country.

Mr Albescu came to Australia as one of the first refugees to arrive in the so-called "blood boats" four years ago. Initially, adapting to life in Australia was hard for Viktor. "I was turned almost half a century ago, when I was eighteen," he told this reporter, "so I still look like a young adult." It seems that this made it difficult to fit in; his apparent peers were all interested in going to the beach, lifesaving and surfing, daytime cricket and football, all activities necessarily off-limits to him. After many failed attempts to fit into his community, he finally obtained a job as security guard for a well-known night club in Oxford Street, Paddington. He first came to the attention of local authorities when the crime rate in the immediate area fell dramatically within months of his employment. During his time with the club, Mr Albescu has intervened in countless fights and deterred criminal elements from visiting the club. The neighbourhood, once best known as black spot, is now famed as a safe and family-friendly area of Sydney.

"He's great," says club owner Rico Giuliani. "We should give them a go, as the Australians did for my parents when they came to Australia."

Additionally, Mr Albescu has worked tirelessly in the wider community to promote vampire-human relations, setting up outreach programs and hosting numerous information evenings to allow both races to get to know one another on a more personal level. "Vampires are excellent to have on your table at a quiz night," he has pointed out, "as many of them are so old that questions about history are a doddle for them."

The Prime Minister said of Albescu, "he is the perfect example of the good, decent Australian vampire, and a role model not just for other vampires, but for us all."

In honour of Mr Albescu's sensitivities, the award ceremony will be held at night.

SUMMER BAYING FOR BLOOD!
FIRST VAMPIRE ACTOR TO JOIN THE CAST OF *HOME AND AWAY*

There's a new girl in Summer Bay. That's nothing out of the ordinary on long-running and much-loved Australian soapie *Home and Away*, which thrives on fresh blood . . . except that the Bay's latest arrival thrives on blood, too.

While alive, Sharon "Shazza" Bowgenne trod the boards with the Bell Shakespeare Company for several years, and since becoming nosferatu, she has appeared in advertisements for Fangtastic Toothpaste and No-Explode Sun block, among many others, before getting her fangs in the door at Summer Bay, playing kooky coroner Hemo Globe.

"I just kept trying, and finally it was that perfect combination of right place, right time," Shazza says, sipping on a bottle of cola-flavoured carbonated cow's blood, her long talons clinking against the glass. "It was that simple—persistence, hard work, and talent really can overcome anything, even rigor mortis."

Shazza is reluctant to comment on how long she's likely to stay in the Bay, saying only that she's got a lot of acting years left in her. Given a vampire's average lifespan of, well, forever, and that she'll never look any older, there's no arguing with Shazza's professional staying power.

Nobody could possibly claim Shazza has bitten off more than she can chew.

SHINING SUN EXTINGUISHED

The leaders of the God's Shining Sun anti-vampire organization are in police custody, charged with fraud, inciting hatred, and attempted murder.

Both Rabbi Seth Goldstein and Imam Argi Hilaly were arrested in their Sydney offices yesterday by police, along with several other members of the organisation.

The fraud charges relate to tax returns claiming exemption due to being a religious, non-profit organization, an exemption the ATO has denied them. "The Shining Sun are a cult at best," an ATO official said, "and a terrorist organisation at worst."

Police have yet to comment on the other charges, which would seem to stem from their recent rallies in metropolitan areas around the country.

SUCK ON THIS!
AUSSIE VAMP CRICKETERS SLAY SRI LANKA IN 20/20 NIGHT SERIES

Our new vampire cricket team, the Willow Bats, have handed Sri Lanka's undead cricketers a resounding defeat at the WACA overnight, winning by twenty runs.

The Sri Lankans started strongly, with their main fast bowler, Banduka . . .

. . . game seemed all but lost, but when Jorgi "Toothy" Constantinescu came to the crease, all that changed.

"Toothy" wielded the bat like a vampire slayer with a stake, knocking the Sri Lankans to the tune of eight sixes and twelve fours.

. . . bowled the last of the Sri Lankan batsmen out with six overs to spare, beating the Night Tigers by twenty runs.

"It's a proud day for Aussie vampire sports," match organizer Bob Tarrant declared. "There's clearly an audience for these events, and we will . . .

ZOMBIES GO HOME! AUSTRALIAN HAEMOVORES
REJECT HAITIAN ZOMBIE INTEGRATION

As the first boatload of zombie refugees arrives off the shores of our far north-west, vampire Australians are speaking out against allowing the creatures asylum here.

Ms Felicia Bishop, president of the Australian Undead Equality Party, yesterday issued a public statement to the effect that the party would not support the integration of illegal Haitian Revenants into Australian society.

"The official line taken by the AUEP on this matter has been prompted by threats to the wellbeing of ordinary undead Australians should these zombies be allowed to come here," Ms Bishop said.

"With these zombies commonly—and, I might add, erroneously— referred to as being 'undead', there's a very real danger of genuine Australian undead being misidentified, of actually being actively associated with these walking corpses. Given the suspicion and dread with which zombies have been regarded by biotics in the past, I'm sure most reasonable people would understand our concerns. Letting the zombies in would represent a backwards step for Australian haemovores, and for our society in general."

"It's also worth pointing out that these creatures [revenants] do not even subscribe to the cultural expectations of ordinary Australians— some of them are flesh-eaters, for example. Others are known to not be genuinely 'undead'—merely drugged-up biotics, misrepresenting themselves in order to gain a foothold in our country.

Australian Immigration Services officials have yet to offer comment.

AFTERWORD TO "THE TIDE"

"The Tide" is a genuinely collaborative story, the only way it could have been properly told. It began as an odd idea of mine, a tale told through newspaper clippings of a history of vampire immigration in Australia, an unsubtle dig at the repeated cycles of anti-immigrant propaganda that constantly seem to flow through the mass media in this country. From hated outsiders, to misunderstood and feared shadowy threats, all the way to accepted members of society, the articles, written by myself and the ten other fine writers who kindly put their hands up to be a part of this, tell a story that should be all too familiar to anyone who's lived in Australia, and especially those who've emigrated here.

Yes, it's a story with a Message™.

It was also a story that was a tremendous amount of fun to write, I think all of us involved would agree. And hopefully it's also a story that's a tremendous amount of fun to read, that our childish enjoyment comes through in the articles. Thanks to all the contributors, Alan, Felicity, Patty, Devin, Chuck, Andrew, Lezli, Daniel, Carol and Kaaron.

MUTINY ON THE *SCARBOROUGH*

SHONA HUSK

I should be dead. I'd been left to die. They could've bribed the magistrate, the guards of New Gate gaol or the guards on the ship. They didn't. My own kind had turned their backs and left me to my fate.

They were hoping I'd suffer the agony of blood depravation and die on the six month voyage to Port Jackson—many convicts did. There were many times on the trip I wished I was dead. The stink, the hunger and the guards' brutal lottery of who to beat that day for a bit of fun. I'd had more than my fair share of turns. I was too tall and I healed too fast.

The fresh air and the glimpse of the sky between boots when I was able to look up almost made it worthwhile. The savage hunger for the blood I needed to mend the damage that followed every beating wasn't. Have you ever been so hungry you'd eat anything? And I mean anything. Your stomach overriding your mind and good sense?

There were rats. I'd save some old bread crusts and let them nibble on my fingers until I could catch them and tear into their warm bodies, spitting out the bones as I went. I'm sure the other men thought I was crazy but they hadn't seen anything. And I'm sure that if they knew I was eyeing them up as my next meal they would have tried to kill me themselves.

I'd promised myself I wouldn't kill any of the men chained down in the hull; they were more wretched than me. Starving and sick. But when the man next to me died I couldn't help myself. In the darkness I hoped no one had seen what I'd become. I was sucking on corpses to stay alive when once I had been sipping brandy laced with blood and attending the best parties.

I vowed to live through this. At first for revenge on those who had brought me down, then out of simple need to cling to the knowledge this would be over and would be but a blink in my life. I'm not immortal, just damn close.

But I am human. The only difference is the food I crave. It has to be fresh; meat needs to be almost raw. And I need blood. I can go weeks without. Then the craving will sneak up and ride me like the devil himself. Usually it doesn't take much to satisfy the hunger. A few drops—unless I'm starving.

The guards picked the wrong day to haul me up for a crawl around the deck while they set their boots to my ribs and their whip to my back. There was no blue sky that day. I saw the world in black and white and red. The guards' pulses pounded so loudly in my skull I couldn't hear their words. When I raised my head and saw the look of unconcealed terror on their faces, I knew my eyes must be white with blood lust. The pressure in my jaw became unbearable so I let my fangs descend. I wasn't so far gone as to let them show—not yet.

When the first one got his bollocks back and took a swing at me, cuffed and kicked to the deck, I took him on. I was weakened from months at sea, the beatings and the lack of food and inactivity, but I was desperate.

My iron cuffs smashed into his cheek. His bone cracked as his skin split. Blood welled, sweet, hot, sticky and crimson, better than any opium pipe. Red trickled down his slack face and he fell to the deck. For the first time in my life I was ready to kill to get blood. I let the hunger take over.

His gutless friends set upon me to exact punishment They were just like any thug outside a tavern looking for a brawl. The promise of a red-hot feed spurred me on. When they kicked, I kicked back. I was going to feed or die. They wouldn't let me live. They would whip me until I couldn't scream, then throw me overboard to drown.

I growled and bared my fangs. Those that were still conscious scrambled back and I leaped after them more animal than human. Two more were dead before the smartest one loaded his musket.

The bullet scraped past my ribs but I kept walking, stalking my prey. I wasn't going to let a bit of burning lead stop me. The guard dropped the musket and started praying and waving a cross at me as if his personal beliefs would hold me back. With his back to the railing he decided he'd rather take his chances in the ocean than face me.

I let him jump.

He swam bravely. But I saw no land on the horizon and none of the other ships that made up the second fleet. I'm sure I shared my supper with the sharks.

I didn't bother with the dead. I wanted to feel the blood pumping into my mouth. The guard I'd knocked unconscious I drained dry. His pulse weakened beneath my fingers while my wounds began to heal, hating myself the whole time. I'd become a killer.

Exactly what humans expected from my kind.

Hiding in the cabins were the rest of the crew, the cook, the surgeon, the ship's master and other men and boys. To them I was undead and unstoppable. And they were trapped on a ship with nowhere to run. I'm sure the crew expected me to kill them. They watched me but none were brave enough to confront me. I forced the cooper knock my irons off by threatening death. He'd seen what I'd done and obliged with a tremble and a prayer. He knew what I was . . . did he care why I'd been driven to do it? Did he care why I was here?

No.

Once convicted no one gave a damn anymore.

I sat on the deck all night while the ship drifted aimlessly. Her sails snapped and popped in the breeze. Sharks swam alongside waiting for the next meal. Around me blood stained the wood dark. Some was mine; most of it was the guards. Gradually the blood lust cleared and colour returned, bringing guilt and sanity.

By morning I was healed and the sunlight was too bright. The downside of drinking blood was the sensitivity to light. I wasn't going below deck again but I needed shade or I was going to burn and die.

I can be killed. A shot to the heart, decapitation and sunlight are all effective. Most of the time I can tolerate daylight but last night's excesses had made me vulnerable.

Yet the darkness had given me clarity.

I had to finish what I'd started. I washed and dressed as a guard. Then I called the rest of the crew.

"Obey me or swim." I said with a hint of fang for show. That hint of fang is what had gotten me into trouble in the first place.

Seems a particular Lord knew about vampires and had hired them to do the work he had no stomach for. Debts had to be paid with blood or money. Some vampires were happy to be bought. I wasn't one of them. The Lord was less than keen when his unwed daughter was seen on my arm at more than one party. I stole something from her that could never be replaced and he had me hunted like a fox for punishment. Vampires walk a fine line, we protect our own as we don't want too many knowing we exist but if those rules get broken . . . well, you end up like me.

A murderer in charge of a ship and men.

I couldn't return to England, my life there was over. People would look for the ship if I stole it and made a run for America. Then there were the men still chained below deck. So we sailed on to the fledging colony.

All of the crew believed more vampires lurked below and I didn't dissuade them of that opinion. I let them think I'd bitten and made a whole army. Some vampire myths work to our benefit. Those of the crew that got cocky I killed. I had no choice. If I wanted to live and be free, I had to be as ruthless as they expected.

My act worked. I concocted a tale about an attempted mutiny. No one breathed a word of truth when we sailed into harbour and unloaded our miserable human cargo into a landscape that was sharp and unforgiving.

I'd arrived in vampire Hell.

My murderous turn wasn't going to go unpunished. I was stuck here for the term of my unnaturally long life; the first vampire to arrive in Australia. But I wasn't the last.

AFTERWORD TO "MUTINY ON THE *SCARBOROUGH*"

"*Mutiny on the* Scarborough" *was an idea that had been in my head for a couple years. After watching* The Incredible Journey of Mary Bryant *I began wondering how a vampire would survive transportation. While the story remained in my musings, every time I read something about convicts it would come back. During that time I wrote other vampire stories so when the* Dead Red Heart *call for submissions was made I knew the story I wanted to write and I knew what type of vampire I was writing, all I had to was put one into a historical context.*

I researched the first and second fleet, but the second fleet really drew me as the 'what if' game started again. What if some of the high mortality rate was because of a vampire on board, and what if the reported attempted mutiny was actually caused by a vampire getting free? What had this vampire done to deserve transportation?

Now my vampire has landed in Port Jackson I would love to follow up with his life in the new colony because I'm sure his story isn't over.

SUN FALLS

ANGELA SLATTER

I tap the fingers of one hand against the steering wheel, beating out a rhythm to replace the one that went missing when we got beyond the reach of any radio reception. It helps me to ignore the noises from the back seat.

The window is down so I can blow away the smoke from a hand-rolled ciggie. Barry hates it when I smoke in his car. Few things in the world Barry loves more than this old Holden, with its mag wheels, racing stripes, flames painted on the bonnet, and the fluffy dice dangling from the rear view mirror like a pair of square, furry testicles. He adores it better than any woman. I wouldn't be allowed to drive if it weren't an emergency of the *most* urgent kind.

Me? I think he looks like an idiot driving it, like some clueless pimp. But I'm not stupid enough to tell Barry that. Nope, not stupid enough at all. And it's not as if I'm paid for my opinion. In fact, I'm not paid. Just here to shut up and earn my keep, as Barry says. Just like my Mum did before me and her mum before that, all serving Barry for as long as we can remember.

Two hundred years give or take. It's a long time to be a slave.

Outside it's cooling down, which is a blessing because the air-con died a few hours back. The sky is splashed garish pink by the setting sun and now it's low enough to not hurt my eyes. I push the cheap sunnies to the top of my head, hook the ear pieces into my hair so they stay put. I enjoy the rush of the breeze moving in and out of the car. In those brief moments when the engine doesn't howl, I can hear the sounds of the night: cicadas, possums, snakes, lizards, hares, wallabies. All manner of nasties that don't come out in the sunlight.

Kinda like Barry.

I can't hear the words he's shouting, but he knows the dark's come and he wants out. I've got a fair idea what he's saying. *Terry, open the fucking box.* There'll be that for a few more k, then *Teresa, love, sweetie, please open the box. Please let me get some fresh air. It's cold in here.*

I leave it just until I sense he's about to move to threats, then I reach behind, keeping my eyes on the road, feel around on the back seat, find the cooler and flip the lid off. It lands on the floor with the sort of noise only falling polystyrene can make, both offended and humble, a sort of squeal like it's not happy but doesn't want to bother you.

"Thank fuck for that!" Barry's got quite a voice on him for someone currently without lungs. "Are you deaf?"

"Couldn't hear you, Barry. Engine's too noisy." And the machine doesn't make a liar of me—it rumbles and protests like an old man with emphysema. It's been a long trip.

"Well, this thing better keep going, I can't afford to get stuck out in the middle of nowhere in this state."

Barry's "state" has been a cause of concern for a couple of days now. There have been gang fights on the streets of Sydney—not the usual sorts, not the drug peddlers or the slave traders, not the gun runners or the money launderers. Not this time anyway. Rival gangs of bloodsuckers, all trying to survive, to reach the top of the tree. All trying to be the big dog and negotiate with the breeders, those few Warm who are in the know (even with the current state of societal decay, there are some things you don't want the general populace to find out). But there are those who understand the night isn't a safe place, never has been, not since the First Fleet came and nicked the nation from under the nose of the indigenous population. That even on those ships, the greatest enemy wasn't scurvy or the lash, it was the things, just one or two, that roamed the lonely hours picking off the weak so as not to draw attention to themselves. Those who slept nestled in hidden compartments until the daylight passed.

Barry was one of them. Nasty bastard by all accounts (I've read the diaries my grandmothers kept). Didn't make too many of his own kind initially, just found a thin girl, none too bright, pregnant and fearful, someone he could bully and boss, someone who could do what was needed when the sun ruled the sky and who thought his protection worth the price of her liberty. Minnie: my ever-so-great-grandmother, a silly little pickpocket too slow to not get caught, who sold all our freedoms with her one stupid decision.

She couldn't read or write, but her daughter could, so Minnie told the story and her girl wrote it down. And so on and so on—we've all kept notes of some kind, some more literary than others. The Singleton women have quite a collected work now.

After Minnie's dimness, Barry decided we'd be more useful if educated, so fancy schools for his girls, university if you wanted it (I have a science degree for all the good it did me). He never turned any of us, just keeps us, generation after generation, like family retainers . . . or pets. We don't run. I asked my Mum why, but she just gave me that sleepy junkie smile. In her own way she did run—she just found her escape at the pointy end of a needle.

I've thought about it a lot in the years since and I reckon we stay put because we're told from the cradle there's nowhere else to go. How do you outrun the night? How do you go on living when closing your eyes means you might wake with a weight on your chest that doesn't go away? It's easier to live in the eye of the storm than to try and outrun it. And, ashamed as I am to say it, the protection of the devil you know is preferable to being meat to something else. There are worse things in the dark than Barry.

Of course there's always the theory that girls without fathers will attach themselves quite willingly to father-figures. Barry's a bad dad if ever there was one, but he's always looked after us. Can't argue with that.

So we shut up, do what's expected or find a way out. I'm never quite sure if Mum intended things to go the way they did. The drugs numbed her, but she could function, and Barry turned a blind eye. I guess I always thought it would go on like that forever until I got the call to say Barry had found her one night, stiff and cold under the pergola, propped against the BBQ with the little silver happy stick still in her arm. So, the big recall for me. Goodbye, uni; goodbye, honours degree; goodbye normal life.

But I digress.

Barry and his state.

He thought himself safe; thought himself well-protected. He'd built up his empire and believed himself king of the vampires. Didn't occur to him that his bodyguard—not me, I'm just a kind of housekeeper—might not be content with the status quo. That Jerzy might want a change of pace, of lifestyle, of regime. That Jerzy might take the great big Japanese sword Barry liked to keep hanging on the wall of his study and use it to separate Barry's head from the rest of his body before the other bodyguards had a chance to tear Jerzy up like a hunk of shredded pork. Then, untethered, they all bolted out of the big house with its Greek columns and stamped concrete driveway, its seldom-used-in-daytime swimming pool, blackout blinds and luxuriously appointed cellar, leaving the wrought iron gates open and me to wander in from the kitchen to find all the excitement had passed.

What should I see but Barry's head still intact? His body nothing but a pile of cinders and ash, but the head was all in one piece. And talking. Well, less talking than screaming and yelling obscenities. That's when I went to find the cooler, as much ice as I could and Barry's car keys.

And here we are, heading towards the arse-end of nowhere because Barry says so. Because he says there's a place he can find help, a place where life begins again.

† † †

The road is more dirt than black stuff now and it's starting to rise, just a little. Around each bend, the incline gets steeper and the car protests more loudly. Soon, I should imagine, it will make its wishes known with the mechanical equivalent of a big *fuck you*.

"So, tell me how this is going to go again, Boss."

Dawn is starting to grey the sky and Barry's gotten lethargic as you might expect. He's quietened down and I should probably put the lid back on his box—the last of the ice I'd dumped in the esky turned to warmish water hours ago, but I don't guess he'll drown. Looks like he's immortal, if not invulnerable.

"It'll all be sweet, Terry. I'll be good as new," his voice is low and sleepy.

"Fine and dandy, Barry, but what are the details? What about me?"

"What about you? This isn't about you, you dopey bitch." More awake now.

"Never said it was, Barry, but: point of order. We're walking into this place. What's out there? More of your brethren? You're not really in a position to protect me, are you? I'm a canapé on legs. So, *what's out there?*"

"Nah, Terry," he says but he doesn't sound very sure. "It'll be okay, nothing there, no one. Nothing to worry about."

And for the first time in my life I don't believe Barry. I don't trust him to look after me and it gives me a funny feeling in the pit of my stomach. Of course, that could be hunger—that last apple was three hours ago and I'm down to a packet of muesli bars and a tube of Pringles. "Sure, Barry. Sure."

No one, my arse. I know enough about bumps in the night and deserted dead hearts to know nothing's ever really empty. If Barry knows about this place, so does someone else. *You're not king of the vampires here, Bazza, you're just a talking head.* I pull over to the shoulder of the road, reach back and put the lid on Barry and his polystyrene swimming pool. I get out of the car and look around, stretching my long body as my back protests and my worn-too-long cargos and tee stick to my skin. I can smell my own sweat and the determined stink of the cigarettes that ran out not far out of Sydney. I stare into the bush. It's changing as we head up the mountains, getting greener, darker, denser, wetter. More like a rainforest. Not sure what I expect to see . . . nothing there, no movement, not even the twitch of a leaf in the breeze. I feel weird though; I feel watched. *Imagination*, I tell myself. *Bullshit*, I tell myself.

I slide back into the driver's seat and turn the key in the ignition.

The only answer I get is the exhausted metallic grinding of a thing that's gone as far as it can go. I lean forward and rest my head against the steering wheel, smelling the stale-sour scent of hands gripped too long about the leather cover. My spidey senses tell me this road trip will not end well.

† † †

I've got Barry's box in one hand and in the other is the long Japanese sword that parted him from his body. It seemed like a good idea to bring it along—just made sure Barry didn't see it, sore point and all that. The water bottle hanging at my waist is making sad little wishy-washy sounds. Not much more than a mouthful left and I'm thirsty. The need for nicotine is dancing under my skin.

The air is cool and damp, the clouds are sitting on the road and it's hard to see too much in front of me. The condensation is plastering the fringe to my forehead. It's mid-afternoon and I don't know where I'm going, I'm just following the road. Can't open the box to ask Barry; he's been in deep sleep for hours now. I just keep walking, although my boots have rubbed blisters onto my soles and the outer edges of my little toes.

Up ahead I can hear a sound, sweet and clear. Running water.

I pick up my pace and stumble off the road, down a slight slope to find a clearing, a little creek running through it. There's a fire pit that looks like it hasn't been used in a long, long time. I refill the water bottle, drink deeply, then peel off my boots and socks and plunge my feet in. It's icy and hurts only for a little while before the numbing cold makes everything seem okay. I lean back, raise my face to where the sun should be and imagine it on my skin. Problem with being in service with a night crawler is that you don't tend to see too much daylight. Oh, you have to run errands and some of those are unavoidably day-oriented. But mostly, you become as nocturnal as your master. Feels like shift-work. Do it long enough you either get used to it or go nuts. Or a bit of both.

Behind me there's a sound; behind me, where I dropped Barry's box (the katana I kept close). There's that distinct polystyrene noise and I turn to see the biggest freaking possum I've ever seen in my life. It looks like a large dog, a Labrador maybe, on its hind legs and it's got the lid off the cooler and one paw buried deep inside. It pulls Barry's head out by the messy black hair.

There it dangles at the end of possum claws, eyes closed, lips slack and a little open and the neck so cleanly severed you could almost admire it as a nice tidy job. I stand slowly. The possum sniffs at Barry's nose, licks it then opens its mouth and sinks sharp white teeth into the substance of Barry's pert little snoz.

I take a good few fast steps and bring the katana sweeping upward and the possum paw drops to the ground, which leaves Barry hanging briefly by his nose in the grip of the teeth of a very unhappy marsupial. Possum spits out its meal and gives me a look that makes me think twice about getting any closer. Then I remember that I've got the sword and about four feet in height on the thing. But it's fast and the remaining claws sharp; my cargos and the leg underneath get a nasty gash before I manage to take the stinking thing's head off.

I have a rest, bent over, hands on knees, breathing hard while I watch blood dribble out of my injured flesh. There's a yell and I fear a possum support column may have arrived. But it's only Barry, waking up.

"What the fuck happened to my nose? Do you have any idea how much this hurts? What the hell did you do to me?"

"Oh, Barry, you don't want to know. Now, which way? There are no signs for Sun Falls."

"Just keep following the road." The he pitches his eyes downwards, trying to get a good look at the state of his nose. I manage not to laugh as he goes a little cross-eyed. "Fuck this hurts."

†   †   †

A bonfire and five figures gathered around it: a woman, an old man, two young men and a teenage girl. Raggedy stragglers, left out here with orders to guard the place, I guess. They're vampires, though, so it doesn't matter if there are five or a hundred. The rush and roar of water is clear from somewhere in the darkness. I can feel a damp spray I think might come from the falls.

I washed the wound and wrapped my leg up tight, but I know they can smell it before I step into the circle of light. There's a collective growl that must be something like a gazelle hears before a pride of lions brings it down. I might be able to take out a couple before they get to me. The fire catches the edge of the katana and pinwheels in Barry-unboxed's wide open eyes. The pack stays back, however. I must look as though I know what I'm doing—well, you can fool some of the vampires some of the time, I guess.

The woman stands and takes a few steps towards me.

"Hello, dinner," she says. "How obliging of you to turn up."

"You might want to re-think that," I say, and raise my boss's head.

Barry pipes up, "Lynda, keep your hands off her. She's no one's meal."

"Is that you, Barry?" The woman squints. Her hair is wound into filthy dreads, not all of her teeth remain and the breeze tells me she's not washed in some time. Hillbilly vamps, who'd have thought it? Feeding on the occasional lost tourist, stray cattle, giant possums. "Aw, Barry. What the fuck happened?"

"Long fucking story. I need to use the pool," he says shortly.

"The pool? No one's done that in a hundred years—you dunno what's gonna happen." She gets a cunning look in her eye. "What's it worth to ya?"

"How about a snack?"

Told you Barry was a nasty piece of work. But you know what, I'm less afraid of him than I am of them. One thing I do know is this: no matter how much he lies to everyone else, he's always kept his word to my family. He said I would be safe. He's also the only thing protecting me from the cast of a bloodsucking *Deliverance*.

I'm flanked by two underfed youths with straggly beards and, if I didn't know better, a look that says "Inbreeding keeps it in the family". One of them carries a torch plucked flaming from the fire. They don't need it to see, hell, they don't need fire at all, but I recognise in the building of the bonfire a remnant of their warm days, a little thing to hang onto. A memory of *back when*, of kids playing at grown-ups, of a time when heat meant comfort, meant life. Creatures pretending one day there might be light.

The falls are a couple of minutes walk away, down a path strewn with sticks and pebbles, occasionally hidden by touchy-feely ferns. When we reach the bottom, there's a shallow pool and a whole lot of spray where the water crashes down. One of my escorts points to a break in the foliage, right next to the cataract; the other pushes me roughly forward. My Docs slip and slide on the damp rocks. I keep my balance though; with a head in one hand, a sword in the other, and Barry cursing me the whole while it's no mean feat. I walk around behind the curtain of *wet* and see an entrance, a glow coming from inside it like a jack-o'-lantern.

There are no torches here, I notice, but the walls glow. Phosphorous? I wait until we're far enough down the tunnel for my guard of honour to not hear.

"Barry, you ungrateful bastard. I carry your sorry metaphorical arse all the way here, nearly get eaten by a mutant possum and this is the thanks I get?" I shake him by the hair and glare into his blue eyes. "You think I'm an *hors d'oeuvre?*"

"Calm down. Wait—possum? Is that what happened to my nose? You let a possum eat my fucking nose?"

"Focus, Barry. Seriously, do you think I'm going to drop you in the all-healing, all-fixing pond so you can serve me up to that lot?" I shake him again and he winces. "Or are you gonna snack on me yourself?"

"Don't worry about it. Once I'm whole again, no one's going to mess with you."

"You didn't answer me!"

"I might need a little blood when I'm done," he admits. I give his head a good rattle and a few choice profanities, and he yells, "Not much! Not much! Just a little to top up. I promise!"

"What are we talking? A thimbleful? A shot glass?"

"Just a—bit. Terry, I promise I won't drain you, I won't turn you."

What choice do I have? The devil I know or the ones I don't.

The pool is at the bottom of the slope, in roughly the centre of a small cavern. The liquid in it is milky-white with the same sheen as mother-of-pearl, and the smell is a little like household cleaner. A bit bleachy—more *Domestos* than *Dettol*.

"What's that?" I ask, trying not to breathe too deeply.

"Stuff. You know—stuff."

"You knew about this how?"

"Stories, Chinese whispers, old diaries—your lot aren't the only ones who keep records you know. Nothing precise, nothing exact, just hints."

"You *read* our diaries?" I shouldn't be surprised.

"Yeah, yeah, yeah, I'm a bad person. Throw me in."

"But what if it doesn't work?"

"Not really in a position to be picky, am I? Fountain of youth, a wellspring, a cauldron of plenty. There are legends and they all say it brings life."

I don't point out to Barry that strictly speaking he has been for some time well and truly beyond the usual span of any creature. Well and truly outside the spectrum of what we call "life".

"So," I say, "life?"

"Life. Now hurry the fuck up and toss me in."

I walk around the edge. It's about five metres across and bubbling enthusiastically. If I drop him, maybe he'll just drown—this is a bit deeper than the esky—which still leaves me with a problem.

"Here's the deal, Barry: I'll put you in but in return you let me go. I'm no one's lunch, I'm no one's slave, I'm gone. I'm out. I do whatever I want."

"Terry . . ."

"You want life or not?"

"Yes, fuck it!" He gives a growl of frustration. "Alright. Agreed. I can find better than you at the local whore house anyway."

"Touché."

I kneel beside the pond and lower Barry in, resisting the impulse to drop him from a height to see how much of a splash he'll make. Some of the fluid leaps up like a nipping fish and lands on my fingers. It stings like ice. I grit my teeth and keep going, don't release the head until he is thoroughly submerged.

I try to straighten up, withdraw my arm, but I feel sharp teeth in my wrist. Barry, you bastard. That, however, is the least of my problems: the water has me. Blood spurts from my nose and turns pink as it hits the milky pond. It's like I'm in the grip of an electrical current. It tugs at me and tugs at me until I over-balance and it pulls me beneath the surface.

I feel as if I'm dying forever.

My last sight before I'm overwhelmed is Barry's head tossed and churned, jumping about like popping corn. Angry fingers of fluid force their way into my mouth and race down my throat, filling my lungs like inhaled fire. My skin seems to peel off, each hair follicle is a tiny pin in my scalp. Surely my eyes burst.

When it stops hurting, the water lets me go.

I crawl out and lie on the surprisingly warm rock. I'm whole, intact if somewhat soaked. I rub a hand against my shin, right where the possum bite was and feel . . .

And feel . . .

Nothing.

I roll up the leg of my cargos and strip away the bandage. There's just a pink mark that might have been a scar but fades as I watch. The katana is where I left it, and I pick it up, prick at my finger with its sharpness. Something silver oozes out from the cut and just as quickly the opening closes over.

A great spout of water comes from the pool and a body lands not far from me, gives a displeased groan.

Barry, whole again, tall and handsome and muscular and . . .

And no longer pale as if he tries to tan beneath the moon.

He rolls on his back, coughing, making a noise like an espresso machine. He *breathes*. I poke at him with the katana. A tiny drop of blood blossoms on his skin and he swears. Rich, fresh, oxygenated, *living* blood.

"Oh, Barry," I say. "You were right."

He sits up, runs his hands over his arms and legs, wondering, not understanding. "But . . ."

"It does give life, Barry. You've been dead a long time." I can't keep the laughter out of my voice.

"But . . . Fuck!" He stands up, pacing. "Okay. I don't have to outrun them, I just have to outrun *you*."

"Here's the thing, Baz, I don't think they're going to be interested in me anymore." I rise, do the thing with the poking and the quick silvery bleed. "Close as I can figure it, nature abhors a vacuum. The pond finished what you started, taking my blood and all, then . . . replaced it."

I start up the path, cast a look behind, "Long time since you've been meat. How's it feel?"

AFTERWORD TO "SUN FALLS"

The problem with vampire fiction is that there is now so much of it—or rather the problem is how to do something different with it nowadays? The days when Stoker's Dracula or Le Fanu's Carmilla could stand out in a fairly unpopulated field are long gone.

When I was thinking about writing this story, I kept wondering about the problems vampires would have in Australia—I mean, sunshine is not a vampire's friend and Australia is the sunshiny capital. I figured that the key to the vampire's survival was going to lie in the protectors s/he gathered. I thought about how Australia must have been for people coming here on the First Fleet—you've already been arrested and incarcerated in England in jail or one of those floating hulks; now you've been completely uprooted and sent to this weird place. If protection was offered to you when you're so scared and alone, mightn't you sell your own future and that of coming generations just to be safe?

I realised then that this was the story of the protectors, not the vampire. I wondered what happens when the latest in a line of protectors gets tired of the gig and has a personality that's just about ready to rebel. When the writing flagged and I was going to give up, it was my Significant Other who said the fatal and inspiring words "giant mutant possum"—how could I not go on? Thus Terry got her journey into the mountains with a talking head in an esky. So, blame it on the giant mutant possum.

SUCH IS LIFE

JEREMY SADLER

Samuel Bennett didn't like the arrangement at all. The Inn was darkened, deep in shadow where he, Superintendent Sadlier and the troopers were bathed in the moonlight. When they arrived they found the original trooper commander, Superintendant Hare, at the railway station, shot in the wrist, pale and faint. That left the blacktracker leader O'Connor in charge. They found him in the cover of a ditch, well back from the Inn, with a small group of troopers.

"John Sadlier," the big Superintendant introduced himself to O'Connor. The Superintendant indicated Bennett. "Special Inspector Bennett. Your report?"

O'Connor rose to address them. "They fired at us when we 'rrived, then went inside. We 'ave the building 'rounded, sir."

To Bennett, the statement was ambitious, as there were but a handful of troopers and blacktrackers spread around the Inn, reinforced now by the troopers just arrived. If the situation had not been so serious, Bennett might have smiled. A siege, like the old days.

"One 'a them left out th' back," O'Connor continued as he pointed toward the Inn. "Went into th' bush."

Bennett interjected. "You let him go?"

The man was upset. "We fired on him, sir! He wouldn't go down!"

Sadlier examined the Inn for a few moments and then turned. "I shall not risk the men in an assault," he said. "Nor the many people who have gathered to watch." He pointed his hand toward the rest of the town, where Bennett for the first time could see a crowd had gathered. "I will telegraph Melbourne for a cannon."

Bennett wanted to question the wisdom of such a decision, but knew he could not; he held no authority there.

Sadlier sent a trooper to the railway station to telegraph Melbourne, and then they sat and waited in silence for some time, as the sky to the east continued to brighten. They were roused suddenly by a shout.

A figure appeared then from the scrub to the side of the Inn, large and hulking, wearing a long coat. Ungainly, he walked around to the front of the building.

He was tall, and Bennett saw he wore some kind of helmet on his head, made from a dark metal, with a slit for vision. He could spy under the long coat the same metal around the man's chest.

Armour, he thought. How ingenious.

The figure raised his right arm, in which he carried a revolver, and fired. The shot went over the head of the troopers; the man fired again.

This second shot prompted the assembled troopers to open fire themselves, and Bennett heard a metal sound as bullets hit the armour and deflected. The figure stumbled a little at each hit, but kept his feet. Bennett saw some bullets hit the figure's unprotected arms and legs, however they had little effect. Bennett knew mere bullets were not going to be enough to stop this figure.

He drew his revolver and took careful aim down it, for an exposed leg. The figure saw him and faced him fully, even smacked the butt of his revolver against his chest plate and said something, though Bennett could not hear it. He began to advance, and Bennett fired.

Just as Bennett pulled the trigger the armoured man stumbled from other bullets, but Bennett's aim had been true and his bullet hit the figure in the leg. Bennett saw a splash of black liquid, heard the figure cry out, and the figure fell onto his back.

Troopers yelled out and a few charged forward. First to reach the figure was a big burly Sergeant whom Bennett recalled was named Steele; as the other troopers landed on the figure to hold him down, Steele grabbed the helmet and roughly pulled it off.

"It's Ned Kelly!" Steele shouted, and grabbed Kelly by the throat and beard, his revolver pressed up against Kelly's face.

"Don't you kill him, sir!" It was Bracken, the local Constable, who had his own pistol out but pointed it to the ground. "Kill him and I'll kill you!"

Steele withdrew. Bennett and Sadlier arrived. Other troopers were still firing into the Inn, and Sadlier ordered his men to grab Kelly and drag him to cover.

Distance from the Inn achieved, Sadlier ordered his troopers back to the line. As Kelly watched them from the ground, Sadlier gave Bennett a meaningful look, and then turned and walked back to the line himself.

Bennett went down on his haunches next to Kelly. He noted the wounds from the trooper bullets had already closed over, little more than scars that would soon disappear. "Hello, Edward."

Edward Kelly smiled. "'Ello, Samuel." He paused. "I may lose the broad Irish with you, I would hazard." He motioned toward his leg, where the wound from Bennett's bullet hissed, smoked and spat flecks of black blood. "Blessed bullets are new."

Bennett reached behind his back into his satchel and produced a wooden stake. He tapped Kelly's armour with the pointed end. "They are, and so is this."

Kelly laughed, a guttural sound. "Magnificent idea, yes? No getting through it with that." He nodded toward the stake. "Does it remind you of anything?"

Memories of armour shining in the hot sun, massed armies, charging horses and bloody battle came to Bennett's mind. White flags with red crosses.

"An older time," Kelly continued. "A better time for men like us."

Bennett stared into space a moment longer then blinked the memories away. "*Vade retro satana. Sunt mala quae libas.*" The Latin felt good on his tongue, steadied him. "Your craft won't work on me."

Kelly nodded. "I remember."

"How many did you convert?" Bennett asked.

Kelly smiled, and Bennett saw the sharp canines through the beard. "That's the question, isn't it? I knew our adventures would bring you."

Bennett looked up to the east. "Sunrise soon." He looked down again. "I've been directed to take you alive, if possible. The civil authorities demand a trial."

"Ah . . . I thought as such. They want a show." He raised his eyes to the sky behind them. "The sun won't kill me, if I understand your threat well enough."

Bennett nodded agreement. "You do, and I know. But it will hurt. How many did you convert?"

That smile again. "That is the game, Samuel! Threat and counter threat, attack and parry."

Bennett felt anger rise in him. He swallowed and controlled his emotions. After a moment, he said: "You cannot escape."

"My dear Samuel, what makes you think I wish to do so?"

Bennett looked at the . . . *thing* on the ground before him. "Your first priority is always survival."

Kelly sighed. "Perhaps in the past, but no longer. We are both old, Samuel. Time for Edward Kelly to die." He paused. "There were four of us, but I converted only two of them. Young Joe I did not change, you will find him dead inside from your trooper's bullets."

"What of the rest of the Kellys? The family?" Bennett asked.

"Their minds are so weak, Samuel," Kelly said. "Was but a trifle to manipulate them. I fed off some of them, but did not convert them."

Unbidden, again, memories of times long gone, armoured knights on horse. Bennett dismissed them.

"So the man they say is your brother?"

"Daniel, yes, he's in there. And another young 'un, Steve Hart." He sighed. "Them I changed. No more."

Bennett searched the face for signs of the lie. Previous experience told him how manipulative this *thing* was. "Will they surrender?" He tapped the armour again with the stake. "Like you?"

Kelly shook his head. "No. They are convinced this is to be a mass killing, a feast."

Bennett thought on that for a moment. The "Kelly Gang" had been travelling around the bush for several years. Some deaths, various other crimes. This was much larger than anything they had done before.

"And what of you?" he asked finally. "What is this for you?"

"An end to the show. I'm tired. It is time to depart the stage." He turned his face away. "You have your information. Leave me be."

Bennett stood up. "Tell me how I can resolve this."

Kelly turned back, snorted and closed his eyes. "That I cannot do. Those two . . . they will not go quietly."

Bennett sighed. "So be it." He made to walk back to the line of troopers.

"Samuel?" Kelly called.

Bennett stopped and turned.

"The sun."

Bennett nodded, walked back, and with effort dragged Kelly into the shade of a tree, just as the tip of the sun breached the horizon.

The far hills to the west were bathed in gold. The valley in which the town lay still swam in a pre-dawn mist.

"What a beautiful view," Kelly said softly.

Bennett grunted, and left.

†   †   †

More police arrived some time after sunrise as troopers continued to fire at irregular intervals into the Inn. Some civilians escaped and almost became casualties. Eventually, Sadlier ordered a ceasefire.

The Superintendent met with Bennett out of earshot of troopers. Sadlier was one of the few who knew Bennett's role in the Kelly operation. "What now, if they won't come out?"

Bennett glanced over at the prostrate Kelly, still in the shade. "I have no answer, sir. I can say they will come out, eventually, but it may take days."

Sadlier glanced at the Inn. "We do not have days. We cannot let them control the situation."

Bennett waited. He suspected the Superintendent already had a plan.

Sadlier pulled his fob watch from his pocket and examined it. "I will give them until 3PM," he said finally. "Then, I will fire the building, with them in it."

Bennett nodded slowly. "That won't kill them."

"But it will rob them of their position," Sadlier said, his tone gruff. "Then we may deal with them."

Bennett did not react to the use of "we". Instead, he said, "Yes, sir," and then went over to Kelly.

"Time wears on," Kelly said.

Bennett grunted as he adjusted Kelly's position to keep him out of the sun. The blessed shot wound on his leg continued to ooze and spit. The other, normal shot wounds had all but disappeared.

Bennett went back to the line of troopers. He saw across the way Sadlier in discussion with a man of the cloth. Bennett eyed the man from a distance, until Sadlier noticed him and motioned him over.

"Special Inspector Samuel Bennett," Sadlier said formally. "This is Father Matthew Gibney. Apparently, he was just passing through, on the train to Albury, and heard about the goings on here. He offers his assistance."

Father Gibney shook Bennett's hand. "I'll certainly help where I can."

"I thought perhaps," Sadlier continued. "He might tend Kelly over there, look to him while you are otherwise engaged."

Bennett looked from Sadlier to Gibney and back again. How much did this priest know? Certainly he would have been taught about the existence of the . . . evil things at seminary. But there were many more matters which were kept secret.

"Very good," Bennett said finally as the other two waited for his answer.

"Excellent," Sadlier said. "If you would be so kind, Mr Bennett, to take the Reverend Father to him?"

Bennett nodded. "This way please, Father."

The pair approached Kelly, in the shade of an overhanging tree. Still some distance from the prone figure, Bennett placed a light hand on Gibney's arm.

"Father, there is something you must know before we proceed."

"Yes?" Gibney was perplexed.

"You must be on your guard, Father. Pay no heed to what this . . . man says to you. He will use words to muddle your mind, make you believe him, even do things against your will. May I suggest, sir, you hold your rosary in your hand?"

Gibney looked at him, startled. Several rifle shots echoed around; Gibney jumped with each one. "Surely he is—"

"He is evil personified," Bennett interrupted, flatly. He watched Gibney reach into a pocket and retrieve a rosary, holding it bunched in his hand.

Kelly watched them approach and when they were close said: "Samuel?"

Gibney knelt down next to the prone figure. "My son, how may I be of assistance?"

Kelly looked from Gibney to Bennett and back again. Gibney reached a hand out to place it on Kelly's arm, a gesture of reassurance. It was the hand that held the rosary.

"Get away from me!" Kelly hissed, his teeth bared. He shuffled his body with difficulty, still in armour, away from the touch. "Samuel, get this . . . man of your God away from me!"

Gibney's mouth fell open, and he looked back up at Bennett in surprise. "But . . . he . . ." He crossed himself.

"Yes," Bennett said, his tone still flat. "I suggest you keep your distance, Father."

Gibney stood and turned on him. "Who *are* you?"

It was the question Bennett had hoped to avoid. "I am as said, a Special Inspector." He guided the priest away from Kelly.

"But you know things," Gibney continued as he glanced back over his shoulder. "You know about . . . that."

"May I suggest you tend to the civilians, Father," Bennett said. He directed the man toward the clustered group of people who had escaped the Inn. "I am sure you have many questions, and I may be able to provide answers later."

Gibney nodded slackly, and left Bennett to join the group of civilians. He began to move among them and talk.

Bennett returned to the troopers.

†   †   †

As the sun moved over the sky, and more police arrived, Bennett adjusted Kelly's position a few times more. They exchanged no more words. The thing seemed content to stare into space and moan a little about the blessed bullet.

As the time approached, Sadlier selected one man who gathered up hay to act as a torch.

"One covering volley, men," Sadlier ordered. "When I give the word."

That volley was fired at ten minutes to the hour. Then the lone trooper's torch was lit and he ran to the front of the Inn.

Behind, the civilians who had escaped the Inn began to make a ruckus. Father Gibney broke off from them and dashed to Bennett.

"They say there is someone still in there, someone other than the Kelly gang," he said.

The trooper was at the front of the Inn and dropped the burning hay on the front step. He then beat a retreat. For a few moments in appeared the fire would not catch; then it did as it licked up around the front door.

"Stay here Father," Bennett said. He drew his revolver and dashed forward.

"Come back at once!" Sadlier shouted after him, but Bennett ignored him.

He reached the front door of the Inn but found his way blocked by the flames. Quickly he ran around the side, then to the rear door. As he ran, he pulled his stake from his satchel.

He shouldered the door aside, his revolver held before him in his right hand. In his left he held the stake. He could hear the flames on the far side of the building as the front wall burned and the fire licked at the roof.

Inside, the noise of the fire was a loud roar. It would have masked his efforts to bash through the door. He saw armour, much like the set that Edward wore, piled in one corner. As he stepped into the room, he heard a shout.

"Let 'em come!" a voice screamed.

A figure stepped into the room then, a man, tall and solid with a beard. He stopped. Bennett recognised him from description: Steve Hart. He wore no armour.

"You!" Hart screamed, and stepped forward.

Bennett raised his revolver and shot Hart twice. The man made a guttural sound, like a laugh, and then paused and looked down in surprise as the two wounds hissed, smoked and burned. Then he collapsed onto his back.

Bennett stepped forward and raised the stake. Hart's hands convulsed over his chest, scratching at the two wounds which continued to smoke. His dark eyes focused on Bennett, and the Inspector spied the final evidence that settled his mind—the twin points just behind the lips.

"*Non nobis Domine,*" Bennett shouted as he dropped to his knees over Hart, his voice rising with each word. "*Non nobis, sed nomini tuo da gloriam!*"

With that he plunged the stake home into Hart's chest.

Hart screamed an inhuman screech that tore at Bennett's ears. His body writhed and convulsed so strongly that Bennett was knocked aside. Black thick blood sprayed from Hart's mouth and the wounds on his chest.

Bennett came to his knees as the screech died away to a gurgle, and finally the body lay still.

There was movement, at the door through which Bennett had entered. He recovered his pistol and aimed.

The door moved and Reverend Gibney appeared, sweat on his brow from the heat. The priest looked down at Hart's body, with the stake still in the chest and the two bullet wounds and the pool of black liquid that slowly spread around it.

"In God's name!" Gibney shouted. "What have you done?"

Bennett regained his feet and pushed the Reverend back toward the door. "Get out, Father!"

"No!" Gibney yelled in return. "They must be saved!"

"You cannot save them!" Bennett yelled. The fire was so loud it was difficult to hear; the smoke so thick it was almost impossible to speak. Bennett coughed. "Don't you die here too!"

Bennett turned as he felt a presence behind him, and a large arm smashed into the side of his head. He fell, his head a fog.

Dan Kelly stood over him, his hair and clothes smouldering, his eyes aflame like the building in which he stood.

Bennett fired, blindly, emptying the pistol. As his vision cleared he saw Dan Kelly on the floor next to Hart's body, and like Hart he grabbed at wounds on his leg and abdomen, wounds which hissed and smoked and spat black blood.

Bennett shook his head as he clambered back to his knees.

Reverend Gibney dropped to the floor next to him. "Can you walk?" he shouted.

"Get out!" Bennett yelled. He reached over, grabbed the end of the stake in Hart's chest, and pulled. Black blood splashed them both.

The fire was almost upon them all now. Bennett, unsteady, dragged himself over to where Dan Kelly lay. Kelly shivered like he was cold; his hands clawed at the bullet wounds.

"*Non nobis Domine, non nobis, sed nomini tuo da gloriam!*" He yelled the words, slurred them all together, and used his whole weight to drop the stake into Dan Kelly's chest.

He did not wait, this time, as the inhuman wail drowned out the roar of the fire. The roof in the next room collapsed, the fire was all around them. He found his feet and took hold of Reverend Gibney for support. Together they pushed their way back out the door and ran.

The roof of the inn collapsed, and the whole building was consumed in flame. The two of them staggered further on until they were well enough away and then collapsed, coughing.

"Sir!" Gibney was saying between rasps. "The last prisoner was not in there! They found him outside."

Bennett coughed. He had risked his life for nought. If the fire had forced the two out they could have been taken outside; if they had burned, he could have staked them before their bodies healed.

Gibney was still next to him. "So tell me: who are you?"

Bennett replied by lifting the left wrist of his jacket. There, tattooed to the inside of his wrist, was a small red cross. Gibney's eyes widened with surprise, and he met Bennett's gaze. Every man of the cloth knew that symbol.

"*Pauperes commilitones Christi Templique Solomonici,*" Bennett said, his tongue fumbling over the particular Latin phrase he had not spoken in so long. He let the sleeve fall and grabbed Gibney's arm. "I was never here, Father."

Gibney's face filled with realisation, and he nodded.

Just then troopers arrived with water, and helped them back from the flames.

† † †

Kelly sat alone in the cell when Bennett came. The Melbourne Gaol guard opened the cell door with his fat keys and then went to stand a respectful distance out of earshot. The cells around them had been emptied. There was only Bennett and Kelly.

Bennett carried a chair into the cell where Ned sat on the low cot, placed it near the door, and sat.

Kelly looked up. "Come to gloat, Samuel? Not like you." He was dressed only in the simple prison garb.

Bennett smiled. "Here only to see this to the end."

It was Kelly's turn to smile. "The circus here is finished. The people got their show."

Bennett shifted, uncomfortable. "There is something I wish to know."

Kelly smiled further. "And that is?"

Bennett frowned. "You could have fled. Why did you come back?"

Kelly chuckled. "We all have a place in history, Samuel. What happened at Glenrowan will be remembered." He sighed. "Living as we do . . . it's not for me anymore. Time for it to be over." He shrugged. "Time for Edward Kelly to die."

Bennett sat silent for a long moment, lost in thought. He was interrupted by a noise outside the cell, the jangle of keys and the scrape of a metal door.

"Ah," Kelly said as he indicated the cell door. "And yet, the moment does arrive."

Bennett stood up, moved the chair out of the way, as two guards, the Warden and a priest appeared at the cell door. All of them regarded Bennett for a moment. Bennett stepped aside and motioned for them to take the prisoner.

The two guards entered the cell and shackled Kelly. The Priest began to read from his Bible, a passage appropriate for the condemned prisoner.

As the two guards took him out the door, Kelly paused and turned to face Bennett. "It has come to this. Will ye be watchin', Samuel?"

Bennett nodded. "Yes."

He sighed. "I shall see you, then." With that, he was gone.

† † †

Bennett stood on the floor below, in a crowd of others, as the ceremony was carried out. The priest and his attendants were gathered to one side as the Warden put Kelly in position. The executioner stood to the side until the Warden was clear, then placed the hood on Kelly's head, rolled up, like a cap. It was followed by the noose, carefully placed.

"May God have mercy on your soul," the priest finished.

The Warden stepped up to Kelly.

"Any last words?"

For a moment there was silence. Then Kelly spoke, but it was a mumble, barely audible to anyone beyond the immediate vicinity.

The Warden stepped back then nodded to the executioner, who grasped the metal handle.

"What did he say?" a reporter who stood near Bennett asked his companion in a whisper.

"I'm not sure," the other replied. "Was it . . . Such is life?"

The floor fell, the rope went taut, and before a crowd of witnesses, Ned Kelly died.

† † †

Bennett watched as the body was taken down and carried out toward the gaol hospital, which also served as the mortuary. The doctor had checked Kelly's body to confirm he was dead. Bennett knew the procedure now would be for the doctor to remove Kelly's head, to make a death mask, and dissect the body before burial would be finalised. Bennett was to be there first.

When he stepped out of the gaol house where the hanging took place, the yard was empty. The two guards had already carried Kelly into the hospital. Bennett paused in the warm sun of the summer day, stretching his toes. He was tired. Many, many years of chasing Edward across continents had finally come to fruition. Perhaps now his superiors would see to his rest.

First one guard, then the other, came out of the hospital and disappeared in the direction of the guard house. Very shortly the gaol doctor would arrive.

He resumed his walk to the hospital and stepped inside.

It was dark and cool. One body lay on the table in the centre of the room. Bennett walked toward it.

"The time has come, Edward," Bennett said. He retrieved his stake from his pocket.

The body was covered by a blanket, with only the feet and the top of the hooded head revealed. Bennett glanced at the shoes. They were boots, much like those worn by the guards.

He grabbed the blanket and flung it away. The body wore the gaol garb in which Kelly had been hanged, the hood covering its head. He placed the point of his stake against the appropriate point on the chest and was about to speak the ceremonial words, when he stopped.

Kelly had worn shoes.

He looked at the feet. Boots.

He leaned over and lifted a trouser leg. The wound from Bennett's bullet, even with the round removed, would never have healed properly.

There was no wound.

A cold feeling crept into his chest. He jumped up to the head of the table, grabbed the top of the hood, and pulled hard.

The hood came away easily, and the head hit the table with a thump.

Not Edward Kelly.

He looked around the room. There were no other bodies.

I knew our adventures would bring you.

He dashed to the door of the hospital and looked out. The courtyard was deserted. The only people beside himself who had been here were the two guards.

The two guards!

What makes you think I wish to do so?

He ran fast to the guard house.. There was one guard on duty, whom he did not recognise.

"The guards!" he yelled at him. "Where did they go?"

The guard looked at him quizzically. "Beg pardon, sir?"

"The two guards who carried Kelly to the hospital!" The cold feeling had spread, enveloped his whole chest. "Where did they go?"

The man looked at him with a vacant expression. He did not know. Or did not remember.

They want a show.

He dashed through the guard house, through several gates manned by guards who all looked at him vacantly when he asked the same question. Finally he was at the main gates, which opened onto Russell Street.

Time to depart the stage.

He stepped out. The street was busy with people, buggies and carts and horses. Some had gathered to await news of Kelly's death. He looked back and forth, back and forth, as he searched the faces. None he recognised.

Time for Edward Kelly to die.

Bennett cursed under his breath. And so he had died. Before reporters, a priest, a Governor and a large number of witnesses, Edward Kelly died that day.

AFTERWORD TO "SUCH IS LIFE"

Around the time I began brainstorming for Dead Red Heart *news came that Ned Kelly's remains, lost since his execution, may have been unearthed in the grounds of the old Pentridge Prison in Melbourne. The idea struck: what if Ned Kelly was a vampire? That the remains could not be identified just reinforced my idea that Kelly escaped his execution and abandoned his identity. That the monster lives among us is a concept central to vampire lore.*

I found that almost all of the Kelly story, from the bush fashioned armour to the Glenrowan siege, Kelly's date with the gallows to the loss of his remains, fit like puzzle pieces together with the image of Kelly as a vampire.

Samuel Bennett, the only fictional character, is the kind of old soldier I love to write. Who is to say a crusading vampire hunter was not among the constabulary that day? What history would he and Kelly share?

The story of Ned Kelly has grown over time to become Australian legend, and the opportunity to weave that folklore together with the vampire myth was just too compelling to pass.

APOLOGETOI

CHRIS LAWSON

Another body had turned up heartless and exsanguinated, only this time the corpse and the wash of blood had been left on the steps of the Pyramid of the Eagle in full view of the Black Swan River and the city below. It was a punch to the face of the Commissioner, who had promised on national television to stamp out the sacrifices.

And so it was that Senior Investigator Petru Razvan and Investigator Herbert Lockwood came to be padding the streets of North Bridge, doing their best to look serious and resolute while having no plan of action other than to traipse around the obsidian bars on Texcoco Street looking serious and resolute.

The street was jumping that night. News of the sacrifice had filtered through the city and drew hundreds of traditionalists to dance like gods and slug back obsidian gin until they passed out, and for some of them to hope that their unconscious forms might be dragged off in the night and added to the sacrificial pile. The news seemed to have summoned an even greater number of people who had no particular interest in the old religion: drunkards, anarchists, sociopaths, university students, journalists, beggars, buskers, and pickpockets, not to mention the just plain curious descended upon the street and choked it with a swirling liquid of humanity so viscous it was nearly impossible to move.

Razvan and Lockwood were there so that the Commissioner could say something was being done, but they were as useless as crocodile toupees. A murder could have unfolded twenty steps away and they would have been powerless to stop it.

"In here," said Razvan, dragging Lockwood by the arm into The Jaguar and Unicorn, one of the pubs on the street that was stained-toilet seedy but had never been a favourite with the traditionalists. "I need a drink, by god."

"On duty?" asked Lockwood.

"If we were doing real police work then maybe I'd call it 'on duty'."

"Fine. I need a leak. Please make sure you finish before I get back so I never see you drink it."

The crowd inside the pub was just as thick as it was out on the street. It took Razvan a full ten minutes to reach the bar. He ordered a double Oxblood. The bartender stared at him hard and cold and made no move to serve him. Razvan noticed that the bartender had feathers knotted into his beard. There had been a change of management at The Jaguar and Unicorn.

"We don't serve Oxblood here," said the bartender.

"I guess you don't," said Razvan.

"Obsidian gin is on the house tonight, if you're interested."

"No thank you." Razvan could feel the weight of the crowd behind him, trapping him. He tried to move away from the bar but could not.

The bartender flicked a towel across his wrist and drew it tight like a noose. "With all due respect, Investigator, I think maybe you're in the wrong neighbourhood tonight."

Razvan prickled. He could sense the mood shifting in the people around him. He shoved hard against the man behind and moved into the small gap that opened up. He pushed hard, using the weight of his body like an icebreaker to open tiny channels in the sheet of people and then to split them enough to move forward. He could feel the dangerous mood radiating outward faster than he could push through the crowd. He could smell the rush, the mix of fear and vengeance, and he knew that in this crowd there would be more than a few who carried ceremonial knives, mostly for show, but there was no telling what would set the spark among the tinder.

Razvan forced his way towards the toilets, to where Lockwood had gone. Then he felt it behind him, a change in the way the crowd moved and jostled. Someone was following in his wake, moving towards him. Razvan stopped and waited. He put one hand on his pistol, but firing a shot in a crowd was a bad idea at the best of times; in this crowd it would be suicidal.

There was a burst of motion behind him and a long stone blade lunged at his back. Razvan twisted slightly, leaning against a man to his left, and the knife slid by harmlessly; then he reached down and snapped the wrist that held the knife. There was a cry of pain and the clatter of stone blade hitting terracotta and with that the crowd suddenly eased. Razvan walked and patrons stepped aside, even if they had to squeeze themselves into tiny nooks between people to do so.

At the door to the toilets, Lockwood burst out, still buckling his belt.

"Sir, we have to get out of here," he said.

"You think?" asked Razvan.

"You should see the graffiti in there. It's hardcore . . ." his voice trailed off as he noticed the staring crowd and the metre of emptiness around Razvan. "Oh," he said.

"Let's go," said Razvan.

They made their way out of the Jaguar and Unicorn and off Texcoco Street by the nearest side alley. As the crowd thinned out, Razvan allowed himself to relax.

"What happened in there?" asked Lockwood.

"Nothing that needs reporting," replied Razvan.

"You all right, sir?"

"No, damn it, I'm not all right. I didn't get my Oxblood Ale."

They walked east into the old industrial graveyard where factories had been left to die. They walked to get away from the Pyramid of the Eagle, which seemed to watch over them from the summit of Kings Park. The ziggurat glowed orange from floodlighting, with flashes of blue and red from the police lights of the crime scene crew, and seemed to float in the distance no matter where they went.

Razvan never got his Oxblood, but a tiny corner all-nighter sold them beer, puppy kebabs and breath mints. They sat on a park bench a few blocks from Texcoco Street, far enough to be out of the fray, close enough to respond if paged, with the Pyramid's line of sight blocked by a water-stained concrete wall that ran the length of the street, and they drank together.

Razvan was the grandchild of a minor Wallachian noblewoman and a Nahuatl priest. Their affair had been quite the scandal. She was stripped of her titles and he was expelled from the priesthood, whereupon they sailed for the Southern Hemisphere to make a new life together. Some days Razvan took pride in their fierce determination to carve their own way in the world. Other days he felt the haem pangs and wished he had inherited his grandmother's blood privileges alongside her Wallachian genes.

Herbert Lockwood was the descendant of a pamphleteer who upset the Lord Protector of England with a particularly lurid gazette that made the mistake of making accusations of corruption that were, beneath the spittle-flecked ranting, undeniably true. The pamphleteer, being too nettlesome to leave in place and too prominent to hang, found himself transported to Perth.

For both men, the run of their lives had been corralled by decisions made by people far away and long since dead.

Razvan and Lockwood sat on the bench the rest of the night, venting their anger at having been pulled from an important surveillance, and trading stories, mostly of the incriminating variety, about their fellow officers.

Just on dawn, Lockwood's phone buzzed. "There's another body," he told Razvan. "Off Texcoco, corner of Metepec and Itzli."

"Let's go," said Razvan.

As they made their way to the new crime scene, the city awoke around them. The first buses rumbled down the streets, taxis started to be outnumbered by cars, the early cyclists, runners, and dog walkers came out of their homes and onto the footpaths.

Razvan and Lockwood crossed Texcoco and saw that the crowd had eased. A few hardy souls staggered about, and there was a dusting of Eagle sympathisers passed out in the street, making easy pickings for anyone inclined to add to the offerings already made.

Off Texcoco, they made their way through weatherboard cottages and tiny playgrounds that marked a sudden end to the ecosystem of North Bridge and into everyday suburbia. The bakeries and newsagents were rolling up their metal screens and putting their signs out front, although it would be hours yet until the offices and solicitors' firms opened.

Razvan stopped and held up his hand to Lockwood.

"What is it?"

"I can smell blood. Lots of it."

"We're standing right outside a butcher's."

"Human blood."

"You're sure?"

Razvan scoffed. "Of course I'm sure."

"Where?"

"I can't tell yet, need to look around."

Lockwood and Razvan paced the length of the street, followed a small alley to the right, found nothing, came back to where Razvan had first tasted the air.

"It's not here now."

"What? It's gone?"

"No, not gone, but a lot weaker. It's moved."

Lockwood pointed up the street. "Found it!" he said.

Half a block further on, an old woman walked against the flow of people coming into the shops for their morning supplies. She wore a light floral dress that billowed around her waist and she walked with a wobbling, side-to-side gait, as if her hip joints could only move in one plane. Her right hand held a blue plastic bag, a disposable supermarket bag holding something wet and dark that swung forward and back fro, and where the bag had touched her right leg it left a huge bloody stain on the back of her dress.

"Let's get her," said Lockwood.

"We'll follow her first," said Razvan.

Razvan and Lockwood kept their distance. They did not want to spook the old woman and there was no chance she could throw Razvan off the trail. Downwind, he could have smelt the blood from blocks away. While they walked, Lockwood called it in on his mobile phone.

She led them to a small Edwardian cottage on the lip of a railway embankment. They waited until she had stepped into the house, then moved up to the house.

"How long 'til a car gets here?" asked Razvan.

Lockwood echoed the question then said, "Ten minutes."

"Pass the phone." Razvan put the phone to his ear and said, "Permission to enter, sir . . . I know, sir, but we have no idea what's going on in there . . . I don't think we should wait . . . Much appreciated, sir." He gave the phone back to Lockwood. "In we go."

Lockwood knocked on the door. There was no answer. He knocked again, louder.

"Who's there?" asked the old woman.

"Senior Investigator Petru Razvan and Investigator Herbert Lockwood. Open up."

"Do you have a warrant?"

"We have reason to believe there may be a crime in progress on this property."

"I can assure you that is not the case, officers."

"Then you won't object to letting us in."

Then a male voice spoke, deep and old and dry as dust. "Let them in. Better we talk inside than have the whole street listen."

The door opened and the old woman stepped back to let the investigators enter. Inside the house was dark with blades of sunlight reaching in through small gaps in the shutters. It was hot and humid, and smelled like a delicatessen. From the rafters hung strips of drying meat. The walls were lined with shelving and the shelves were filled with books and codices. One wall of shelving was devoted to glass jars of organs and bones floating in a liquid that was various shades of tawny.

"Ye gods," muttered Razvan.

The old man spoke. "It's not too late to walk away, officer."

He stepped forward and a sliver of light ran across his form. As soon as Razvan saw the light sweep across the man, he knew he had made a mistake. They should have waited for the car.

The old man had painted his face black and marked his temples with smeared blood. His long hair was matted with gore. He wore a grey singlet that revealed a tattoo on his left shoulder of a feathered wolf, which meant he had fought with the Belavezha Wolves in the Cleansing of Florida nearly fifty years ago, and that meant the man was old, older than anyone Razvan had seen walking before, and dangerous. The blood in his veins would be so thick he would be chewing warfare by the bucket to keep his circulation flowing.

The old campaigner was a mirror opposite to Razvan. Where Razvan's ancestors had been cast out of the clashing empires of Bucharest and Tenochtitlan, this man had born with a Wallachian bloodline but fought with the Aztecs. He was a janissary, a radu bey, a man with a foot in two cultures, and the Belavezha Wolves took only the most uncompromising of converts.

Razvan had walked in with his hand on the hilt of his pistol. Now he moved his fingers slowly around the grip and onto the trigger.

"I can't do that, sir. We've already called in your address."

"You can call back, say it was the wrong house. Give us time to clear out."

"Don't move," said Lockwood, showing too much agitation.

"My friend," said the old man, "all our sacrifices are willing adults."

Razvan said, "Under the new codices, you are committing murder whether the victim consents or not."

"They are not victims," snarled the old man. "They ask to be sacrificed. They come to us and beg to join the rituals, to become gods for a day."

Lockwood drew his gun. "Sit down and we wait."

The old man sighed. He turned to the old woman and said, "You take the young one," and with that he leapt at Razvan.

Razvan ripped the pistol from its holster and fired. The first shot went wide, the second tore open the old man's thigh, but the man kept coming. The next shot opened his hip, the fourth landed square in the old man's chest, and finally the old man fell. Black blood oozed out of his wounds, torpid as syrup.

Razvan looked over his shoulder. Lockwood lay face down on the carpet, pale and unmoving and slick with blood. His gun lay unfired beside him. The old woman stood over Lockwood's body and looked back at Razvan.

"Stay where you are," ordered Razvan, aiming straight at her heart.

Ignoring him, she moved slowly to where the old man lay dying and held his hand. Razvan lowered his gun. The old woman would be no trouble now. He went over to Lockwood and that he was beyond resuscitation. He pulled up a vinyl-backed kitchen chair, sat down, and called for an ambulance to follow the police car. "Officer down," he added just before he snapped shut his phone.

The old lady sat down as well, holding her man's hand even though it now hung limp.

Razvan looked about the cottage. It was a reliquary of human remnants, a temple of bones and organs and strips of meat. There were bottles of charred heart ash, jars of body parts, jellied flesh, sun-bleached femurs, and jewellery made of wrist and finger bones wired into their natural anatomical relations. Each artefact had been carefully prepared according to prescribed rituals. Had Razvan and Lockwood not stumbled onto the house, the body parts would have been distributed to the faithful over the next few days. The Commissioner would be pleased and Lockwood would make a handy martyr of his own.

The police car pulled up outside the house. Its lights flicked colour across the curtains that shaded the front windows. The constables would be inside soon and Razvan had a question he needed to ask before that happened.

Razvan asked the old woman, "How can you do this? All the blood and death and wasted lives? And for what? Some stupid gods?"

The old woman let her man's hand fall and replied, "It's all too beautiful to be wrong."

AFTERWORD TO "APOLOGETOI"

One of Cortés's conquistadors wrote: "They take him who has to be sacrificed, and first they carry him through the streets and squares, very finely adorned, with great festivities and rejoicing. Many a one recounts to him his needs, saying that since he is going where his God is, he can tell him so that he may remedy them. Then he gives him refreshments and other things. In this manner he receives many gifts, as is the case when some one has killed a wolf, and carries the head through the streets. And all the gifts go to those who offer the sacrifice. They lead him to the temple, where they dance and carry on joyously, and the man about to be sacrificed dances and carries on like the rest."

To the Christian empires of the 16th century, the Aztecs presented a terrifying challenge to their notions of piety. They Aztecs practised the most barbaric rites, and yet they were not savages. They had a highly ordered, complex society with notions of honour and propriety to rival the arête of ancient Greek athletics. Aztec hydro-engineering created the marvellous floating city of Tenochtitlan, unequalled anywhere in the world. The absolutely worst thing, though, was the care and deliberation the Aztec priests applied to their activities. Here was a deeply religious civilisation dedicated to mass ceremonial murder, children included.

To this modern humanist, the Aztecs are just as horrifying but for different reasons, for what the Aztecs showed is that sophisticated and honourable people will engage happily in the most execrable practices so long as those practices are normalised, transcendental, and wrapped in a pretty ritual.

The 15th century Wallachian nobility is another horror entirely.

PUNISHMENT OF THE SUN

ALAN BAXTER

Annie sat at her window, staring across the darkness. No moon and high, thin clouds made the world beyond stygian and dead. Like her life.

She knew the tack shed sat not far away. Beyond that stretched dry, dusty paddocks with dry, dusty horses, ribs like xylophone keys through thin, scabby hides. The orange desolation dragged on as far as hope would last in every direction. Too young to leave this desiccated hole, she grudgingly endured.

A strike of light in the distance and Annie's heart skipped a beat. Her slumped pose in the window became rigid attention as she stared through the dark. Impossible to tell how far away it had been, she grew desperate to see it again.

Then another. Annie gasped, throat thickening with fear. A man, hands cupped around a lighter, his face briefly lit in orange glow and contrasting shadow. She could see two pinpricks of ruddy brightness, glowing and fading, well beyond the yard.

She forced her sight to penetrate the dark. Every time a man drew a lungful of smoke, the cigarette acted like a weak torch, easing back the night. She saw other movement, more than two of them. They carried something, wrapped and heavy, moving easily, unencumbered by the darkness or weight. Across the distance she heard a metallic rattle. They were at the feed shed across the south paddock. She couldn't see it, but every inch of this station lay burned across her mind like a scar. They were putting something in the feed shed.

† † †

Annie rose soon after the sun. As hot, early light crept across her bed she dragged on shorts and t-shirt and trotted through the house.

Her parents sat at the kitchen table, poring over paperwork. They drank acrid coffee while toast burned under the grill and her father moaned about taxes and levies. Annie headed for the door.

"Where are you going?" her father asked.

"Going to see Pebble!"

"Get back here!"

Annie stopped, set her jaw. She turned back, huffing a deep sigh. She stood in the doorway, framed by sunlight.

"Well?" her father said.

"What?"

"You know very well what! No play till your chores are done."

"I'll do them later."

Her father scowled. "You'll do as you're told!"

Annie gritted her teeth, desperate to investigate the shed. "What difference does it make?"

Her father scraped his chair back, half rising. "The difference is I told you to do them now!"

Annie looked to her mother, eyes pleading. Her mother just shook her head. "Neither of you care about me!" Annie yelled. "You only had children to do all your work for you! I hate you!"

Her father growled, stepping around the table. Annie bolted before he could say or do more, heading into the utility room and the tools for her chores.

† † †

An hour later she finally got time to herself. Everything seemed to be about cleaning and fixing and tidying. A few more years and she'd be gone.

She skirted the tack shed and climbed the gate of the south paddock. Sunbaked red earth puffed fine ochre dust with every slapping footstep as she ran. She approached the feed shed and slowed. Her heart danced in her throat and a chill leaked down her back. So fascinated by what she'd seen, her only thought had been to find out what those men were up to. Now came a second wave of thought, heavily tainted with trepidation.

She glanced back towards the house, squat and peeling in the already ferocious sun. Perhaps she should tell her dad what she'd seen. But what did he care? Always telling her what to do.

Swallowing her nerves, taking a steeling breath, she opened the shed door. Sunlight flooded into the musty darkness within, dust swirling in the shaft of day. She walked carefully into the gloom, looking all around the huge space. Plastic buckets and battered shovels lined the walls, bales and giant plastic feed bags made haphazard mountains all around. Everything sat as dull as her life. Except for a heavy looking canvas, dumped into a corner.

Annie reached a hand towards it, taking a corner, lifted it back. It lay empty, deflated against the shed wall. She saw a piece of thick, yellowing paper on the floor. A note, hand written in dark red ink.

You slew an elder and your punishment is sun.
Survive this trial and your punishment is served.
Fail to survive and your punishment is served.

That didn't make sense. What kind of punishment was sun? Who was the note for? She sighed, looking around the musty shed. Her eyes narrowed. Did she hear a scrape then, a sound of movement? Sharp lines of incandescence marked gaps in the planks of the walls, painting bright stripes across the floor. She walked among them, looking into the shadows between the feed bags and hay bales. It would take hours to search every nook and cranny.

The distant sound of her dad cursing drifted through the air. She sighed again, and headed back to the house

† † †

Annie's dad was furious. Her mum stood in the doorway, hands clasped. "What do you mean, all of them?" she asked.

"I mean all of them! Every fucking car, bike, quad. Even the tractor and the back-hoe. Some fucker's been in and ripped up the engine in every vehicle we own."

"Why?"

Her father spun on his heel, leaning across the yard in his anger. "How do I know why?"

Her brothers stumbled from the house, rubbing sleep from their eyes. Useless, dopey teenagers the pair of them. "Wha's goin' on?" Trent asked.

"Some of your friends having a lark?" Annie's dad yelled. "Someone's been in during the night and ruined every vehicle we've got."

"Why would it be our friends?" Josh, the eldest, seemed genuinely offended. "Maybe it's yours, pissed off that you never cough up for a round on the rare occasion you go to the pub!"

Their dad pulled back one hand, striding across the dusty yard. "Why you little . . ."

"Enough!" Annie's mum's voice cracked across the hot day, freezing everyone in their tracks, always the ultimate authority. "What's wrong with you? Josh, you need to learn some respect. Bill, calm down and call Jerry at the police station. See what he has to say."

Bill pushed past his sons. "As if he'll be any bloody help."

† † †

Annie sat at the kitchen table while her father fumed and her mother cried. Her brothers, quietened, looked on. The ruined remains of two satellite phones sat between them.

"Do any of you know why someone might have done this to us?" her father said. They all shook their heads. "Every vehicle ruined, the phone lines cut and the radio antenna is gone." He pointed at the smashed sat-phones. "To do this they came *in* the house."

Annie thought of the distant cigarette glows in the dark. She'd seen the men there, but hadn't heard anything else. Would they have done this? She fingered the strange note in her pocket, wondering if she should tell her father. But if she could figure this out on her own perhaps they'd all stop treating her like a kid. She bit her lower lip nervously.

"Is this some kind of warning, Bill?" her mother asked.

Her husband gave her a sharp look, said nothing.

"Can't we fix the phone line?" Trent asked.

"No. They've smashed the connection on the roof." Annie's father drew a deep breath, standing. "We need to act. I'll take a horse over to Bradley's place, use his phone to call Jerry and get the police here. They can bring stuff to repair our vehicles and phone. I'll use Bradley's ute to get back. Josh, that puts you in charge."

Josh nodded, looking young and terrified.

Annie's mum looked stricken. "Bill, it'll take you ten hours to ride to Bradley's!"

"What else am I going to do? I can do it in eight."

Josh grunted. "You'll kill the horse. Our nags aren't built or trained for that."

"So be it."

Without another word he headed out, Josh running to catch up.

"It's all right, mum," Trent said, setting his jaw. "We'll look after you."

"You're a good boy, Trent. Help your father."

† † †

Annie's restlessness became unbearable. "I'm going to feed the ponies."

Her mother looked up, nodded. "Don't go any further than that."

"Okay."

In the yard her brothers were arguing, trying to jury-rig an antenna. Only a year apart in age, everything became more about competition than cooperation. Annie's stomach felt like heavy water. Anger had driven her to hold her tongue. It felt like a terrible mistake. She had to solve this.

She reached the shed and heard scuffling as she pushed the door open. She froze on the spot. Holding her breath, straining her ears, she stood still for close to a minute. Nothing.

She pushed the door wide, walked cautiously in. Everything seemed as it had before. What had she heard moving? It had sounded too big for rats. She stalked through the bales and bags, looking into corners and gaps. As she got deeper into the shed, away from the flood of sunlight through the open door, the shadows grew denser. Gaps in the shed walls here and there still cast bright slashes across the floor and feed, everything in between a soft, dusty twilight. Enough to see by, too dim for detail. Maybe she should open the doors at the other end, let more light in.

She pushed between two stacks of bales and something whipped past with a hiss. The sound like someone in sudden pain, sucking air in through their teeth. A smell of burning hair drifted through the gloom. Annie's heart hammered. She turned in a circle, trembling. Low panic gripped her as she retraced her steps, trying to look everywhere at once.

Outside the hot day seemed as refreshing as a mountain stream.

† † †

Her brothers looked at her disdainfully. "Something in the feed shed?" Josh asked.

Annie nodded.

"What?"

"I don't know. It rushed past me."

"Did you get scared by a big, old rat?" Trent asked. The brothers exchanged looks of derision.

Annie ground her teeth. "What's wrong with you two? Don't you care about all our stuff being ruined? Something's going on!"

Josh barked a humourless laugh. "Yeah, of course. Dad's pissed someone off again and they're fucking with us. He probably owes someone money and all that stuff last night was 'a message'."

"What are you talking about?"

Trent sighed. "Dad's in big debt. This whole station is in trouble. We reckon he's got caught up with a loan shark and they're scaring him into paying up."

Annie looked back over her shoulder. "But what about the thing in the shed?"

"What thing? You're just spooked."

"No! I saw men last night, in the dark. They were smoking cigarettes and doing something over there!"

Josh and Trent's eyes widened in shock. "What?" Josh sounded incredulous. "Why didn't say anything before?"

"Because dad pissed me off and I wanted to figure it out myself to prove I'm not a kid!" Annie looked at the red, dusty ground.

Josh threw his shifter down. "Fuck me, Annie. You *are* a little kid. You should have told dad! When he gets back, you tell him."

She nodded. "What about that?" She pointed at the feed shed. "Someone's in there!"

"Why would someone hide in there, Annie? You're spooked. Go inside."

† † †

Her brothers fought and argued over the radio and eventually gave up. Her mother coped as she always did, making too much food, baking, roasting, boiling things down to jam. Annie worried. Her dad would be furious when he got back.

Her mother ran out of things to cook as the sun began to set. She sat at the kitchen table, hands tormenting a tea towel, staring out across the yard. Annie put an arm across her mother's shoulders. "Dad'll be back soon. It'll be all right."

Her mother smiled, though it did nothing but move her lips. "Sure, honey."

The sun dipped below the horizon, dusky twilight turning everything to deep brown shadows. "It's not really dark yet," Annie said.

Her mother shrugged. "Twilight or dark, same thing."

"Dad'll be back any minute."

"Where are your brothers?"

Annie looked out. "Trying to fix up Josh's bike last time I saw them."

"Call them in for me?"

Annie headed around the house towards the big garage where the ute, bikes and quads were kept. Something whooshed past her in the gloom. With a gasp and a swell of nerves she stopped dead. She saw Trent walking towards her. "Was that you?" she called out.

"What?"

"Something just brushed past me really fast."

Trent shook his head. "Stupid kid."

"Mum wants you two inside."

"Whatever."

A crash and yelp of pain sounded from the garage. Another crash, then a cry cut short. "What the fuck . . . ?" Trent turned. "What are you doing in there, Josh, ya dickhead?"

Annie felt a wave of foreboding spread up her body. "Trent, don't . . ."

He frowned at her. "Don't what?"

She felt fixed to the spot. Trent pushed open the side door of the garage. With a yell like he had been burned he staggered backwards. Annie started to cry.

Trent turned and ran for the house. "Annie! Get inside now!"

"What's happening?"

Trent ran, pumping his arms, face white. "Run inside, Annie!"

A dark blur shot from the shadows beside the garage. Trent arched forward as the shadow hit him in the back, legs still running as he lifted into the air. He screamed, high-pitched like a girl. Annie cried out. Trent hit the ground and a tall, pale man knelt beside him, one hand pressed into Trent's chest, holding him down. The man had blood over his face, dripping from his chin.

Annie screamed again as her mother came running around the house. Her mother's scream mingled with Annie's as the man fell upon Trent, shaking him by the throat like a dog with a rabbit.

Annie's mother skidded in the dust, raising something dark and shiny into the night. "Get off him, you bastard!" Thunder and fire burst out.

Annie winced, closing her eyes against the sound. She opened them as her mother fired the second barrel, but the man was nowhere to be seen. Trent lay still, his throat a shiny black mess in the gloom, his eyes staring wide into the darkening night.

Annie screamed. "He was in the shed!"

Her mother dropped her gaze to stare at Annie. "What? Do you know . . . ?" She whipped away from Annie's side like a sheet of paper caught in a sudden gust.

Tears flooded Annie's vision. Through the haze she saw her mother land near the chicken pens, legs twisted beneath her, mouth crooked in a snarl of pain, unseeing eyes staring at the ochre sand. The shotgun was nowhere to be seen.

Annie fell to her knees, sobbing and gasping. A sucking, slurping began to her left, where Trent lay in the dirt, but she refused to look. Her mind trembled. She wanted to curl up and sleep, never to wake again.

Another sound came distantly to her ears. A chattering rumble drifting on the hot night air. She jumped to her feet, running as fast as she could, waving her arms. "Daddy! Daddy, turn back!"

She saw her father's face behind the wheel, leaning forward, eyes narrow in concern. The ute skidded to a halt and he almost fell from the door, dragging a .303 with him. "Annie, what's happened?"

Annie sobbed, trying to speak. "Men last night . . . someone in the shed . . . Trent and mummy . . . he's coming . . ."

Her father grabbed her, looking hard into her eyes. "Where is everyone?"

Annie cried so hard she couldn't speak. Her entire body shook, her knees threatened to fold up. She felt vomit rising.

Her father picked her up, put her into the passenger seat. "Stay here. Lock the doors and don't open them for anyone."

He ran off into the darkness. Annie shook her head, whispering, "No, no, no."

A howl of soul-tearing anguish echoed back to her. She heard shouts, then gun shots. As her crying hitched to a quiet trembling, everything around the station fell to silence. Complete darkness settled over the ute, impenetrable. She could only see her reflection, gossamer faint in the windows.

Movement outside made her hold her breath. A shuffling, a slight cough. She dropped into the foot well as the passenger's door jiggled, locked shut. The scuffling retreated around the ute. She looked up, eyes widening as she saw the driver's door closed, but not locked.

The door opened and the pale man slipped in, smiling at her. Two teeth extended long over his bottom lip, sharp and shiny white. His face was clean but his shirt front and collar stained a darker blue than the rest. "Hi Annie."

She stayed down, curled as tightly as possible, shaking so much her teeth chattered. He leaned across and unlocked the passenger door, pushed it open.

"I've been watching you, trying to figure it out." He laughed. "I'm too full for more. Even a little one. But I'll see you again . . . one day."

Annie stared, frozen.

"Get out."

She uncurled her legs, sliding off the footplate and dropped to her knees in the dirt. The ute shuddered into life, big engine roaring. With a spin of tyres it drove into the night, leaving Annie kneeling in a cloud of dust. Within moments the darkness and silence had settled over her again.

AFTERWORD TO "PUNISHMENT OF THE SUN"

When I was thinking about what to write for this anthology I had two things in mind:

1. Australia is a wide open, sun-drenched land, and
2. Vampires are supposed to be nasty, feral creatures that feed on people, not lovely sparkly sex symbols.

It was important to me to factor these things into my story. When I started working with those ideas, the concept of vampires using the wide open, sun-drenched spaces to punish their own seemed both obvious and uniquely Australian. You couldn't punish a vampire in this way in Britain, for example. Subsequently, a vampire fighting for its life in this situation would act in a violent and completely ruthless way. Once I'd coupled that with a struggling family on an outback station, the story came together and the result is "Punishment Of The Sun". I hope you enjoyed it.

RED DELICIOUS

FELICITY DOWKER

The boy's arms were inside the dragon, and shadows stalked him with intent to kill.

His brown hair was pulled back in a messy ponytail, his eyes closed, his lanky jean-clad legs splayed on the muddy spur road. The metal flank he leaned against was not really that of a dragon, though that was what he'd called it as his friends had chained him to it. He seemed a fiery spirit himself, his hot exhalations pluming white in the freezing night air.

Ivy saw what the boy couldn't see yet: two big men moving toward him, one gripping an iron bar, the other a cricket bat. She crouched in the trees, waiting, watching. Eucalypts towered around her, spindly ghosts in the moonlight. She inhaled their menthol scent, and smelt pines, too; Leatherwood, Blackwood, Celery Top, Myrtle, Sassafras, Huon. Melodic names that reminded her of Saturday mornings spent at Salamanca Market on Hobart's waterfront with her parents, browsing the stalls' wood, sheepskin and opal wares, listening to Arauco Libre's lively Chilean music, eating steaming donuts laced with cinnamon and sugar—and, oh, Dagwood dogs skewered on wooden sticks, oozing thick tomato blood.

All that sensation, all that light. One and a half decades ago, when she'd been 18. She was still 18, but back then, she'd also been alive.

She remembered the sharp brine of the Derwent River in the air, fairy lights in the trees, and a dreadlocked woman at one of the stalls handing out SAVE THE WELD fliers. "Huon Pine are a remnant of the supercontinent Gondwana," the woman had said. "Undisturbed, they can live for more than 3,000 years." How impossible that had seemed to Ivy at the time. Now she wondered how many more thousands of years than that she herself would linger.

Forever, perhaps, whatever that meant.

She stopped breathing. It was unnecessary, and it brought yearning for all that was lost to her. Better to focus on this night, full of the forest's noises and the promise of blood.

Earlier, she'd watched Ponytail and his friends' machinations, completed by jerky torchlight; digging the hole, pouring quick-set cement, inserting shackle rings, driving a doorless old car over the top of their handiwork, securing Ponytail to it, and leaving him.

And now, the two brutes had appeared.

"You tree-huggers and your bloody 'dragons'," Iron Bar said, and Ponytail gasped. His feet twitched, sending a huntsman spider the size of Ivy's hand scuttling for cover. Gorgeous creatures. Didn't spin webs, just hunted.

"Who's there?" Ponytail's head snapped back and forth.

"*We* don't call 'em dragons, though," Cricket bat said. "*We* call 'em "how far off the ground do we have to lift that car before the hippy's arms pop out of his sockets"."

Ivy stepped out of the trees. The forest leaned in on both sides of the logging road, blocking the moonlight. Ivy could see just fine, but Ponytail, Iron Bar, and Cricket Bat could see only murky outlines— not that any of them saw her at all.

Ponytail was rigid against the car body. "What are you doing out here in the middle of the night?" He tried to sound brave, bless him, but he only sounded desperate.

"Hunting," Iron Bar said, slapping the bar against his palm. Cricket Bat chuckled. They stood directly in front of the boy now.

"I'm not hurting anyone," Ponytail said. "This is a peaceful protest. There's no need for violence."

"You hurt our families every time you *protest* against our livelihood," Cricket Bat said. "It's only fair we hurt you back."

"And what about what you're doing to this land? What about—"

Ivy didn't get to hear the boy's arguments, because Iron Bar adopted a baseball batter's stance and swung the bar in a huge arc at Ponytail's head. Blood exploded outward from the right side of his face, his head snapped to the left and ricocheted off the car body, and he slumped in his chains, unconscious. Iron Bar spat on him.

"Bullseye!" Cricket Bat yelled, and raised the bat above his head like an axe.

Ivy closed the gap between them in a blur of rapid movement, leaves whirling in her wake, mud spurting into the air. Iron Bar and Cricket Bat spun around, gaping at her. They saw the shape of her long tangled hair flying on the wind, the impression of dark checks on her flapping flannel shirt, but most of all, they saw her pale yellow eyes, glowing in the darkness like miniature moons.

"So you're here to hunt?" She said. "Great. So am I." She shouldn't talk to them, shouldn't prolong this, but the harder their hearts were beating when she bit into them, the bigger their arterial spray would be, exploding against the back of her throat and gushing into her, life itself. And oh, but she wanted life.

"Get the hell out of here," Iron Bar said, but it sounded like a question.

Ivy shouldered past them, craning her head over Ponytail's shoulder, looking down into the car, her eyes lighting their own way. In their confusion, Iron Bar and Cricket Bat didn't touch her. Two holes were torn in the wreck's underbelly, through which Ponytail's arms were placed, chained to the shackle rings in the cement.

"Ah." Ivy straightened, turned to face the men, standing between them and their victim. "Must dent your working day in a big way, moving them every time they do this."

"Didn't you hear him?" Cricket Bat pointed at her with his bat. "He said get the hell out of here. This is nothing to do with you."

"Oh, but it is." Ivy smiled. They didn't see her fangs; to them, her teeth were just white smudges in the night.

"What, he your boyfriend or something?" Iron Bar took a step closer. "Well, he shouldn't have played in the forest with the big boys. And neither should you." Another step. Another.

"Yeah," Cricket Bat said, raising his bat as Iron Bar reached for her with blood-spattered fingers. Behind her, Ponytail gurgled as he woke.

"I don't see any big boys here," Ivy said. "Just sacks of shit who feel tough when they beat on chained-up kids."

"We'll show you what big boys we are, sweetheart," Iron Bar said, dropping his bar to the ground and reaching for Ivy's throat. She reached for him in turn, and for a moment they looked like lovers locked in a heated embrace. She broke his neck before he could scream, the crack like a gunshot, carried away by the wild night wind. He fell bonelessly to the ground. Cricket Bat roared. She held her arms wide, welcoming him. He swung at her with his bat, but she slapped it aside like a mosquito, sending it flying into the forest. His arms dropped to his sides and he stared at her, stunned.

"Oh, come on," Ivy crooned. "You've got more than that, *big boy.* Show me."

Cricket Bat crouched, dropped his head below his shoulders, and rushed at her. When he reached her, she snatched a fistful of his hair and yanked. His body continued its charge, bouncing off the car next to Ponytail, who shrieked as it fell to the ground, blood jetting from its neck stump. Cricket Bat's head dripped and swayed in Ivy's hand like a grisly piñata. She held it above her, letting blood patter on her face, tilting her head back and opening her mouth, sighing as the red droplets coated her tongue.

"Oh my God," Ponytail moaned behind her. "Oh my God."

She lowered Cricket Bat's head and turned to look down at Ponytail. He sobbed and muttered, the ruined right side of his face still bleeding heavily, his mouth moving with obvious difficulty.

"It's ok," Ivy said, kneeling before him.

"Oh my God," he said again, then: "Thank you."

"Don't mention it," she said, and, reaching out with her free hand, broke his neck. Her teeth slid into him at almost the same moment his vertebrae snapped, half his lifeblood gone down her throat before he even knew he was dead.

† † †

"Red Delicious." Tesla flicked through the dog-eared appointment book on the front desk, hunching her right shoulder to wedge the phone's handset against her cheek. "I dunno, dude, we're booked out months in advance. We might be able to squeeze you in if it's small . . ."

Ivy took her foot off the pedal, the tattoo gun in her hand falling silent, and watched Tesla over the bare hump of her client's rounded hip. Tesla was tiny, looking only 12 of her 19 years. Her fire-engine-red hair stuck out in fuzzy spikes where the phone was pressed into it. Ivy smiled at her. Tesla didn't smile back. She was still pissed about being left to run the shop alone last night while Ivy hunted and fed—though of course, Tesla didn't know that was what Ivy had been doing.

"I love this song," Ivy's client said. Jane, Jill? Ivy didn't much care. "*Pure Massacre.*" The girl hummed along. Her blood spotted her skin like an orchard of tiny rotten apples, reeking of codeine abuse. Ivy sprayed water on the half-finished tattoo, wiped the blood away with a paper towel, and flung the soiled towel in the bin at her feet.

"Silverchair were great, once," Ivy said, bending her head, the tattoo gun buzzing in her hand as she recommenced her work on the girl's thigh. She stopped breathing so she didn't have to smell the girl. "Frogstomp was their only good album."

"You would say that—you've really got that 90s grunge vibe going on."

"Thanks," Ivy said, resisting the urge to press harder with the tatt gun.

"You know what I mean," Jane/Jill said. "Hey, I like your shop logo. It's hardcore."

"Thanks." *Shut up, shut up, shut up, you little bag of rotten blood, shut up.*

"What is it, exactly? It's a bit twisted, I can't tell. No, wait, I can guess—it's partly an apple? Cos your shop's called Red Delicious. And the Huon Valley is the Apple Valley, and Tasmania is the Apple Isle, right?"

"Good guess." Maybe pressing harder with the tatt gun wasn't such a bad idea.

"So what is it?"

"What?"

"The logo? Apart from an apple, I mean."

Ivy sighed. "It's a bleeding heart, shaped like Tasmania, with a tattoo needle stem at the top."

"In other words," Tesla said, finished with her phone call, "It's a fucking apple, ok? Now unless you want a shaky tattoo that goes all the way to the bone, I suggest you shut it and let Ivy work in peace, yeah?"

Jane/Jill gaped, her eyes darting from Tesla to Ivy, then buried her face in her arm and was silent. Ivy raised an eyebrow at Tesla. Tesla smirked. All was forgiven, then.

Israel's Son blared through the shop. Tesla sang along as she worked on a stencil for her next client. Ivy smiled. Being dead had its downfalls, but running your own night-time tattoo shop wasn't one of them. She'd built a solid rep in the five years she'd owned Red Delicious, and people never baulked at the opening hours. They figured geniuses were always eccentric, and coming into the shop under cover of darkness added to the mystique, as did Ivy's "cool yellow contacts and fake fangs". The customers all left satisfied and they all paid top dollar. Dead or not, a vampire still needed to make a living.

Jane/Jill's swirly floral obscenity was almost done. The girl winced and twitched melodramatically as Ivy worked, the white butcher's paper stretched under her crackling on the red vinyl it protected. The phone rang, and Tesla answered. She always did. Aside from it being part of Tesla's job to handle the phones, Ivy had the same issue with phones that she had with mirrors. They didn't work for her. No reflection—visual, verbal, or otherwise.

"Red Delicious. Hi, mum. No . . . calm down . . . *what?*" Tesla dropped the phone.

"Tes?" Ivy stopped tattooing.

Tesla looked at Ivy, her eyes wide and moist. "Mum says Pete never came home last night."

"I thought your brother often went MIA."

"The police called Mum. They think they found Pete in the Weld. She has to go identify the . . . the body."

If Ivy's heart was beating, it would've stopped. "What would your brother have been doing in the Weld?"

Tesla was too distressed to notice Ivy's odd reaction. She retrieved the phone, her mother still on the other end, and said she'd be home in fifteen minutes. She hung up.

"Tes?" Ivy laboured the point. "Why would Pete have been in the Weld?"

"I don't fucking know," Tesla snapped. "I . . ." She clapped a hand over her mouth, grabbed her bag, and left.

This was bad. Ivy liked Tesla, a lot. She also liked keeping her work and her feeding separate. That was why she hunted in the Weld in the first place. It was close enough for a vampire to run to within minutes, but far enough away to make running into the few humans Ivy still knew—at night, no less—so unlikely as to be impossible. Her two halves were never to touch. What's more, hurting Tesla was unthinkable. The girl was like a punky puppy, and if Ivy was honest with herself, she probably didn't just like her, she probably loved her.

It might be the love of an owner to her dog, vampire to human, but it was still love.

But Ivy had never met Tesla's brother. She didn't know what he looked like. It was possible, during last night's hunting trip, or a previous one, that . . .

"Get out," Ivy muttered. Jane/Jill looked up at her in confusion. "Your tattoo's done. No charge."

"But . . . can I have a mirror to look at it? And I couldn't possibly not pay."

"I said, *get out.*"

Jane/Jill looked into Ivy's "cool yellow contacts", and obeyed. Fast.

† † †

Ivy needed to go out in the light.

Like most young vampires, she'd been obsessed with losing the sun when she was first turned. Even in Tasmania, Australia's sun was harsh. It hadn't been easy, but she'd found a way. She couldn't change her body since dying. Hair and nails grew back, wounds healed, but for some reason, tattoos stuck. Something to do with the interplay of vampire blood, metal-heavy ink, and the deep layer of dermis she injected it under. Ivy had decorated her skin with tattoos everywhere she could reach—largely red, because it had the most metal—and had Tesla tattoo the areas she couldn't. She'd done her face and neck in white ink, from shoulders to hairline. It meant that with a thick hat, a lot of sunscreen, and several layers of clothing, she could walk in the day for limited periods of time before the burn started to get too deep to bear and sweet-smelling smoke started to seep from her pores.

She ran to Tesla's house and hid behind a wattle bursting with yellow flowers. A female voice, an older version of Tesla's, drifted from an open window in the one-sided conversation of all telephone users.

"I know." A sob. "It's horrible. Those mutilated bodies. Someone's child, each and every one of them, and I know it's awful, but all I could think while I was looking at them was *thank God they're not mine*. Tesla's gotten it in her head that Pete's up there, though, in the Weld, because the bodies keep turning up, and he's still not home, and she's driven off up there in such a state . . ."

Ivy ran for the Weld, invisible with speed, the trip brief as ever, but still giving her a moment to think. She never left bodies lying around. She wasn't *stupid*. She buried them deep, and covered her tracks with inhuman expertise. It had troubled her when bodies had started being found in the Weld weeks ago, but the authorities had been curiously eager to write them off as animal attacks, accidents, exposure, drunken fights among campers gone wrong. It sounded flimsy to Ivy, but people bought it.

And now Tesla's brother was missing, and Tesla was in the Weld looking for him. It would be bad if Ivy had inadvertently killed Pete, but niggling at the back of her mind was the question: if she hadn't, what had?

† † †

It felt like hours had passed before Ivy found the first body. Her skin had begun to feel hot, even in the damp, dim forest, and she thought she detected a hint of the roast pork smell that meant she'd begun to fry in the blood of her victims.

The body was a girl in her late teens, face untouched except by dirt and leaves. The rest of her hadn't fared so well. Her clothes hung in ragged streamers, and her flesh had been torn from her bones in chunks, especially around her neck and inner thighs. She looked like she'd been mauled by a powerful animal. Of course, there was nothing bigger than a fox in the Weld. Maybe a wild dog or two, escaped from a nearby farm, but that was a stretch. Certainly nothing equipped to do this.

Ivy hadn't killed this girl. She never forgot a victim's face.

She darted through the forest she knew so well. She found more bodies, and recognized none of them.

The heat in her skin deepened, became a definite burn. Sickly-sweet odour filled her nostrils as she inhaled. Her head swam and her limbs felt floaty. She'd have to turn back and seek the shelter of her dark bedroom above Red Delicious, with its blackout curtains, double brick walls, heavy door, and a bed that sang to her across the kilometres.

"Hello, Ivy," a male voice said.

Ivy stiffened. "Ethan," she whispered.

"You're adorable, you know that?" Ethan wandered out from behind a tree as if this were all part of his morning stroll. "Fifteen years as a vampire, and you're still here in this redneck hole, clinging to your human memories, keeping human pets."

"Why are you here?" Ivy stepped sideways, circling, keeping the male vampire in front of her at all times. He was tall and broad, clad in blue jeans and a battered brown leather jacket, his hair short and spiky, his mouth set in a pleasant smile that was betrayed by his long canines and creamy-bright yellow eyes. He wasn't wearing a hat, and his skin looked untouched by sunscreen. He was ancient, though he looked no more than 30. His skin withstood the sun far better than Ivy's. His voice had a strange accent, somewhere between Irish and American.

"I got bored. It happens, every decade or so. Thought I'd see how my newest daughter was doing. But you're not doing anything, are you? You make me wonder why I bothered giving you this gift at all."

"You didn't give me anything. You took everything from me."

Ethan rolled his eyes. "Always the same old song from the newbies. "Wah! I didn't want to be a vampire!" Get over yourself."

"You killed my parents!" Ivy's hands curled into fists as she stepped closer to Ethan. "You murdered them, and you turned me, and you had me *feed on their corpses*! Then you left. What did you expect me to do?"

"Be a *vampire*," Ethan hissed, closing the gap between them. "Not the snivelling, creeping, human-loving thing you are. This always happens. Humans always disappoint, even once they're vampires. A tattoo shop? A few loggers and hippies taken in the woods now and then? *That's* your eternity?"

A weak cry sounded nearby. Ivy's head snapped around in the direction of the sound. Tesla!

"Oh, yes. I haven't finished with that one. Came looking for her brother who, unfortunately, is rotting somewhere in these woods already. He died begging. But I liked her. She had guts. So I didn't spill them." Ethan laughed at his own pun. Ivy snarled. "I was almost done with her when you showed up. She's drained, but I haven't refilled her yet."

Ivy's mouth hung open as the meaning of Ethan's words dawned on her. "You've . . . *turned* Tesla?" She'd smelt blood on the air, but it had been masked by all the other strong scents in the area—decaying flesh, old and new blood, Ethan himself, her own slow-burning skin. Now she focused, and yes, there was Tesla in that blood, and pain, and horror, and grief. Her lips peeled back and she bared her fangs at Ethan in open aggression.

"Well, no, she's not turned yet, she's just dying. Without vampire blood, she'll be worm food, probably within minutes." He wiped his mouth with the back of his hand, a smear of red stark on his white flesh. "She was a *tasty* one, too."

Ivy leapt, but Ethan was ready for her. He caught her like a father might catch his child as she ran into his arms, and threw her in the air.

She flew for a moment, small whorls of sweet smoke spiralling dizzily in her wake, and then crashed into a tree. Bark exploded around her upon impact, the tree splintering and toppling to the ground. Ivy shook her head, panting, and got to her feet. Blood trickled from a cut on her forehead, obscuring her vision. She ran a finger along the cut as it healed, catching the blood before it stopped flowing, and licked her finger.

"You're burning, my daughter," Ethan taunted. "Better run back to your burrow and hide. I'll look after your little pet while you're gone."

"Ivy?" Tesla's voice was thin, but closer now. The undergrowth rustled as the girl dragged herself closer to Ethan and Ivy. "Help me. I'm cold."

"Help her, she's cold!" Ethan mocked.

Ivy rushed at him again, feigning right. In his arrogance, he didn't doubt her move. He lunged right to counter her, and she curled around and came at him from the left, wrapping her arms and legs around him, sinking her teeth into his throat. He screamed, and grabbed her head in his strong hands. He pulled, and Ivy's skin began to sizzle in earnest as her neck stretched. But Ethan's blood was powerful, and it gushed down Ivy's throat, strengthening her and weakening him with equal speed.

He might still have beaten her, if the group of ten loggers hadn't chosen that moment to burst into the clearing where the battle was taking place, chainsaws, axes, and picks in hand. One of them carried Tesla, the girl pale and bloodied, her hands clinging to his neck like little bird claws.

"It's him," Tesla cried, "That's the one who attacked me, the murderer who's been leaving bodies up here!"

Ivy detached from Ethan's throat with a slurp and regarded the loggers with glowing yellow eyes and long fangs coated in gore. They stared at her as Ethan kept his vice-grip on her head. The smell of pork filled the air, and Ivy's skin radiated red, like sunburn gone radioactive.

"That's my friend," Tesla whispered. "She was trying to save me."

Looking at each other, then Ethan, then Tesla, then Ivy, then at each other again, the loggers finally decided to act first and question later. They waded in, weapons raised high. Ethan released Ivy and tried to turn to defend himself, but Ivy clung to him like a spider monkey, and he staggered, giving the first logger time to bring his axe down on Ethan's head as several other loggers started up their chainsaws.

Ivy let Ethan go, the weakened older vampire falling to the ground as the humans closed in around him, ignoring his screams. She ran to Tesla and gathered her in her smoking arms. The girl was unconscious now, but Ivy whispered to her as she ran, nonetheless.

"It's ok," she said, as the Weld fell behind them and they neared the safety of Red Delicious. "It's ok."

† † †

Ethan blinked, tried to knuckle the blood-encrusted sleep out of his eyes, but found he couldn't move his hands. He turned his head from side to side and saw silver manacles encircling his wrists, the chains tethering him to the surgical table he lay on. Something rattled when he tried to move his legs—more manacles around his ankles. If he pushed his skin against the silver too hard, it sizzled and smoked. There would be no muscling out of his bonds.

He opened his eyes wider, taking in his surroundings. Red vinyl. Pin-ups. Silverchair blasting from the wall-mounted speakers. Photos of tattoos on the walls. A weird image that might've been a heart or might've been an apple emblazoned everywhere he looked. Blackout curtains drawn across the windows.

Ivy and Tesla, smiling down at him with matching fangs.

"Wha," he said, and found that his throat burnt so much he couldn't go on.

"That'll be the wild rose and hawthorn branches we've shoved down your neck," Tesla said. "Great thing about the Huon and the Weld and, well, pretty much everywhere in the Tassie wilderness: plenty of natural vampire deterrents to be harvested. Easy to avoid if you're running past them and know they're there, not so easy to avoid if they're inserted inside you."

"You'll find talking painful, and screaming impossible," Ivy added. "But please, feel free to try. It never stops being funny."

Ethan did try, and a fire raged in his throat that required him to squeeze his eyes shut and be still for a few agonised moments before he could move again.

"Bitches," he rasped.

"No," Ivy said. "Vampires. Wasn't that what you wanted us to be?"

"How?" Ethan ground out the word.

"Simple. Ivy brought me back here, gave me her blood. You'd already drained me, so that was that. I was one of you. And to be honest, I'm quite pleased about that, which will probably piss you off more than anything." Tesla handed a bottle of clear liquid to Ivy, reaching over Ethan to do it. He bared his fangs at her, and she chuckled and patted his arm.

"And then," Ivy continued, doing something with a metal object that Ethan couldn't move his head far enough to see properly, "We went back to the Weld. If the loggers had still been there, well, sadly, they would've had to go, despite their fortuitous assistance. But they'd gone, and they'd left you there in an undignified pile of bloody flesh. They'd messed you up pretty bad, but they hadn't removed your head, and they hadn't put wood through your heart, and they hadn't set you alight, so you were still alive, though they didn't think so."

"They'd obviously just left you there to rot. Guess they figured we wouldn't mind," Tesla said. "And they were right."

Ethan hissed, coughing as the fire scourged his throat.

"So we brought you back here, and we made sure you couldn't yell or escape, while we dealt with the rest of the mess you created," Ivy said, unscrewing the bottle and carefully pouring a little of the liquid into a plastic cup, where it mixed with the red ink already there. The sharp odour reached Ethan, and he sucked in a startled breath. "We found all the bodies you'd left up there, and we buried them."

"I took my brother home to my mother," Tesla added, her voice soft. "And she told me I looked paler than usual, and asked if I was alright. Can you imagine? I deliver her son's mauled body, bloated and already decomposing, and she asks me if *I'm* ok. I've lost a mother as well as a brother, because I can't see her anymore. The grief might destroy her."

"But you've gained a sister," Ivy said, dipping a long metal needle into the cupful of ink.

"A different sort of mother," Tesla agreed.

"And when your mother's time comes, if you decide to, you can turn her, too."

"Please," Ethan said. "Not . . ." He coughed as his throat refused to let him continue.

"Garlic?" Ivy inserted the needle into the tattoo gun and pumped the foot pedal experimentally, smiling as it buzzed into life. "'Fraid so, *dad*. I think we'll start with a nice, big chest piece. The ribs are the worst, you know. Some people throw up, others pass out, some just cry like babies. You're a big strong vampire, so you'd normally be fine, but with the garlic I just put in the ink, well . . ."

Tesla nodded and pointed to a large sticker on the wall above Ivy's head: YOU BET IT HURTS!

"We'll start with a nice traditional heart with "mum" on a banner in the middle, for my mother, and for Tesla's, you son of a bitch," Ivy said, brushing her hair out of her face and leaning close to Ethan's chest, tattoo gun in hand. "From there, we'll do a stylized memorial tatt for Pete. I haven't decided what we'll do for my dad yet, but we've agreed that all the names of our victims go on you, too, as they happen. You're going to be our in-house pincushion. That's a lot of garlic ink."

"But you're vampires too," Ethan whispered. "You kill too."

"Two wrongs don't make a right," Tesla said. "You made us. The sins of the father aren't going to be visited on the daughters, they're staying right with the father."

"Sucks to be you," Ivy said, and she and Tesla shared a giggle at the pun before Ivy put the needle to Ethan's pale skin.

It turned out that he could scream, after all.

AFTERWORD TO "RED DELICIOUS"

I'm from Tasmania, so the requirement that the stories for Dead Red Heart be in some intrinsic way Australian was a delight. As a writer, you don't want to churn out the exact same thing all the other writers are submitting, and I was fairly confident that few, if any, would write about Tasmania for this anthology—or if they did, I hoped my love for my island home would infuse my story with enough oomph for it to still earn a place. (Yes, I know Australia is an island, too. Hush.)

In addition, I've always loved the vampire mythos, and still do to this day, despite cries that our fanged friends have been overexposed. That's like saying a person can have too much chocolate, and we all know that's crazy talk, right?

I'm also passionate about body art. There just aren't enough tattoos in speculative fiction, and the tattoos that do show their inky faces are much maligned as token, clichéd, sexist or sexy, classless, or just plain ugly. Like most tattooed freaks, I don't much care about that, to be blunt. How others perceive body art is their problem. But it is art, and I jumped at the chance to wear my tattooed heart on my sleeve, in print. Art begets art.

Initially, I hoped to make some sort of commentary about conservation and logging in Tasmania through the subtext of "Red Delicious" (I particularly wanted to pay homage to the Weld Angel, but couldn't—Google her, seriously) but as always happens when I try to be too clever for my own good, I don't think that really worked out. I might've wanted to provide powerful insight, but Ivy just wanted to bite people, run a cool tatt shop, and have a bloody good time.

I did manage to include one important truth in "Red Delicious", though . . . Frogstomp really was Silverchair's only good album.

JUST A MATTER OF ECONOMICS

YVONNE EVE WALUS

I pretended to be one of them so I could gain entry to the conference facilities. All my credentials were in order, and I knew how to nod a greeting to look the part. The bulky guards let me through the massive wooden door without a second glance.

I made it in, but I felt no high of victory. Searing shards of hatred exploded in my spine. The hotel was teeming with them. My skin shrank back, pulling tight around my chest, urging me to turn back.

Vampire! Vampire! The childhood taunt reverberated against my eardrum. Revulsion shot up sour into my mouth. *Vampire!* I would show them yet.

"Are you all right, sir?" A waiter with a silver bowtie stood at my elbow.

"Quite," I snapped.

"May I offer you a drink?"

He did not carry a tray. I shuddered. "No, thanks."

Time to stop drawing attention to myself and get on with my plan. Act the part. Mingle. Listen. Draw conclusions.

One delegate put away his phone. "Thought I'd check the Internet for the latest news," he said. "Nothing new."

"The Democratic Province of Fiji doesn't have much of a Web presence," answered another. "*I* watched the VCNN. The disease spread to Vanua Levu and three other minor islands, but it hasn't yet hopped the border into the Democratic Province of Vanuatu."

"Bugger! I have land on Vanua Levu—"

"History is repeating itself," I couldn't be certain whether it was part of the same conversation. "In the early 2000s, it was Foot and Mouth that attacked the stock."

The sniggers that followed raised my blood temperature to boiling point. I stared out the window, getting a grip.

Outside, the sun had already set. The rapidly darkening Australian sky hung liquid over the bush. But inside the conference building, I smelled none of the powdery air, heard none of the evening cicadas. We may as well have gathered in a metropolis hotel, instead of United Australia's trendiest Wildlife Reserve.

A firm believer in hiding in plain view, I chose a seat in the second row from the front and opened my conference folder. A three-day old news-snippet was superimposed onto the first page. *Danger approaching our border*, the headline screamed.

And then, in smaller font: *The outbreak was first detected two months ago in the Democratic Province of Tonga, but the disease has now spread—*

My mind slid over the remainder of the article. I knew all that. That's why I'd insinuated myself here.

I paged over. Another headline: *Government's head in sand, foot in mouth.*

Text followed: *In a press conference yesterday, a government spokesperson quoted outdated statistics to bolster the official claim that AIDS has not reached epidemic scale in Australia. Although HIV tests are available on request, no data has been recorded in accordance with the Privacy Act. Officially, the problem doesn't exist.*

Among those quoted to have spoken out against the government, I found a statement made by our organisation.

"Your attention, please." The MC brought us to order.

The plenary speaker was a young female with a blaze of hair so fiery it distracted me from her opening words. I usually need more than good looks to feel sexual desire and I had never been attracted to one of *them*, but this girl was . . . something else. My seat was close enough to spot a promise of freckles on her stubborn nose.

Yowser. Me Tarzan, she Jane.

Her presentation covered the very topic that had made me risk my life at this conference, yet only fragments reached my brain. Typical male, me.

". . . overwhelmed by the response. Ninety-five percent volunteered for the tests . . . HIV's negative propaganda . . . preliminary results." As she spoke, she activated the data screen.

Stock quota. Test results.

Disbelief punched me between the eyes. Could it really be? Eighty percent of the population infected?

An icy wave crawled up my back. And it wasn't a gust of the air con.

". . . treatment . . . land-wide panic . . . mass emigration . . . cannot afford that."

Afford? I mused. *Cannot afford that*?

". . . the latest strain of the virus . . . spreading more rapidly than its predecessors . . . resilient . . . full-scale research into a new cure . . . more complex with each mutation."

I had been right. They *were* financing the research. They *did* want to find a cure.

"What about vaccines?" asked somebody far back.

The speaker's hair bounced from side to side in a shock of auburn flames. "Too late for that," she grimaced. Impatience lent a new dangerous spark to her gaze, a new twist to the already intriguing lips. My humming body enjoyed the second-row view.

She paused as she sipped the thick crimson liquid from her glass. "With the proportion of stock already infected, vaccines wouldn't make much difference." Her eyes combed the room, her face lighting up in a smile of recognition time and time again. Once, her gaze bounced off like a basketball. I looked in that direction and recognised Alvir. The richest one of the lot. The head of the most powerful clan, the owner of the majority of the South Pacific territory. Rumour had it that he controlled many of the Democracies' presidents.

I turned back towards the podium. The redhead was looking directly at me now, wary, challenging.

"The disease is still confined to the islands. We could step up border security and minimise infiltration . . ."

The screen came to life again and displayed a map of the region. The mercury-like light pointer moved along the Gold Coast and Sunshine Coast all the way to Townsville.

"Here's the fence. Its optical expert system can recognise the means of violation—an animal, a human, a boat." More slides. "The software identifies the section of the breached fence to the nearest metre. However, the resource constraints do not allow us to respond . . . . submitted a request . . . change the setting to *stun* or *lethal* . . . need authorisation by the highest channels . . . more drastic measures—"

Applause interrupted her.

It couldn't be my imagination. A flicker of loathing crossed her face. She looked up from her notes, straight at Alvir the Wealthy.

"We'll reconvene in two hours' time," she announced. Her lips looked very dark and very full. "During your midnight recess, I would like you all to consider the options."

I shuffled out of the conference room in a daze. This couldn't be happening.

"Hey you!" I heard a voice behind me.

I'd been spotted. My mind whirred maniacally. What gave me away? The note taking? The emotion in my eyes when I listened to the dry figures? The fact that I had avoided the carafe all evening?

I turned around, my face impassive. Or what I hoped would pass for impassive.

"Yes?" I demanded.

"ID."

I produced it, an elaborate document detailing my background and family history. It was based on a true identity. The organisation to which I belong is very thorough in such matters.

The owner of the identity was dead. The organisation is not only thorough. We can also be ruthless.

"Password!"

I gave the one for the night, as well as the general one.

Even that wasn't sufficient. One of the bulky security guards donned a mask and held my arms, while the other sprayed something into my face. Garlic oil. I twisted in the man's grip, retching and choking.

"Sun torch," ordered the man who held me.

My skin reddened as soon as the beam hit it, then began to sizzle. I yelped and kicked at my captor's shin. I felt the vice around my shoulders soften. A hand pulled me to my feet.

"A thousand pardons, sir," the guard said. "We thought—"

"I know what you thought," I wheezed through clenched teeth. My stomach was still in my throat, both from the garlic and from the narrow escape.

At least they hadn't tried a mirror test. But then, the reason I felt safe infiltrating a rustic setting like this one, was precisely the low probability of shiny-surface décor.

† † †

Concealed by a fake rock formation, Cass watched the stranger's ordeal. For a while, she stood perfectly still, pondering, analysing her emotions. Was she relieved or disappointed that the sex dish had turned out to be one of them?

She'd been so sure of herself. Although the guy looked the part, what with his white skin and fangs, there was a certain *something* about him. Something different. Excitingly covert. Frail and primeval and—yes, decidedly animal-like.

But all she had was intuition. And he had clearly passed the tests. So perhaps it was just her hormones talking.

"Thanks," she grinned at the bouncers and tossed her head, letting her hair ripple along her exposed neck and shoulders. "One can't be too careful these days."

"Milady," they answered in unison.

Oh boring, boring, boring! Why couldn't they wink at her? She'd been informal enough with them, and often enough.

Look at me, she wanted to shout. I'm more than my father's daughter. Royalty or not, I'm female. Attractive. Who cares about the stock, who cares about the epidemic and the financial consequences? The night is starry and you guys have gorgeous muscles, we can frolic in my private swimming pool and . . .

"Cassy, my deah," she heard a stern voice behind her. "Why didn't you complete the phesentation? I thought we'd decided—"

"It's Cass," she interrupted without turning her head. "C-A-S-S. A fact you might care to remember if you're hoping to marry me."

She marched off, still without a glance in Alvir's direction. She despised him almost as much as she despised his idea, his solution to the epidemic crisis. And yet she knew if she allowed herself to remain in his company for too long, she'd succumb to him. Not because she had any desire for *him*, but because she had plenty of desire per se . . . and no other male dared to respond to her advances. They all feared Alvir.

Damn, damn, damn. It was this Austrâlian air affecting her. She'd been used to the chills of Christchurch on that remote southern island across the sea. But after the tsunami scare the previous decade, Papa had moved the entire clan to the paradise that was Central Australia.

And paradise it had been, despite the sudden onslaught of immigrants, all driven out of the Pacific by the fear of floods and permanent climatic change. Paradise rediscovered. Till now.

She opened the door to her father's suite without knocking.

"Papa," she put her arms around the stout figure. "Will you do me a favour? It's about the guy I've just—"

"Hnph."

Ah, she'd forgotten. He was still seething because of the way she had treated Alvir in the morning, just before going to sleep. Well, she could just imagine what he'd say about her latest offence.

She wasn't going to give in without a fight. Hell, she was not going to give in, period. She knew her father owed Alvir a dreary sum of money after his latest gamble with the Reserves. He said it had worked with the American Indians. Unfortunately for him and Cass, though, it hadn't with the Pacific Islanders.

"Father," the official term now, no more endearments. "I am not going to marry Alvir. You may as well accept it. I won't be sold off to him like a chattel."

"Sold? Who's talking about selling you, my pet? Alvir is a good fellow, a decent fellow. A girl could do a lot worse."

A girl could do a lot worse indeed. A lot worse. That stranger, for example. The one who had passed all the tests but still felt dangerously wrong. Cass remembered the way he'd drunk in her every word and gesture at the conference. She felt a delicious shiver fizzing up and down her spine.

The stranger was not a good prospect, not by a long shot. He was not aristocracy. He did not wear any wealth insignia. Still, he must have been important, or they wouldn't have let him attend the conference. A mystery man. An animal.

"Yes, Papa," she said meekly, her eyes shining. "A girl could do a lot worse."

†   †   †

I was startled when the door of my room squeaked open. No knocking had preceded it, no audible footsteps. Although I knew it was silly, for I carried no incriminating materials with me, my instinctive reaction was to evaluate the room's appearance. The conference folder and my notes on the bed—those were perfectly safe. My personal artefacts in the adjoining bathroom—nothing wrong with them either. And fortunately, no mirror anywhere.

Only then did I look at the intruder. "Please come in."

"Hello," said the Titian beauty in a slightly foreign accent. "My name is Cass. Would you like to have a swim? The heat is positively oppressive indoors."

"Er," I said with all the verbal dexterity I could muster.

"I'll interpret it as a yes," she said. "And let me warn you: I can interpret anything I choose as a yes. Even a no."

Her smile was like a spider's web. Soft. Exquisite. Inviting.

I stood up. "How will you interpret a yes, then?"

"Follow me and I'll show you."

I did.

The surface of the swimming pool shivered with currents created by the water jets. The tiles, together with the underwater lights, made the surface as blue and as opaque as the African sky at high noon. Nothing reflective about it, thank heavens. I slipped into the water as if into silk.

A muffled shot made my shoulders tense up. Then I heard the cascade of froth.

"Champagne is the only thing I miss," she said as she slid into the water next to me, her white bikini taut and translucent. "I've never cared for the sun and I can live without garlic bread. But nothing shouts decadence as loudly as a bottle of bubbly." She poured the champagne over her skin, emptying the entire bottle into the pool.

The wine was from a small exclusive estate in the Yarra Valley. Its aroma was strongly yeast and faintly Stilton.

I licked her shoulder. "Delicious."

"The champagne?"

"That, too." I meant it. Her skin tasted like a forbidden slice of heaven. Or hell. Either. Both. My body burned for her as though it had forgotten she was one of them.

Cass' thigh brushed mine. Challenging. Inviting.

Confusing.

"I'm afraid you won't like my proposition," she said.

My brain stopped working. Perhaps it was getting too little blood. I suppressed a groan. "On the contrary," I murmured, my tongue still against the cold marble of her shoulder. "I have a feeling I am going to like your proposition very much."

"I meant the presentation I'm about to give. The solution to the latest HIV outbreak."

I couldn't believe it had slipped my mind. "Tell me."

She did. Plainly and simply. As though she were discussing a shopping list.

So much for exotic creatures. But then, tigers were exotic. Especially tigers imported into Australia.

Pull yourself together, man, I thought. Act cool. She doesn't know. She can't possibly know. Tomorrow, you can leave at daybreak, as soon as they open the gates for the regular visitors. You can go back to headquarters and tell them they'd been right and you were wrong. Vampires were not helping humanity to solve the AIDS problem. No reason to delay the purge.

"I see," I ventured at last. "The solution would certainly be, um, effective. Even if, shall we say, a bit on the extreme side?"

"You mean the waste? Financially, we will suffer, no doubt. And those with the largest herds, will naturally suffer the most. Which is all right with me," she giggled unexpectedly, "Papa is almost ruined anyway thanks to his political aspirations. He had this hare-brained scheme to lock up uncontaminated stock in Reserves."

Politics?

"Your father was behind the Human Reserves idea?"

"He poured all his capital into the Segregation Party's coffers. The campaigns, the bribes, the pilot projects. He should have known it would never fly. The world is still recovering from Reverse Apartheid on the African Continent. But that's in the past. What matters now is that we protect our food supply."

"You don't have to do it like that," I argued. "The blood of an infected individual is as good as that of a healthy one. And as safe to drink. It's mere superstition that the—" I almost said *victim*, "that the meat should be healthy and clean."

"Don't you understand?" She took a sudden dive under the surface, and when she emerged, she was ten metres away. Her wet hair licked her shapely skull with a golden blaze. "We won't be culling the HIV positive specimens to protect *ourselves*. We'll be eliminating them to protect *the healthy ones*. Nothing personal. Just a matter of economics."

Her words were still sinking into my Cass-softened brain, when suddenly there was no more light and no more background gurgling of the water jets.

"Damned electricity," muttered Cass. "We'll have to wait for the backup generator to kick in."

As she spoke, moonlight filtered in through the Australian darkness. I could already see the contour of her mouth . . .

"Aha," she pointed triumphantly. "I knew it!"

I followed her finger with my eyes. The water was dark now, and perfectly still without the water jets. In the ribbon of moonlight spilt onto the swimming pool, I saw my own reflection.

Only my own reflection, of course. Cass did not have one.

Fear paralysed my brain for a split second before the adrenaline kicked in. When you hunt vampires, their speed and stealth are your two biggest challenges. The first rule of engagement drummed into novice Buffies is to lure the vampire out where you can see him. Or her.

I could see Cass all right. Dazzling. Dangerous. Titillating.

My fingers locked around something hard and solid. The champagne bottle.

"So," she whispered. "My first vampire hunter. What are you going to do to me?"

I honestly had no idea. It seemed silly to hit a vampire with a champagne flask. Especially a vampire as alluring as Cass.

She came closer and my brain cells scrambled. "Tell me . . . how did you fake the garlic reaction?"

"I've always been allergic. And sun makes me blister. When I was at school, my nicknames ranged from Vampire to Count Dracula. Kids thought it was great fun to blow garlic fumes at me and watch me puke. They also tried holy water and crosses, but without much success."

Cass laughed, leaned in. Her breasts touched my chest. The champagne bottle pressed tighter into the palm of my hand. "So that's why you hate us?"

Yes. No. I shifted my grip on the bottle. Did I really hate Cass?

"No."

Her arms twined around my neck, her lips cooled my ear.

"We don't slaughter all our stock," she said. "Some we keep around indefinitely. For . . . various . . . reasons." The tone was suggestive and her spicy breath sent a titillating shiver down my spine. "Would you like to be my stud bull?"

In retrospect, I guess I should have been offended. But I wasn't. Far from it. It was the blood thing, too little of it in the brain.

"Say yes," Cass whispered.

"Yes."

"No," hissed another voice.

Alvir's large frame appeared before us- seemingly out of nowhere. "Lunch time?" he sneered.

For the first time that evening, I felt truly frightened. Adrenaline still tingled in my fingers, but my ears rang with the dull *mmbf-mmbf-mbbf-mmbf-mbbf-mmbf-mbbf* of my heartbeat. A mouse stared down by a cat in a tight corner.

"Yum," said Alvir. I saw the sharp tip of his tongue.

"Typical Alvir," snapped Cass. Her voice was behind a wall of cotton wool. "Food is the only thing *you* ever think about. Now get out of my suite. This party is by invitation only."

"You can't fight me, Cassy. Youh daddy would not be pleased."

"I'll just have to suffer the consequences of his displeasure then." The fire in her eyes scorched through my cotton wool wrapping.

Alvir tsked. "You don't undehstand. If it wasn't foh me, youh clan would be insolvent. I can make you destitute with a snap of my fingehs. Do you know what being destitute means to a vampihe, Cassy? An etehnity without money? Daddy knows it well enough. It's just a matter of economics, you understand. He p-hactically begged me to take you—"

The movement of her hand was so fast that I missed it. All I heard was the slap as her hand connected with his face.

He raised his arm to his cheek, his eyes on Cass.

Now was my chance. I swung the champagne bottle's neck into Alvir's chest with all my rage, all my terror, and all the sexual frustration surging through my body.

It worked, all right. Vampire hunters are good at staking. Alvir's body melted like a gigantic slug sprinkled with salt.

My knees shook with relief and I sank, rather than lowered myself, onto the patio tiles.

"My hero," Cass said. The words were mocking, belying the come-hither curve of her mouth.

I couldn't afford to trust her expression. It's one thing for her to know I was a slayer, quite another to witness a killing. My eyes sought hers. "What happens now?"

Cass shrugged. "Daddy will be pleased. Now, where is that damned backup generator?"

Feeling very manly, I located the main switch and turned the power back on. Alvir must have switched it off to confront us in the dark. When I came back, his shrivelled-up body wasn't anywhere in sight. So much for immortality. *All things that shrivel and die must face the tempest, echoed inside my brain.* A song? A quote? What happened to vampires once they died?

If I chose to stay with Cass, sooner or later I would find out first-hand. If I chose to stay . . . Did I even have a choice?

Cass. I still knew nothing about her.

"Why do I get the impression your resistance to Alvir's idea wasn't about the money your father owed him?" I asked.

Her face contorted in a wince. "I was in Britain when they burned the sheep at the beginning of this century. Combing out the foot and mouth disease with their fiery comb. It's something I don't want to witness ever again."

I understood. It didn't help my dilemma. I had come to the conference hoping the vampires had finally discovered the cure for AIDS. If I got back and told the others that the vampires were useless to the cause, it would be open season again. And Cass . . . The sharp twinge in my chest informed me I didn't want anything to happen to Cass.

"But what about the AIDS epidemic?" I hazarded.

"It would be a short lived virus if it killed off all its hosts," shrugged Cass. "I'm sure it'll mutate into something less virulent as time goes by."

"What if it doesn't?"

"Then I guess I'll just have to go vegetarian."

And then she smiled. Her sharp canines gleamed. A gorgeous predator. To die for, in fact.

"So what's it going to be, lover boy?" she asked. "Do you want to stay with me? For ever?"

"Yes."

She winked. "I'll take that as a yes then, shall I?"

AFTERWORD TO "JUST A MATTER OF ECONOMICS"

It's actually my husband who's into vampires. Whether they adhere to the folklore created by Anne Rice, Whitley Strieber, Twilight or True Blood, he is fascinated by their longevity and super-powers. Personally, I don't fancy the idea of cuddling up to a cold, dead guy (undead, I can hear my husband correcting), which is why the hero of this story is a vampire slayer.

I cannot deny, however, that there is something romantic, or indeed erotic, about a super-fit man visiting my bedroom in the dead of night to play with my neck, red velvet cloak optional. And so, it should come as no surprise that my vampire-slayer gets turned in the end.

I'll never write about zombies, though.

QUARANTINE

PATTY JANSEN

"Hello? Helloooo?"

Rob's voice resonates in the general store.

Wan light casts a silver glow over the shelves with flour, cans of tomatoes, toilet paper, and other such life's necessities. A bay of fridges hums peacefully against the back wall.

There is no one behind the checkout and there hasn't been since he came in. It hadn't worried him; he knows where the photocopier is and doesn't need help fixing it. But now he needs someone to sign his worksheet.

"Helloooo? Olivia?"

He picks up his box of tools and walks into the car park, disturbing a family of bush turkeys. Clawed feet go scratch, scratch, scratch in the dirt as the birds run into the nearby scrub. His car sits surrounded by puddles of ochre-hued water, diamond drops of humidity on the roof.

A wall of rainforest looms on the other side of the road. Wisps of mist hang over the tree tops. To the right, the road snakes down into the rainforest. To the left, the asphalt is cracked and overgrown with weeds. The Exclusion Zone boundary is just a few k's from here.

Signs on the shamble of buildings behind him proclaim the Paluma General Store—that's where the photocopier is—Paluma Real Estate, Rainforest Inn. The latter has been boarded-up for months.

Where the fuck is everyone? "Hellooo?"

He goes back inside, clutching his worksheet book. Past the checkout into the door that leads to Olivia's house. The light is on in the kitchen. A copy of the local newsletter is on the table, a photocopied rag on two pages. Rob notices how crisp the ink is. Not bad for such a rickety machine, eh?

"Olivia—"

As he walks around the table, his foot connects with something soft, like he's accidentally kicked the cat, only bigger, and more inert.

Like somebody's meaty arm.

Attached to a body.

Shit. "Olivia!"

She's wearing her usual striped apron; her face is relaxed and bears no signs of a fight.

Rob drops to his knees and runs his fingers over the cold flesh of her neck. First place to check with these freaks around. There are no bite marks.

On the floor of the store room is another body, a man in shorts and work shirt with a courier logo. The checkout girl lies half over him, a couple of newsletters spread over her prone form. Both are cold, too. No bite marks.

He runs outside.

"Hellooo? Is anybody here?"

Through the window of the real estate agency, he can see the secretary, face down on her desk.

And he hears the silence, rainforest sounds amplified to match the roaring in his ears. Whipbirds calling, a catbird wailing, and the musical croaks of frogs.

Fuck the worksheet. He wants the police.

Of course his phone doesn't work. There has never been much reception here, and when the Exclusion Zone boundaries went up, other things took priority over phone reception.

Rob gets in the car, turns the key, revs the engine, and guns out of the place, fast.

Into the rainforest.

He's trembling, his sweaty hands on the wheel. It's a good 70k back to Townsville. The first twenty or so down a narrow and windy rainforest road. It starts raining. Tyres slide on the wet asphalt. Boxes of cartridges rattle around in the back. Hairpin bends pass in a blur, walls of rainforest turn shades of smudged green.

† † †

The young woman runs onto the road as if coming out of nowhere. White skin, black hair plastered to her face.

"Fuck!" Rob slams the brakes.

The car skids sideways.

Misses the girl.

Crosses onto the wrong side of the road.

Slides into the soft road verge and stops there. Steaming.

"Oh, fuck!"

Rob clutches the wheel, immobilised by the seatbelt locked across his chest. The sound of the engine is like a roar. In the rear vision mirror, he sees the girl scramble to her feet and examine her knees.

He releases the seatbelt, heart still thudding, and opens the door. Steps into the squelching mud.

"Are you OK?"

Rain falls on his head. The girl is brushing mud off her dress. Behind her, the wet grey ribbon of road winds around a sharp bend and vanishes into the rainforest. Somewhere out of sight a waterfall roars.

The girl looks up. Black eyes in a pale face, wide with fright. Skin almost translucent. One of *them*.

"Oh, shit." Rob scrambles back to the car. Opens the back door. Fumbles through his stuff. Bags, boxes of toner.

His hand closes on metal. He points the rifle. "Not a step closer."

She freezes. "I don't want to harm you." She looks about twenty but sounds younger.

"I'll believe that when I see it."

"I'm serious. I need a lift." She hesitates, wiping hair out of her face with a long-fingered hand. "Please. I *have* to get out of here."

She is trembling. Black liquid oozes down one leg. That isn't mud; it's blood. Vampire blood. Hand prints on her thighs. Smudge marks of fingers. There is blood on her dress, too. A rape victim.

"Please, help me. He's going to kill me."

Shit.

"Where . . ." He clears his throat. "Where do you want to go?" Never mind who 'he' is. Rob doesn't think he wants to know.

Her shoulders sag. "I don't know." She is crying now. "I don't know anymore. I thought we were safe, but . . ."

— 129 —

"But what?" In the Exclusion Zone, safety is but a commodity to be traded for other essentials, like food. To her, Rob is food.

"I don't know. They came out of nowhere and started killing."

"Hang on." That doesn't make sense. None of the bodies he saw showed signs of violence. "Who was killing who?"

"The dominant men from the camp were killing the others. Younger men. Women. Children."

Rob didn't know there was a vampire camp up here, but then again, they usually keep quiet. They live in family groups, and have lots of children.

Rob contemplates his options, but he can't refuse a woman in distress. Not when she's been violated. Not even a vampire. Damn it. "Get in."

He has a feeling this is one incidence of chivalry he'll regret.

She slides into the seat, tears running down her cheeks. "Thanks." She wipes her face with the back of her hand, spreading blood. "My name is Gloria."

Rob nods and slips behind the wheel. Tyres slip in the mud. A smell of singed vegetation permeates the car, but the foray into the muddy road verge seems to have left no damage.

He concentrates on driving for a while.

"So," he asks finally, "Do you know what happened?"

She shakes her head. "All our hosts are dead. The men are going crazy. That's why . . ." She spreads her hands. "We're all hungry."

"How long ago have you fed?"

"Two days ago."

Rob slams the brakes and the car skids to a halt for the second time. "Get out."

"No." Her eyes are wide and pleading.

"Get out," Rob repeats, more forcefully. "I am not a host and I have no intention to become one—"

"I won't, I promise."

Rob does his best *I don't believe that* stare. He thinks of his rifle, powerful enough to shoot crocodiles, but which he's left in the back of the car, out of reach. Damn. His father always said he would never make a soldier.

"I promise, honest. I have a host on the highway. At the petrol station. Take me there."

Shit. "OK, then. To the petrol station. No further."

"Deal."

† † †

Rob says nothing all the way down the mountain. He's driving as fast as he can, casting occasional glances at Gloria. He wonders how she will feed on this poor sod he's taking her to. From what he's heard, vampires feed often in small portions. She could easily bite him. He's also heard that it doesn't hurt, and that the sex is amazing.

And he *so* doesn't want to think about stuff like that right now.

He pulls up his left shoulder as if to shield himself. The exposed part of his neck feels larger-than-life.

She's trembling, clutching herself, and occasionally she tightens her arms about her waist. He wants to ask if she's pain, but he can't think of a way to do that without sounding interested. Bad things come from being interested in vampires, not the least of which losing his job.

If I spot you with one of them, you're out! Mal says, and Mal's toner and photocopier business is one of the last in town that's still pure. Hates vampires, Mal does, even though they're fast becoming his most important customers.

Rob's already breaking that rule, and jobs are hard to come by in the Exclusion Zone. Too many people, not enough money to pay them. No one leaves, no one comes in. It's the classic response modelled on the pest containment models used by the Department of Agriculture. Used on fruit fly. In fucking paw paws. Once the vampirism virus is eradicated and the boundaries lifted, maybe he'll move elsewhere. Go to Brisbane or something.

If he ever gets out of sharing a car with a hungry vampire.

If there's anything of the country still left.

It's not until he's well onto the highway that he realises Gloria isn't saying anything. She's shivering worse than ever, her arms clenched around her stomach.

In an impulse, he touches her arm: slick with sweat. He's never touched a vampire before and is surprised her skin feels alive. But too cold.

God, where else did this bastard hurt her?

† † †

By the time they get to the petrol station, she's slumped against the passenger door. A man comes outside when Rob stops the car. At the sight of Gloria, he freezes. A woman comes up behind him, her hands on her husband's arm.

"Please, go away," the man says. "We have nothing for you here."

Gloria is getting out of the car. The hem of her dress is stained with black blood. Rob feels sick.

"The host . . . My son is dead," the man continues; his voice wavers. "We found him this morning in the shed."

Gloria moans and mumbles while steadying herself on the car door.

A heavy silence hangs between them. Everyone knows what will happen if vampires become too hungry.

The woman steps forward. "Take me."

Rob shakes his head. "It has to be a man." He knows that much, and he knows he should volunteer—these people have already suffered too much—but in the brief moment he hesitates, the man says, "Take me."

Gloria totters towards him and takes his hand.

The boy's father straightens up. "You better know what you're getting yourself into, lady. I'm going to kill you."

The woman presses her lips together, and nods, as if when her husband fails, she will do the job.

Rob feels even more awful.

But you can't kill a vampire. All that garlic and sunlight stuff is rubbish. Vampires laze about the park during the day. When all you need is blood, there's no need to work; humans do it all for you. All you need to do is fuck and make babies, and vampires are doing plenty of that.

Gloria and the man disappear into the house.

Rob can't bear to watch, or meet the woman's eyes. He's a coward.

He follows her into the shop, a shabby sort of place with lino floor, fluoro lighting and plastic chairs. The windows are dirty and there are specks of gecko shit on the chipped Formica tables.

"Not seen you here before," she says.

"No," Rob says, while guilt piles on. He's never bothered to stop here and it looks like the place could have used his patronage.

The woman nods, although it's not clear why. To take her mind off what's happening to her husband, maybe. There are cries from elsewhere in the building. The woman's face remains blank, but her eyes tell a different story. "Come from town today?"

"I left early this morning." Rob shrugs, feeling stupid. In fact, this entire conversation is stupid.

"Seen anyone on the road?"

Belatedly, Rob notices anxiety. "Why?"

"There's been no traffic."

"No traffic from town at all?"

She shakes her head, listens. "Wait—can you still hear them?"

The house has become eerily silent.

Rob goes into the next room, the son's bedroom, empty. The next room: a storage area for the shop. The owner is on the floor, slumped on top of a bundle of newspapers. Dead.

Rob whirls at a small sound behind him. Gloria stands in the doorway, completely naked.

She looks from the owner to Rob, her expression genuinely shocked. "What happened?" There is a softness to her voice he hasn't heard before.

"I don't know. I found him here."

"I was looking for him. He gave me blood, but he . . . didn't collect his payment." The look on her face leaves no doubt about the nature of the payment.

Rob feels even more wretched. Not only did the owner sacrifice himself, he honoured his marriage to the very last. He killed himself rather than give in to her.

"Do you want to—" Gloria begins.

"Go fuck yourself." Rob is surprised to find how much effort it costs him to say that.

"Really." She drapes herself against the doorpost, arching her back so that her small breasts push forward. She's perfect, and virtually begging. Rob knows that this is what the vampire girls do, but still feels blood stirring in him.

"Fuck it, Gloria, haven't you got anything better to think of? The guy and his son are dead."

"Yes, so it looks you're going to be it."

Rob staggers back from the doorway, blood roaring in his ears, and runs. The dank corridor, the shabby shop, are no more than blurs before his eyes.

"Go out to the car!" he yells at the shop in general.

There is no reply. The boy's mother lies face down on the table, also dead, her head on the newspaper.

Newspapers. The cashier at Olivia's shop had a couple of newsletters across her body. Olivia had a newsletter on the table. The owner lay across those same stacks of newspapers.

Hasn't he read something about vampire blood used as ink?

The only blood associated with vampires is the human blood they drink. No one ever talks about a vampire's blood, the blood that stains the hem of Gloria's dress. Mal once said something about vampire blood.

†   †   †

The streets of town are deserted, the shops dark.

At the park along the beachfront, a group of young vampires is about to cross the road. Young men, one woman, thin and pale like Gloria, and very, very pregnant.

"Here's your mates," Rob says. But he feels uneasy. Normally, the vampires lounge in relaxed fashion. There is nothing relaxed about these ones. A man is holding the pregnant woman, who struggles to free herself. She's scratching at his bare arms, black blood under her nails. Then she stops, clutching her stomach with her free hand. The way she stands there, her legs apart, her knees slightly bent makes Rob feel sick. She's bearing down hard, perhaps minutes from giving birth.

He should do something and tell the brute to leave her alone. But he's not strong enough. The man will bite him. Hell, she might even attack him.

"They're not my mates," Gloria says. Her voice is weak, her face sweat-sheened, her eyes wide.

"Don't you want to help her?"

Another man is now holding the woman's free hand. She's fighting and kicking and screaming. "That's no way to treat a woman." Not even a vampire.

Gloria shakes her head. The woman is bearing down again, and now a lot of others are rushing to the scene. Men start fighting each other. The woman is screaming.

"We have to do something!" Rob half-opens the car door.

Gloria clamps hands over her ears. "Take me out of here!"

"But they'll kill her, or the baby."

"Take me out of here!" She's hysterical.

Rob pushes the accelerator. He turns the corner and stops again.

Next to him, Gloria is coughing and trembling. A trail of saliva runs from her mouth. "That's what they did to . . ." She coughs into her hand, gulping breath, her shoulders heaving. "Sorry, I didn't mean to . . ." Her next cough is wet. A stream of frothy vomit dribbles between her fingers onto her lap. She sways, and for a moment he's afraid she will faint.

God. He adds up the facts. That's what they did to her. Almost ripped the baby from her womb. Killed it, drank all its blood.

†   †   †

In the bathroom of his house, Rob cuts his wrist, holds a cup to catch the dripping blood until it's filled up. It makes him feel sick and dizzy. He applies a pressure bandage to his arm.

Gloria's eyes are half-open. He slides an arm around her shoulders, shivering where his skin touches hers, and puts the cup to her lips.

She drinks. Slowly, blood staining her mouth. Her eyes remain half-closed, but she empties the cup. Rob puts it on the table, watching adhering blood slide down the glass, not sure if he's done the right thing, not sure if it was enough.

She's asleep now, and he watches her perfect face and pale neck. Her mouth is slightly open, and he can just see her pointed teeth. Knows that if not today then tomorrow or the day after, she will sink those teeth into his neck while he fucks her. He becomes hard just thinking about it. Wants to fuck her right now. Wants to feel the pain of her bite in his neck. What a way to hold onto your lover. Pain and sex, that most exquisite combination.

But then he will be a host, and possibly the only adult host in town. His blood can keep two or three vampire girls in good health, but maybe as many as ten clinging onto life. Not only that, he will get the girls pregnant. They will feed on the children. Not all will grow up to be vampires. That way, vampirism will not die out.

He goes and stands by the window, looking over the empty street.

At a soft rustle behind him, he turns.

Gloria stands there. "You fed me."

He nods, shrugs, hopes she won't ask him why, because he has no idea. He turns back to watching the empty street.

"Thank you."

Her hand touches his shoulder. It's surprisingly warm through his shirt. He turns around again, and finds that she has shed her dress.

"Look, don't—"

"It's only fair," she says. "I can't pay you any other way."

Resistance is futile.

†   †   †

Mal is in the office. Rob almost cries when he sees *someone* still alive, but Mal looks tired, and smells of sweat.

His desk is a mess, packed with the ever-present tangle of invoices, toner cartridges and scientific papers.

"So, there you are," Mal says. His expression is dark.

Rob feels that Mal can see through him, that he knows Rob has sat beside Gloria while she slept, that he knows about the crumpled bed and the smell of sex in the room.

"What's this?" Rob asks, but he recognises the black substance in a small bottle. Vampire blood.

"You want to get rid of them, eh?" The tone of Mal's voice is loaded with meaning Rob can't fathom. Mal is an ex-epidemiologist who lost his job when the Exclusion Zone went up. Isolate the problem, that was how the Agriculture Department dealt with diseases.

Rob nods, failing a better reply. He does want to get rid of them, but more importantly, he wants to know what killed all the non-vampires, even those who weren't hosts.

Mal laughs. "The only thing that's strong enough to kill a vampire is another vampire. The only way to make them kill each other is to make sure they're hungry. The only thing they eat is human blood. So what's the answer to the puzzle?"

Rob shrugs. None of the possible answers sound pleasant. All involve killing Gloria.

Yet he knows you can't form a relationship with a vampire without becoming dependent. Gloria might be happy to drink blood from a cup for now, but sooner or later he will have to pay. In fact, the thought of it fills him with morbid fascination.

But he forces himself to think rationally.

And reason tells him that people must leave the Exclusion Zone. And they can't, because they could be carrying the virus, that's what the zone is for. Which means people must die. Because only when there are no people left will all vampires die.

He looks at the text in the book open on Mal's desk.

There the quote Mal has shown him before, in small cursive script: *Those who have to misfortune of being the first to read a text written in vampire blood will die the most terrible death.*

Mal sells toner for printers and photocopiers. More importantly, he sells ink for the *Bulletin.* That's Rob's task: keeping the machines supplied.

Hot anger rises to his cheeks. "And you sent *me* around spreading this stuff?"

"You want to get rid of this vermin? You gotta make sacrifices! The department thought that they would isolate the problem and it would go away, but vampires make more vampires. You know that a vampire can become pregnant two days after giving birth?"

Rob knows. Belatedly, a thought comes to him. "But why doesn't the print kill me?"

"Oh, it would have killed you, had you done your work properly. But you never tested your replaced cartridges, did you? So now I'll have to deal with you in a different way."

He reaches under his desk and pulls up his crocodile-shooting gun.

In a few steps, Rob is at the desk and tips it upside down on Mal's lap. While Mal tips backwards, the gun goes off with a deafening bang. Ceiling plaster rains down. Mal scrambles on the floor for the gun. Rob picks up a golf club from the corner, and hits Mal over the head as hard as he can.

Mal flops down on his belly, and doesn't get up.

Rob leaves the office feeling sick.

But there is a group of vampires waiting near his car. Female, hungry.

They're too strong to overwhelm, too many to outrun. He doesn't want to run; he wants to fuck them. They will fall pregnant, like Gloria, and they'll survive, because of him

He goes back into the mess that's Mal's office. Takes a cartridge from the box. Puts it in the photocopier. Places the front page of today's paper on the glass.

He hits print and picks up the sheet that comes out the side.

It says: *Quarantine to be lifted within a month.*

AFTERWORD TO "QUARANTINE"

Vampires don't exist, right?

Well, I think we've been looking for them in the wrong way and in the wrong places. Even a child could tell that vampire myths could never be true. By biting another creature, a vampire turns the other creature into an individual competing for the same food source. Sorry, but that makes no evolutionary sense at all.

No, this author has the insider knowledge. Because once upon a time, I lived in Townsville, and on hot and unbearable days, we used to drive up to Paluma and swim in Crystal Creek. I tell you, there is stuff up there you don't want to know about. Some of it was subject of talk in the circles of boffins at QDPI, James Cook Uni and CSIRO. Quarantine, one of my colleagues said, was the only thing that would stop it, and I tell you, QDPI knows a lot about quarantine. But nothing was ever done. So this evilness is still there, like a ticking time bomb. Go on, drive past the building of the Townsville Bulletin with its large glass facade through which you can see the printing presses, and shudder. Be warned.

OUT OF THE GRAVE

AMANDA PILLAR

Kacey Martin knew that her day—her whole week, even—was going to suck.

And suck big time.

Shaking her head while holding her breath, she took a step closer to the dead body. Squatting next to the puddle of ooze and gore, Kacey studied the teenage corpse in the twilight. Oh, the coroners at the Vampire Investigation Unit were going to have a field day over this, Kacey thought. Underneath the surface mess, there was a baby vampire—undead for maybe a month, dead for maybe a day.

Kacey stood and walked a few steps away from the body, where she took a breath of decay-laden air. Looking around, she took in the rest of the park, which was largely a square of dead grass, with some play equipment huddled in one corner. Not the normal scene for murder.

But there was nothing remotely normal about vampire deaths.

"The ME is going to hate this," Kacey said to her partner, Morris. She flicked a glance over her shoulder at the tall, silent vampire who wore his blues with a flair that made them look fashionable, and waited for his response.

When he realised she was looking at him, he raised an eyebrow.

Kacey sighed. Morris was, well, Morris. That was about as expressive as he got. "Have you made the call?" she asked him.

The black eyebrow returned to its customary position. He waved his iPhone through the darkening air. "Of course."

"Did they say when they'd arrive?" Talking to Morris was sometimes more excruciating than pulling teeth. And she'd pulled teeth before.

"Twenty minutes."

Kacey looked around to see if there was a convenient pole she could smack her head against. Finding none in the park, she sighed to herself. Peering at the dead vampire, she tilted her head as she looked at the stake jutting out of its chest. Beneath the bloody gore, the stake had been painted in stripes of colour; red, blue and white. They might be able to get some prints off it, but she nibbled her lip in doubt. Vampire killers tended to make sure they left clean crime scenes.

Gang work, she'd bet a week's wage on it.

"Where was the parent, do you think?" Kacey asked Morris, not that she expected an answer. Turning to her silent partner, she ground her teeth in frustration when she saw that he was looking everywhere but at the body.

"No idea." Morris said after a few moments. When he looked at her, he raised both of his dark eyebrows. "What's the matter? Your teeth sound like they're turning to dust."

Oh, *now* he gets verbal. "Are you even paying attention to the fact that there is a dead body at your goddamned feet?"

Morris' eyebrows stayed where they were, and his blue eyes twinkled briefly. She blinked, thinking she'd imagined it.

"Yes, I am. There are hundreds of human children's tracks, but only one set of adult footprints near the body, but plenty over at the play equipment. No smell of vampire anywhere, apart from the stench of the dead body."

"Okay then," Kacey shrugged and deliberately looked away. She believed him—Morris would have been able to smell another vampire from a mile away.

"You really don't like me, do you?" Morris said.

Startled, she jumped and felt her shoulder brush his. Electricity surged through her when she realised that Morris had come to stand right next to her, and she hadn't heard a damned thing.

"I don't *not* like you," Kacey hedged, straightening her blue shirt. She fiddled with her holstered Smith & Wesson. She deliberately didn't touch the stake strapped to her gun belt, not wanting to give Morris the wrong impression.

She frowned as she thought about the problem that was Morris. It was hard to dislike someone when they were so inhumanly beautiful.

She really tried not to care about his looks, but it was like ignoring the memory of a double-coated Tim Tam. Impossible. Almost six feet four, Morris was covered in muscle and had long black hair he normally tied back. Add those features to a sharp, almost aristocratic nose, bright blue eyes, lips to die for, and you had one killer combination. It was hard to hate someone so pretty, and she had tried.

"You may not hate me, but you don't like me." Morris took a step away from her. She could see him look from the dead baby to her and back again.

"It's not because you're a vampire," Kacey said quickly, guessing what he was thinking.

"No?" His lips settled into a very slight sneer.

"No," she said. "But until you guys came out of the grave, I was working a nice job in homicide, working my way up the ranks."

"That was five years ago," Morris said.

Only five years? She thought. Wow, time flies when you're *not* having fun. But maybe that was also because she'd had her fair share of cases to look after. More than ever. More than before, anyway.

"Yeah well, your lot's quest for recognition fucked my life-plan. I was being fast-tracked to become a homicide detective."

"Now you work for the Vampire Investigation Unit with all the homicides anyone could ask for."

Kacey flicked a glance at Morris to see if he was joking, but his face wore the usual blank expression.

"I don't want people to die," she said.

"Sure."

Kacey frowned. "I don't do the job because I like working with dead bodies; I do it because I like catching killers."

"Even killers who murder vampires?" Morris was staring at her, hard.

She swallowed.

He took a step closer to her, and she thought she saw some emotion flicker through his eyes, but it disappeared fast. "Oh, I get it. You resent working with me because rather than finding killers who attack your own kind, you've been stuck working cases where the victims aren't human, so they don't count, is that it?"

Kacey realised her mouth was hanging open. She shut it with a click and winced. She could *taste* the dead baby now. She wanted to deny Morris' claim, but she couldn't, because what he'd said was true. She wanted to help her own kind, not persecute them because they were trying to remove the creature that was one step higher on the food chain than them. But at the same time, she didn't *approve* of what they were doing.

And that's why she'd been given the job.

Morris turned away from her, muttering something inaudible.

"Why do *you* do the job?" she asked.

The tall vampire froze, his shoulders stiff. "Like you, I didn't get a choice."

"What do you mean?" Kacey asked, but he didn't reply, because the sound of sirens was coming up the street. She glanced over her shoulder at the blue and red lights as they approached Tanner's Reserve. After a few seconds, she turned back to Morris. Later, she thought.

† † †

"Martin, you coming?"

Kacey looked up from the paperwork spread out over her desk and hit save on her laptop. Paperless office my arse, she thought, then focused her attention on Sergeant Yarrow.

"Where you going?" Kacey asked. He was wearing civilian clothes and had his keys in one hand.

"We're going for a drink." His white blond brows were drawn together, and his tone indicated that he'd told her this already. Probably more than once.

She looked at the pile of papers on her desk and sighed. She should finish the paperwork about the dead baby, but it could wait. Grabbing her keys and jacket, she decided she could almost taste the beer on her tongue. Morris, on the other side of her desk, raised his eyes at her movement.

"You coming?" she asked before she realised what she'd done.

A faint smile flickered across his face and then to her surprise and Yarrow's, he nodded. "Sure."

There was an awkward silence for a moment, but Kacey forced a smile. "Let's go then. There's still a few hours until dawn."

Morris stood and followed them out. Chapel Street was packed, the hotted up cars gliding along in slow motion, caught behind trams and traffic lights, the owners nodding their heads to music that could be heard on the street. Damn subwoofers, she thought.

"Grillions?" Yarrow asked.

Morris and Kacey nodded; it was close and not overpriced, for St Kilda. The staff also didn't care if their clientele were police— or vampires. Following Yarrow, they walked the fifty metres to the upstairs pub. Wilson and Byte were already there. They held up their pints and called out hellos when they saw Yarrow and Kacey, their smiles freezing in place when they realised Morris was there as well. But only for a second.

"Why, it's M and M!" Senior Sergeant John Byte said. He was a typical cop in appearance; short hair, hard chin, flinty eye.

"Clever," Kacey muttered and sidled up to the bar. Glancing over at Morris, she raised an eyebrow. "Want anything?"

"Do they have Beez Neez?"

Blinking once, Kacey turned to the barman, who was dressed in an extremely tight black shirt, and asked for a Beez Neez and Carlton Draught. He was eyeing Morris like he was an expensive chocolate bar, just waiting to be unwrapped. She brought the two beers over and handed Morris his. She sat down at the small table with the three men and one vampire.

"So, heard you got a dead baby today," Wilson said. He was dressed in jeans and a T-shirt, leather jacket slung over the back of his chair, short brown hair spiked carelessly.

"Yeah," Kacey said and took a drink.

"Accident?" Byte asked.

Morris shook his head. "Not unless they fell on their back and then someone tripped over with a stake in hand."

"A stake painted in red, blue and white." Kacey said.

"Damn it, that's the fourth this week," Yarrow said.

"Fourth?" Morris was sitting very straight in his seat.

"Fourth gang killing. More dead vamps than that, and more dead humans from wrangling with vamps who didn't want to be bothered. Those idiots at the AAV are going to get themselves killed." Yarrow took a sip of his beer and ended up with a foam-moustache.

"You think the AAV are behind the gang murders?" Kacey asked.

The Australian Anti-Vampire movement. They were the little brother of the American AAV and they were nowhere near as hard-core. But they were escalating. The stakes were a dead giveaway. Ha ha.

"You drink Beez Neez?" Wilson was staring at Morris as if he had grown another set of fangs.

"Yeah, so?" Morris glanced down at his beer.

"Does it, uh, go down okay?"

Kacey snorted.

Morris slung a sidelong look at her that burned. "Sure."

"But it doesn't satisfy you." Wilson had just been transferred to the Vamp Police, and it wasn't half obvious.

"No." Morris was back to being chatty.

"Got much planned for the weekend?" Byte leaned across the table, cutting Morris out from Wilson's line-of-sight.

"Gotta take the kids to the movies," Yarrow said.

"Whatcha seeing?"

"I dunno, some animated thing."

Kacey only listened with half an ear, spoke when she needed to, but otherwise, just tried to relax and enjoy her beer. Seeing dead baby vampires wasn't easy; especially when only a few months earlier they'd been human. And usually young.

†   †   †

After waving goodbye to the guys, Kacey shoved her hands in her jacket pockets, and turned down Chapel Street towards her apartment.

"I'll walk you home." Morris said.

"I'm right," Kacey mumbled. She started walking. Morris kept pace beside her.

"You're drunk."

"Am not." Damn the footpath for not being straight.

"Are too."

She squinted over at him, and then lost control of the footpath and bumped into Morris' side. It felt like warm steel. Kacey moved away quickly. "I had just as much as you did."

"Exactly."

"You're not drunk." He couldn't be, he seemed to be propping her upright.

"No."

"Can you get drunk?"

"No."

She giggled.

"What's funny?"

"Just thinking about what you'd be like if you were drunk." Morris, drunk? The total badass three-sheets to the wind? She had trouble seeing it, but she knew it would be hilarious. Or dangerous.

Probably both.

"Why would that be funny?" he asked. He wrapped an arm around her and half-dragged her the fifteen minute walk home. She arrived at the old brick apartment building feeling cold down one side and blazing hot down the other—the one that was pressed to Morris.

"I'll walk you up."

"No, you won't." Kacey started fumbling in her pants' pocket for her keys. Fishing them out, her numb fingers had trouble determining which key was which.

With a sigh, Morris took them from her and opened the glass door. "Let's go."

Kacey eyed the terracotta tiled stairs with a frown and shrugged. She'd climbed these stairs drunk before, but she couldn't really remember how she'd managed to not tumble down them again—not without Morris to push her upright whenever she seemed to list. But she was getting the hang of it. In fact, she seemed to glide up the last flight and across the landing to her door.

Morris opened the door for her and prodded her through. She leaned against the wall to take her boots off, but ended up sliding down to land on the entryway tiles on her butt. She wrestled with the boot until it came loose and then sat there clutching it in her hand. Kacey heard Morris sigh and take the shoe from her.

"Come on; time to get you to bed."

"I can put myself to bed," Kacey muttered. In fact, the floor looked pretty darn good.

Morris heaved her upright and then almost dragged her through the small lounge and kitchen to her bedroom. He then started unzipping her jacket.

"What are you doing?" She grabbed for the jacket but it disappeared. She frowned at her shirt.

"Taking your clothes off." Morris' voice was like deep velvet, Kacey decided.

Long fingers entered her vision and began unbuttoning her shirt.

"I can do it myself," she said, batting his pale, sinewy hands away.

"Can you really?"

Kacey tried to undo the buttons, but they kept sliding out of her fingers. "Normally, yes. I'm really good at it."

"I'm sure you are," Morris said and she flicked a glance up at his face. He was smiling. It put a whole new level of devastating on the attractive radar.

Before she knew it, her shirt was on the floor next to her jacket. She crossed her hands over her chest protectively. He didn't seem to notice. He was loosening her belt and her pants were sliding to the floor.

"This is not how I pictured my night ending," Kacey said to the top of Morris' head. She had to grab his shoulder for support as he slid a sock off her foot.

"And what did you picture?" Morris stood in one smooth motion, her socks in hand.

"Oh, you know," she waved a hand airily, "getting smashed at the pub and getting laid." She didn't mean it, though. She'd just wanted a few drinks and an early night.

"Really?" Morris was smiling again, and it was lopsided, devilish.

"No," she said, taking a step back. When Morris looked like that it was . . . dangerous. For her. For every woman on the planet, and half the men.

"Maybe I can help you fulfil your night's objective." His voice was a deep purr as he took a step closer to her. She gave a shaky laugh, but he silenced it by kissing her. And it was the best kiss of her life. Cool breath, tasting slightly of beer and him, and a tongue that should have been illegal.

In fact, she thought later that night, *he* should be illegal.

† † †

Kacey woke to a head that was filled with tiny miners, tapping away with correspondingly small hammers. Small *pointy* hammers. She groaned and clutched at her skull, curling into a ball on her bed. Too much beer. Way too much beer. Damn miners.

She tried to remember what had happened after she left the pub, but it was hazy. Morris had walked her home, she knew that. Moving her head to look at the bedside clock, her brain felt ready to implode. Squinting, she saw that it was eleven AM. She didn't have to be at work until five-thirty. Moaning, she pulled the blanket over her eyes and went back to sleep.

† † †

"How's the head?" Morris asked.

Kacey turned to the sound of his voice and saw that he was sitting on the edge of her desk, arms crossed over his pale blue shirt. He was smiling at her.

"Ah, okay." She wasn't really sure she was capable of thought when he looked at her like that. *Why* was he looking at her like that?

"Really?" He had that damn eyebrow raised again.

"Yeah, little achy, but otherwise okay." She gave him a wan smile. It had taken two Beroccas, four cups of coffee and a few Panadols to feel even half-human. She wasn't going to drink again. Ever.

"Morris!" Wilson called.

Kacey winced. She saw Morris look at Wilson, who was walking over to them, keys in one hand. Just signed on.

"How ya doing, man?" Wilson slung his jacket over the back of his desk chair, which was—at the moment, for all the noise he was making—too close to hers.

"Fine."

"You can sure drink! Man, the hangover I had this morning . . ."

Kacey tuned the conversation out. She didn't want to talk about hangovers, let alone the alcohol that had led them there. She shuddered.

"You okay?" Morris asked.

"Yeah," she said, not looking up. She heard Morris stand and walk to his desk, which was directly opposite hers.

His phone rang.

Kacey almost slithered off her seat to the floor, clutching her head. She heard Morris speak, rapid-fire bursts that ended with him slamming the phone down. Suddenly he was back at her side, leaning down over her. His blue eyes were intense lightning. "Are you up for a call out?"

"No." Kacey answered honestly, but stood and threw her jacket over her shoulders. "But I will be."

She followed him out the door, trying not to look at his arse. *What is wrong with me?* She wondered. She normally wasn't so aware of Morris as a man. Hell, he wasn't even a man.

Morris was waiting in the car for her when she arrived, so she slid in and buckled up. "Where are we going?"

His brows drawn together in a frown he said, "I got a call from an old source. He says that there are some baby vampires being housed out in Knox Park. And 'housed' is a euphemism."

"But—why?" Kacey asked. Baby vampires were volatile and loved nothing more than snacks of fresh blood.

Morris didn't reply. Kacey tried to keep track of the street names, but they were hard to read in the dark. They soon left the CBD and were heading into the outer suburbs.

Morris sighed and said into the silence, "Babies are, well, they're not like full vampires."

"No, but they take a year or so for the full change, don't they?" That's what she'd been taught. Hell, that's what they still taught in the Academy.

"Yes, and during that time their blood is . . . potent."

"Potent?" Kacey asked, frowning.

"Well, baby vampire blood is like heroin." Morris sounded like he was grinding his teeth.

"*What*?"

"It's a drug. One we don't want people knowing about—imagine what the government would do if they realised our young were walking opium poppies. Or the AAV."

"Does anyone in the VIU know?"

"The vampires do."

"Shit."

"That's one way of putting it."

"But I thought vampire blood was deadly," Kacey said.

"Adult blood is. You drink it and you either become a vampire or die trying."

"Shit."

She saw Morris raise both his eyebrows briefly.

"Shouldn't you have taken Anton or someone, rather than me?" Kacey asked. Anton was one of the other vampires stationed with the VIU. He was even quieter than Morris, but he was good at his job.

Morris' hands tightened so hard on the steering wheel she thought it might break under the pressure. "No."

"Why?" Kacey turned to look at the scenery, rather than stare at Morris. He'd tell her if he wanted to, or he wouldn't. Unkempt nature strips rushed by, lit by the sodium-glow of streetlamps. Verges were covered in old TVs, mattresses, couches and various other unwanted goods. Hard rubbish, Kacey realised. At least, she hoped that was it.

"Anton and I don't get along."

"Any reason or just because?" Kacey had learnt that vampires tended towards a solitary lifestyle, unless they made babies. Then they'd live in covens.

"He's a tool."

Kacey thought about that, and about everything she knew about Anton, which wasn't much. She assumed he'd ticked all the right boxes, to get into the VIU. "Right."

"He thinks that vampires and humans can be friends." Morris' face was blank.

"And you don't?" Kacey asked.

"No."

"But—"

"Look, just because we have sex with humans, it doesn't mean that I think humans and vampires can get along in long run."

Kacey blinked. "Why do you have sex with humans then?"

Morris turned to look at her, his eyes burning. "You don't remember?"

"Don't remember what?" Kacey asked, feeling the blood drain from her face.

His lips thinned. "Nothing."

She thought back over the events of last night and frowned. She couldn't remember when Morris left. But she felt warm, tingly. And he'd been rather . . . nice . . . today. "Did we have sex?"

His lips had almost disappeared. "Yes."

"Did you drink from me?" Kacey's voice rose to a near shriek.

"No."

She was silent, feeling her heart beating fast. "Thanks," she managed to mutter.

"You initiated it."

Shock seized her. "I did not!"

"Yes, you did. You said that your goal of the evening had been to get smashed and get laid."

Oh, *god*. That had been her catch phrase through her clubbing years, not that she'd had sex all that often. Gotten drunk, sure, but the picking-up part hadn't gone well. Guys didn't like a woman who knew how to kick their arses, she'd found.

Kacey sighed and said dryly, "Well, thanks for helping me out."

He smiled a little half-smile then, and it transformed him. "Anytime."

She had a feeling he meant that.

The car began to slow down and he pulled over to the side of the road. He turned the lights off and let the engine idle for a moment before switching it off. "Two blocks down, that's where the babies are being kept, according to my source."

"Shouldn't we have a TRG team or something?" Kacey fingered the gun and stake at her belt.

Morris grinned, an unholy light in his eyes. "I am a TRG team."

She rolled her eyes, but he was probably right. Morris could kick some serious arse, and the times she'd seen him fight, she figured he'd been taking things easy. "Too bad you can't try out for the Olympics."

Morris barked a laugh. "If the government could get us in, they would. You know how much Aussies love gold medals."

"True. So, why aren't we letting anyone else know about this . . . drug op?"

Morris sighed. "Let's say we can't let the humans in the VIU know, not yet, and my superiors want this cleaned up fast."

"Your superiors?" So, he didn't just work for the VIU.

"Other vampires . . . older vampires."

"How often do these ops come up?"

"Not often."

And the dealers never survived, she didn't need him to say that aloud. Kacey decided that she didn't want to know more. Later, hell yeah, but right now, her head was spinning.

"Okay then, let's go."

They climbed out of the car and Kacey felt self-conscious, even though it was dark and they had parked in the no-man's land between lamps. The houses on either side of the street were nearly all made from brick, their curtains shut, yards filled with rubbish and used car parts. No one was out. Letterboxes hung bent and broken and dogs barked wildly. The neighbourhood was a shithole—the bastard love-child of Frankston and Dandenong, she thought, abandoned and raised by abusive foster parents.

Kacey followed Morris along the street and kept close as he veered off into a dark gap between fences, down an easement. A few metres into the easement, Morris jumped a fence that was half-collapsing under the weight of the ivy clinging to its side. Sighing, she followed him. Feeling more like a burglar than a cop, she kept close to him as they quietly made their way across a rubbish-strewn backyard and over another fence.

With each step she took, a knot began to form and swell in her gut. She didn't like this, haring off into the night, skulking through backyards like criminals. Morris leapt another fence, barely even touching the top as he flew over. Kacey grunted as she heaved herself over the rotting palings. Sometimes being human sucked, she thought, as a sharp jab struck her finger. Splinter.

Over a fence and into another trash-laden yard, and then they were staring between broken palings into the backyard of a house that looked in even worse repair than its neighbours. Light shone out the gaps between curtains.

"This is it?" she asked quietly.

"Yes."

"No one's watching us?" For once, she was glad for Morris' taciturn nature.

"No."

"You sure?" Kacey asked. Morris might have the sight of an eagle, but they were surrounded on three sides by houses.

"Well, I can't hear anyone nearby."

"What do we do?" She'd never gone on a two-people raid before. She wasn't sure it was allowed. But hell, the humans at the VIU hadn't even known baby vampire blood was a drug. Or that Morris' superiors periodically wiped these sites clean.

"I can't smell or hear any humans in the house at the moment, but this place stinks of vampire and human." He nodded in the direction of their target.

"We go in, break the babies out?" Kacey didn't really like that idea. If there were babies, they might think she was dinner. They didn't exactly understand the meaning of restraint.

"I go in, you wait here. If I need you, you'll know."

She tried a bit of eyebrow raising herself. "You dragged me all this way just to sit and watch?"

"You're back-up."

"Great."

"You want to come into a nest of babies?" he asked.

She ground her teeth. "Not really."

He nodded and with the whispering sound of cloth, was gone.

Kacey watched as he disappeared inside the house. He was gone moments before she saw the rear door fly open and a young woman rush out. Kacey tensed, not sure if the girl was part of the operation or one of the babies. The vampire's red hair was obscenely bright, her face pale and stark in the glow of the light, like a tortured angel. Bruises ran up and down her bare arms and legs, and she looked thin, emaciated. Kacey'd never seen a vampire in such terrible condition. The girl paused in her flight and began sniffing the air, turning towards her.

Oh hell, Kacey thought. *Don't think I'm dinner.*

Before the vampire reached her though, she heard the snap of a twig behind her. Spinning, her stake raised, she saw a flash of steel and then felt the sharp, swift pain of impact. Breath rushing out of her, Kacey stared into the eyes of her attacker, light from the house reflected back at her.

"Are there any more of you, princess?"

He's got me in the gut, she thought.

Fuck. Fuck. Fuck. Mother fucker.

He was human. She'd bet her money on that. A vampire wouldn't let her blood trickle onto the dead grass.

"You!" A low, female voice hissed. Hatred almost warped the word beyond recognition.

Kacey wanted to turn, but she was kept immobile by the knife in her gut. Her attacker looked past her, at the voice, and then twisted the blade. She cried out, the pain deep and raw. Hot fluid ran down her front, no longer just dripping.

The hand holding the knife let go with a jerk, and Kacey fell to her side, seeing everything in hazed slow-motion. The redheaded vampire still had a human-softness about her, didn't yet have the immortal beauty of her kind. Definitely a baby, Kacey realised, as the girl jumped over her, landing squarely on her attacker, pinning him to the ground. White flashed, then there was a male scream, sheer terror. Blood then, spurting, not her own.

Blackness.

†   †   †

"Come on Kacey, drink!"

Pain. A red haze of agony.

"Kacey! Open your mouth."

Morris? She thought. She went to ask, but something was pressed against her lips, something warm and slippery. Hot liquid gushed into her mouth and it tasted bitter. She tried to draw away, but her head was pressed in a vice.

"Drink, Kacey."

She swallowed, one mouthful then another. "What?" she gurgled. The pain began to fade, her body coated in a slick glove of blessed numbness.

"It's my blood."

Her mind stirred through the pain. *Become a vampire or die trying*, something whispered. But she didn't want to be a vampire and she didn't want to die. Wasn't there another option?

More blood, and then she felt light, free, the agony gone.

"Don't you dare die, Kacey!" Morris again, she thought.
Her heartbeat was loud in her ears.
"Kacey!"

AFTERWORD TO "OUT OF THE GRAVE"

Vampires are still the new black—and for good reason, if you ask me. They're a fascinating mix of the unknown, death and sexiness. From the moment I put pen to paper to begin my writing life (some fifteen years ago now), vampires were my favourite topic. Nothing has changed.

When Russell announced his anthology, I was captivated by the concept: sunny Australia with the night-dwelling vampire. Then the ideas began, mostly of what I didn't want. I didn't want a secret society of vampires out there, I didn't want my vampires to be all about blood and gore, and I certainly didn't want my vampires to sparkle.

Plus, my heroine, Kacey, was more of a see-it-to-believe-it kind of girl, so the vampires had to already be "out".

That's when the story began.

DESERT BLOOD

MARTY YOUNG

The world began to bleed as the sun melted into the horizon. Hell was leaking, its blood seeping up from the sand and the sunset itself to reflect in the slow moving Cooper Creek next to them.

"This day can't end soon enough," Sharon said as she brushed limp hair from her shiny brow. She was slumped in a camp chair next to him, under the shade of a coolabah tree. A stubby of West End Draught was in her hand, but that was empty now.

"I'm sick of the bloody sand," She continued. "Sick of getting it down my pants and in my mouth, and having to dig into it to collect these bloody samples."

Toby grinned. "I told you what to expect."

"I know, I know. But you go on about the wonderful desert all the time so I had to see for myself. And now I know you're just mad."

"But right now, this isn't so bad, is it? It's cooling down, the flies are gone, and the colours—"

"Another beer wouldn't be so bad, either." Sharon lobbed her empty stubby on the ground at Toby's feet.

Toby shook his head at his wife, slouched there like every other exploration geologist with which he'd spent desert time. How far we've come, he thought, amused. She'd been so posh when they'd first started going out. Clean fingernails and all. When was that, eight years ago now? Nine? How this job changes people.

He was about to say as much when something dropped down from the trees to land between them.

"Jesus!" Toby cried, jerking back in his seat and toppling over. He heard Sharon scream as he crashed to the ground. He rolled, clambered to his feet in time to see a man, naked, red-skinned, and hairy, leaping at her. Sharon fell over backwards, her arms flailing. The ragged man followed her to the ground, his deformed hands outstretched, his mouth opening impossibly wide.

Toby yelled and went after him. The odd-looking man looked up and Toby saw the desert within those eyes, an eroding landscape of sand and dust. The sight caused him to stagger, and that was enough for the man to swing at him and send him tumbling against the base of the tree.

Toby's head cracked on the trunk and suddenly there were stars, stars and darkness swimming towards him faster than the sunset, screaming towards him, forever screaming.

"Sharon—" he groaned, reaching out for his wife as the monster took her away.

Then there was only darkness. Night. Desert emptiness.

†   †   †

Toby sat up with a start, certain he'd heard something. He listened to the great desert but in a few heartbeats knew there was nothing of interest lurking in the dark, not tonight. It was as silent as only the outback could be.

He lay back down and stared at the stars as the long ago memory drifted away once more. His eyes traced out Scorpio, then followed its tail to Sagittarius and across to Capricornus.

"Still waiting on you," he whispered as he pulled his old blanket up about his chin. It felt like he'd asked the stars to guide him a millennia ago but they had yet to offer help; perhaps another millennia had to pass before they got the message, and then more time to relay their answer. They were a long way away after all.

Well, no matter; he would be out here waiting. Time was the only thing he had left. His backpack had been discarded sometime in the past and with it, his sleeping bag and the last possessions of an old life. Even the blanket over him would soon fall apart.

A tongue of wind licked his cheeks and broke his arms into goose bumps. Savouring the feeling on his sunburnt skin, Toby closed his eyes to the stars and let the wind blow him into sleep again. Sometimes, deep in the dark with his eyes firmly closed, he could almost believe it was Sharon's breath he felt as she lay next to him, sleeping.

†   †   †

"They're just stories, mate. Old Aboriginal legends. They ain't true, an' you're crazy thinking they are." The old man from the store said in a stray memory from a lifetime ago. He was another ghost, come to haunt again. The desert was a graveyard of spectres like him.

"Listen Mr Davies, I know it's not my place to say anything, but not all of us believe you were responsible. It's like Lindy Chamberlain all over again. Damn shame, what happened."

The fella's beard was grey and grew down past his caved-in chest. His eyes were a glassy yellow amongst skin of leather. There was a fly on his cheek but it didn't seem to bother him.

"Go home. Forget about make-believe monsters an' let the cops do their job."

Home. With its spray-painted messages: *murderer, killer, fucking dingo lover—*

No, he could never go home. Not while she was still out here.

The fella scratched his cheek, finally unsettling that fly, which circled about his head and landed on the other cheek. "The outback's a big place, y'know. People get lost out here all the time, one way or another. You're not going to find what you want."

The old guy turned and went back inside the desert store. The fly screen door screeched shut behind him with a bang that scattered the memory.

†   †   †

Toby traced the outlines of the trees with his eyes as the ghost faded from his mind. River red gums, red Mulga trees, all growing from red sand—this whole damn world was red. A constant reminder of what had happened.

He stretched, rolled his neck; it cracked twice. The sound was an explosion that revealed a flash of yet another dusty memory; of police, detectives, sitting across from him, one of them cracking their knuckles in a way so common on tele as they grilled him.

"Do you know how many murders happen in the outback?"

"Why'd you do it, huh? Not getting enough at home?"

"It's so easy hiding a body out there. Hard for us to find, right, by the time the animals and the sun all have their way?"

Corellas called from the trees as they took flight for the day. Toby watched them pass overhead. He could remember the detectives' eyes, the looks of accusation, even the tightening of the skin around their eyes when he hadn't given them the admission they'd wanted, only a story that made even less sense in its retelling than it had first-hand. A story that sounded outlandish now, so long after it had happened.

A short, hairy man dropping from the trees, with a huge mouth ready to gobble up his wife? C'mon sir, surely you don't expect us to believe that?

Did *he* even believe what he'd seen—or thought he'd seen?

Eventually the Police had given up questioning him though, even if they hadn't believed him. The only truth they could gather was the lump on his head where he'd hit the tree. There'd been no evidence to hold him any longer, no motive for her murder, none of Sharon's blood on his clothes, not even her body, so they were forced to let him go.

And all too soon, they were forced to put aside the case and move onto something else, a crime with leads to follow. We won't give up but we just have nothing to go on, they'd told him at the end. The desert's too big to keep searching.

Sharon's face was going, too. Each time the memories came, her face was less defined than the time before and he knew the desert would soon have her. She had grown transparent in his memories, a monster's visage superimposed upon her. What came more readily was the image of the raggedy man staring at him with erosion in his eyes, and that huge mouth, like a snake's.

They're vampires, someone had told him, a stray voice on the phone a million years ago. *Yara Ma Tha Who, that's their name. They drop from the trees and use the suckers on their hands and feet to drink their victim's blood, an' you know what happens then, right? You've seen the movies.*

Vampires. Desert madness. Sometimes Toby wondered just how much the desert had truly taken from him. But still, there was hope to be had in that legend, and he clung to it.

You're a fucking murderer and I hope the cops rape you—

Toby climbed to his feet and stared at the water. The creek was full from recent rains, flowing steadily. He walked into it and quickly submerged, letting the cool water slew off the remnant memories. Only one he clung to, and it was the one memory he recoloured every morning. This one he wouldn't let the desert fade to grey.

Time passed, and sand spread. Dunes rose and migrated with the wind. Trees died and new ones grew. Memories rose and set like the sun, random reflections of a world he no longer knew.

But he didn't give up.

He walked the desert, following the winding path of Cooper Creek north-east from Innamincka, the small desert settlement near the Strzelecki Desert, to Cullyamurra Waterhole in the eastern corner of South Australia, where he caught yellowbelly and sometimes catfish in the desert lake, soaking in the cool water when no one else was around. He dove down as far as he could but never reached the bottom, and at night he sat among the trees, waiting for the Bunyip to rise from the waters and come seek his company.

Alone, he made his slow way to the Nappapethera Waterhole in the south-western part of Queensland, forty-three kilometres from Innamincka, before eventually returning to the township itself, where the horror had begun.

He lived off the land, off grubs and fish, birds and lizards, sometimes snakes. He picked berries when he found them, and stole from campsites when he needed. His hair grew, his bead grew. His clothes fell away and his naked hide blistered, eventually turning a brown-red like the rest of him. Like the land all about, drawn from blood.

He travelled south from Innamincka to the Minkie Waterhole, a smaller lake than the Cullyamurra, only to double back once more. He slept among the trees, sometimes high in their branches to watch those who camped below, staying there for days at a time before moving on.

One night, as he perched amongst branches, he felt the other.

That swollen presence crowded in upon him and the great expanse of the desert grew claustrophobic under its weight. With his heart thudding and his knuckles going white where he held the tree, he searched the darkness. The last flames of the campfire below made the shadows and trees dance with twitchy movements, but already the sensation of being watched was fading like his memories. Then it was gone.

Silently, Toby let out his breath and felt the crushing weight of rejection. He closed his eyes and swallowed his scream.

Sometimes, deep in the night as he waited upon the stars, he tried to remember how happy he'd been, him and Sharon, but those memories were gone now. Taken by the desert like it had taken his tears. This desert he had once loved.

Time passed, but still he walked. Through days and weeks, and the cycles of the moon, he followed the river, seeking the desert legend.

"I'll find you," he whispered to the trees he shared the night with, to the corellas who took flight come dawn and settled back again upon dusk.

There were aborigines out here, and tourists too, seismic survey crews and geologists. The barren desert was filled with life, and though he tried his best to remain hidden, he became legend himself, the sick white man of the trees who had come to the desert to die, so the campfire whispers went. Stories grew about him, tales of this ghost forever seeking what it had lost to the outback. Flittering amongst the red gums, coolabah, and mulgas, vanishing when spotted, only to appear somewhere else along the Cooper. Still looking, still searching. Innamincka's ghost.

Sometimes, when the night was still, his voice could be heard calling from the dark; "Yara ma, Yara ma, which way have you gone?"

† † †

And finally, one day, his call was answered.

† † †

He heard a car approaching, the diesel engine an unmistakable sound. From the perch he'd used last night in the tall red gum, Toby watched the strengthening lights swing towards him, then stop.

"I wish we hadn't stopped back there," the woman—Sally-Ann, he remembered—said as she pushed open the door and climbed out of the Hilux. She stared at the twisted trees lining the banks of the river before shaking her head. "All I can think of is what that bartender said."

"Maybe it's Burke's ghost, or Wills' ghost—no, maybe it's both of 'em. They've become joined at the hip in the stories so maybe they've become joined in death, too."

"So would you scream or laugh if the ghost of a joined twin was coming after you?"

The fella—Mike—slammed his door and then stared at her. "You're some kind of cuckoo, do you know that?" He went around to the back of the car and opened the doors there. As he hauled out the two small tents they'd set up here last night, he said, "Look, I wouldn't worry about what that old freak said. He was probably just having fun at our expense."

"I figured that much. It makes you wonder, though."

"About what?"

"About what could be out here."

He shrugged at her, then said, "C'mon and help me with this."

The tents went up. Soon, they had a small fire going and their camp chairs close to the warmth of the flames as the desert cold rose up about them.

The scene was so similar to last night, to last week and month, to the years and other people before them, back to when the universe was created. Men, women, men, women, they were all the same. All so vulnerable huddled beneath the desert trees. Toby didn't need to see their eyes to know who they were, and knowing made no difference. He'd been like them, once. Him and Sharon.

The woman below pulled on a sweater and moved herself closer to the fire. "Do you believe in ghosts?"

The guy shook his head. "I'd like to think I have an open mind, but whenever I hear a story about one I never believe it. Like this one. If there was something out here, we'd know about it by now. Someone would've made a movie about it."

"Like Picnic at Hanging Rock."

Mike grunted, then finished his beer and tossed the empty can into the flames.

"I reckon there's more to this world than what we know," the woman said. "A lot of people die out here so why can't there be ghosts? There's nothing to say ghosts have to haunt cities."

"They'd be lonely buggers if that's true. You're not coming down with the willies, are you? Not you of all people? We were here last night and nothing happened."

She laughed. "Tonight's a different night though, 'cos now I know about it."

Toby watched them stare off into the darkness held at bay by the flickering light. The fire made shadows dance like wild natives, and the crackling and popping of wood sounded like ritualistic song and banging drums.

He settled amongst the branches, waiting. He waited as the stars moved silently overhead, his message still unanswered. Waited as the couple beneath him cooked a meal, the smells making his stomach growl dangerously loud.

He thought about dropping down between them and taking their food. He'd have to knock the man out first. The woman, he could overpower.

†   †   †

The sound of a yawn brought Toby alert some time later. He shook his head to clear it, then stared again at the couple below. The tent flickered in the dying flames of the campfire.

The man was stretching.

"I'm hitting the sack," he said.

"Yeah, I think I'll do the same," she said.

"What time do you want to get going in the morning?"

"About seven? It'd be good to get started before it gets too hot."

But Toby had stopped listening because there was someone behind him. Close. Almost pressed against his back.

A tide of words flooded his mind, sentences he had practiced saying at this moment as he'd lay staring at the stars, waiting for her to finally come to him. He knew she'd appear when she was ready— when she was allowed.

But his words had become dry husks.

A cold hand touched his shoulder, squeezing gently, then sliding down his bare arm. Toby gasped and felt goose bumps erupt over his flesh.

"What was that?" The man from below said.

"Such suffering," a voice whispered in Toby's ear, making him shiver. Cold lips brushed at his earlobe and made him groan.

"Sharon," he said, finally finding a word. He went to turn but there was a jolt to his side and suddenly he was falling. Branches slapped at his face, punched his chest and stomach, knocked against his head as he fell to the ground.

A woman screamed and Toby remembered Sharon had screamed too.

The man swung something at him as he tried getting to his feet and whatever it was caught him across the temple, exploding stars and night. He staggered, clasping the side of his head and already feeling blood. Then he was hit across the shoulders, again on his thigh, and he went down. The world spun. He saw the man drop the thick branch and run after the woman, who had climbed into the Hilux and started the engine, and then Mike, it was Mike he remembered, was scampering into the cab too, and they were reversing and swinging around, dust billowing, and they gunned the engine and the truck bounced away over the dirt track, back towards the nearby township. The horn blared, and blared again. It kept on screaming, like Sharon had done. She hadn't stopped until blackness had taken him, and then he hadn't known what had become of her.

He had hoped, though. Dared to believe in vampires. And now—

He struggled to sit up, desperate not to lose her again, but a shadow dropped silently from the trees to couch over him.

Time spiralled. The world swam to catch up. Stars were born and exploded.

Toby stared up into the eyes before him. The moon was in those eyes, the moon and the universe, shining down upon him. And deep amongst that eternity was something vaguely human, raised to the surface by his suffering.

"It's not you," he said, feeling his world fall apart again.

The ragged man before him smiled and there *were* teeth, sharp, pointed, shiny teeth filling that mouth. The legends were wrong, Toby thought with panic.

There were sounds in the distance, drawing nearer. Revving engines, frantic voices. Huge spotlights blasted the dark.

The thing standing over him reached out and touched his cheek with its deformed fingers. Toby flinched. Its smile never wavered. Then it straightened, turned, and vanished into the night. Gone back into the desert once more.

"Wait!" Toby cried after it. "Please—"

But headlights were already catching the nearby trees and Toby knew it wouldn't return. Not here.

He allowed his eyes to close for a heartbeat before rolling over and quickly crawling towards the river.

He knew who had been behind him in the tree. Even after all of this time, with his memory of her eroded by the desert, her touch was unmistakable. He'd have known it had a million years gone by.

The raggedy man had let her come to him, given them scant seconds in a life of eternity, but for what purpose? To say goodbye?

No. Not that. He wouldn't allow it to end like this. He wanted her back, and he'd have her, too. One way or the other. He wouldn't give her up.

He slipped into the water like a crocodile and let the current carry him away, off into the darkness of the desert.

ATERWORD TO "DESERT BLOOD"

I'm not sure where or how this actual story came about, only that it was inspired by David Unaipon's "Yara Ma Tha Who", which Angela Challis and I reprinted in Macabre in late 2010. Unaipon's story recites the aboriginal legend of the Yara Ma Tha Who, and it has been debated numerous times whether or not these frightening creatures are actually vampires. I can certainly see how they could be viewed as such. But for "Desert Blood", I liked the idea of a man losing himself and what made him human in his desire, or need, for revenge. He basically becomes the mythical monster he is hunting. This was one of those wonderful stories that sits perched at your fingertips and the moment you begin typing, it pours from your fingers, through the keys, and onto the screen all in one go. It's also set in one of my favourite places and that's Innamincka, outback Australia. It's beautiful there and along that river system—though the townsfolk may not welcome me back if I keep writing ghoulish stories set there!

THIN AIR

SIMON BROWN

I knocked on the window of his compartment. He looked up from his bible, distracted, and gave me a puzzled look. I lifted my chin and pointed to my dog collar.

He slid open the door. "You're from the Bishop?" he asked, frowning.

"I'm Father Costello," I said, extending my hand.

"From Kendall? I wasn't expecting you until the end of the line."

"I had business in Wollongong."

He finally took the hand. "Father Fury. Well, Bill."

"Mick," I replied, taking the seat opposite him.

The station guard blew his whistle and the train set off.

"Does the line go all the way to Kendall?"

"No; it stops at Berry. But Kendall's only an hour's drive from there."

Fury swallowed. "Umm, did Bishop Carroll explain . . ." He let the sentence drift.

I shrugged. "I was told I had an assistant priest for a few weeks." I smiled to make him at ease. "Kendall's a small parish. You'll fit in just fine."

He tried to smile back. "I'll do my best," he said.

†   †   †

Mrs Tingwell, my cook and house cleaner flitted from job to job in the presbytery like a dragonfly on a pond. About mid-morning her husband Frank turned up and they talked urgently and quietly for a minute before he left. I heard her trying to stop herself crying.

I called her into my office, sat her down and asked her what was wrong.

"It's Violet."

Violet was her daughter. She was nineteen, as big-boned as her mother, a studious, clever girl who worked every other day as a receptionist at Doctor Purdom's surgery, and in between travelled to Nowra to attend secretarial school.

"How could Violet be troubling you?"

"She didn't come home last night," Mrs Tingwell said.

"Ah. Was she out with anyone?"

"Anne Harvey, Father. A girl who's also with Doctor Purdom. They always go out for a sandwich and a cuppa after work. Sometimes she gets home after Frank and I go to bed. But we don't worry, Father. Violet's a good girl, you know that."

"Of course I know that."

"Only this morning she weren't there. Frank's been out looking since he woke up. He's already seen Doctor Purdom, and Anne Harvey, and they don't know where she is. I don't know what to do."

"I'm sure she's all right, Mrs Tingwell. Why don't you go home and wait for her there?"

But Mrs Tingwell wouldn't leave. She didn't want to be home by herself.

†   †   †

Violet never came home. She was the second in two years. They simply disappeared. In the big city the disappearance of two women might not get much attention, but in a country community the loss of anyone young is a great tragedy, and to lose them to thin air struck deep into everyone's conscience, as if we were all guilty of it in some way. The first was Elizabeth Bellini, twenty-one years old, plain and round but always laughing. Then came Violet.

It was made worse because of the war. As with every town in Australia, Kendall suffered. Many of its young men were gone to fight, and now and then we'd hear of one of them being wounded or killed or captured, and it was like our future being taken away, cut after cut. But the disappearance of Elizabeth and Violet sliced much deeper into our common life.

I helped in the search for Violet, and consoled her grieving parents, and when the search was finally called off, I promised them I would preside over her funeral should a body ever be found. In the meantime they would live in hope, which is the cruellest refuge.

The people of Kendall did their best to push her disappearance to the back of their minds. After all, there was a war on, and although no one doubted we would defeat the Axis in the end, the war was not going brilliantly for the Allies. There wasn't much official said, and that in itself let us know progress could be better. Our daily lives were threaded along the course of the war like rosary beads on a string, and in the end there was little room for anything else.

There were moments, sometimes minutes at a time, when you could forget the rest of the world existed. Kendall's beach was largely deserted, and unlike those closer to Sydney still without barbed wire. Sitting on its white sand, staring out over the Tasman Sea, its gentle swell rising and falling like the notes of a lullaby. it was almost possible to remember what life was like before Poland and Pearl Harbor and two missing girls.

† † †

One Saturday a month later, I was in the presbytery office working on my sermon. Mrs Tingwell interrupted to tell me that Bishop Carroll was on the telephone.

"What does he want?"

"I don't know, Father," she said in a tone suggesting it would have been presumptuous for her to have asked.

I followed her out to the hallway and picked up the heavy black receiver from its cradle. "My Lord?"

"Any news about the missing girl, Father Costello?"

"Elizabeth Bellini?" I'd been thinking about her today.

"God's sake, Father. Victoria Tingwell."

"Oh. No; no word at all." I glanced at Mrs Tingwell, who was pretending to polish the hall rail.

"It's her mother who works for you? She answered the phone?"

"Yes, my Lord."

"It must be a very hard time for her and her husband. Have they any other children?"

"No."

"So much the harder, then." There was a long pause on the other end before he continued. "Father, I have some understanding of what you must be going through, as well. Two young female parishioners lost in two years. A dreadful thing."

"Yes."

"The pressure on us as the community's moral guardians is especially difficult during times of war and tragedy," he continued.

"I'm fine, my Lord."

"Of course you are. I'm coming your way this Tuesday. I'll stay the night, if that's suitable."

"I look forward to it. Is there a particular reason . . . ?"

"Excellent. Tuesday, then." The Bishop hung up.

I stood there for a moment with the dead receiver in my hand, Mrs Tingwell still hovering nearby. "He's coming for a visit," I told her.

"The Bishop? Here?"

"Yes, Mrs Tingwell. On Tuesday. And he'll be staying the night."

"I'd better get the extra room ready, then."

†   †   †

That same night I was called to give the last rites to old man Bates, a dairy farmer who'd sold up in his eighties and retired to a bungalow in town with his youngest daughter, Hattie. When I got there, Doctor Purdom was just leaving; he shook his head to let me know there was no chance Rourke would bounce back like he had a dozen times before. I went into Bates' bedroom. He looked like a mummy, dry skin stretched around bone, the flesh all burned away by decades of hard work. His eyes were half-closed, and his thin lips shaped words that never sounded. I figured he was too far gone to hear anything, but I gave the sacrament, which at least comforted Hattie, herself over fifty years old. When I was done I accepted her offer of a cup of tea, and we went into the kitchen.

"What will you do?" I asked her.

"Stay in the house. He's given it to me."

"You could move in with one of your brothers or sisters. They wouldn't mind."

She sighed so deeply it sounded to me like someone retrieving water from a deep well. "I'd mind, Father. After all these decades, some time alone would be welcome."

I understood, so didn't press the matter. Like a lot of youngest daughters, she had been expected to stay a spinster and look after her parents when they got old. At first she'd bucked them, even gotten engaged in her 20s, but her fiancé was blown away at Hamel in 1917 and she gave up the struggle after that.

We talked awhile, about her father and the farm she grew up on, about all her nephews and nieces and grandnephews and grandnieces whom she loved dearly but ideally from a distance.

Before departing, I looked in on Bates one more time. He was puffing like a horse that'd run a four mile race; he was on his way out. I left Hattie to her last grieving and stepped out into the night. One of her brothers was just arriving, looking angry that his father would choose this time of night for his dying.

The moon had set and stars spilled across the sky. It was very late, and nearly every house was dark. There was a light on in the Tingwell's house, though. As I walked by I saw Frank alone in the living room, sitting in a reading chair in his pyjamas. He was sitting there crying, the tears rolling down his cheeks, his shoulders shivering tightly.

† † †

Bishop Carroll arrived mid-morning on Tuesday, his big black car drawing notice on the streets of Kendall. He drove it himself; most of his staff had been cut back because of the war. Mrs Tingwell rushed out to get his luggage, which turned out to be nothing more than a single carpet bag, and took it to the guest room.

He greeted me genially enough, but he seemed much more careworn than last time we'd met. His face, already narrow, was pinched, and his white hair was brushed back over his head like a hospital sheet. I'd always thought of him as a short, dapper man, but now he looked decidedly thin except for a new paunch over his belt. When he smiled he showed small, even, yellow teeth.

"It's nice to see you again, Father Costello," he said with his strong Kerry accent.

"Welcome, my Lord," I said, and led the way to the living room.

As he always did, he slowly cast his gaze about, studying the contents of my bookshelves, then took the plumpest seat. He nodded to the Bakelite radio near the window. "That's new."

"I wish it worked better. Reception isn't always brilliant down here. Something to do with atmospherics."

"Really?" His eyebrows lifted. "Atmospherics?"

He asked it in a way that made me feel foolish for even suggesting the word. "So I'm told. I don't pretend to understand the science."

"Well," he said, using the word to suggest a lot more could have been said, and placed his hands in his lap. They seemed too large for his straw arms, great paddles that would have looked more at home on a carpenter or plumber.

Mrs Tingwell poked her head around the door. She was all bone and angles, and looked large enough to swallow our guest whole if she had a mind to. "Are you hungry, Bishop Carroll? Shall I make you some sandwiches to go with your tea?"

"Not just now, thank you," he said in a tone that dismissed her. Her head disappeared and the door closed behind her.

"How is she?" Carroll asked, nodding towards the door.

"Coping, in her way. She works twice as hard to exhaust herself."

"She is here fulltime?" Carroll asked.

"Three days a week. It's all I can afford to pay her, and her husband has great need of her in his butcher shop. The war's taken all his apprentices."

"Bloody thing," he said.

"Bishop, it is good to see you, but you're not one for social visits. Why have you come, my Lord?"

Carroll took a deep breath. "I have a priest who needs placement."

I could not hide my surprise. "You want me to move on? I have only been here three years—"

He waved me quiet. "No, no, nothing like that. He will be here to assist you, that's all."

"I don't need any assistance, my Lord. This is a small parish, as it is."

"I know you must have been under great strain of late, with the disappearance of two girls." He shrugged. "And the war and all, of course." His tone challenged me to contradict him, but a parish priest knows his place.

"Who is he?" I asked.

"His name is Father William Fury. He is almost retired. Not long to go at all. But he needs some work to keep him busy in his last few years."

"A few years?" I blurted out, alarmed.

"Not all here," Carroll said quickly. "A few months, no more. Just until I'm sure."

"Sure?"

Carroll cleared his throat. "Sure that you've reached an even keel, Father."

"Is this priest to be my parochial vicar?" I asked carefully.

"Oh, no. You'll be entirely in charge. That isn't changing. He will be your assistant priest, and will look to you for guidance."

"He's not done parish work before?"

Carroll shook his head. "Not as such."

"Is he a refugee, my Lord?"

"From overseas, yes. From Cork. But that was a long time ago. Until recently he was a teacher at a boy's school in Sydney."

"He doesn't want to teach anymore?"

"I must be blunt with you, Father. He has fallen into temptation, and though repentant cannot return to his old profession."

"I don't understand. What temptation . . ." And before I finished the sentence I understood what Bishop Carroll was trying to say. "No. You can't."

"Your parish is small. Few children. No local school."

"My Lord, you can't be serious."

"He's sorry for what he has done. He has been absolved in the confessional. That is enough."

The Bishop would say no more; he had driven long and far, and needed to rest. He said we would talk again later. While he slept, I went for a walk to clear my head. The day was overcast, with heavy clouds rolling in from the sea. There was a cold edge to the wind. Kendall lay quietly under the growing gloom. Even the magpies and lorikeets were quiet in the trees. The beach looked murky in the dim light, and the sea was almost flat, the tide creeping rather than washing in. I smelt old seaweed and brine and rotting cuttlefish.

I wanted my conscience to find me a way out of accepting Father Fury, but my conscience led me down blind alleys. Once I'd thought being a priest gave you a life neatly divided between what was right and what was wrong, and that all my choices were black or white. I've learned that being a priest means that all our choices are grey.

Mrs Tingwell met at the presbytery door. "He's gone!" she said.

"Who? Bishop Carroll?" I glanced back at the street and noticed his big black car was no longer there.

She nodded. "Almost as soon as you left. He told me he had urgent business and that you would understand."

"Is that right?" I couldn't hide the disappointment in my voice. I had no choice at all, now.

"He said I was to pass on his thanks, and that concerning the matter you'd discussed together . . ." she frowned, trying to remember his exact words ". . . he said that the grace of forgiveness was God's greatest gift, and that he'd be in touch to finalise the details."

†   †   †

Father Fury and I arrived at Berry Station late on a Monday night. The station guard tipped his hat to us. I led the way to the van in the car park.

"Tingwell Butchery," Father Fury read on the van's side. "Beef and Lamb."

"It's the best I could do on such short notice," I told him, unlocking the doors. "I'd have picked you up in Wollongong if I could've gotten hold of enough petrol rations."

"The train was fine," Fury said.

We drove into the Nowra and then south along the Princes Highway, passing very few cars. The road was narrow and twisty.

He asked me in a strangely high voice, "And Bishop Carroll told you nothing about the nature of my leaving Sydney?"

I shook my head. Truthfully he had not, at least not in so many words.

"It is not my place to know, Father, although if you wish to tell me I will listen."

"No, no. Perhaps one day."

We drove is silence for a long while, and then I said, "I have a favour to ask."

"Ask," he said, sounding almost desperate to return the favour of giving him refuge. "Anything."

"I want you to hear my confession."

Fury said, "Me?", as if he could not believe anyone would ask that favour of him.

"I would have asked Bishop Carroll on his last visit, but he had to leave in a hurry."

I heard him swallow. "Well, of course."

I turned onto a forest trail and stopped the car. Keeping my hands on the wheel I began.

"Bless me, Father, for I have sinned. It has been seven weeks since my last confession." I paused, then said lowly, "Actually, more than two years since my last full confession."

Father Fury sat in the dark cabin, making no sound or movement. He was a black shape, hunkered against the passenger door.

"Go on, Father," he said quietly.

"Last night, about an hour before evening mass, I killed a woman."

He caught his breath, and I could hear the blood drain away from his face. I felt a great release, the unburdening that comes with final commitment.

"Her name was Hattie Bates. She had come to the church for confession. I followed her out of the church and along the darkening, glistening alley that winds its way along the glebe. I took her before she reached the Kendall's main street, wrapping my hand around her slim, pulsing neck and pulling her up with me into the mid-branches of an ancient ironbark. There, twenty metres above the earth, I drank her dry. In the end there was nothing left of her except her husk, like an old paper bag filled with brittle sticks; I stuffed it into an owl's hollow in the tree trunk, where I'd previously hid the remains of Violet Tingwell and Elizabeth Bellini.

"You don't know their names, Bill, but everyone in Kendall does."

"Why?" he croaked. "Why are you telling me this?"

"I'm confessing. It won't stop me from feeding again. But I feel better telling someone about what I've done."

"This . . . this isn't a confession. You're not sorry."

"I may not be repentant, Bill, not truly. But I do need absolution. We all need absolution. But no more interruptions. I haven't finished."

"After killing Hattie Bates, I had time to return to the sacristy and clean myself before the start of evening mass. I was so filled with Hattie's life that I regurgitated some of her blood into the chalice when I was changing the Eucharist, but none of the parishioners noticed."

Fury groaned. His left hand was fumbling for the passenger door handle. I slowly reached out and grasped his wrist, squeezing it so tightly that the bones ground together, the joints cracking audibly. He screamed.

"You know, Bill, I don't dream anymore. Sleep for me is a perfect blank. I can't even daydream. I used to daydream all the time. When I was young, I used to dream about being a priest, of giving myself completely to God. That's a terrible vanity, you know, to think that any of us is worth giving to God.

"Now I wonder if my . . . condition . . . is His punishment for my vanity, and that by making me something less than human He is forcing me to learn something of humility. I do wonder about it, and the nature of my passion, perverted from religious zeal to a thirst, a desire, greater and darker than any I could have imagined before. I do wonder about the kind of love God might possess for creatures like me."

I pulled Fury towards me. His breath gusted onto my face. I could smell the fetid germ in it, the decay that had set in when he fell to temptation.

"I cannot share my parish, Bill, and certainly not with someone like you. I may take the lives of the innocent, but unlike you I do not damage their souls."

I put both hands around his head and twisted it almost right around. There was a snapping sound, the smell of his bowels evacuating, and the smallest ghost of a light behind his eyes guttered out.

I could not consume this one. It would have soiled me. Instead, I buried him deep in the forest, among the ancient mountain ash. His remains would not be found for years, maybe decades, maybe not ever. He will have disappeared into thin air.

† † †

I drove along the coast road, always trying to keep in sight of the sea. There was something about the sea that made me feel calmer, somehow more sure of myself. I stopped at the northern edge of Kendall beach and sat on the brightest and windiest patch of sand. I stared out towards the horizon for hours. I prayed, but never heard a reply. As always, God left me alone with the sand and flies.

AFTERWORD TO "THIN AIR"

"Thin Air" was first called "The Colour of Air", and was started about fifteen years ago. I could never find a way to finish the bugger until pushed by desperation and deadline. I cut out about 4,000 words, changed the ending, moved the emphasis and sent it back in time to WWII. And suddenly it was working and actually easy to finish.

I'm glad this story is off my chest, but can't help feeling very pleased with the way it grew up.

KISSED BY THE SUN

JODI CLEGHORN

Anke leaned against the cistern, head resting on the concrete wall, listening to the disjointed conversation of the women hunched over the sinks, peering at anaemic reflections in the filthy mirror. They were the visual equivalent of running your fingernails down a blackboard. She couldn't look at the emaciated former beauties, expending life essence like body fat. The crop tops and low-slung jeans exposed sunken stomachs, protruding hip bones and gnarled muscles, bodies cannibalising themselves in an orgy of drugs, sex and all-night dancing. The first night in Fortitude Valley Isolda warned her never to drink from an amphetamine chick: the vacuum of life made them toxic.

Anke wondered how long Brian would wait. Isolda's bizarre behaviour should have scared him off; sniffing the air before him and telling how good he smelled. But the boys in this meat market were willing to ignore all sorts of social transgressions to score a girl who'd ride their cock all night like a Duracell bunny.

The toilet door slammed open cutting off the inane chatter.

"What are you looking at?"

"The door marked exit." Anke shuddered recognising her maker's voice.

"Really."

"How about you avail yourself of it?"

"Fuck you."

"Leave!"

A snarl punctuated the command, followed by the rapid shuffle of feet, swearing and the whine of the door hinge. The cubicle door flew open, shaking the entire row of partitioned walls and doors, and Isolda grabbed her progeny by the shirt front, hauling her off the toilet lid.

"He's been drinking rum. I specifically told you no alcohol. The blood must be pure."

"I couldn't stop him."

The older vampire released the fabric and fixed her fingers around the tiny blonde's slender neck lifting her off the ground.

"You made no such effort."

"I don't want to bleed him."

Isolda hurled Anke against the wall, the toilet disintegrating in an explosion of plastic, ceramics and water. She lay twisted among the chunks of dismembered porcelain, fangs buried into her bottom lip, glaring at her maker.

"I don't care if you don't want to," Isolda snarled, dragging Anke's head up by the hair, Death riding shotgun on every word. She leaned closer; lips curled back and fangs bared. "Your days as a spoilt human are over. Dead and gone." Isolda yanked the younger vampire to her feet. "Now you have me."

"And if I don't want you?"

"I'll kill and replace you." Isolda shoved a black bag into Anke's chest. "Three pints by dawn. Don't disappoint again."

The door opened and a riptide of competing beats, lyrics and melodies dragged Isolda into the fetid, throbbing depths of the dance club. Anke followed, head low and eyes downcast.

Brian sat on the threadbare corner of the couch, shoulders folded in, staring at the bottom of an empty glass shifting from hand to hand.

"Come," Anke said, snatching the glass and dragging him off the seat. They plunged into the cigarette smoke, fake fog and the crush of bodies. Anke turned back and saw surprise, relief and gratitude vie for equal air time on Brian's face.

"Hey . . . you're wet," he yelled into her ear, trying to slow her down. "Is everything okay? Your lip?"

"It's fine."

"Where are we going?"

"Anywhere but here."

"I need to find Alan."

"He's gone. Let's go." She stopped and tugged at the bag on her shoulder, trying not to think about the contents. Brian hesitated and she said, "You want to stay?"

"No." He squeezed her hand. "Let's go."

She slipped her hand free, aware of the difference in their body temperature despite the overheated room, and headed for the front door.

"Can we go to your place?" she asked. "I don't want to go home."

"Sure, it's just up on St Paul's Terrace."

The Empire Hotel spat them onto Brunswick Street. Brian rubbed his raw eyes and took deep breaths of the cool night air. Anke hurried towards the intersection of Ann and Brunswick, knowing lingering out the front of the pub was bad news. He broke into a jog to catch up with her.

"Do you want to grab a taxi?" he asked, meeting her at the traffic lights. "I don't mind paying."

"I prefer to walk. Will we be alone?"

"I think so. Hey, Anke." He grabbed her arm as the lights changed and tried to stop her, but she eluded his grasp.

"If you're not into this, it's fine."

"I'm into it."

They were half way across the road, drunks swerving in and out of their path. A girl wailed on the street corner, long streams of black tears staining her cheeks as her friend tried to console her.

"It's just you seem—angry."

"I'm pissed with Isolda." Anke stared at the crying girl, now crumpled on the footpath.

"Yeah, Alan shits me. He's more Trent's mate than mine. I only came down because Trent got an internship and I could pass for him to use the ticket."

"And my boyfriend dumped me."

"Oh shit, look—"

"Isolda said something and he went back to Switzerland."

"No wonder you're upset. Hey, look, it's okay if you want to go home, I'll walk you and maybe we can do lunch some other time."

Anke turned and propelled him into a doorway set back from the street. She was closer to him than she knew was sensible in public, pressing her slight body against his broad torso, the intoxicating scent of his blood filling her nostrils. The odd beating of his heart made her gums itch; a strange syncopated rhythm running counter to the actual pumping of his heart. Silent phantom beats woven between the steady pulses. Her fangs ached to tear through the soft skin above his carotid pulse.

But she thought of Isolda and stepped back.

"Alone is the last thing I want to be . . . unless you don't want to be with me."

"No. No, God, I want to be with you." The half-pained expression finally left his face and he leaned down, brushing her lips with his, trembling hands cupping her face. "I so want to be with you."

"Come," Anke said, pulling away from him, the itch morphing into tiny shots of pain in her gums. "Public displays of affection are dangerous."

† † †

His warmth cooled on her naked body.

She sat back on her heels inside his eviscerated torso, his chest yawned below, broken open with her own hands. His blood congealed on her face, breasts and hands, pooling in her navel. Only his head remained recognisable, long crimson streaks marking his cheek, the width of her fingers where she stroked his face, willing him back to life. His blue-green eyes, stared up at her and she burnt them into her memory.

The dirty curtain breathed in and out of the window, as dawn raced to greet her. The green digits on the clock radio changed. Vital minutes slipped through her fingers.

It shouldn't have turned out like this. She needed just three pints, taken while he slept in post-coital bliss. It should have been easy. But she'd asked Brian to touch her in places she'd never dared ask anyone before. His nervousness and willingness tore open something inside her. She wanted more. At first, a warm body to snuggle up to, then the desire to remain after dawn, asleep in his arms. To be loved, wanted, cherished as she'd been before Kiel abandoned her.

Now she belonged to the night; Isolda's bloody handmaiden and there would only ever be one night with Brian. The yearning for a human life and the chaffing of Isolda's yoke made her brave. She'd take just a little of Brian home, her little secret from Isolda, to comfort her and dull the ache left behind by Kiel's blood.

She straddled Brian, eased herself onto him and moved slowly. A little blood was not enough when she buried her face and teeth in his neck, and the blood flowed hot and sweet over her tongue. She knew

Brian was her escape from loneliness, just as she had been Isolda's escape from Switzerland.

But Isolda had will-power and control, coupled with the knowledge of a thousand undead years.

Shaking uncontrollably, she picked up the phone and dialled home. It rang out. The handset slipped through her bloody hand, falling among the unused medical equipment on the bedside table. She picked it up and hit redial. The line picked up after a minute.

"Isolda, help me."

†　†　†

Anke hated Surfers at this time of year. Every year Isolda brought her to Schoolies to purge Brian's death. Every year she felt the rawness of guilt and the haunting of her naivety among the crush of so many pounding heartbeats.

Thousands of teenagers milled on Cavill Avenue; couples kissing, boys mouthing off and groups laughing, crying, singing, arguing and screaming drunkenly. Car horns pierced the general din, sirens wailed and dance music seeped out of the air-conditioned nightclubs and bars onto the simmering street. The humidity clung like fresh blood on the skin.

The older vampire moved with the swell of people, tacking across the pavement toward the traffic lights and the wide expanse of moonlit beach beyond The Esplanade. Anke struggled to keep up as every second male tried to manhandle her. Even in life she'd struggled with crowds. Jostled, shoved and groped, she washed up beside Isolda.

"It degrades with every passing year," Isolda said and looked on with boredom at the endless procession of cars and boys hanging from the windows.

Behind them someone vomited loudly.

"If you hate it so much, why come?"

"Because I can."

Isolda thumped the large silver disc on the traffic light with the side of her fist.

"We should be back in the Valley. We've got a shipment due in three days."

"I want the sun."

The lights changed and Isolda strode out ahead. At the edge of the sand they kicked off their shoes and stepped onto the warm sand with a reverence not shared by the swarm of teenagers streaming around them. For a few minutes they stood in peace, side by side, the moon large and on the rise, platinum cirrus clouds caressing the sky.

A champagne cork shot into the air. A girl screamed out, "Ow, my eye. I just hit my eye," in between fits of hysterical laughter.

Isolda scowled and walked towards the water, moving around the congregation of drunks. She stopped when her toes kissed the retreating tide, her eyes set on the silver swell of the surf.

"We are returning home," she said, finally. "Tomorrow."

"What?"

Anke twisted the hem of her dress around her finger, all too aware of Isolda's intolerance of questions, and the mercurial moods which underpinned her sadistic nature. From past trips, she also knew her maker was most unpredictable and dangerous during schoolies when she specifically hunted for blood loaded with sun and recreational drugs.

"I won't become a day walker drinking sunshine-infused blood."

"But it makes you feel good. You only have to look at our accounts to know that. I remember the blood in Europe. It was different. We're so close to figuring out correct exposure times." Anke fought to find the correct words. "I know it's not a quick fix."

Isolda pointed her toe and drew circles in the wet sand. "You speak from only a decade of drinking this blood. You would not be so swift to jump to conclusions if you counted your time in eons."

"Perhaps it's volume rather than exposure. There are other possibilities. Transfusion? We can't give up. This is what you brought me here for."

The water swept up and wiped away the circles. "I have a chartered flight out of Coolangatta."

"And you never thought to consult me."

"What concern is it of yours? You go where I go."

"Not this time," Anke turned to walk away but her path was immediately blocked.

"I do not forgive having that which I gracefully give thrown back in my face."

"What have you ever given me?" Anke's fingers tore through the hem, wishing it was Isolda's throat.

Isolda brushed a stray strand of auburn hair behind her ear. "Freedom from sickness, old age, an eternity of—"

"Slavery. That's not a gift. I'd rather be dead"

"You seek the true death? Then go," Isolda stepped aside, her hand brushing the air.

Anke hesitated. "You're letting me go?"

"If death is what you resolve to embrace, then yes." Isolda turned back to the ocean, "I suggest you pack lightly tomorrow night."

The final words followed Anke as she ran, snapping at her heels; past the human refuse littering her path, through the drag of sand and onto the sticky tar. Brakes screeched and she hurtled on, pushing aside teenagers who loomed in and out of her field of view. She fell, got up and stumbled on through the disorientation and cacophony of competing thoughts. Her entire body buzzed with the sensory over load of instincts thrust into survival mode. Voices crowded in on her, every touch of another body exacerbated the smell of blood and sun, heart beats pounded in every direction and her control faltered until she recognised a rhythm lost years before.

She separated from the swell of the crowd and stood near the steps of McDonald's not daring to believe what she heard. With her eyes closed, she pushed aside the distractions and focused her heightened senses to home in on the echo of Brian's heartbeat.

As she did, the conversation flooded back: *He's more Trent's friend than mine. I only came down because Trent got an internship and I could pass for him to use the ticket.*

He had a twin, their hearts joined at conception, shadowing each other and beating in stereo beyond death.

She forced her way back into the crowd, looking back and forth for Brian's face. Bodies hit like bumper cars and pushed her this-way-and-that. Someone swore. A hand went up her skirt. Girls giggled. Someone pinched her arse. Anke ignored it all, the world contracting to a single heart beating the rhythm of redemption.

And there he was, loitering on the steps of Baskin-Robbins, a white shirt buttoned over a sunburnt torso, red board shorts colour-coordinating with his face. Their eyes locked. The self-awareness of his age amidst the schoolies fracas kept his sunburnt features frozen and he looked away embarrassed, entering the sea of teenagers, caught in but simultaneously fighting the tug of debauchery.

Anke followed him up the Esplanade and Cavill Avenue, hanging back when the merry-makers dispersed and just the two of them walked up a street of high-rise holiday apartments. He stopped and looked back. Hidden off the street in a visitor's carpark she listened to his heart beat speed up and then slow. The drumming pulled away from her, like a radio being turned down gradually.

Down the street she ran, stopping in the courtyard of a small cluster of older-style, low-set holiday apartments. She slipped through a gate, around a pool lit aquamarine from below, opened a glass door, climbed a short flight of carpeted stairs and stopped at door number seven. She raised her fist to knock and caught herself midair.

I have information about your brother.

Your brother didn't die in the fire.

He was never a missing person.

Your brother was murdered.

I killed your brother.

She knocked and the final moments in Brian's bed played before her on the beige door. The phone, bloodied from her hand dropping on top of the empty collection bags. Brian's eyes staring up, blue-green and still; the billowing curtain and the green digits on the clock.

The door opened a few inches. Trent frowned, recognising her immediately from their brief exchange on the street.

"I'm not the police," Anke said, sticking her foot in the door for insurance. "Can I please come in? I need help."

† † †

A breeze picked up, cool and salty. Trent walked beside the tiny blonde, their footsteps squeaking on the sand. From time to time he glanced sideways at her and Anke looked back but neither said anything.

Once they had passed the main section of the Esplanade he took a deep breath and said, "You appreciate I'm having a hard time . . . comprehending what you told me back in the apartment. Ten years of not knowing and a total stranger knocks on my door with all the answers."

"And you appreciate the night is almost over and you haven't said yet if you'll help."

"It's the bit about being a vampire. See, I can believe you knew Brian and maybe who killed him. Perhaps the guilt is eating you up, so you believe it was you who actually killed him."

Anke hissed and launched herself at Trent, knocking him back into the sand and landing on his chest, fangs out.

"Shall I bite you? Make it real."

"Holy fuck!" Anke felt his strong body squirm beneath hers, each movement digging the hole beneath deeper in the effort to fight free. She glared down at him, enjoying his fear.

"If you ate Brian, why should I trust you? What's stopping you from killing me too? I mean, I should go to the police."

"And tell them what?"

"That . . ."

The futility of the truth was obvious to both of them.

"I need you." Anke stood up and offered a hand. "I promise I won't bite." He ignored the hand and got himself to his feet.

"This is fucked." He kicked at the sand, hands clenching and unclenching. "Fuck. Fuck. Fucked."

"You think I chose this? For the first time I have a say over what happens to me and what options do I get . . . death or Isolda."

Trent stopped kicking at the sand. Anke bit down hard on her lip and a small amount of blood ran down her chin. She wiped it away with the back of her hand.

"I don't want to go and know Brian's death was for nothing. I loved him in my own way. I argued with her about using him. I didn't want to." She stepped closer and laid her head against Trent's chest, the familiar heart beat comforting. "If she'd let me choose someone else, he'd still be alive."

Trent's arm wound around her, fingers caressing her hair and the side of her chilly face.

"Promise me you will kill Isolda so she doesn't do this to anyone else."

He held her for a long time eventually dropping his hand from her head, and said, "Okay . . . but not for you, for Brian."

"That's all that matters." Anke pulled away from him. "Come," she said and walked towards the surf, the outgoing tide leaving greater stretches of sand behind.

They passed unconscious teenagers and partially naked bodies entwined beneath beach towels, and stepped over empty Cruiser bottles, beer cans and cigarette packets. The salt water crashed against their bare shins, swirling around their ankles, retreating, sucking the sand from beneath their soles. Trent reached for Anke's hand.

"When I was human I dreamed of the beach. I'd never seen the ocean so Kiel promised to bring me here."

"Do really think Kiel left you?"

"I think Isolda killed him, and forged the Dear John note so I'd be mad and not chase after him. I think she's terrified of being alone."

"But she let you go?"

Anke stood on tip-toes and traced the tendon in his neck with her fingertip, pushing aside the collar of his shirt to expose the clavicle. Her face twitched in time with the gentle throb of the carotid pulse. Lips pressed into Trent's skin, she drank in the sun, the salt, the freedom of day. She kissed his neck, the pulse in his neck speeding up as the sea water swirled at their ankles, feet sinking into the soft sand.

"How many humans have you killed?" he asked and Anke pulled away, dragging her feet from their wet graves, rinsing the sand in the next surge of water.

"Brian is the only one." She watched the tiny bubbles left behind by the water, a moment of life before disappearing forever. "I've never hunted to kill, only to secure a blood source. We extract three pints via cannula and sell it in small vial-sized shots to an established market in Europe."

"But before. What about Europe?"

"I never hunted. Isolda brought me blood while we waited for Kiel to organise our transfer to Brisbane."

Her fingers lazily traced the sunburnt expanse of skin between the flaps of his open shirt, coming to rest over his heart.

"I swear there hasn't been a day I haven't thought about Brian and what I did."

"I felt him go that night. It's a twin thing. The police said he was missing because there was no evidence of a body . . . but I knew."

Trent wiggled his feet free and retreated to the dry sand, sitting with his legs bent up, wrists slung over knee caps. Anke knelt in front of him and pulled a slip of paper from her bra.

"This is our address and the coding for the security system."

He took it and looked for a long time at the blue biro figures. "Why don't you kill her, if you're so hell-bent on avenging Brian."

"I will be dead soon."

"You're really going to kill yourself."

"I don't want to return with Isolda. If I am still alive this evening I will have no choice but to go. I thought I couldn't do it, but with you here, I have the courage to see the sun one last time . . . knowing Isolda will get what is coming to her." Anke shifted back and nestled between Trent's legs.

A stain lightened the edge of the horizon, giving definition to the divide of sky and sea. Trent's heart thundered in the back of her skull and she wondered how painful the end would be, mentally multiplying the agony of past exposure experiments on her arms and legs to her entire body.

Green numbers on a digital clock flashed before her eyes. Brian's blue eyes. Dawn was closing in; this time she was rescuing herself from Isolda.

She shuddered and Trent wrapped his arms around her.

"I'm a fire hazard."

"I'll take my chances," he said, nuzzling her neck, losing himself momentarily in the perfume of her skin. "I believe if you want anything bad enough it will come to you."

"It's too late to be wishing on falling stars. When the sun comes up I'm going to burn."

"Are you scared?"

"Not now." She reached up to cover his hands with hers. "Thank you."

The pale smudge widened over the horizon. A meniscus of light appeared, followed by the first sickle of dazzling sunlight. Trent turned to look at her. He half expected her skin to smoke; instead the beginnings of a peach glow spread across her ghostly skin. And a smile he couldn't quite fathom fixed her face.

"Stand up." He pulled her to her feet and took a few steps toward the sun, and the water, gently leading her in, until they were knee deep in the surf.

The golden orb rose inch by inch. Anke closed her eyes. She couldn't bear to see her skin bubble and smoulder. But the pain came from within, a dull throb gathering intensity, radiating outwards, and a slow burn rising in her throat. She hunched over; a thousand glass shards shattering in her unused veins as the first true rays of sunshine caressed her milky skin.

She gasped and fell to her knees, engulfed by a pain she couldn't comprehend. A rogue wave hit her, knocking her under the water. Trent scrambled to pull her up.

"My heart," she spluttered, her head breaking the surface. "Feel." She pressed his hand over her breastbone, struggling to find her feet against the pull of the ocean. "It's beating again."

Her chest rose and fell in agonising, atrophied, heaves but she smiled, hanging onto Trent's arm, life flowing back into her, the waves alternating between crashing into them and dragging them out with the tide.

"Oh God, I'm breathing. It wasn't a lie."

Trent covered her mouth with his lips. They moved slowly in time with each other, her body warming beneath his hands.

She pulled back, gasping, clinging to his wet shirt, the tide pulling away from them.

"Oh god, it hurts, but I'm alive. Breathing."

He pressed his ear close to her lips.

"So you are."

He put his hands on her shoulders, caressing them. "Kissed by the sun. See, I told you if you believed in something enough."

She laughed, bouncing up and down in the water, splashing as the sun rose higher. The pink and tangerine highlights in the sky were mirrored in her face when she stopped to shake the water from her hair and push the skirt of her black dress below the water, where the air pushed up beneath it. And then she was under again. The water closing over her head, hands reaching down for her.

Fingers clamped around her throat. Water filled her mouth and nose. Her heartbeat exploded in her ears. She thrashed beneath him, her now-human fingers clawing ineffectually at his. He dragged her into shallower water to keep his balance, keeping her pinned below. Amber eyes bulged, beseeching him to let her go. Silent screams tore from her lips. Columns of bubbles boiled to the surface, slowing until the last one rose and disappeared and her body went limp.

The sun cleared the horizon and Trent let go, the waves pulling her body into deeper water, long blonde hair floating around her head in a golden halo. He staggered away, slumping down on hands and knees in the shallows, breathing hard. He got up and walked away from the water, remembering the slip of paper she'd given him. The paper, sodden and transparent still bore Isolda's death warrant, the blue biro address.

Ten long years he'd waited, believing if he wanted it bad enough he'd get it. And now he'd started he wouldn't stop until everyone got what they'd waited for.

Sunshine.

Redemption.

Revenge.

AFTERWORD TO "KISSED BY THE SUN"

More than a decade ago my soul-sister told me about the amphetamine chicks in The Valley. The image of them—pale skin, emaciated bodies, hardwired to speed and music—never left me. They were the perfect social set for vampires to infiltrate in Brisbane. But why would a vampire choose to come to here, to my adopted home town?

Isolda, like so many emigrants, comes for the climate. She is obsessed with the idea sun-infused blood will transform her into a Daywalker. After a thousand years of darkness she wants the ultimate in immortality and will do anything to get it.

Her untrusting nature leads her to turn a human with strong ties to a lover and use them as her ticket to Brisbane. Kiel's going through a messy divorce, in love with young Anke and in the final throes of preparing for a six month stint in the Swiss Pavilion at World Expo '88. He's the perfect target for Isolda; useful in the short-to-medium term and dispensable after that.

The story came easily in the early drafts, before the lack of a consistent POV was raised as an issue by my beta readers. What I saw and heard came via the males in the story—Brian, Alan and Trent—who came and went at different times. It was suggested I change it all to Anke's POV, but she and Isolda refused to talk to me (with the exception of Brian's dismemberment.) Not every scene could be filtered via the male lens. The struggle between Isolda and Anke is as much a reflection of my struggle with them, as it is of their own personal battle against each other.

Don't get me wrong though, I wanted Anke to have a happy ending—which she almost did! No matter how hard Anke fought against the lot she'd been given, and no matter how hard I fought for her at the keyboard, it kept coming back to the same thing . . . she was damned the moment she laid eyes on Kiel.

Sometimes our free will is our undoing.

BATS

JANE ROUTLEY

Cicadas shrill so loudly that my eardrums are ringing. White sunlight blazes through my heavy lids. Someone's calling.

"Hello?"

A woman's voice. Footsteps on the wooden stairs. I wince away from the light. My head is like a lead weight and my tongue tastes rank.

I'm lying on a sun lounge and, wouldn't you know it, I'm right under the only shaft of sun that has penetrated through the branches over the verandah. The glare has that hot midday feeling. From the crick in my neck I must have been lying here since last night. My whole body aches, but my brain's still out for the count.

"Ooh, ooh? Anyone home?" calls the voice. The habitual cry of the country woman. Footsteps creak around the verandah towards me. The house is a classic old Queenslander; stilts, rusting galvanised tin roof, worn-silver weatherboards, and an all round verandah.

"Hello? Ms Dargeville?"

Shit! My stage name! I fling out my heavy arms in a hungover prelude to running and hiding, and knock over an empty bottle, which falls with an almighty thud and rolls and rolls and rolls until it hits the verandah rail.

Ouch!

"Ms Dargeville!" A brown-skinned face pokes shyly round the corner of the house. The rest of the body sidles round after it. She's about my age with crows feet, salt and pepper hair and a round middle-aged body in a faded floral dress and flat sandals. Not much attempt to stop the passing of time. There but for the Grace of God . . .

The little side table teeters as I grab shades to cram over my eyes.

"Hi. Sorry to bother you," she says. Her eyes are taking in everything; the dirty glasses, the vodka bottles, me prone on the sun lounge in my grubby silk night-dress. This is yesterday's nightie, no it's the day before's. Good God, hope I don't pong too much!

"I'm Jenny Hammond, your neighbour from down the road. Just came in to see how you were settling in. I brought you the last of my mangoes."

She holds out a white plastic bag full of big orange fruit. Mangoes—about 515 kjs each if they are large—too high K to eat.

Wellmeaningness shines off her; which means I'm trapped. I've never been much good at chasing people off. David always does . . . always did that for me.

I hunch over my knees and mutter, "Thanks. Kind of you."

"Put them here, will I?" she says, leaning the plastic bag against the wall by the back door. "Do you need anything? Do you know where to find everything? Would you like to come over for tea?"

Oh God, a dinner invitation! I just can't!

"I'm right, thanks," I mutter. "I'm not here long. Got lots to do."

A slight crease appears between her eyebrows. Is she getting the message? Have I been horribly rude? Will she think I'm being racist?

The glowing smile wavers a little. Then she brings out the other thing she's carrying, offering it forward—a familiar theatre program with the elegant logo of the Bell Shakespeare Company on the top corner.

"I saw you in *Romeo and Juliet*," she says. "I'm a big fan. I've followed your career since *Home and Away*. I was wondering if you could sign . . . Oh thank you so much. It's okay . . . I've brought a pen."

After that she leaves. What a thoroughly decent person!

People still like me. The warmth of that thought gives me the strength to make some effort at the day, to stagger off the sun lounge, swallow some antacid, have a slow heavy shower, change into a sundress and eat some crispbread.

That empty feeling is back all too soon. I knew it would be. It will always be there now.

By dusk I'm back on the sun lounge, drink in hand, re-living that appalling moment in the restaurant four days ago, when I discovered that David had given That Little Bitch the role of Mina Harker in his planned revival of *Dracula*.

"Couldn't you be a bit discreet," I'd hissed. I mean fucking her was one thing—but giving her my lead—it was humiliating—he'd be offering her co-directorship in our new company soon.

"Darling," he'd said. "I think you're too long in the tooth to play Mina, don't you?"

The scheming bastard! That was why the nice restaurant! He'd thought I wouldn't make a public scene. More fool him! You'd think he'd have known better after ten years together. I threw a grilled chevre salad marinated in herb olive oil with coriander salsa and a peppercorn jus over him and gave him both barrels—screaming, positively screaming, about how he'd had the best years of my life, how he'd used me up, how he had no business humiliating me like this.

I shouldn't have yelled. I should have noted how well heartbroken tears had worked for That Little Bitch. But I couldn't be doing with such lily liverish milk soppery, so I left him, though not before I'd seen That Little Bitch smirking on the latest cover of *Australian Vogue*. Was she going to take all my roles from me? I wasn't going to hang around to witness that. I cut and ran and came here to my grandparent's old farm house deep in the wilds of tropical North Queensland.

That bastard. That damned smiling villain. Remorseless, treacherous, lecherous, kindless villain. Make a discarded first wife of me, will you, you fucker? Where's the mobile?

Damn, I threw if off the verandah after that first drunken midnight call. Fuck. Fuck. Fuck.

No matter. A little vodka clears us of this pain.

The old house is overshadowed on one side by grey-green monster bottlebrush trees with huge springy tentacles. The harsh shrieking of the fruit bats which nightly descend to eat and quarrel over the red blossoms echoes the fury in my mind. When the bats have used their needle sharp teeth and tongues on them, the flowers are left ruined, thread bare, the colour of dry meat. Pure Australian Gothic. Pure Alys Dargeville.

† † †

I wake to blackness and rustling plastic. The verandah creaks. Someone's here. My eyes spring open before my brain has time to register anything.

The light from inside the house shows a dark shape crouching at the back door. I shriek.

It turns and springs up, hissing, a man's figure, a man's height.

"Go away!" I scream, and the figure runs. It jumps up onto the verandah rail, spreads its wings and launches out into the darkness, its heavy body crashing away through the branches.

I shout with all the anger vested in me as I lob an empty vodka bottle after it. Then I stagger into the house, locking the door behind me. I might be self-destructive but I'm not stupid.

†   †   †

For the first time since I've been here, I wake up in the bed. A gaggle of schoolkids is walking down the red dirt road in front of the house, their high, bright morning voices cutting though my skull like knives.

Gulping down aspirin in the bathroom, I stare at my face in the broken mirror. I look every year of my forty despite the botox. I broke the mirror on my first night here and I knock another shard out now. How can my luck get any worse? Fucking David.

After a couple of coffees, my brain crawls round to thinking about what I saw the night before. Men? Wings? Men with bat's wings? Hallucinations are not a good sign. I give serious thought to cutting down on the vodka.

The plastic bag with the mangoes is torn and the fruit have rolled all over the back verandah. Someone has been here, but a common or garden prowler with bat wings? Pleeease! He probably just swung off the verandah on a branch. Though the branches are very skinny. Would they hold a full-size person?

Behind the house is a tangle of bushland, though jungle might be a better word. Anything could be out there. I prowl around the house and find the door key so that I can lock myself in at night.

In the front of the house the bleak yellow-green sea of sugar cane stretches out to a relentless blue sky, all colour washed out by the hot white daylight. My grandparents farmed these fields but my mother and her sisters sold them off and now the roofs of other houses ride the swaying sea of cane. Jenny Hammond must come from one of them. Perhaps the one with the big mango tree over it.

What has possessed me to come to this godforsaken place? A place where it seems I'm now going to be murdered in my bed. Just let someone try!

But I should leave. Sober up enough to go somewhere nicer. But is there anywhere nice in this stale, flat and unprofitable world?

It's back on the wagon for you, my girl. Hallucinations are no laughing matter. I have a vodka and tonic—hair of the dog—and a Kraft cheese crispbread sandwich as well. Full fat cheese. Fuck the kilojoules. Who cares what I look like now?

I bring the mangoes into the house, meaning to put them all "Home Beautiful" in a bowl in the kitchen, but there isn't a bowl and as I poke around the house looking for one, I lose track of them. Someone, a tenant perhaps, possibly my mother, maybe even Gran, has left a big collection of potboilers—Jacqueline Susan, Harold Robbins, Patricia Cornwell, all the old favorites. And a book on how to keep your man which I so don't need just now. Looking at it makes me feel like a stretch of sand trying to hold onto the retreating waves as the tide goes out. It's all leaving me—David, my career, the theatre company we started together, my youth.

Vodka in hand, I seize something called *Interview with a Vampire*—a book about my dear, dear David perhaps—and curl up on the couch.

It's a good choice—juicily purple and just absorbing enough. By dusk I'm doing well; several vodka and tonics behind last night's tally. I turn on the lamp and read on. Moths bounce against the flyscreen. The windows are just glass louvers and the nights are too warm to close them. The swaying of the trees under the assault of the bats makes the only breeze.

Sweat trickles down between my breasts as I read about hot, still New Orleans nights—which sound just like hot, still Queensland ones, only more elegant—and Anne Rice's beautiful vampires, immortal, forever young, bored with their tedious immortality. Lucky ingrates! If I could be forever young, I'd still be playing Ophelia and modeling for *Vogue* and lunching with celebrities and David would still love me. And maybe this time I'd make him jealous by drinking champagne with some fresh young Hollywood brat packer, all six-pack and curving biceps. I had my chances back in the day, but I wasted myself on true love and fidelity.

Or maybe I'd just bite the bastard and suck out his life like he sucked out mine.

Something heavy thuds onto the verandah and boards creak. I'm locked in the house and I've left the verandah light on for a sense of safety. I lift my head and peer up over the edge of the couch.

There he is, his wiry-lean body hunched over as he creeps barefoot along the boards outside the window. The fluorescent verandah light gleams dully on dark skin and slicked-back hair. A wild man of the woods. His torso is bare. A chill tingles down into my belly. I smell a sharp muskiness as he creeps carefully past. Then he's out of my sight. The backdoor rattles and a low hissing makes me reach for an empty bottle but there's nothing more. No assault on the feeble lock or the feebler glass. Just the pad, pad of feet and the creaking of weight on timbers. A bead of sweat rolls down my cheek. I crane my neck further, careful not to make a noise and see that the man is still there, balanced easily on top of the verandah rail, with his back to me, chin on his knees, hands resting on his feet, surveying the verandah up and down. He's naked. His cock dangles between his lean muscular legs. His face in profile is pointed, like a fox's. Or a bat's.

He spreads out his arms and just like that they are leathery wings and he launches off the verandah rail and is suddenly smaller and flying; just another big bat flapping away to quarrel among the trees. Even though I shake my head and pinch myself and slap my own cheek, I know I'm awake and sober. I've just seen a man turn into a bat. It's like a light show has started up in my brain, a blinding, scintillating knowledge.

I'm hardly aware of making, and drinking, another vodka and tonic.

†   †   †

I leave the verandah light on for the next two nights and wait on the couch in the inside dark, and both nights he comes. Both times he patters across the verandah and tries the verandah door. He doesn't try to break in. Instead, he crouches on the back rail, absently sniffing and nibbling at the hanging callistemon blossoms—as if waiting or watching—before suddenly, without a flash of light or a flourish of music or anything else Hollywood, he turns into a big dark bat.

I know what he is, but is he ageless and immortal? I long to ask him, just as the young reporter asked Louis in Anne Rice's book. But how can I? There's nothing civilised about this creature. Does he even speak English? Perhaps this wild predator of the forest has been here forever, preying on kangaroos and Aborigines, on early white settlers. On lonely drunks.

Yet I am certain I am safe in the house. They can't enter without an invitation. Everyone knows that.

As much as I feel anything through the vodka and tonic haze—I'm still too raw to get back on the wagon—I feel a certain weirdness. Not fear. I feel like a traveler who's just come out of customs. I know this country from books and films. I just never expected to travel here. Especially not in far north Queensland.

I dream of the black man-bat, sleeping and waking, while reading of vampires in New Orleans and while lying hazed out on the sun lounge. David and the empty beach of age and loneliness are receding and now I face a bright firmament filled with shooting stars. There are more things in heaven and earth, Horatio, and isn't that a glory!

On the third night he turns from his perch on the rail and sees me watching him. I'm paralysed. He stares for a long, long minute. It's as if a message has passed between us. He nods his head and is gone. Beautiful predator.

†   †   †

What I'm contemplating scares me. I drink too much and find myself raving at David and what he's driven me to. It's evening and I'm crawling round on the red dirt in front of the house, searching in the grass for my mobile when someone calls my name.

A man is walking his children back from the schoolbus. I've seen them before. He's aboriginal, but too round-faced and chubby to be my lean night-time visitor.

"You all right, Ms Dargeville?" he says, helping me up out of the grass, hand firm but not inappropriate on my arm.

I try to stand straight and steady.

"I dropped my phone," I explain with dignity.

"Kids, see if you can find the lady's phone, will ya?" The kids drop their schoolbags and dart away beneath the house. Only the youngest stays. She swings from hand to hand around the man's body as we talk. He introduces himself as Matt Hammond, Jenny Hammond's husband and tells me about the kids. As he speaks, a broad line of bats begins to stream to out of the jungle behind the house, passing above us and away across the darkening cane fields. The sun is setting red.

"Lot of bats here," I say, scanning the flock, looking for one that is bigger than the rest.

"Yeah. They come during mango season and stay for the bottlebrush flowers. You gotta keep your windows closed or you'll get 'em in the house. Dirty thieves."

"They don't bother you?"

"Nah! We keep 'em away. Nets." He grins and winks. "And blackfella magic."

"I'm hungry," says the smallest child. Maybe she's said it a couple of times already. The kids are back at the man's feet, tired of looking for my phone. It's dark now.

"We better be getting back. Mum'll have the tea on. You wanna come, Alys?"

I excuse myself.

As he goes, he calls back, "Don't worry about the bats. Flower season's almost over. They'll be gone soon."

His words electrify me.

† † †

What was that line from that movie? Never grow old, never die. Also, fortune favours the bold. Also, it's now or never. That night I regard my face in a shard of mirror. Could I spend immortality in this face? I could be thinner. The vodka diet has taken a toll, though so far only with a slight paunchiness round the belly. Can the undead lose weight? Can I risk waiting longer? He might leave when the bats leave and then my chance is gone.

I prepare myself as if for a red carpet opening. Arrayed in my best white silk night-dress, I work at my make-up and hair until they're perfect. I open the back door, lock the screen door and wait on a chair in the hallway, a glass of Russian courage in my hand. The night is warm again. I wait more nervously than on a first night, afraid he won't come, afraid he will. I wait through several more drinks. Will it hurt? Will it work? I fall to dreaming of a glamourous vampire life, of blood red lips and black velvet gowns by gaslight, of the vampire Lestat under neon light.

The screen door rattles. The dark figure is silhouetted in the doorway. I jump up and he steps back. He's going to flee.

"Stop!" I cry leaping towards the door.

Against the verandah rail he does stop. I stand at the door and beckon, calling him back.

Slowly he straightens and comes, padding back over the boards, musky smell enveloping me as he closes in. His glance is sidelong, his face foxy.

I wish I had a script. I'm an actress not a playwright, damn it. I don't know what words to use.

I reach out my hand to touch the screen, and haltingly, he places his dark hand against it. He's warm to touch.

"I will let you in," I say. His eyes widen and he tilts his head as if waiting for more. He must understand me.

"But only if you make me like you," I say. "Will you make me like you?"

He squints at me as if questioning, his face foxier than ever. He reaches down and rattles the doorhandle.

"Only if you make me like you." I say.

He looks at our hands pressed against each other against the screen door.

"Do we have a deal? A deal?"

He regards me sideways out of those dark alien eyes. At last he gives a measured nod.

I open the screen door, my slippery drunken hands struggling with the snib. I stand ready, in a hurry to meet my fate, arms outstretched, eyes squeezed shut. Please don't let it hurt too much. Please don't let it hurt. Let's get this over with.

The man steps into the house, pushes me aside, and pads away into the dark hall. Without a backwards glance, he pushes me aside. Pushes me aside as if I was something in the way, as if I was rubbish, as if he has no interest in what I have to offer. I hear hands scrabbling at the hall table. I hear my purse hit the floor and then a couple of mangoes come rolling towards me.

I've been rejected. Again.

This is last straw!

Hot red anger screams into my veins. My fingers turn to claws. I launch myself like an avenging angel at that lean dark shape and seize him.

"Dammit, you fucker! Don't do this to me."

Fingers grip skin. The stench of musk and sweat. In the darkness, flailing arms are everywhere. I hang on tight, feet digging into the boards, dragging after him, as he shrieks and breaks for the open door. I cling on, down the hall and through the doorway, even as I feel limbs shrink away from me, and leather wings flapping wildly in my face.

"No you fucker. Bite me! Bite me damn you."

Even as white hot teeth tear into my wrists and hands, I clung on and on. Until I trip over mangoes and my hand slips. Then he's away, his heavy body speeding like a ball, out and over the verandah rail, a big dark bat flying into the darkness.

My carefully manicured hands are ripped to ribbons, covered in blood, but I've got what I wanted. I don't need him anymore. I bind myself up with silk torn from the bottom of my night-dress, crawl back onto the couch and wait for the change.

†   †   †

God, those bites hurt. All the finest nectars of the Russian steppes can't sweeten the throbbing.

†   †   †

The oldest Hammond child finds me the following day. Walking home from school, he hears my mobile phone ringing in the grass beneath the house and brings it up to me.

The first thing I know of it is the squeak that wakes me up. I see a boy standing in the doorway.

"No," I cry, afraid for him. He's only a child and I'm turning into a monster. It feels like hell which is what it should feel like. I guess. I'm relieved when the child runs away. I lie there wondering if the daylight outside will hurt me and an eye blink later the house seems full of Hammond parents, shaking me and asking questions and bandaging and pulling me around.

"It's nothing," I protest. And "No, Not into the sun."

They bundle me into a car and drive me into Townsville hospital, where doctors wash and stitch and bandage me and shoot me up against tetanus and something called Lyssavirus, which it turns out is Rabies, and put me on a watch for Hendra virus. And give me something to help with the DTs.

I don't turn into a vampire. Not once. Not even a bit.

Nor does David rush to my side, the bastard. My brother comes instead. Oh joyful day. Though I have to admit he is useful and almost kind.

A couple of days later, when everything is white and clear and clean, Lyndal Hobbes rings again. That had been her on the phone when the Hammond boy found it. She probably saved my life. Uncharacteristic for an agent.

"You need to work," she says. "I want you to audition for this new thing called *Hoochie Coochie*. I know you can sing and dance. I've seen those old episodes of *Young Talent Time*. And don't give me that bullshit about being a serious actress. That was always David's thing. Now you've ditched him, we can get you some real money."

My brother and Jenny Hammond pack up and clean the house.

"Hell of a mess," says my brother. "Jenny was very apologetic. Seems they didn't realise the back door was open and the fruit bats got in and got at the mangoes and spread them everywhere. I sent her some flowers and the biggest box of chocolates I could get. You owe me seventy bucks."

Mangoes, I think; Jenny Hammond's mangoes rotting peacefully away on the hallway table. Suddenly everything becomes horribly, humiliatingly, embarrassingly clear. He was after the mangoes all the time.

Because fruit bats, of course, like to eat fruit.

Not blood.

My very soul curls at the thought of my misunderstanding. I should go back and thank the Hammonds in person, but I can't face it. I simply send a signed picture and flee back to Melbourne.

AFTERWORD TO "BATS"

I've been trying to write an Australian vampire story for years, ever since I sat at the window of a student room in James Cook University, watching the fruit bats bickering in the huge bottle brushes and longing to write a story that evoked the velvet feel of the tropical night on my skin. It took me a while to realize why I couldn't get fruit bats to metamorphose into vampires. It was only when I thought up Alys Dargeville that I found the way in to the material. Three cheers Alys! Long may you tread the boards!

BLACK HEART

JOANNA FAY

It was time to die. That was why she'd come here, to the red land. The sky swept over her, horizon to horizon, uncompromising scarlet. The colour of her unlife, like the sands stretched wide to meet it.

She walked from the thick-scented burr of life, where tin roofs rusted under ghost gums. She didn't need the moon, or the way it lit her path to streaks of black and headlight-white. Silence met her as it always did—tiny crouching mammals froze at her passing. Night-time insects flickered away on some primeval instinct. Moth-wings brushed her cold silk hair an instant, then scattered.

She didn't stop for dawn. She was so old the sun's punishing rays couldn't crisp her skin. In her reborn youth, this light would have destroyed her tender marble whiteness. Now she was granite to the smallest pore. Day could only send a mottling grey across her unclothed arms and neck, craze them to a vision of womanly flesh carved out of stilton, or blue castello. Just a hint of ash, painless, brushed from her skin by the wind.

She could have set fire to the house behind her. Instead she walked away from the reek of bodies four days dead in the heat, let blowflies feast on the husks she left. It was the flies' incessant hum that drove her at last from the cover of brick and tin, not the smell.

Nothing moved her anymore, and she had nowhere to go. She was the last. Boredom, the dull onward stretch of eternity had taken even Stephan at the end. When the final thirst, infant blood, lost its enchantment, his heart turned black. Her mind's emptiness filled with it, a festering thing, leaden.

"Sarah," Stephan said. "It's sucking me down."

His legs buckled under the weight of his sinking heart as it pushed him into the waiting earth. The grass had still been faintly green then, back in late spring—but it shrivelled to brown straw under his fall. He didn't cry out, didn't try to resist the ground's embrace. Just pressed deeper into the cracks, until rubble clattered down across his back, clumped the faded yellow of his hair.

Sarah watched his grave in silence. The sun climbed and fell, not reaching her. She stood through another day. Not a tear dropped. The second night she started off along a gravel track running around the rim of a hill. It stank of cow pats in the darkness, reminding her of the taste of cattle blood taken in desperate moments. She kept walking.

The land changed faster than she. On the sixth day she crossed an invisible line, one of those dotted borders on the roadmap Stephan had found. They'd committed it to memory, played lethal games across fragile divisions. State or territory, now it was a matter of indifference. All she noticed was the land's deepening red. Sparse but stately trees ringed the last house, isolated under a rise.

The door was open, fly-wire screen shut of course. Her feet made no sound on the veranda slats. The fly-wire creaked a little, but it was dusk, and the TV was on in the next room, its flash and flicker reporting some new catastrophe, floods up north, the falling dollar, a boatload of refugees. That last picture—their quest for liberty stirred her briefly; memories of freedom she'd once lusted after. How it had burned in Stephan's eyes too. But his unbeating heart defined other, darker boundaries. Such things had a price.

The spell broke. The newsman's voice blurred into a drone as irritating as the flies. Sarah stepped close behind the couch. Neither of the men's heads moved, their gaze riveted by disaster to the end. She killed quickly and drank them both, the old man and the younger, left their bodies skewed on sofa and floor. That was when she felt it, the first tendrils of blackness, creeping through her heart like a silkworm's thread.

Fear, a momentary frisson up and down her spine, then gone. Even though she wasn't yet heavy, she was like one paralysed. She sat on the sofa's faded arm, as if truly a creature of stone, unmoving. Not breathing, so the stench never reached her, only that final maddening sound. Stirring, she looked back at the bodies, thick with insects, and pushed herself to her feet. The fly-wire was open, whining in the first faint breeze. Sarah tasted the scent of sand and scrub, and decided on her direction.

Chill, arid wind. It called her, started to whisper as soon as she stepped out the door, off the veranda. She faced it, closed her eyes a moment under the moonlit stripes.

Sarah.

Stephan's voice ran through her bones, lodged in her glacier flesh. He was waiting—she would meet him in heat, red brightness. She began to walk. The silhouettes of ghost gums, by a trick of the light perhaps, shrank back from her path. Through the gate, across the paddocks, grass so dry it crunched underfoot.

Sunrise, when it came, pooled around her toes, graced the land to an illusion of softness, rimmed it in subtle apricots, tinted the trunks of the thinning trees to palest pink. These colours reminded her fleetingly of the snow-lands, far under northern lights. Stephan's eyes flickering under the aurora's dance, the tilted curve on his lips a thing of purity in those moments. She stared, entranced. He laughed. Only a tiny bloom of scarlet on his jaw had marked the vision of his beauty as *something other.*

Sarah walked. The blackness came again. This time its wisps began to lace a pattern into the unmoving walls of her heart. Fine crocheted tablecloths she'd seen on arriving in this land, genteel doilies strung with beads over cream jugs, dainty silver bowls of sugar. The lacework growing in her body could have been pretty, except that its dark, thin yarn was starting to pull too tightly, and its fibre was poison.

The memory of blood.

Not hers; that was too long past. But all that she'd taken, welling, congealing into destruction should her will falter. She supposed it was fitting. The fear again, one flutter against the weight bearing down in her chest. She kept walking. Day fell. Night rose. Days. Nights. She saw few living things. The shadow of a wedge-tail high above, dark angel shadowing her trail. The thump-thump of a mob of roos, drumming the earth's heartbeat up through the soles of her feet.

She thought the land was changing faster. Now her flesh, its frozen time unbinding into looped and knotted threads, forced her to suck air like a fish in a dried river-bed. Her heart pressed against her ribs, demanding space. Blackness bled into her running arteries, shivered through her veins. Shadows swam across her vision.

The earth was finer between her toes, turned to dust the colour of survival. Through the haze, Sarah saw crimson stretching to embrace her. Wide to the horizon, sun sinking in blood. Everything was perfect. She let the weight take her at last, pull her to her knees in the dirt. The ground sank under her impact, and kept sinking. Blackness pushed her into a crouch until her nose touched baked sand. Was this how the land would take her, curling her into a fearful child? With an effort, she straightened her legs, felt thirsty heat joined to her belly.

Water welled in her eyes, in the dryness. Her body was a river, barely contained. She let out a sob.

It's all right, Sarah love.

Soft dust shivered back from her face. Stephan's eyes met her, free of bloodlust, their colour soft ochre. He lay underneath her, warmer than the earth under dusk-light, waiting. Sarah smiled. The black walls burst inside her. She closed her eyes and pressed her mouth to his parted lips.

AFTERWORD TO "BLACK HEART"

"Black Heart" began its journey as a single image, and a question. Both were inspired by the anthology's title, Dead Red Heart, *which sparked a picture of a female vampire standing in the "red centre", alone, surrounded by dirt of that searing, iconic colour. When I asked what she was doing in this landscape the colour of blood, I realised she'd gone there to die. The "how" of the story unravelled backwards from that image, just as Sarah's unlife was beginning to unravel.*

"Black Heart" is an end story, a journey as simple as the act of walking, although what is occurring in Sarah's undead body and deadened mind is far more complex. There are no battles, crosses or stakes through the heart, just the backwash of a quiet internal violence, the long glut of blood turned septic, as Sarah walks in and out of memory and time.

I wanted the relationship between the two characters, the vampire and the land, to slowly transform from mutual alienation to final embrace. The initial relationship, driven by repulsion, is portrayed in the maddening hum of flies around corpses, the shrinking of plant and animal from Sarah's path. As she becomes attuned to the poison spreading from the emptiness of her chest, the "otherness" of her vampiric state, her history, is juxtaposed by the landscape's reflections—the heartbeats of her victims in the thud of passing kangaroos, the shadow of death in a tailing wedge-tailed eagle. The imagery of the land becomes sparser, more arid with her progress, a counterpoint to the sparking of her emotions. And when Sarah is ready to surrender, to be consumed in a final act of longing, the land is waiting.

RENFIELD'S WIFE

DAMON CAVALCHINI

It is my mistress's saliva that stops the blood from clotting. Sweet rivers of chemicals intermingling with the other woman's blood, holding back the tide from the wound. Safe in my little wooden hut, surrounded by the protective blanket of the rainforest, no one can hear us. I stand in my appointed corner, feet scraping on the splintering floorboards, watching as the woman thrashes against the knotted ropes that cling to her, binding her to the eating chair. Ignoring her protests, my mistress continues to feed, gorging her hunger on the woman's exposed flesh. The electric hum of desire singing in the air. She's only one person, just another lost tourist. But as we have been living off the local wildlife for the past few months, she is as juicy as any forbidden fruit.

I walk around the edges of feeding, not wanting to interfere, glancing again at the rough hessian rope, making sure the bulging knots are holding firm against the woman's protests. The whole canvas of her skin, not just her face and neck, presents varied opportunities for my mistress to bite. About five foot eight with blond hair and a look of ruffled despair, the woman is another victim of nature's never-ending dance of death and renewal. A lonely traveller kidnapped under the rainforest's tropical shawl.

I rarely see any of my mistress's brothers although I know they exist, chattering away in other parts of the forest. They avoid us, not caring for my presence. Besides, the males don't need the blood, you see. They can survive on the rainforest's rich berries and hunched fruits. It is the females who need to drink the wine of humanity to survive, to breed. Before my eyes the age-old ritual continues, the essential struggle to recreate yourself, to make a family, to survive. Procreate or die.

The woman struggles, trying to shake free of the ropes that bind her. But her outbursts are fading, each shake slightly less violent than one before. Watching her eyes, I can see that she wants to strike out against her attacker. An oil-stained cloth in her mouth gags her resistance, causing her to choke on her own fear and bile. A sheen of sweat polishes her tanned skin, adding a lustre to the flesh and a scent of spice which only makes my mistress hungrier. The sweat of human fear is tastier. Sweeter. Her skin is beginning to peel, burned by the constant exposure to the sun. As my mistress feeds, I watch the terror in the woman's eyes and the silent, desperate plea for release from the tsunami of experience crushing through her body. From my vantage point besides a dust-covered bookshelf, I slowly shake my head. She is neither attractive nor remarkable. Deliberately so. We don't want to offer the ever watching media any special reason to be interested in this particular case.

I've seen it all many times before so I walk outside and leave my mistress to her needs, grumbling a few words to myself just to hear my own voice. It is easy to forget how to speak hiding here and there are still times when I need to communicate with others, to pretend to be normal. A baited lure dangling before the unsuspecting members of my own kind.

Spears of sunlight pierce the veil of trees. Rainbow dressed leaves flitter under twilight's steady glare. If you open your mouth, you can almost drink the moist air, feeling the dew condense on your tongue. Or cuddle it. The squeals and coughs of various animals sing a natural symphony to life. The golden casque of a cassowary disappears into the undergrowth.

Nestling between the rough, moss-haired bark of two ancient eucalypts, like a lover's head between legs of their desire, I can see where my hut sleeps securely. A faded CSIRO logo peels from the roughened wood of the walls, flakes of paint occasionally drifting to the ground like coloured dandruff on the brown mud of the ground. Originally established as a place to watch the unfolding wonder of life, it now serves as a nest for our existence.

My heart starts beating a little faster, dancing to the now rhythmic beat of the woman's screams. My mistress will have removed the cloth for the final kill. She likes to hear the terror, to feel the vibrations of their curses as she drains the last of their resistance. Leaving just another foolish visitor lost in the tricky embrace of the Daintree. Normally my mistress would control herself and the lost tourist would wander from the warm moisture of the forest after a week or so into the blaze of snapping camera flashes and a huddle of television cameras. The wounds on their flesh would be attributed to the teeth of a myriad of wildlife and the gentle needles of plants that attacked them as they wandered, dehydrated, through the forest. Any blood on their clothes is simply a badge of their survival and the memories which haunt their dreams, the nightmares they can never share, are ignored as the result of hunger and fear.

But this time my mistress is hungry and the urge to procreate overwhelming.

Mounds of wounded flesh rose on my arms and neck, reminders of the times when there was no one else to satisfy my mistress's desires. I say mistress but you may as well call her my wife so often does my blood sustain her. We are bound. I love her. We had never shared the words or conducted any kind of ceremony. Such things are not part of her nature. We just are. Together. I love every delicious bite, every drop of my blood that dribbles over the ravines of her teeth. Decades ago I had entered the forest's embrace, unaware of the true mysteries held in its mossy fingers. As a young entomologist hoping to specialise in hemipterology, the warm colours of the Daintree seemed to me to be a kaleidoscope of invertebrates. Crustaceans, worms, beetles, ants, spiders, mites, scorpions, amblypygids, centipedes and millipedes, not to mention the snails and slugs, burrowed their way into the complex ecosystem that had survived virtually untouched by the machinations of man. Siren-like cicadas singing my dreams of a PhD into reality.

The screaming from my hut stops, replaced by the normal whispers and murmurs of the forest. I close my eyes, breathing these last few moments of rest. Even the nearest colony of crocodiles is at least a two day journey from the hut. The slowly stuttering waters crayoned brown with mud from the recent rains. I will head out as soon as my mistress leaves. The further away from the hut that body is found, the better. Hopefully it will never be found at all.

Every so often people from the CSIRO would come and visit the hut, camping inside while they conducted whatever research they were doing. We always moved out, hiding in the gentle care of the rainforest, and let them go. That was the deal I had made with my mistress so long ago. One of the few conditions of our relationship. While the deaths of a few foolish tourists could be hidden by the sapphire-misted mountains and the ring barked forest, all tragic to the moon, the loss of a scientist would be harder to hide.

Even I was forced to briefly return to the world to remove myself from its bland stagnancy after my wife found me thirty odd years ago. Forced to cut myself from the bureaucracy of everyday life before I could join her in the humid forest. I had come here, young, eager to make a name for myself, hoping to use the ancient footprints of the evolutionary past to draw a map for the future of humanity. I was looking for a blueprint written in insects. Increased knowledge. A desire to improve my mind. Instead I found something older than I ever dreamed, with a history that swallowed my science like a jacaranda drinks the mist.

Her.

She had lived in the forest for millions of years, oblivious to the rise of social media and civilisation. Empires grew and fell around them barely brushing the silken hairlike strands of her awareness. No Christian crosses or Stars of David worried her or her kin; they didn't know what they were so they had no reason to fear. Only the harsh burning sun causes them to hide, safe under covered embrace of the forest's trees. I know I am little more than a convenience for them, the latest in a long line of handy servants. I don't care.

An explosion of sound, the squawking cries of startled galahs, the nervous hiccoughing of tiny tree frogs, vibrates through the forest as my mistress leaves. Moss covered tree trunks bend to escape her path. A wombat grunts and buries itself in a mound of fallen leaves and bushes shuffle as the wallaroos scamper for another place to play. With a deep sigh, knowing that only a drained body awaits me inside the hut, I grab my old, torn body bag and go to collect the corpse.

† † †

I hear the whispers as I walk through the dirt-dressed street of what pretended to be an outback way station. From the skies above, it looks like a hole in a blanket of green. While the forest provides most things, it is painfully short of coffee and chocolate bushes. People stare at me. The crevassed bushie with the faded blue singlet and the rock scratched boots. Years of walking through the rainforest unprotected by suntan cream had stained my skin deep brown and I scrape some patches of mud from my knee-length shorts as I approach the tin roofed buildings.

Mick's says the sign. No one needs to explain what Mick's is. Mick's is everything. Post Office. Bank. A clearing house for communicating with the rest of so-called civilisation. Somewhere off the Upper Daintree road, east of Bloomfield and south of Degerra, the place had a pub, Mick's, and no name.

"Hey, mate," drawls a voice from behind the counter. Mick doesn't even look up from the pages of a two month old People magazine. I raise a hand, my open palm acknowledging his greeting. On a wall, hiding behind the Tim Tam laden shelves, there is a row of doors, gateways to boxes behind them. On one of them are the letters RMR. My initials. "There's a box for you out the back," Mick calls out. "And I've packed up your usual stuff if you want to bring your ute round the back."

I distractedly grunt a thank-you. Not that Mick cares. He goes back to his magazine, reading an article about the NRL with the headline 'Who needs a Big Willie when you've got a great Tongue' referring to the latest round of player trading.

There's a letter in my mail box. Addressed to her. She doesn't get mail. As far as I know, she cannot even read. She certainly doesn't speak. I just know what she wants, as if the ideas arrive in my mind, skipping the artifice of language and plugging directly into my brain. My fingers run across the edges of the envelope, twisting down to trace the v-shaped smile of the lip at the back. There's no return address. No identifying information. There doesn't need to be.

Mick looks up again. "Anything interesting," he calls out, displaying a negligent curiosity. "I didn't know if was a wrong address or what but I stuck it in the box for you anyway."

"Not really. It's for someone I used to know."

"Need me to send it back."

I wave the envelope at him, indicating the lack of details. "No need. I'll look after it."

He shrugs, disrupting the dandruff that lines the shoulders of his faded flannel shirt. Finger-painted dust Mandelbrots stain clichéd art across the exposed singlet. Mick looks exactly how people expect him to look. At home, I'm sure he dresses in jeans and a t-shirt. And drinks shiraz instead of Fourex for all I know.

I pick up some other supplies from the shelves, things I had once thought that I would never need again. Walking to the counter, I hand over my possessions including one of deodorant dispensers that spray a mist of scented beauty into the air.

"Planning a party?" Mick asked as an electronic beep recorded the prices. "I thought you didn't care about this stuff?"

"I'll need some extra cans of gasoline as well."

Mick's eyes narrow as he hands my credit card back. "What's going on, mate? This ain't like you. Is it something to do with that letter?"

Lifting a 5 litre cask of insect repellent onto the floor, I look around the shop. I wonder if he knows that this will be my last visit. "Yeah. I know who it is from and what they want."

† † †

Dusk's gentle light cries farewell to the heat of the day as I enter the research hut. Placing my purchases on the table I stand still and breathe. There is no-one there. Not even in my mind. I throw the letter on a wooden table leaning heavily against the wall. The envelope catches on the splintered surface, little claw-like tears scratching its surface. There is another envelope, just like it but thirty years older, lying abandoned in a drawer of my desk.

I wrote that one.

I unpack my provisions, stacking them neatly in the limited cupboard space or under my camp-bed. I should turn the generator on to ensure the batteries are charged properly. The patterned sunlight through forests hood holds things steady while I'm away but it isn't enough to fully recharge the deck of batteries that power the hut.

Tomorrow. I'll do it tomorrow.

I should also clean the various insect droppings, loose leaves and sheets of dust and life. More jobs for tomorrow.

Or for my replacement. That is what the letter represents. I know why. I have aged, my blood no longer boosts the rich sweetness of youth nor the refined maturity of middle age. I turn 60 next year and my blood is going stale. My mistress needs new flesh. The latest tourist probably convinced her of that. Or convinced her kin.

I close my eyes and she is there. A black mist shaped into the form of a woman. A charcoal drawing, made with a twig from a camp fire. Imprecise and imperfect, I can see the little jutting mounds on her skin as she keeps this form.

My heart skips an erratic thump as I fall in love again.

"You know." The words form in my head, not in English, so clear that it is a language that transcends all languages.

"Yes," I reply, still using my voice even though it is not necessary. She smiles, amused by my small rebellion.

"The other slaves give up the need to open their mouths."

"I need the practice for when I collect the supplies from town."

She nods, a ripple of anticipation canyoning down her black flesh. Unlike the others who came before me, I knew other loves. Other obsessions. I came here, long ago, looking for bugs to teach me about the ways of life and the intricacies of nature. I found more than I ever imagined. These creatures were beautiful. Deadly but beautiful. How could explain that I wanted to live? I am just livestock to them. Two legged cattle roaming the land until the time comes from me to become the latest BBQ.

My wife could never understand my reluctance to die. That was the way the forest worked. Co-dependence. There is no malice in her decision. I can no longer provide the duties for which I was kept. In the same way people in the city takes an arthritic pet to the vet or a farmer kills a pig to feed their family, my fate has been sealed from the moment I accepted her offer to become her slave. The law of the forest.

And I understand the necessity of what must happen next. The very concept of divorce is foreign to her. I am useless. I am finished.

My wife glides around the hut, a creaking grunt echoing as she shuts the windows. The door seals with a click. There is no escape. We are trapped here, together, as it must be.

My wife and her family can never be revealed to the masses of humanity. They would be killed. Just like my wonderful insects. Scientists still don't know how the evolution of insects relates the to the evolution of other animal groups. They are the loners of the animal kingdom, the children who only play with their own kind. Their ties are closer with plants. Yet we think of them as pests, we try to kill them with chemicals and genetically manipulated bioagents. On the whole, humanity fails to learn from insects. Fails to appreciate the awe of something different.

I sit on the camp bed in the corner and briefly close my eyes. "I am ready."

"You have served well."

"Thank you."

I turn my head to look at her. My mistress, my wife, begins to break down, her body shattering into hundreds of tiny mosquitoes, a previously unidentified *Culex* subgenus. The reverberating buzz fills the room. She doesn't like sunlight, preferring the cooler hues of dawn and dusk. It doesn't matter. There will be no more days for either of us. Original bloodsuckers, more than 150 million years old, they evolved in ways no-one had conceived. In meeting her, I absorbed more, learnt more, than I ever dreamt. Through her, I become better. She is my evolution.

The first mosquitoes bite into my skin, the poison coating my flesh killing them instantly. With a violent screech that threatens to shake my mind into a billion pieces, my wife swarms.

† † †

Slowly, deliberately, I release the chemicals from the pesticide into the air, the invisible gas filling the sealed space. It is based on *Allium sativum L.*, minced dehydrated garlic.

I smile. There is no escape. For either of us.

Hundreds of tiny bites pierce my skin, no longer feeding, just seeking raw revenge. Wave after wave fall to the ground. My wife cannot reform her human shape and open the windows or free herself.

I cannot breathe without swallowing some of her. We merge in a way we have never merged before.

My eyes close, huge welts from the multitude of bites pressing them shut. This is death. The bounce of my heart is slowing, the air in my lungs turning stale and frustrated by the inability to escape.

Unable to talk, I whisper my final words in my mind, knowing she will hear, hoping she will understand.

"I love you. Until death do us part."

AFTERWORD TO "RENFIELD'S WIFE"

I've always been fascinated by the character of Renfield. If "Renfield's Wife" has a purpose, it is to remind people that the Renfield of Dracula *is a truly tragic person who suffered his madness long before he fell under the influence of the Dark Prince. In Bram Stoker's* Dracula, *Renfield is a "zoophagous maniac" hoping to absorb the life energy of animals by eating them. He starts by eating flies, then develops a scheme of feeding the flies to spiders, and the spiders to birds, all the time hoping to gain more and more life. When he is not allowed a cat, he eats the birds himself.*

My modern Renfield extrapolates the madman to a scientist and, hopefully, takes his obsession with insects along a different path.

This is probably the wrong place to mention that I'm getting married next year. This, of course, did not influence me in writing the above story except for the fact the last line has been dancing around in my subconscious for the past few months.

Nicky—you inspire me in lots of ways that don't involve bloodsucking fiends despite your enchantment with Joss Whedon and True Blood *and for that I truly do mean forever after.*

For those who know me, I've spent most of the past decade on the other side of writing—administering and helping other writers develop their stories rather than writing my own. A huge thanks must go to Russell and all of the other talented people involved in this anthology. It is a great way to return to the light side of the force. Thanks for reading, I hope you enjoyed the story and 'avagudweegend.

LISTENING TO TRACY

JEN WHITE

JUNE 2011

She had been up on the third floor of Archives for hours, transcribing the decades-old voices of desperate people trying to explain what hell was like. The flattened landscape, the steel telegraph poles bent double, the planes thrown upside down, houses turned to toothpicks, street after street of it. The search for survivors, and for the dead. And car after battered car, speeding down the Stuart Highway. She imagined the adults in the front seat staring straight ahead, fags hanging out of their mouths, the blank-faced kids in the back warily watching the passing scenery, stopping every few hundred miles to refill. Free petrol, all the way down, they said. And volunteers coming from everywhere after seeing what the cyclone had done. People pulling together in a time of crisis, needing to do something.

Bree took her headphones off and stretched. Her hands were trembling. She stood and walked over to the large windows that overlooked glass towers, broad trees, busy people scurrying along the streets, and the ocean flat and still in the distance. Darwin suited her. Bree had lived in many places, but this place felt most like home and she planned to stay. Despite the heat and light there was a complexity here which intrigued her, something fecund and heavy, a dark sensibility, at the centre of this vibrant town.

She sighed, massaged her temples, slightly displacing the frangipani in her long black hair. Her head ached but she wasn't yet ready to stop listening to the voices. She felt she had to honour their experiences in some way, to bear witness. He should be doing this himself, she thought, meaning her employer, Brent Gray, a local historian who wanted to write the definitive book on Cyclone Tracy. He's missing it all, the terror and the anguish and the heartbreak. He's missing the humanity.

She returned to the tapes of Tracy, the slightly dated Australian accents, the shock, the despair, listening until she all but forgot where she was ... *and I started shaking, just like that. Now, I'm not normally a shaker, no way. But I just couldn't stop. What the hell was wrong with me? I took a deep breath and leaned against the car. And then it hit me. I was the only living thing for miles. Not an animal, not a bird, not even a bloody insect. Nothing alive in the whole northern suburbs but me. It was sheer bloody loneliness and, believe me, it was unbearable. I got back in the ute quick smart and high tailed it out of there. Never went out on me own again. Always took someone with me, or took me dog. I'll never forget it.*

† † †

DECEMBER 1974

I watched my wife and daughter, dressed in someone else's mismatched clothing, walk across the hot tarmac towards the waiting plane, knowing it could be months before I saw them again. And the next day I had to watch the volunteers landing in the same plane, resentment rising in me, sweat pouring off their soft southern bodies the instant they felt the heat. Most of them wouldn't last the distance, I knew.

We had come to this town a year ago. I'd been offered the job of bank manager, an opportunity I wouldn't have had for years if we'd stayed in Sydney. We were just starting to find our feet when, in the space of a night, everything shifted under us, changed beyond recognition. Like hundreds of others, I had said my hurried goodbyes to my family knowing that I had to get them away from here to somewhere stable. And me, who knows? Who knew what the future would hold for any of us now.

I had commandeered an old tourist bus, using it to pick up two dozen or so of the volunteers and take them to the local Travelodge where we were putting all the blow ins. My own house had been destroyed but I didn't fancy the Travelodge. I couldn't stand the idea of being shoulder to shoulder with the volunteers, the ones who had lost nothing. Instead, I found myself an old style Darwin house that was still standing, high up off the ground, with louvres all around allowing the air to move easily through the rooms, and overhead fans that would be useful when we got the electricity back on. From the north windows I had a glimpse of the ocean and from the south, east and west, the devastation. And me of an evening, staring out blankly over the darkness, getting good and drunk. Better than lying in bed listening for hours to the damn silence, waiting for I don't know what.

And then the cleanup began. Clean up! Strange description for what we really had to do. Get essential services up and running. Hunt for the living and the dead. Dismantle anything dangerous. Dispose of anything rotten. And clear the streets. Major-General Stretton had been put in charge, but we didn't need to be told how to do our job. Start in the middle and circle out, focus on the areas worst hit, and try not to get sick or injured

It was the same thing every morning. We'd arrive at headquarters, grab our partners and assignments, and head out. I got one of the blow ins. Fletcher, his name was. A puny, washed out kid who'd blow away in a gust of wind. Lucky he hadn't been here for the cyclone.

"Where you from?" I asked him.

"Down south," he said briefly.

I laughed at that. "Everyone's from down south," I told him.

He smiled. "Down towards Adelaide," he replied.

Fair enough, I thought. Doesn't want to give too much away. We're all trying to get away from something up here in one way or another. So I left it at that.

Fletcher and I headed out to the north of the town, slowly manoeuvring around the fallen trees and the sheets of corrugated iron, the furniture, the Christmas trees, the toys, and everywhere bloody tinsel. And drip, drip, drip. Gave you the creeps. Everything was still sodden, still drying out. Drip, drip, drip.

"Hard to believe it's the same place," Fletcher said, a pale, thin arm leaning on the window.

"It's not," I told him. "That town's gone."

I shut off the engine and we got out of the truck, heading towards the only house in the street still standing. We needed to be careful. Yesterday one of the men had been savaged by a traumatised dog, and he was in real trouble. A dog bite in this environment could turn bad very quickly. A dog bite could kill. But what was even worse was that they'd had to kill the dog. That went against every instinct, to end life in a place where there was such need for life.

"I thought I liked the quiet," Fletcher said, "but this is just too much."

"It's a relief to me," I told him. "Better than the sound of corrugated iron flying through the air. I'll never get it out of my head."

We were getting closer to the house. I hated this, never knowing what you might find. Oh, Christ. A refrigerator lay stuck in the ground. Last thing you want to see after a cyclone, a refrigerator. When people are desperate they'll hid in anything, even airtight white goods. Already three bodies had been found in fridges, one of them a child.

"Wait," I said, but Fletcher moved forward quickly. He didn't seem to care. Ignorance is bliss, as they say. I held back while he pulled the fridge door open, releasing a god-awful pong.

"It's all right, Jeff," he shrugged and motioned me forward. It was just a putrid leg of ham already turning liquid green. We buried the damn thing, as well as a dead cat, before we moved on. That's what it was like for weeks, one disgusting stink after another all day long.

† † †

JUNE 2011

Bree drifted slowly past the market stalls alongside her mate Todd, the evening breeze soft against her skin. Like thousands of others, Todd had come to Darwin for work. He was making a fortune in the mines. It would set him up for life.

Bree wasn't really with it. After listening to the transcripts for days she was experiencing a serious sense of dislocation.

"Where are you?" Todd asked.

"Thirty seven years in the past," Bree told him.

"Not those bloody tapes again," he said, impatient with her. "They're doing your head in."

Perhaps he was right.

Bree had always known about Cyclone Tracy, of course. It was part of Australia's history. But until now she had not understood in such a visceral way how real people, real lives, had been so powerfully affected."It's tragic," she said to Todd.

"But it's all over now," Todd said. "It's a long time ago. Look all around you at this great town. It survived. Hey, more than that. It thrived."

The stories were so vivid. They made her feel as if she was just skimming the surface of her own life, brought her vague everyday sense of dissatisfaction into sharp relief.

"But maybe we've lost something too," Bree said.

She was becoming familiar with some of the voices. With the women gone it had become a man's town. Conflict seemed common, fights breaking out over nothing. They had been through so much, after all. How do you express the inexpressible? Maybe you have to fight it out. It was Jeff she listened to mostly. He was one of those who had stayed on from the beginning. She wondered about that. Jeff had only come to Darwin 12 months before the cyclone, hardly long enough to be considered a local or to feel any deep commitment to the town. And yet he had remained. It slayed her, the way people pulled together in times of crisis. She pictured what it must have been like, groups of men totally engrossed in addressing the chaos surrounding them, working systematically to clear the town, involved in something that required the whole of one's consciousness and dedication, total focus on the moment. Perhaps it was a kind of relief, to be able to lose sight of the long view, just for a time.

"Swings and roundabouts," said Todd. "It's the way of the world."

"I dunno, Todd. God, what am I even doing here? Temp job after temp job. It's all so aimless."

"Don't look back, Bree. Look forward." Todd told her. "If you keep looking back you get dizzy."

Todd sounded, thought Bree, as if he knew what he was talking about.

† † †

JANUARY 1975

Occasionally, when I got sick to death of my own company, I'd join some of the others at one of the makeshift bars that had sprung up. Frank and Whitey were usually there, and Jonesy and Klem. One evening I dragged Fletcher along too. After all, we had something to celebrate. We had driven to the edge of town that day, a lot further than we usually went. Fletcher said he felt like seeing something different, and since he was normally so easy to please, that's what we did. We drove along the outskirts, where town meets bush, each lost in our own thoughts.

"Stop," yelled Fletcher suddenly.

I nearly jumped out of my skin.

"Look, there," he pointed.

"Can't see a thing, mate," I told him, squinting into the bright day.

"There." He wiggled his pointed finger, as if that would make it easier to see whatever it was. I kept on staring, and then I saw it. Movement. A group of Aborigines. They were a family: an older man and woman, two other men, a pregnant girl, and three kids. Turns out they were Arnhem Land people. They had come into town the day before Christmas and got stuck here. They'd been living off bush tucker since the cyclone, and looked pretty skinny, but they'd being doing all right. Better than I could have. We brought them in and gave them a feed and a place to stay. We really lucked out finding them like that. Dunno how Fletcher spotted them in all that grey green bush. If he hadn't had his whim, if we'd been a minute or two later or looking the other way . . . well, it doesn't bear thinking about.

He was good like that, Fletcher. He spotted things I'd never see. "Here," he'd say. So I'd stop the truck, and Fletcher would jump out, peering through the chaos for who knows what. We found a couple of people like that, a few dogs, even goannas. I used to joke with him that we'd find a croc one day, and then we'd been in trouble.

I asked him how he did it. What did he know that the rest of us didn't? "I use logic," he told me in his quiet way. "I try to think about where something would be if they wanted to hide, be safe. Then I listen and I look. Nothing mysterious about it."

Fletcher didn't drink. He sat there among the group of us nursing a water. I looked around. Gangs of dirty, tired men pouring grog down their throats, shouting and laughing and grimacing, trying to forget what they'd seen. Trying to forget they were afraid. I was sick to death of everything by then, and I could feel myself getting cranky at Fletcher, sitting there with that bloody water, still and silent, watching the rest of us like a hawk. I knew I shouldn't have brought him. Just one can, mate, I felt like yelling at him. It's not going to kill you.

I asked him why here was here, meaning here in this town."Just doing my part," he said.

"Yeah, but you could have just donated five bucks," I told him. "Like everybody else."

He sat there for a moment staring at his damn water. I didn't think he was going to answer.

"It's hard to explain," he said after a bit, "but I suppose I just wanted to be part of something. For so long it had just been me, you see."

I nodded, even though I didn't have a clue what he was getting at. Me, I'd never felt more alone. I didn't push it, though. When it came down to it, it was none of my business why he was here. Everyone had their reasons. All I cared about was whether a man did the job or not. And Fletcher did. He had a strong stomach, and he could go all day without whinging about food or water. Plus he hadn't fainted once. He was a natural. He was even good at rats. I hated the buggers. He'd spot them, break their necks, get rid of them. Fletcher was a bloke you could rely on in a tight spot. Fletcher was worth six men.

That was good enough for me. And he didn't badger me all day with small talk. Let me get on with my own thoughts. We made a good team.

Not everybody saw it that way, though.

"You know what your bloody problem is," Whitey told him after one too many.

Fletcher shook his head in that mild way he had.

"You're a bloody body chaser," Whitey said, poking a finger at Fletcher's chest. "That's how yer get yer thrills. Yer don't belong here. Bloody outsider."

Whitey stood, knocking his chair to the ground, sizing up to Fletcher.

"Bloody suspicious if you ask me. Haven't even got a tan. What d'yer wear, suntan lotion? Bloody poofter!"

We all stood then. I could see Whitey was getting ready to give Fletcher a good one. I moved in front of Fletcher. Christ, I thought, if Whitey even touches him, Fletcher's not going to get up again. But before anyone could stop Whitey or even try to hold him back Fletcher had moved past me and downed him. Quick as anything. Knocked Whitey clean out. Fletcher was stronger than he looked. Frank and Klem ended up dragging Whitey out. We didn't see Whitey again for a couple of days.

Fletcher made an enemy that night. But so did Whitey.

† † †

JUNE 2011

They met in a local cafe. Its signage was all garish blues and yellows and oranges, and it did without air conditioning, but it served the best rendang in town. The place was noisy and Bree had to lean close to hear his words.

"It's just trauma," Gray told her. "First they pull together, then they fracture. You see it over and over again. Anyway, you're getting hung up on individual stories. It's the grand sweep that's important."

"But there's something here," she insisted.

She didn't know how to explain it. What was it? A niggle, a suspicion. An irritation of some kind that warranted further investigation. All her life she had been lead by instinct, and now instinct was shouting out to her loud and clear: "Watch this space." But how to say this to an academic?

Sweat gathered between her breasts. Gray smiled at her and leaned back in his chair. She felt naive, unsophisticated. What would she know, anyway? She didn't even have a degree.

"Are you sure you want to keep doing this?" Gray asked her. "It seems to be getting to you."

"Of course I do," she said. "And look, I'll be okay. It's just powerful stuff. Raw emotion." It was suddenly very important to Bree that she have continued access to the tapes, the voices. "I'll handle it, you'll see."

† † †

MARCH 1975

Over time the animals gradually returned. First came the mosquitoes, of course. Then the other insects, then the vermin and the frogs. And pretty soon cats were running wild in the rubbish tips, and gangs of dogs, and a dingo every now and then. And mobs of dragonflies everywhere just as the Wet was turning into the Dry. It really felt like things were finally happening. We continued on with our work, clearing roads and the like, building demountables. Felt like we'd been doing it forever. I kept expecting Fletcher to pick up and leave, get back to his normal life, but he didn't seem to be going anywhere.

Weekends there was fishing, hunting, getting as far away as possible from all the human muck we were constantly confronted with. I asked Fletcher along a few times but he always said no, he wasn't the hunting type. "That's not the point of it, mate," I told him. He just shrugged and shook his head, still as pale as the day he'd arrived in town. Well, a man's entitled to keep himself to himself, I thought, and left it at that.

I was keeping to myself more and more too. Things were getting to me. I could feel myself becoming too angry too often. The others were always going on about the blow ins, the southerners. They've come all this way to help us, you bloody idiots, I thought. Seemed like they weren't happy unless they were getting stuck into someone. Especially Fletcher. It was Fletcher this, and Fletcher that.

"Can't a man be a bit different?" I asked them.

"Not that different," Whitey said. "He doesn't drink. Won't go hunting. He's as white as a ghost. Hell, he is a ghost. He's a bloody spook. Why the hell is he here? He's after something. You mark my words."

"Why is he so pale?" Jonesy agreed. "Why is he so thin?"

"Maybe he's from Sweden," I said.

"Then why doesn't he say so," Whitey shouted. "Thinks he's one of us. That's something he'll never be. He gives me the creeps."

"Either say it to his face, or bloody shut up," I told Whitey. But he went on and on, worrying at it, like he couldn't stop himself. Spreading ill will.

It got to the point where I had to warn Fletcher to watch himself. "Don't go around on your own," I told him. "At least not in the dark anyway. These blokes have been taking the law into their own hands for a while now. They might not know when to stop."

"But I like it here," Fletcher said, a puzzled look on his face. "I'm glad I came. It's hard to explain, but it feels like a forgotten place, a town where you can be yourself because no one's watching."

"No one's watching," I agreed. "You're right about that. The rest of the country doesn't give a damn about us."

"I feel like I could stay here, live an okay life. Anyway, I'm just here to help. I thought you'd all appreciate it, my helping, I mean. I thought I might even find somewhere to . . . you know . . . belong."

He seemed to mean it. I felt sorry for the bloke. "The mistake you're making here, Fletcher," I said, "is looking for logic. There's no logic to it. Just a bunch of scared, tired men wanting someone to blame."

I could see I gave Fletcher something to think about. For the rest of the day he was even quieter than usual, if that was possible.

Watch out, I thought. When a mob senses difference, watch out.

I remembered then how Fletcher had knocked Whitey out so easily. Perhaps he's not so defenceless, after all, I decided.

† † †

July 2011

Bree sensed a wariness at the table. She shouldn't have mentioned it. There were those still living in Darwin who had been through the cyclone, and still suffered. It was late afternoon, and Todd had asked a few friends over for dinner. They sat out on the balcony, the overhead fan cooling them slightly.

"My dad stayed on afterwards," Anna offered. Anna drove the huge trucks that hauled minerals from site to site. A middle aged woman, she looked far older than her years, her face a mass of pouches and wrinkles. "I wish I could have. It was worse somehow being so far away. We didn't know what was going on, and when you don't have much information, you start imagining all sorts of stuff. Dad used to tell us stories about it. He told us there were man-eating dingoes roaming the town, and that they'd grown as large as tigers. He told us that the zombies used to like the rubbish tip 'cause there were lots of cats there."

"Nah," said Bree. "What I'm hearing, it's not like that. It just feels like I'm not getting it, not quite understanding the social dynamics. I feel like I'm beginning to know some of the people a bit, though. There was this one guy, really good at what he's doing, clearing debris, finding animals, helping to build the town up again. But he makes people uncomfortable. It's like they're scared of him or something. Your dad never mentioned anyone like that?"

"No, he only told made up stories. The truth was too confronting. I hardly knew my dad when we got back together. I don't know what happened, whether it was me that had changed, or him. But something had. Anyway, I don't like thinking about it. A town that's not a town. A city without people. It's wrong." Anna downed the rest of her drink.

A screech overhead, and suddenly there was blood everywhere, over the dips, and in the drinks, covering their hair and faces and clothes. A bird had flown into the ceiling fan, decapitating itself. They jumped up and away from the table, halfway between horror and hysterical laughter.

"Bloody Darwin," Anna yelled

"Everyone in the pool," Todd ordered, and they ran for it.

† † †

MARCH 1975

The Aboriginal family disappeared quick smart. They didn't want to hang around. They blamed whitefellas for the cyclone. There was a lot of fear around, a lot of uneasiness.

Plus they couldn't stand Fletcher. I checked on them a couple of times. I took Fletcher with me the first time. The women shooed the kids behind them when they saw him. They wouldn't meet his eyes, wouldn't turn their backs on him. Maybe it was because of how pale he was. In a lot of Aboriginal cultures white skin means spirit world.

Maybe I should have left too. I talked to my wife once or twice a week. Any more and it was too painful. Every day got harder and harder, but I had to do it. Couldn't live with myself if I didn't.

On Klem's birthday I thought I'd make an appearance at the pub. He'd been doing it tough ever since the phone call from his missus, the one where she told him she was leaving him. Poor bugger.

The night was sticky, the air thick as honey. I saw Fletcher in the distance, across the road, walking in the opposite direction. He seemed at home in the dark, strolling casually down the street. I told him to be careful, I thought. What the hell's he doing? I lifted my hand, about to try to attract his attention, but thought better of it. He knew his own business. I'd see him tomorrow anyway, no doubt.

I joined the others and got Klem a drink, and we sat there and talked about the day we'd all had.

"Where's Whitey?" I asked.

"He's coming," Frank said. "We had a bloody hard day. He's prob'ly just done in."

"I'll go and get him," I offered. "He'll be pissed off if someone doesn't."

I eased up out of my chair and wandered out the back to the rooms, knocked on his door and waited, enjoying the slight buzz of the alcohol. When he didn't answer, I twisted the door handle, pushed the door open into a typical Darwin motel room, peeling veneer, grubby carpet, rusting television. And there was Whitey's feet sticking out past the bathroom door. I rushed in, knelt down. His throat was a mess of fleshy ribbons. I felt his pulse. There was none. He looked so pale, even in the darkness.

I can't remember much about what happened next, but I know someone called the cops and they took care of it and I was left with that vision in my mind of Whitey stretched out across white tiles, dead in a place where we'd seen too much death, and wondering why there was no blood. He should have been lying in a pool of it. There was no drain in the floor. I couldn't figure it out.

Last thing I felt like doing the next day was going out, but I did because what was the alternative? Lie in bed all day on my own in the heat in a house that wasn't mine with Whitey's blank mug in my head? No thanks.

I must have looked pretty rough, even more than usual. Fletcher asked me if I was all right.

"Not so good mate," I said. "Whitey got killed last night."

"Sorry to hear that," Fletcher said.

"Thanks mate," I told him, "but don't worry about pretending with me. I know he gave you a rough time."

"Yeah, he really did," Fletcher replied.

We got stuck into the work after that, just like we always did. We were spraying for mosquitoes, and by the end of the day we'd inhaled so much of that stuff we were just about hallucinating. Still, something didn't feel right with me. It was more than Whitey. It wasn't until I was home again and had showered away some of that stuff that I remembered I'd seen Fletcher out the night before. And I also remembered that he hadn't asked how Whitey had been killed.

†   †   †

JULY 2011

Bree lay awake at night wondering at the nature of what she was hearing. She could understand the other men feeling threatened and confused by this Fletcher. She felt something of it herself, a creeping unease, even at this distance. But was she just focusing on irrelevancies, her transcribing an act of cherry picking. Was she unconsciously selecting facts to create narrative where there was no narrative, mystery where there was no mystery?

She needed other points of view, she decided. That was sensible, right? Check the facts. Double check. Don't rely on just one source of information. Maybe even put an ad in the local paper.

Wanted, she wrote over Sunday brunch. *Information on an unusual incident that took place in Darwin in February 1975. If you were here then, please contact me on . . .* and her email address. Vague enough to give no obvious prompts, specific enough for those who were there to know what she was getting at. Yes, that would do.

She waited a week, two weeks. She had almost given up expecting a response when she received the email.

I think I might know to what you are referring. I would be so very happy to meet and talk.
Sincerely, Gerald Weston

No slang, no shortcuts, no text talk. An old guy for sure. It sounded believable. She replied immediately.

Thank you for replying to my ad. I have been researching this period and I want to really make sure that I give it the time, effort and respect it deserves. Any information you can give me would be invaluable. Would it be possible to meet at the Courtyard Cafe tomorrow evening at about 7pm? It is only two doors down from NT Archives. I am working late and hopefully this will be convenient for both of us.

Somewhere public, she thought. So very sensible. Plus they serve good wine. She received an email soon after agreeing to the meeting.

†   †   †

MARCH 1975

Fletcher's reaction to the news about Whitey made me see him in a new light. Those rats, for instance. He liked killing them. He liked finding the dead things, or the things that needed to be dead. I had never asked him what he did with them, just let him get on with it. All this time I'd been shoehorning his behaviour into some standard mould, framing him through normal human expectations. And he had been doing a pretty fine imitation of a human being himself. But something was missing in him, some essence that you rely on for the most part when you deal with other people, that you don't even think about until it's not there. And if it's absent, well . . . everything becomes totally unpredictable. I kept remembering him sitting there silently beside me, the work we did together. Who knew what had been going on inside him.

Hold on, I told myself. I don't know a thing for sure. But in the next instant I had to admit it. I knew in my gut that Fletcher had done it.

And what did he do with the blood? Surely he didn't . . . no, not that?

Maybe he'd really meant what he said when he talked about wanting to belong. But that need didn't go too deep. He had other stronger needs.

There was nothing I could do about it except keep myself from becoming a target. I knew I should have gone out with him as usual the next day to avoid suspicion, but I just couldn't do it. Couldn't bear to think about hours and hours in that truck sitting so close to . . . who knows what. I made my excuses, food poisoning I said, and got ready to fly out. My wife and daughter. Ah Jesus, it had only taken a monster to get me back.

† † †

JULY 2011

I heard much later that Fletcher went missing soon after. No one thought much about it. Men came and went all the time. That's just the way it was. I wonder about that now, about the others who went missing, about what really happened to them? I s'pose I'll never know. Bree removed the headphones, wondering for the first time about Jeff's sanity. Gray had talked about the effects of trauma. Perhaps this was what she was hearing. Paranoia, suspicion, looking for someone to blame, needing a scapegoat.

Bree looked up, rubbed her eyes. She had been so focused on listening that she hadn't noticed the darkening sky through the window. She was suddenly very aware that she was alone on this floor. Rapidly, she began gathering her things. This was the evening she was to meet that old guy, Gerald Weston. She would get there early, she decided. Have a drink, calm her nerves.

When she looked up again he was there, just near the window, his pale skin shining.

She froze. She knew this was the one she had been hearing so much about. I'm too late, she realised in that brief moment. Too late in understanding, too late in taking action, too damned late. In hindsight, she realised that he would, of course, have known exactly where to find her. The email had practically screamed her location. How stupid I was, she thought, to think myself safe. How smug to think I could remain untouched by this.

He didn't look like much, she observed, and maybe that was part of it. Anyone regarding him would immediately underestimate him. White, wispy hair, ectomorphic frame, so young. No wonder the others had been both surprised and suspicious at his capacity for hard work, his endurance. He looked as strong as a dandelion.

"I'm not a threat to you," she whispered, fear electrifying her.

He laughed at that." As if you ever could be," he said.

"But why?" she asked. If she could keep him talking, reach out to him, maybe he would realise he could trust her. She had to make him see her, understand that her existence mattered. Oh God, she thought. There's so much more I need to do.

"Why what?"

"Why here?"

"Oh, I don't know," he said. "Perhaps some vestigial human instinct that I thought had died bloomed here all that time ago, evidence of that old hive mentality still buzzing. It didn't work out quite like I'd hoped, as you know, but I still liked the place. Like it. I've been here all along in one way or another. I find ways to survive. Frontier towns can be comfortable for us outsiders, those of us who still feel that ancient need to connect in some way."

"How did you . . . ? Where are you from?"

He laughed again. "Ah, still curious. You're so typical that way. As for where I'm from, I'm not totally sure," he said. "But way, way back I remember deserts and dry, and that we survived. Maybe, in our ability to find sustenance in less typical ways, we gradually became something other than human."

"But not completely."

"No, not completely," he agreed. "But enough."

"Enough for what?"

"To be a predator." He moved closer. "To do whatever it takes."

"You don't have to do this," she said.

"Yes, I do," he told her. "I have learned that it is important to reduce the possibility of complications, and you are a complication."

"I won't be, I promise."

"Too late for that," he told her.

Afterwards he gathered up her notes and her memory stick, and wiped the hard drive. What a shame, he thought, that no one would ever truly know how important he had been to the town's survival. But, after all, he decided, there is no connection more satisfying than that between predator and prey.

AFTERWORD TO "LISTENING TO TRACY"

I lived for some years in the Northern Territory. When I first moved to Darwin one of my jobs involved transcribing the stories of survivors of Cyclone Tracy. Reading their words was an intense experience for me.

Like the character Bree in "Listening to Tracy", I had grown up knowing about the cyclone in a general kind of way, but had not really understood how it had affected the individuals who went through it. Ever since that time I've wanted to use this setting in my writing, and when I was thinking of a background for a uniquely Australian vampire story I remembered those stories. I started to wonder what would draw a vampire to this environment, and what would motivate a vampire to stay. The story grew from there. I also thought about the ways in which an Australian vampire might be different from vampires from other cultures. What effect would the Australian environment have? An Australian vampire, I decided, would not need the dark. Australia is a land of searing light, of deadly heat, and an Australian vampire would have adapted to this. For an Australian vampire, daylight would not be an issue.

BREAKING THE DROUGHT

JAY CASELBERG

We had heard the stories when we were growing up, knew how the sun had been made. In those early days before time, when all was dreaming, how the great emu egg had been tossed into the sky and fell upon a campfire, cracking and the vast yolk had caught fire. How the sky spirit decided that the beautiful fire should burn each day and lighten the earth was a part of our history too. We heard all of that before the Big Dry from our folks. They weren't our stories, but we inherited them from the Koori people too, like we inherited the truths we did not really understand.

The parents told us for some reason that we shouldn't go out in the rain, as well. Back then, we didn't understand why, but we learned, soon enough. Drought's a funny thing; you never know when it's going to end, but when it does, the Serpent stirs. We didn't realise then, that other things stirred with him, but they knew. Problem was, there'd been no rain for so long that their caution had slipped away in memory, along with the reasons they'd warned us.

Our place hadn't been hit too hard. We still had sheep; they weren't dying off, but we were living off tank water that came in a big truck about once a week. The paddocks were brown though and the grass was dry and brittle and gradually dying off. A small patch of scrubby bush sat on the old hills behind the place, and that seemed to be faring okay, but the litter beneath it was dry as tinder. The folks seemed to be more worried about the level of water in the dam than anything else, and it was low, a small muddy patch in the middle of a crumbling orange-brown bowl. You could hear the windmill creaking, sucking at the ground on the vague times when we actually had a breeze. My brother and I, we just got on with it, not really attuned to the depth of the Old Man's concern. For us, the flies were more of a worry than the water in the dam. But then, it wasn't our livelihood, not directly anyway, not in a way we appreciated. We sweated and we did our chores. One parched day followed the next in a seemingly endless succession, the smell of dry baked earth and perspiration our constant companions and far more of a theme than the old man's furrowed brow. We'd wander round the property, heedless to the worry going on in the shed, with our pair of blueys following, tongues lolling out of their grinning mouths.

All we knew from the folks, from the TV, from the papers, was that we needed rain. It was time for the Big Dry to end. We needed water like we needed to breathe.

Water. It can hide things. Just like clouds can hide the sun. Clouds are made of water too.

We all grew up with TV. Remember that old TV series *The Wandjina*? My brother and I saw some old reruns a couple of years ago. For its time, it was good.

The Wandjina came from another place, the place where time is no time. The place where time is still no time. In the old TV show, it was space. In the Dreamtime stories it was the Dreamtime itself. Call it another dimension, whatever, it is somewhere other. The Wandjina spirits live in the waterholes, not only painted on cave walls. You look at the pictures, they have big eyes and white round heads. The Wandjina don't have mouths. And why do you think they don't have any mouths? Well, actually that's an illusion. They just look like they don't have mouths. And why do you think they're white? We know it now; it's the sun. In that other place, the sun is different. It's not like ours.

After what happened, we pieced it all together. It's hard to know for sure, but we can guess.

Just about every culture on this earth has its vampire myths. All of them take slightly different forms. A lot of those tales have something about water mixed in with them. Well, water and blood. They go by different names the vampire. I know all this because I looked it up afterwards. Even the ancient Babylonians had their tales. The Sumerians, the Greeks, India, Europe, Jewish folklore, China, all have their variants. The Romanians aren't the only ones with a monopoly.

When you find something like that spread all over the world, you can start to understand that the roots lie in something deeper, some sort of archetype. Why should we be any different? As it turns out, we're really not. That much we know for sure.

They'd been saying for days on the box and the radio that the rain was coming, that the Big Dry was about to end. The first time we heard it was on the radio. Dad used to listen to it when he was working in the shed.

"Hey, Boys," he called. "Come listen to this."

We stood with him in the doorway, listening to the guy on the radio, Dad nodding, his hands shoved into the back pockets of his khaki overalls. Me, I looked up at the sky, but there was not a cloud in sight and it was white blue with the heat. It seemed to be making the Old Man happy, so I didn't say anything, just exchanged a sly glance with Wayne who gave a little shrug—leave well enough alone.

A couple of days later, in the late afternoon, the guy on the radio proved to be right. The clouds had been building for a few hours, and we watched them grow with a sense of anticipation. We were down at the end of the property when they finally turned from ruddy orange to grey black and the light flickered across the bunched surfaces heralding what was to come. Everything went still and even the air felt thick with expectation. Then came the wind, and the heavens opened.

A funny expression, "The heavens opened."

Sometimes, you don't realise the underlying truths held within a few simple words.

Wayne and I simply leaned back on the fence, our faces up to the clouds as the first few, large drops spattered into the dust, throwing up small beads of yellow brown liquid, coated with particles of the dried up earth. One by one, another and another slapped against our faces and our bare arms, on our shirts and our shoulders and our hair. This was the rain, and was it, how. We closed our eyes and lived it. We barely heard the sound of the Old Man's voice through the pounding sheets of rain.

He was charging down towards us, when we finally noticed him, yelling something, but his expression was distracted, as if he couldn't make up his mind, a mixture of relief and joy and yet something else. Finally, he stopped a few metres from us, water running down his face in streams, his thinning hair plastered in lank strands across the top of his head, and blinking the drops out of his eyes. He glanced up at the sky and then back at us and shouted something again.

"Boys, you'd better get out of this."

A puzzled expression flickered across his face, as if he couldn't quite remember why it was we needed to get out of the rain and under cover.

And then we saw it.

Well, Wayne saw it first, and his eyes went wide. I glanced at his expression, followed his gaze and I saw it too.

Standing off to the left was a white streak, barely visible against the grey sheeting rain. Off in the distance, a shaft of sunlight broke through distant clouds. It couldn't have been raining over there any more, not as heavily, because a multicoloured arc patterned itself against the clouds. We peered through the water, trying to make out what was standing nearby. Slowly, gradually, the shape solidified, took form. Man-sized, a little larger, body, head, a strange round head, dark smudges for eyes, the vaguest impression of a nose. I frowned and looked at Wayne, back at the thing. Dad had noticed our attention and he too was looking in the direction we were staring.

He shouted, his voice mixed in with beating water. "Boys, get out of here. Get the hell out of here, now!"

He waved us away, keeping his eyes on the figure.

It was getting closer, and as it neared, its features—or lack thereof—became more apparent. It looked like there was some sort of aura around its head, banding in pale orange and black, but more like a disturbance in the air and the rain than anything solid. It took another step.

"Boys, get! Now!"

The Old Man's second shout was enough to start us moving. Problem was, there was nowhere to go. We had the fence behind us, this *thing* to one side and Dad in front of us. The other side led nowhere except deeper into the property and the last place we wanted to be with that thing after us, if indeed it was after us, but we made a stumbling dash in that direction. Wayne's feet slipped from under him and he fell to his knees. The back of my neck feeling tight like a band, a chill running down the back of my scalp, I scrambled to help him up. I looked back over my shoulder, expecting any moment, that pale creature to leap upon me and do I didn't know what. The look gave me enough time to see what happened next though.

The Old Man was striding towards the thing, a look of determination and hate on his face.

"Not my kids, you don't," he said.

He pulled back a fist as he neared it.

That was the last thing he managed to do of his own volition. The creature reached out with one long, pallid arm, grasped him by the top of his scalp. There had to have been enormous force there or something, because it stopped the Old Man dead in his tracks, and leaned his head back till his face was staring up at the clouds. I noticed then that the creature didn't seem to have a mouth. It was on him a moment later, leaning down, that round, round head bowing, reaching into the exposed neck, placing that blankness where a mouth should have been into our father's naked neck.

Then came two sounds, sounds that I'll never forget. The first was a sucking, slurping sound, and that was followed by a bubbling gurgle, coming from our father's open mouth. His eyes were wide and blank, all the fury drained from him.

I was back on my feet and charging towards them.

"Dad!" I yelled. "You! Get your bloody hands off him."

Though it was hard to tell where the thing was looking with those black hollows devoid of pupils, I felt its gaze upon me. My mad race faltered. The energy, the fear, all feeling swept out of me. I took one or two steps before it all petered out.

Within a couple of seconds more, before I had time to summon the strength or the will to act again, the thing before me faded, became less substantial and then disappeared completely, the Old Man with it.

I stood where I was, for a moment, my mouth open, not sure I had really seen what I'd just seen.

"Dad?" I said weakly.

Wayne was beside me then.

"Where is it?" he said. "Where did they go?"

I shook my head.

The water falling from the heavens eased, turning into intermittent spatters. It would come down again in a few minutes, but we weren't to know that, or even care.

"Shouldn't we look for them?" asked Wayne. "They can't have gone far."

I shook my head, because I knew better. "There's no point," I said quietly. "They've gone."

I grabbed Wayne by the shoulders and I shook him. "That thing took him, Wayne. It took him!"

Wayne looked at me, his eyes wide.

We stood there like that, staring at each other for what seemed like an eternity, then slowly, slowly we both turned to look at the spot where we'd last seen the Old Man and that *thing*.

We were torn. We didn't know what to do, but then finally the fear got the better of us. We made our way slowly back up to the house, feeling numb, not a word passing between us. We'd known what we'd seen, but neither of us could trust what we knew.

When we got inside, we closed the door, stood there dripping, neither of us knowing what to do next.

Our mother came out from inside and frowned at us. "What are you two doing standing there like drowned rats? Where's your father? He went down to get you." And then our expressions, the blankness on our faces must have registered, because she went pale. "Boys? What's happened? Where's your father?"

Wayne was the first to speak. Slowly, haltingly the words came out, one by one. We couldn't meet her eyes. She grew paler and her mouth sagged open, and then she rushed to the window to stare out at the open fields.

"They told us," she said quietly. "They warned us." Then she spoke without turning around, the next directed at us.

"We stay here. We stay inside until the rain's gone. We stay here. None of us moves from inside this house."

"But what about Dad?" said Wayne.

"We stay here. You do as you're told."

So we waited.

We called the cops of course. Eventually, someone would have worked out that the Old Man wasn't around anymore, that he was a missing person. Well he was that all right.

They even thought he might have slipped and fallen into the dam in the wet, but even after all the rain that came, there wasn't enough water in it to sustain that thought. Somehow, he'd simply disappeared.

None of us were going to tell them what happened, what really happened.

Wayne and I, we run the property now. Mum's never been the same since that rain, since Dad went missing. She's still with us, of course. Both of them remembered what they'd been told too late, and in a way I guess she blames herself. Wayne and I, we'll remember. And if we have kids, eventually, we'll warn them too. We know that much for sure.

Take heed. When you see those coloured bands amongst the clouds, when you see the Serpent moving and fighting against the sun, take care, because he opens doorways to the place that has no time and when those doors are open, things step through. Be sure to look back over your shoulder and check what might be standing there, waiting, ready to feed. It might have been a long time. And it's hungry.

AFTERWORD TO "BREAKING THE DROUGHT"

Australia as a country is a place of extremes, whether it be light, heat and more recently rain, but also extremes of history. The short history of colonisation sits pale in comparison to the longer traditions of the Aboriginal people. I started putting all those factors together to come up as a mix, and then remembered that TV show that used to, frankly, scare the crap out of me as a kid. That gave me the seed for "Breaking the Drought."

There's a dimensionality to Australia in the landscape, the climate and further informed by the concept of the Dreamtime. And, who says vampires don't come from another dimension too? As an Australian, you just get on with it in adversity even when you don't necessarily fully understand the circumstances that drive it. There's a fundamental pragmatism that drives much of what we do as a people amid any received wisdom. Maybe a little of that too has been captured in this tale.

CHILDREN OF THE CANE

JASON NAHRUNG

A sickle moon watches over us as we gather at a corner of the Franklins' cane field. The coasties park on the other side. The cane's just stubble, and dust puffs up under our feet as we walk over the furrows. There's an even dozen of us. Stu has a katana, an old thing his dad's dad brought back from the war offa some dead Jap, and Michelle's got a reaping hook—she carries it light in one hand, not like a full-on scythe that you'd have to use your hip on. Most of us have cane knives. They're all slicers. We figure spiking a heart shot is gonna be way too hard—not because of the dark, we can see just fine, just that it's such a small target when you're dancing—so we're going for arms and legs and necks. Get 'em down and stake 'em. And we've got a little surprise, too. Waiting over in the rusted wreck of the old mill. In there, amid the graffiti and the beer cans and the used condoms, is Paulie with his old man's .243 and a scope you can count craters on the moon through.

Still, I'm nervous. Jerome ain't here to lead us and we're all missing his gangly presence beside us and in our blood; it's a weird feeling, not being able to sense him. It's like there's a numb spot at the back of the brain, like you've forgotten something but you can't remember what it is. He's older than any of us, than any of the coasties; he keeps them on their side of the highway, except for nights like this when someone's called a bingle.

Nevertheless, we walk towards the gaggle of coasties, because we're here now and we ain't backing down just because Jerome's skipped out on us. They're all in black, of course, looking like ninjas at best and emos at worst. Lots of blades. They outnumber us by half again, the benefit of a bigger population, I s'pose. The situation ain't the best but we've got Paulie; he's our ace in the hole.

The coasties wear neon green strips on their arms, as though they've just come from some rave or maybe a weird-arse funeral; it's strange that they'd mark each other like that. Us locals all know each other, we ain't worried about taking a slice and dice from a mate, but I guess in the city, even a shithole like the Sunny Coast, well, who really knows anyone, eh? Still, funny to want to stand out—they should be more worried about us hitting them than their own people taking an accidental swipe.

We square off and I'm one of the lucky ones, only got one against me as we exchange fuck youse. I'm thinking, this would be a good time for Paulie to start evening up the odds, but nothing happens and we all just stand there chucking insults. I'm not sure who starts it but one minute we're swearing at each other and then we're into it. Metal clangs, people cry out, but there's barely a sound of footfalls and no breathing. It's beautiful and brutal under the moonlight. The air fills with the smell of dust, blood and sweet-stale cane. I scream like a motherfucker and get stuck in.

Then Jake—one of ours—goes down. His head's a piece of melon. The sound of the shot reaches us and I think, Paulie, you fucking moron, you've hit the Jakester—maybe the arm bands are a good idea after all. And then Michelle takes a dive, followed by—in the melee, dodging a machete—I think it's Davo next, an ugly third eye where the bullet comes out his forehead.

The shooter's good. Real good. Given the distance and the light, the speed at which we're moving, to pick us off in hand-to-hand is real fucking good, even given they have to be one of us—no breather can shoot like that. Must be a total gun on the PlayStation.

We break and run and the shooter follows us, the gutless bastard, picking us off like cows in a crush. Three of us make it to cover behind Davo's ute and watch as the coasties finish off our mates. They ain't just counting coup and leaving them there for us to unstick and cart off. It's to the death. Heads roll; noggins fold in and bubble away like squishy strawberries: food for the crows; fertiliser.

I imagine Paulie, scrambling up those stairs in the mill, and copping whatever—something silent and quick, for sure, probably a spike to the heart or a cleaver to the head, something to put him down fast.

We scramble back to my Commodore, parked out of sight of the mill, just in time to crank her up and spit gravel before a bunch of coasties arrives. One waves a machete over his head like some kind of victory flag.

"Fuck," Dee says, leaning over from the back seat. There's blood on her face. She licks a dribble from the corner of her mouth. "What the fuck do we do now?"

Stu, next to me, his cheek ripped apart by what was probably an axe, manages to get enough breath into his lungs to say, "I dunno, but we sure as shit can't stay here."

I drive as fast as I can.

Somewhere between there and home, I remember how it was Paulie's idea to hit on the coasties' bit of tail to piss 'em off, that it was him who'd set up this get-even bingle. And I figure I know why Jerome never showed tonight: we've been fucked over.

We stumble back to the old scout hall that's been our home since Jerome took us in and pack our shit. We always knew we'd have to move on. No way could we blend in here once people started noticing our nocturnal habits, the lack of tits and the voices that never broke. Too many faces plastered on light poles. But I'd thought we had a good while longer, yet.

There's no sign of Jerome, our scout leader for want of a better word: Dee calls him Fagin, and to his face too, while Stu and I call him Pedo behind his back—there's none of us over 16. Can't vote, can't legally smoke or drink, but we sure can kill when we need to. The virgin vampires, Michelle says, and pretty bitterly, too. Everyone has a name for Jerome.

I met him in the loos down the gardens, offered to suck him off for a fifty so I could score some weed, but he got me hooked on something far more addictive.

The den's a pretty good set-up. The floor's covered in blankets and pillows, giving it an Arabian Nights feel, and there are books and games and hand consoles to kill the time when we ain't sleeping or prowling. When we come back from hunting, Jerome feeds from us, a bit from each. He always said we'd move on once we'd milked the joint, reached what he called critical mass; maybe go south to the big smoke where there was more opportunity, but none of us was that fussed. We'd all grown up west of the highway, on the farms and in the little towns of the hinterland. None of us fancied leaving home ground. Now we don't have no choice.

I look around at the paintings the young 'uns have done—not a lot of suns, it has to be said, mostly abstracts heavy on red and black, and plenty of night scenes, moons and the like, and stick figures bleeding from the neck and crotch—and the stuffed animals and computer games and picture books. Sometimes, you don't miss what you got till it's gone. I don't miss my old life that much, but these guys—I miss 'em already. I never really believed anything bad could happen to us, not even scrapping with the coasties to blow off some steam. Catch them poaching on our side of the highway, maybe running a raid on theirs to pick a surfie off the beach or some tourist in a back street. Fun stuff. Stick a stake in 'em and leave 'em somewhere outta the sun so their mates can find 'em. Nothing fatal. Not to us. Do what you will and be back before sunrise was Jerome's motto. That and give it up for daddy.

"You ready?" Stu asks, his pack in his hand.

"I want that sniper," I say, not really having thought about it till the words are out. "That bastard did us all in. Then we can go. North to Cairns, maybe, plenty of farms up there, a lotta tourists. Or south, maybe, like Pedo reckoned, get lost in the rat race."

"Cats amongst the rats." Dee likes cats, has them on all her t-shirts. There's one in particular, her boobs make it look like it's stretching.

"Bet there's bigger cats than us down south," Stu says, and chews on a fingernail. "Much bigger."

"We can worry about that later." I like Dee. Her blood tastes like honey. Because we're the eldest, Pedo lets us drink each other; as long as he gets his cut, he doesn't mind so much. "Whaddya reckon?"

"I'm in," Dee says. "We owe our mob that much."

"Yeah," Stu says with a shrug. "Nothing better to do."

We pack the Commodore—sure, I've only got my learner's and unless they bring in night tests I'll never get my Ps, and the car's stolen, but I've been driving since my feet could reach the pedals and God help the cop who pulls us over. On the way out, we hit a couple of farms, feeding up and taking guns and blades and other stuff we think we might need.

Then we cross the highway to settle the score with the coasties, though it's gonna be a tough ask, us just being three kids and all.

The coasties have a nest in a disused skate rink. The place has been up for sale for ages. Nice block, not far from the beach, but close to a creek—it flooded real bad once, when a cyclone came down from the north, which kinda fucked the joint up—and there is, according to the warning signs on the fence, asbestos or something worthy of a skull and crossbones inside. That ain't the half of it.

We come in from the creek side, following a drain that's a bit boggy but has nothing more noxious in it than a rusty shopping trolley.

There's a guard, a young surfie dude, smoking—I guess it makes him feel tough, but it sure helps us see him, both stench and glow—and he goes down without a sound when Dee puts a bolt in his chest. Ace with a crossbow, Dee. We don't take his head because we don't know how wired he is and we don't wanna tip our hand. Poor old Jerome, wherever he is, he musta bled from every orifice with the death of so many of us so close together, all those blood links being severed like that. All those ties that bind, as he likes to say, shared between creator and child. I reckon I'd know if he was dead, that I've got enough of him in me to know that much. That much, but not a lot more. He was a taker, not a giver, Jerome.

Up we creep, finding a handy window, and what a set-up the coasties have got: lights, computers; even a pinball machine. Surrounded by factories and car yards and panel beaters, no one would complain about the noise (and pity them if they did). The coasties could have a disco in here and no one would be the wiser. It's a different kind of party tonight.

They've got Jerome, and there's Paulie and his little sister, Carlie. Paulie has a knife. Jerome, looking even skinnier and bonier than normal, is stretched naked between two posts and is cut up pretty bad. The left side of his chest is a hell of a mess; they've been giving him some heart trouble. I can kinda see what this is all about, now. I s'pose the coasties wanted us taken out, just so we didn't do what the three of us are trying to do: get even. There's a lot of 'em. Their boss is a blond dude, real tanned, spray-on maybe, and he's telling Paulie, if he wants his sister safe from this ghoul, he has to do Jerome. Paulie's been crying and his sister, too; his face is smeared all red, hers is just wet and puffy. There's a chick holding his rifle, real easy-like; she's wearing cammo singlet and shorts, real hot with a pony tail, a real redneck centrefold. But the way she holds the .243, you can tell she isn't the shooter, she doesn't have the love. I'm amazed I didn't know just how ace a shot Paulie is. I mean, I knew he was good, that's why we sent him up the mill in the first place, but he ain't even off a farm.

I'm not surprised that Paulie's here, but Carlie, you bet. I didn't think he'd want her to see this but maybe he doesn't have the choice, not if he wants to skip town. I wouldn't be surprised if his mum and dad have a nasty accident tonight. Something extra in their booze or maybe they'll just be a road snack for their son, a last kiss goodbye before going it alone with his little sis. That's what I figure he'll do, 'cause that's what I did, more or less.

Jerome looks up, must've felt a stir in his blood with us being so close, though his red's spread to hell and back again, and Paulie turns, following his gaze, and stares right at us.

I curse; we'll never get a chance at a little one-on-one with our treacherous mate. It's now or never and we just ain't gonna get to him, not to take his head. So I cover my bases.

I put a round through the centrefold's head. She hits the dirt like a bag of shit. Give the bitch a real migraine when she comes to. Dee puts a bolt in the boss. Paulie positively shits himself, knife useless in his hand, and Jerome looks hopeful, despite the flesh hanging from his body where they've all been having a good taste.

The coasties start for us.

I shoot Paulie's little sister.

Fuck me, but he doesn't half holler.

I shoot him next, just for the satisfaction.

Then Stu starts hurling Molotovs to keep the bastards back—he's got a strong arm, Stu, real good in the outfield for the under-14s—and man, what a shemozzle: screaming, the oily smell of burning petrol, guns going off. Windows shattering. Jerome burning like a candle.

We run, run like frightened roos, ducking and weaving, back through the fence and across the creek where we hope they won't be able to scent us too easy, till we reach the Commodore.

I head north and no one argues. No one says much at all.

† † †

This is how I see it.

Jerome picked us kids because we were young and small and he could shape us. We could kinda accept the new life without worrying too much about what we'd missed, except maybe for us older ones, like Stu and Paulie and Dee and me, but he needed a few older ones to be an example, to keep an eye on the little ones. The little 'uns are pretty useful—sneaky and innocent-looking. Cuteness will get you a long way in the world. I tell you, they can suck a pint out of an oldie in the time it takes to tie a shoelace without 'em even knowing.

I'm not saying what Jerome did was right, just that I understand. At least he was honest about what he was and what he wanted from us. Not just blood, the lazy bastard, though there was more to it than sustenance: it was a power trip. Jerome wanted to be the big man. Well, he was taller than any of us, taller and older and more clever. He taught us everything we needed to know. Paulie said he was a sick bastard and I reckon there might be some truth to that, but I'm not complaining too loud: this life's okay, a lot less hassle in many ways, and it's not like Jerome wanted to, you know, do us. Drink our blood, sure, but that was it. Maybe I'm trying to draw a line where there isn't one. I dunno. What I do know is this: Paulie's gone too far. We were his mates, his family even; you don't shaft your mates.

† † †

Paulie's parents had the only pharmacy in town, right there in the main street between the newsagent and the cafe. Jerome picked him up in Nambour. He'd missed the bus and was waiting for the next, just after dark, and Jerome took a liking. Clumsy, that, not checking, just assuming the kid in the ex-military jacket with the long hair was a blow through. We got plenty on the coast. Not this time.

Paulie made the best of it—no more school, he was cool with that, and didn't really miss pulling shifts for the parentals, nor being clipped round the ear for growing his hair, nor making those before/ during/after dinner G&Ts for the old lady. But he missed his little sister, who his old man called, when pissed, *the accident.*

Dangerous, Jerome said, to have two from the one family go missing. Very dangerous. Until he saw little Carlie. You could see the drool from the end of the street. But he'd misunderstood. Paulie didn't want Jerome to bring Carlie into our happy little family. He wanted him to take out Mr & Mrs and let Carlie go live with someone sober. But Jerome reckoned Carlie could be an exception to his rule. It wouldn't even be a big shift for her, coming from alcoholics to us.

Okay, so maybe Jerome deserved what he got. You got to understand, when they got your blood in them, it gives you a certain predisposition. But in hindsight, yeah, Jerome was a cunt. He liked the taste of youth and he lost sight; I was already damaged goods, but he shouldn't have gone for innocents. I'm glad Paulie cut off his nuts. Not that they were of any use to him, or anyone else, but it's the symbolism, ain't it. But the rest of us—did we really deserve Paulie's wrath? I guess that's the price the coasties demanded to help him take out Jerome, and that our blood wasn't as important as his sister's, not to him. And maybe I can understand that, but given it's *my* blood we're talking about, I have to protest. I mean, he could've run or tried to take Jerome out while he slept. Neither is easy to do when they've got your blood in them. Not a bad little system Jerome had going, really.

Maybe that's why the coasties demanded a sacrifice. To make sure it wasn't a trick. Or simply just to clear the paddock, once and for all. Why settle for just the east side of the highway when you can have it all, from the beach to the hills.

† † †

Cairns has both beach and hills, though it's hotter and wetter than the Sunny Coast. Still, Dee and I figure, we're at the other end of the state, surely this is far enough away. Between the town and the farms, it feels kinda familiar; as good a place as any to settle down, as long as we're careful.

She really does taste like honey.

It's a Friday night, Mr Johnson is in town playing darts, and Mrs Johnson is coming hard on my fingers as I suck blood from her femoral on the kitchen floor.

"You're so good with your hands," Mrs J says between moans, and I can't help thinking, as I always do, my own little joke, that when she told her hubby she'd got someone in to mow the lawn, this wasn't what he'd been expecting.

I hear the screen door squeak open and I know—know, deep down in my blood—it's not Mr J home early. I guess it was always gonna come to this. Paulie loved his sister, more than anything. But still, I don't really understand his chasing after me. I reckon we're even. I mean, it's not like I *turned* her.

We dodge around the kitchen table as Mrs J scuttles outta the way and I manage to lead Paulie outside with a slice across my shoulders to show for it. We dance in the Johnsons' fallow cane field, the two of us trading cuts and thrusts.

I'm copping the worst of it. He's fired right up and I'm sluggish with fresh blood and his serrated machete's got the reach over my dagger. I can imagine him saying my name, over and over, and maybe Carlie's, too, as he filed those jagged points.

"Shoulda known you'd find yourself a new pedo," he says as we circle, and I don't bother trying to correct him. "I found Stu in Rocky."

"Yeah, he split, wanted to try cattle. See if he could do without human blood."

"Didn't work out so good for him. Made him weak." A nice long gloat, and then: "Where's Dee?"

I don't answer, too busy ducking as he slashes, again and again. He opens me up, arm, chest and leg, before we break and circle once more.

"I know Dee's close. I can smell her on you."

"You can't have her. Not without going through me."

"Too easy." His swipe damn near lops me. "Look at you, drunk on that pedo's blood."

"This ain't like Jerome," I say. "I'm doing the taking here. This is one of them symbiotic relationships."

"So you get blood. What does she get?"

"She gets her lawn mown."

I lunge and he twists away. My blade finds air and Paulie slams me into the dirt. I lose my knife ad he looms over me. The machete rises and I know I'm a goner.

Paulie's throat explodes. Blood, flesh and cartilage spray my face. He stumbles, then falls to his knees, and I snatch that nasty little blade of his and turn him into fertiliser, no second chances.

"Thanks, Mrs J." Like any good farm wife, she can shoot straight. I smile my bloody smile and tell her it'll be all right, there won't even be a body to bury. I'll make it up to her.

We've got a real sweet deal out here, me and Dee, and I don't wanna lose that. Who knows, we might even want to start our own little family one day.

AFTERWORD TO "CHILDREN OF THE CANE"

"Children of the Cane" was one of those stories that appeared out of the mind-mist once I'd started thinking about the idea of Dead Red Heart. *I was raised on a cattle property, not in the inland, but on the Queensland coast, where timber and sugar cane were two of the biggest cash crops. The image of shadowy figures moving across the stubble was the first to emerge, and then it was a matter of finding out who they were and what they were doing. I chose the Sunshine Coast because I was familiar with its disparate lifestyles separated by little more than a highway, which reflects the great Australian dichotomy of having this great romance with the outback while in fact being a predominantly urban society. The story also melds the enduring colonial-era trope of the lost child in the bush with the more recent anxiety of child abduction, but in this story, the victims get to outlast their predators, though the cost is high.*

THE SEA AT NIGHT

JOANNE ANDERTON

Joe dug his bare feet into the sand on Maroubra beach as night fell. The dark sea reached forward to wash over his skin and suck at the dirty hems of his pants. A glance over his shoulder showed the beach was emptying. The odd preoccupied couple and fish-and-chips-eating family remained on the steps behind him, but didn't venture onto the sand. Even further back the streetlights flickered on and seemed to congregate, with all the movement and the noise, at the Maroubra Bay Hotel on the corner.

Joe knelt so the tide dampened his knees, and began to dig. He did so with small, practiced movements, filtering sand through his fingers, feeling rather than seeing. He'd spent every evening for years doing this, searching in the warm waves for the parts of him the demon had taken away. He'd come close a couple of times: he'd caught the tips of his own youthful fingers bobbing in the foam, and he'd even found strips of the suit he'd bought for the wedding that never happened, teasing and trailing like seaweed with the tide.

But he'd never found enough to rebuild what the demon had destroyed. So he kept digging. And he was so preoccupied that he didn't hear footsteps on the sand until their owner appeared by his side.

"That's a strange activity, isn't it, for this time of day?"

Joe didn't stop, merely glanced up. The man who addressed him was little more than a thin silhouette in a suit against the streetlights, hands clasped behind him and bent forward from the waist. Joe turned back to his digging.

"And for a fully-dressed man, now that I think of it."

Joe gave a little shrug and shuffled crab-like along the water's edge. "Not fully dressed," he mumbled, "got no shoes."

"Hmm, no I suppose you don't." The man appeared to follow him, but so softly he didn't make a sound. "But that doesn't make it any less strange."

Joe sighed, sat back on his sand-encrusted heels and wiped his hands on the front of his pants. "You going to leave me alone, or what?" He stood, with a creak and a grunt, and turned his scowl on the man. One look at the fresh scars on Joe's face, his reeking mess of matted hair, and the three layers of soiled shirts he was wearing, and surely this bloke would leave him alone.

But this man wasn't normal either. He was pale, too pale for any skin that'd seen the sun. His cheeks were sunken and his eyes large, like a starving child, lips thin and white. His suit was old, moth-eaten in patches and so heavy with dust it floated on the sea breeze, a soft shower glittering in the light from the street.

Caught off-guard, Joe took a hesitant step back. The tall man seemed to flicker, then. One moment he was standing there, hands behind his back and gaunt face curious, and the next he folded in on himself and reappeared, a step closer. Like a bloody piece of paper. He left no footprints, and sounded like the beating of wings.

Joe blinked, shook his head. "Sorry, mate," he said. "I didn't realise you were like me."

The man lifted eyebrows so thin they could have been drawn onto his forehead. "Oh? And what are we?"

"Dark. Dirty. Different." That sounded pretty bad, so Joe tried again. "We're like the sea at night. Doesn't matter how many lights this city turns on we're always there, the dark tide, lapping at its feet, eating away at its precious security." Well, maybe his nonsensical rambling would get rid of the guy anyway. "Sydney doesn't like the parts of it that aren't bright and clean and happy, but that's what we are. So we're like the sea, but at night . . ." He stuttered off into silence.

After a moment the man unclasped his hands and held one out. "My name is Gideon," he said. "At this point in time, anyway." His nails were very short and very clean, and his hand so thin it was almost bones.

Joe lifted a hand but hesitated. His nails were long and currently clogged with sand.

"Oh please," Gideon said, "you don't have to worry about that with me."

They shook. Gideon was cold but his grip strong. "Joseph," Joe said.

Gideon nodded, expression thoughtful. "I'd like to get to know you better, Joe. Can I buy you a beer?" He motioned to the pub.

Joe shook his head. Even if the Hotel security let him inside—with his dirty clothes and his weeping scars and his overall stench—Joe didn't belong in that bright world, with all those people. And anyway, he had to keep digging.

"Oh come on," Gideon said. He folded and fluttered away from the water's edge, towards the street, and despite himself Joe was drawn to follow. "You won't find what you're looking for here, anyway. What you have lost cannot be recovered from the sand."

The steps were empty, now, cluttered only with loose sand tossed there by the wind. The night wrapped Gideon in a cloak that reached out, in shapes like quivering wings, to douse the near-by streetlights one by one. He led Joe through the small park and across the road. All around them, life and movement faded. The old stoners sitting outside the kebab shop took their food inside; the fish and chips closed its doors, despite the oil and the heat; even the bus stop and the pub's outdoor courtyard cleared.

"It's better this way," Gideon said, his voice as deep as the sea. "Don't you agree?"

Two steps inside the Maroubra Bay Hotel and security stopped them. The usual large men without expressions. "This is the point where I turn around and leave," Joe muttered.

One of the security guards nodded to him. "Good idea, mate." He pointed to Gideon. "You can stay, but your friend needs a bath before we let him in here."

But Gideon said, "No, he has as much right to a beer as the rest of you." As he spoke the shadows that draped across his shoulders spread. The lights along the gaudily striped walls flickered and snapped off, all at once. The wide TV screens that streamed surfing and the ever-present sun sizzled into curtains of white noise. Only the lights behind the bar remained, casting the surreal colours and shapes of bottles of alcohol across the room.

"Come on," Gideon tugged Joe forward. "You need a beer."

One of the guards tried to stop them. Gideon brushed him aside like he was swatting a fly, and sent him crashing through furniture to collapse against a far wall. The pub's patrons fled as Gideon approached the bar, leaving dust like a tide-line in his wake.

The barman remained, looking ghoulish in the alcoholic light, though his hands shook as he pulled them each a schooner. Gideon hadn't asked the type of beer he wanted, but Joe decided not to press the issue.

"You may leave now." Gideon waved his hand and feathers rustled in the movement. The barman fled. Probably a good idea.

Gideon lifted the beer to his lips, smiled thinly against the glass. "Go on," he said. "I know it has been years since you drank anything not wrapped in a brown paper bag." His pale skin, stretched so tightly across his skull, turned to a decaying yellow in the light. His eyes were nothing but black hollows and everything but his head and hands was lost in shadow.

Joe sipped his beer. Gideon pretended to drink: he touched the amber liquid to his lips but didn't so much as open his mouth. Add that to the darkness and the mysterious powers and superhuman strength, and it didn't take much to work out.

"So—" Joe was careful to place a coaster beneath his dripping glass "—are you a demon too?"

Something like moonlight flashed in the holes that were Gideon's eyes, then he lowered his beer and pushed it across the bar. "Here, you might as well have mine too. I'm hardly going to drink it, now am I?" When he spoke, his mouth was strange, lips tense and teeth never showing, yet Joe had no trouble understanding him.

Joe shrugged, tossed back his, and took the demon's glass. Did it really matter where the beer came from, as long as it was cold? "I don't know why you've chosen me. I don't have much left to take, you know. Another of your kind got to me first."

Gideon wrinkled his nose in a surprisingly genteel expression of disgust. "I would hardly call the demon that got you one of my kind. And you have plenty left, for someone like me." He leaned forward, face close to Joe's neck and breathed in deeply. "But you surprised me, back there on the sand. I thought I knew men like you." He leaned back. "But you had *remarkable* things to say. So take the opportunity, Joe my boy, and enjoy your beer."

That he could do. So, Gideon was a demon. There was no point panicking about it. Not now.

"Tell me about the sea."

Joe shifted, uncomfortable on the barstool. "The sea?"

"I liked it, what you said. Lapping away at the city's security. You said you felt like that, Joe. And that we were the same. But why would you say that? Was that the demon talking?"

Joe frowned, took a good long drink. Gideon's eyes widened and he snatched the empty glass, flickered around behind the bar and filled it again. A strange sight, all that growing, reaching shadow pouring drinks.

This was more beer in one sitting than he'd had for years. Despite the yeasty sickness gathering in his stomach, Joe was enjoying it. For the first time in almost as many years he was drinking in the company of . . . well, if not friends then at least with someone other than himself.

"The demon isn't here to do any talking," Joe answered, after a moment's thought. "It tore out the best parts of me and left me like this. Scarred. Dirty. Lapping at the edges of my old life like the sea, at night."

A curious twitch of his eyebrows. "How'd it happen?" Gideon even collected a cloth and wiped the bar as he spoke. It made Joe smile. "Warm summer day, of course. When the tide was turning—going in or out, it never matters—and the rips were strong. Too strong, much stronger than you realised. Were you surfing?"

Joe shook his head. "Just swimming. Was never any good on a board."

"And the rip got you. Took you far."

Why was he asking, if he already knew? "Did what I was told, waved and shouted at those bloody flags till I was hoarse. But the rip had hold of me, carried me away from the beach. The land disappeared, the sand fell away underneath and there was nothing but me, and the sea and the hard sky like its reflection."

"Ah." Gideon closed his eyes. "The hard sky like its reflection. Were you a poet, Joe, before the demon took you?"

He snorted beer through his nose at that. "Hardly, mate. Plumber, and I reckon it pays better." He glanced around, searching for food. Too much bloody beer too quickly.

"I'm sure it does. And yet, I have not seen the hard blue sky for, well, for a long time, and you paint it so beautifully." Gideon paused, frowned. "What is it?"

"Seen anything to nibble on?"

A packet of salt and vinegar chips fluttered through darkness and wings to land on the bar before him.

"Perfect." Joe tore them open and offered them to Gideon first, out of courtesy, though he knew the demon wouldn't accept. "Cheers."

"And then?" Gideon whispered.

"Reckon you know."

"Tell me."

Joe shrugged, even though his stomach was rolling at the memory, and took a moment to chew a chip, sharp and biting against his tongue. "And then there was the demon. Thought it was my own reflection, first, wavering before me on the mirror of the sea. Looked like me, almost like me. Me if I wasn't terrified but, well, enjoying myself. Turned out those hands weren't mine, and they reached out of the water and straight into my chest. Took . . . Touched . . . Well, you know. Next thing I was dumped, water in my mouth and sand in everything. And ever since I dragged myself out of that water, that bright and terrible clear water, nothing's been the same."

"Because the demon took the best of you."

"Yep." Another swig, damn the nausea. "Ruined my life. Lost my job, lost my fiancé, lost my house. And ended up like this."

"It ruined your life?" Was that disappointment on Gideon's face? "Do you hate what the demon has made of you?"

"Of course I do." He frowned. "What kind of question is that?"

"The way you spoke about the darkness and sea—with such beauty, Joe the Plumber—I thought you might be different from the rest. Maybe you belong in the darkness." Gideon ran a hand over his bony face. "But you don't, not really. You want to return to the way things used to be, before the demon came. When you belonged to that bright city and its people."

"Yep—I had a life then, you know. So I've got to keep digging. To find the me it took." Joe tried to stand, teetered on the edge of the stool and fell back into Gideon's waiting hands. Damn he could flicker about so fast. "Thanks for the beer. Nice of you, really was."

"Careful," Gideon said. Joe glanced back and caught the tips of two teeth, long and far too sharp, peeking out of the demon's taut lips. "Not so fast." He growled beneath those words, an inhuman noise rumbling from deep within.

"Cheers." Joe patted what should have been a shoulder, but something large and covered in fur—or was it fathers?—twitched and rolled beneath his hand. "You're a mate. A demon, but a mate."

Gideon laughed, and great fangs arched like moonlit scythes out of his maw. A reek like the grave wafted over Joe's face. Gideon steadied him, turned him and held his shoulders so their faces were close. Joe homeless and filthy and ever-scarred; Gideon terrible and dark, lit in places only by the moon.

"Oh Joe, I am not. I *am* the dark you hate so much, so I can't be your mate, don't you see? I thought you might be different, but who would want to be one of us if they had a choice? It's lonely in the sea at night, isn't it?" He leaned in and Joe felt pressure, sharp and strange, against the scabs on his neck. Gideon hugged him tightly, and all Joe's body was cold, everything like ice apart from two points of fire just below the curve of his jaw. "Let me help you," Gideon whispered, words slurred. "I'm sorry if it hurts."

The darkened insides of the Maroubra Bay Hotel smoothed into the flat surface of a calm sea. Joe stared down at his reflection, moonlit this time, pale and looking dead. It screamed at him and thrashed, smacking against water like a tinted windowpane.

"Doesn't hurt—" Joe started to say. Then something clenched inside him. His heart, he thought, beating strangely, smacking against his ribs. But more than that. It was his life, his old self, everything that could have been, everything he had lost, diving back inside him like needles through the two points on his neck. And he gasped, shuddered, tried to pull away. But Gideon held him, and his demon-reflection screamed.

"Not yet." Gideon's voice cracked. The sea and the pub flickered over each other like a bad Photoshop job and Joe strained to look down at the demon, pressed against his neck. Streams of bright tears trailed down Gideon's smooth, pale jaw. "Not until I free you from your demon. From the darkness that hurts so much."

Joe, head fuzzy from the sea and stomach rebelling with the beer, leaned into Gideon and wrapped ungainly arms around him. He hugged the demon, as the demon hugged him, patting his back. "It's okay, mate. Don't worry about it. You don't have to do that. Not for me."

Gideon drew back and stared at him. Blood and tears mingled on his chin.

"Can see you don't want to, mate," Joe said. He held the hem of an inner sleeve against his neck until the bleeding stopped. He healed quickly, since the demon took him, but everything left terrible scars. "So—don't."

"I—" Gideon sounded confused. Strange, for a demon to be confused. "I thought you hated the demon. I thought you hated what it did to your life."

Joe shrugged. "Well, yeah. Of course I do."

"And this is the only way I can help you! I told you: you can't replace what you have lost by searching in the sand. Even if you find yourself, you can never reclaim it all, not while that demon sits so contentedly inside you."

"What?"

"The demon took those parts of you and wedged itself in their place." Gideon made useless, circular motions with his hands, and they still sounded like wings. "That's what they do."

"Oh." Joe scratched at the scars on his arm, the ones that rose up all over his body like goddamned tectonic plates were having a field day beneath his skin. Were all those evenings dredging through the sand an utter waste of time?

"That demon's in you, now, and while you are alive nothing can dislodge it. While you are alive, you will never be free."

"While I am alive." Joe looked up and finally understood. Gideon *was* a demon, after all. "You were killing me?"

Gideon wrung his fluttering hands at his chest, so hard he shed fresh sheets of dust with the motion. "Eating you, actually."

And yet, Joe had seen tears. "Then why'd you cry like that?"

"It's lonely in the sea at night," Gideon said again, voice small and quiet. "I was going to eat you and free you, like I do for all the others I find. But then you started talking about the sea like that. You offered me chips. You called me mate. And I dared to believe, for a moment, that you were different. That you really were like me, and we could be friends. But one mate shouldn't eat the other, am I right?"

"Yeah."

"So we can't be mates, then. Because I can't help you if I don't kill you, and mates should always help each other if they can, shouldn't they?" Gideon wrapped himself in shadow like a child clinging to a blanket.

Joe, more than a little intoxicated, contemplated death. Nothingness. No scars, no stench, no memories that haunted him in the daylight and no desperation that fuelled him after dusk. His lonely, demon-torn life hardly compared.

But Gideon was right. Mates shouldn't eat each other, even with the best intentions. And they didn't leave each other depressed and all alone, either.

Maybe this dark scrap of a life might be better, with company.

"No beer when you're dead, I imagine." Joe scratched at the crawling things in his hair. "And no one to share it with."

Gideon shook his head. "Not the kind of death that I would send you to, at least."

Joe lifted surprised eyebrows. "There's more than one?"

"Indeed." Hope in the demon's eyes. "There are many."

"You could tell me about them, if you like. Over another beer." Joe grinned. Didn't matter if he showed the rotting stubs of what was left of his teeth to a demon with breath like Gideon's. "Your shout, of course."

"Of course." This time, when Gideon smiled, he let his fangs hang out.

AFTERWORD TO "THE SEA AT NIGHT"

Maroubra beach might seem like a strange setting for a vampire story, but I've eaten enough fish and chips on its steps at the end of a stinking hot summer day to know there is something creepy about the beach at night. Well, at least to me. During the day it's a place of shining water and glistening bodies, surfboards ridden and ball games played, heady with the scent of sunscreen. Quintessentially Australian. But when the sun goes down and everyone leaves the waves start to roar and all you can see is darkness stretching on forever. It's that emptiness that gets me, that stillness where only hours ago so many people were playing. Sydney seems to shine so brightly just to compensate for all that unending darkness. This was my inspiration for this story. After all, what are vampires but stillness, lifelessness, where there once was life? And who knows what kind of demons haunt this sun loving, somewhat wild city when night falls?

SKY IN THE MORNING

SONIA MARCON

Alex looked forward to his annual trip down south to stay with his relatives because it was the one enduring reminder that he was once a child. He felt that he was now at an age where his childhood was perceived as naïve and unconnected; it was without iPhones, Facebook and Twitter. He also felt that this reminiscing of a finished childhood was his only secret and whether he realised it or not, he was committed to keeping his younger sister's childhood intact for as long as possible. So, every year on this same train journey, he had no music to listen to, no DS to play with, only the company of his sister, Hailey, and her story books and colouring tools to keep him and her occupied. And that was his choice and the way he liked it.

The relatives were, to Alex, part of the family that extended beyond understanding. His father had a mother who had a brother who had a daughter who had a husband before she died. The husband then remarried giving Alex and Hailey two family members with the prefix Aunt and Uncle even though they didn't rightly fit the namesakes. Even so, Aunt Judy and Uncle Les were the favourites of their relatives. Hailey loved helping Aunt Judy with her garden while Alex adored helping Uncle Les with whatever the retired carpenter was working on. But what both children loved most was the food. Even the mother of Alex's best friend at school, who was European and not a youngster, could not compete with the culinary magic performed by both Les and Judy. Alex had given up asking for recipes from them, though; their answers never changed. Either Judy had found a recipe in a drawer then lost it or Les was told how to cook something by a little bird. The answer was that their recipes would die when Les and Judy eventually did. It didn't stall the children's' curiosity, though.

"What's for dinner?" This question from Hailey had become expected every year when she and Alex had left the train station to sit in the back seat of Les's Holden sedan, and every year it was met with the same cheerful laughter. It was a question that only a four-year-old could get away with.

"Well, let's see. Your Aunt has cut some lovely toenails to have in sandwiches . . ."

"Ewww!" Hailey protested.

"Or your Aunty could knock up her famous Hie Tie Min!"

"Yay!" Hailey cried. This dish was one of the kids' favourites. It wasn't a stir fry nor was it a stew. It was a mixture of meat and vegetables in an Asian inspired sauce served on rice that was as original as its name.

"How do you make that, Aunt Judy?" Alex asked with a smile.

"Oh, it's a recipe I learnt somewhere. I used to have it written down but I misplaced it a while ago."

Alex smiled. "Oh, yeah," he replied making sure the smile was heard in his voice. "Do you still get the meat locally?"

"Of course! There's nothing better than what we get from our local boys."

The local boys were a family of farmers and graziers that went back to when the town was first settled over two hundred years before. Their produce never left this small southern town; what was grown and bred was sold and consumed locally. It was this earnest simplicity that Alex found so refreshing here.

"None of that city produce is up to scratch." Uncle Les piped in. "Not when you're used to the top work our local boys put in."

"Yeah," Alex said, smiling.

Les and Judy lived not far from their local train station so the four of them arrived to the modest brick-and-tile house by the end of their conversation. The town was small enough to function without traffic lights so the journey was continuous and quick. Hailey and Alex shared a bedroom which neither minded; it was a novelty for them both. They took their bags to their room then sat for early dinner. Tea was no later than six pm in this household. As Judy set the food-laden plates down, Les spoke.

"Hold up, Jude. It's warm outside so whaddaya say to eating on the back veranda?"

Hailey breathed in. "Yeah! Can we, Aunt Jude?"

"Of course. If you carry your own plates." Hailey shot from the table, disappearing out the back door. There was a brief pause before she reappeared. "Sorry," she picked up her plate of food and carried it quickly yet carefully out the back. Les, Judy and Alex picked up their respective plates and followed. "I'll take her knife and fork," Alex said as he collected his and Hailey's cutlery.

"Must be a nice change for you to have dinner outside," Les said. "You still livin' in that flat?" This was a question and a comment.

The three of them joined Hailey who was sitting at the outside table looking sheepish. Alex handed her cutlery to her. "Dumbass," he whispered, grinning.

"Knob-end!" This retort was as close to swearing as Hailey dared chance in the company of adults, even though Les swore like a sailor. It was also loud enough to warrant a chattering reaction from the family of rosellas in the backyard Bottlebrush trees.

"Those bloody birds are a nuisance!" Les had a forkful of rice hovering in front of his mouth "They steal the nests from twenty-eights."

Hailey looked visibly offended at this notion, but paused as she processed this information, before asking "What are twennyates?"

The table erupted with laughter. Alex could not work out why Les and Judy had no children. They finished their meal to the sound of life according to Hailey and the syrupy chortle of magpies set to a backdrop of red-tinted sky.

As the daylight diminished, the family collected their plates and went back inside the house. Their entrance was met with the ringing of the home telephone.

"Here we go," said Les, unimpressed. "There's always something from someone. If it's a telemarketer from India, I'll be happy to talk about the cricket."

"I'll get it." Aunt Judy sounded resigned to dealing with Les's contemptuous humour. She picked up the phone. "Hello?"

Judy was silent as she listened, her face showing the concern of someone hearing bad news, then, "What do you need us to do?"

Les and Alex were watching Judy closely, Les with a look of confused concern and Alex with just plain confusion. Hailey was off somewhere, no doubt playing. He looked at Les.

"What's happened?" Alex's voice seemed to snap Les out of whatever he was thinking about. He turned to Alex, grinning.

"Aw, who knows." he said, taking Alex's plate and placing it on the counter. "It's probably one of Judy's gardenin' friends. Prolly dug a hole and fell in it. They're useless as all shit, those women. Why don't ya go watch TV? You can fight over the remote with your sister."

Les was slowly leading Alex out of the kitchen towards the living room as he spoke, stopping when they reached Hailey who was sitting on the floor in front of the TV. "She's beaten ya to it, mate," he said before leaving. Alex stood for a second behind his sister but couldn't bare it. He had to know what the phone call was about. He padded back silently across the carpet until he reached the doorway, then stood out of sight, listening.

"What's happened?" asked Les when Judy hung up the phone.

"Some of the livestock escaped."

"Aw, you're kidding! How many?"

"Three. Maybe four."

"Aw, fuck!" Les paused to compose himself. "See, this is what happens when you let useless fuckwits run the show. Useless, tight-ass fuckwits. Why can't they raise sheep or cattle? Because it's too expensive and the fuckin' greenies get on ya case. So now we've got a handful of fuckin' bloodsuckers loose."

"They can't get far." Judy was shaking and her voice quivered. "There was a harvest today so they . . . they're not complete."

"I don't care if they look like the fuckin' Prime Minister! They're gonna remember who caught them and put them in a cage. We're all up shit creek and you know it!"

"Why?" Alex's voice made Les and Judy jump; they looked like a pair of rabbits caught in headlights. Judy turned and started filling the sink with water. Les grinned and approached Alex who now stood in the doorway.

"Aw, no reason, mate. Just a couple of useless farmers with their dicks in their hands."

Judy turned off the water and faced them, obviously annoyed with Les' ambiguity. "Just tell him, Les. He needs to know, especially if we're all in danger."

Alex looked from Les to Judy. "Why are we in danger?"

Les sighed and rubbed his forehead with one hand in a pained manner. "Because we made a stupid mistake."

†   †   †

Alex helped Les and Judy lock up the house after they had told Alex the story of their towns' meat supply. Then they all got ready for bed. We all still need sleep, as Les put it. They had stayed awake for as long as they all could. They even managed to conjure a believable reason for Hailey as to why all the lights in and around the house were to be kept on. Apart from hers and Alex's bedroom light; Hailey couldn't sleep if she could still see. They said their goodnights and as Les left Alex and Hailey's room, Alex asked a final question while Hailey was off brushing her teeth. "Why do we need the lights on, Les? It's sunlight that kills them, isn't it?"

"It is," said Les. "But we need light to see. They don't. Night, Alex."

"Goodnight, Les." Alex wished he had kept his mouth shut; that last statement by Les said nothing yet everything and raised the level of fear in Alex to a point he could hardly bear. As Les exited the room, Hailey entered and got into bed. "Night, Uncle Les," Hailey said happily, blissfully unaware. "Night, Aunt Judy!"

"Goodnight, love," Judy's voice was muffled by her bedclothes. Les stopped in the doorway.

"See you tomorrow," he said then switched off the light and pulled the bedroom door almost shut.

Alex lay thinking about what he knew when it came to defence against vampires. There was garlic, of course, and sunlight. Was silver useful? He didn't think so. He was thinking about every film he had seen that featured a vampire when his breath caught in his throat.

There was scratching at the window on the wall next to his bed that led from their bedroom to the backyard. No, I'm just imagining it, he thought. Or it's the wind.

Alex then realised something that he wasn't quite sure of, something he didn't know how exactly to feel about. If what Uncle Les and Aunt Judy had said about this town's meat was true, then he and his sister had eaten vampire. Did that mean that Alex was now a cannibal? No, he thought, vampires aren't human. They were once, but then they changed.

What is that scratching sound? Alex thought.

So, if vampires aren't human, what are they? Alex didn't know, but what he did know was that they weren't like him. Does that make it ok to eat them, then, because they were once like him?

Alex didn't know how he could sleep while his brain was whirring or while his window kept scratching. He sat up to look through the space between the curtain and the window sill and what he saw froze him.

Outside, with its nose touching the glass, was the pale face of something Alex didn't understand; it was something he could not liken to anything he had ever seen. It had eyes that looked like they were once brown but were now faded to a pale brownie-grey. Its hair was stuck to a scalp that was flaked and peeling where it wasn't deeply grazed. Its face had a look of focused pain and hate with skin that was smooth, almost beautiful. Its arms, or what was left of them, were raised over its head with the fingers scratching the pane. Alex didn't know how the fingers could move; he had studied human biology at school so he knew enough about the mechanics of the human body to realise that this creature was missing all the parts of its arms that would be used to move fingers. Every part that was flesh and muscle had been removed, stripped completely away leaving the bones visible. Was this what he had eaten? The scratching fingers of the creature stopped and its head slowly turned to face Alex's single frightened eye. When it saw Alex, its eyes widened and its open mouth stretched to what Alex thought was a smile. Aunt Judy and Uncle Les had not been lying about vampires. One of them was now separated from Alex and his family by a single sheet of window glass.

Alex was caught in this stare-off for less time than he felt. Looking at this thing turned his stomach not because of its appearance, but the thought that he might have eaten the meat from those flayed arms made him want to vomit and never eat anything again. Quick as a flash, he launched himself backwards, bouncing once on his bed before landing hard on the floor. His sister sat up. "Alex, what are you doing?" she yelled as he ran out of the room. Uncle Les was right; Alex was thankful he didn't have to search for light switches. The distance between Alex and Hailey's room from Les and Judy's was short, but by the time Alex had begun running he stopped. His attention was caught by the moving figures in the backyard that were visible through the bathroom window. Some were on legs reminiscent of the arms Alex had just seen but most walked on legs that were complete. What those vampires missed was the flesh and muscle that joined their pelvis to their ribcage. Some were even without organs. Something Alex noticed but didn't realise he was noticing was the way the vampires walked. None of them, not even the ones with just bones for legs, walked with any kind of limp or hobble. They all moved like athletes.

Something Alex couldn't help but notice was just how many there were; he tried but there were more than he could count.

He ran the rest of the distance down the hall to Les and Judy's room, but they were up before he got there.

"Don't panic," Uncle Les said as he was laying out a large collection of wooden cricket wickets on his side of the bed. Alex saw that each one had been sharpened at one end; they looked like giant pencils. It was now obvious to Alex why the farmers had chosen a carpenter to help with the new livestock.

"Why are they after you?" Alex yelled quietly. "You said it was a bunch of guys who caught the vampires."

"There is a bunch but they didn't catch them. They made them. We caught them. Jude, where's my . . ."

Bang

"Oh, god. Les . . ." Judy was backed into the corner opposite the window.

BANG

"It's ok. They can't come in uninvited." Les said as he shoved the wickets into a carry-bag.

BANG BANG

"Les!"

BANG BANG

"What's going on!?" Hailey was standing in the doorway of the bedroom.

Les slung the carry-bag handles over one shoulder; it pulled tight against the shirt he wore. "Come on."

BANG BANG

"Where are we going?" Alex asked.

"If there's only three or four of them then we can take 'em. I've got heaps of stakes . . ."

BANG BANG

"How do you know they didn't let the rest out?" Judy yelled. "There's more than three or four out there!"

"How many vampires are at the farm?" Alex asked.

BANG BANG SMASH

"Fuck." Les ran to where Hailey stood and pulled her into the room, and then slammed the door shut. He stood with his back against the door, facing his family. Hailey had been enveloped in

Judy's arms while Alex stood staring back at Les. They could all hear the vampires inside the house; Judy and Hailey jumped each time a smash or thud was heard. Les was breathing hard and staring at the floor.

"What time is it?" he asked.

Judy, Alex and Hailey looked incredulously at Les. "What?" asked Alex.

Les looked up from the floor. "What time is it? How long till dawn?

"Who cares?" Alex said angrily.

"Too long," said Judy. "I know what you're saying, Les, but it's too long to wait. Sunrise isn't till six and we can't hold them off till then."

"But we know it's gonna be a clear day. Last night, evening, the sky was red. It won't be red this morning cause the day will be clear. Red sky in the morning, shepherds warning."

"Red sky at night, shepherds delight," said Alex. "But it's true. We can't hold them back for three hours."

Thud thud

The knocking on the bedroom door made them all jump. Les pressed his back against the door and Alex ran over to help push it closed.

"We gotta think of something quick," said Alex.

"Who are they?" Hailey asked.

THUD

Les and Alex pushed with all their weight on the door.

THUD THUD

"Come on! Suggestions?" Les looked and sounded panicked.

THUD THUD THUD

"WHO ARE THEY?" screamed Hailey, and the pushing on the door stopped.

"Les, you fucker," came a voice through the door. "You lying piece of shit."

"Andrew?" Les' voice was shaking. "Is that you, mate?"

Silence, then "I'm not a 'mate', Les." The word 'mate' was long, drawn out, and full of spite. "You fucked up that possibility when you fucked up our lives."

"Who is it?" asked Hailey in a small voice, to which Judy replied with "Shhh."

"Who have you got in there with you, Les? Have you bullshitted you way into more . . . . .livestock?"

"What's he talking about?" Alex whispered.

"Two kids in there with you, Les? Not much meat on them, mate."

"Les!" Alex looked afraid, yet angry.

"Aw, shit." Les looked on the verge of tears.

"Go on, Les," said the voice through the door. "Tell the kids what you did. Tell 'em how you made us think we were all getting a job. Tell 'em how you locked us is the wool shed with a fucking vampire!"

"I was doing a service! I saved you from prison!" cried Les, no longer able to hold the tears back.

"How did we taste, kids? Like pork or beef? How did you have us? Stir fry or steak? They take all cuts from us."

"Listen, Andrew," Les cleared his throat, composing himself. "You're not gettin' in here so when the sun comes up you're all dead. So you should . . ."

"You're wrong!" The volume of Andrews' voice was terrifying.

"How did you get in?" asked Alex, who was shaking with fear and who was immediately answered with hard looks from Les and Judy.

"Who's that?" asked the voice through the door.

"It's no one . . ."

"Alex," Alex interrupted Les. He saw no point in pretending he wasn't there; the vampires already knew it.

"Alex," Andrew said, contemplatively. "How are ya, mate?"

"Fine," Alex answered, ignoring the continued glares from his audience. "How did you get in, Andrew? Vampires can't enter without an invitation." Alex remembered this bit of information from a vampire film he once saw.

Laughter through the door answered Alex "I never knew that before I became a vampire! Like how sunlight kills us. We only found that one out after Gary and Brooke got caught in it. And we couldn't break any windows here until the little Miss invited one of us in."

Alex, Les and Judy looked at Hailey, whose face was buried in the front of Judy's sweater. She slowly looked up at her family.

"He was at Alex's window," Hailey said in small yet defiant voice. "He looked hurt so I told him to come in and get a band-aid. Then all the banging started and he ran away. I thought he was hurt!" This last statement was broken by sobs.

"Hey, don't cry," said Andrew.

"What do you want, Andrew?" Les interrupted.

"Well, you made us, Les, and you're keeping us in prison. We just wanna be let out."

Alex and Judy looked at Les, who spoke. "Sorry, mate. No can do." This was answered by a huge thump on the door. Judy cried out and hugged Hailey tight.

"Please, Les!" Andrew sounded frantic. "You tricked us! We never wanted this! Give us our freedom!"

Alex had a flash of *Amistad*; the big black guy at the end shouting, "Give us free!" It also gave him an idea. "Were you asked, Andrew?"

"Alex, shoosh!" Les said in a hushed growl, to which Alex answered with a shake of his head and his index finger to his lips.

"What?" Andrew asked.

"Were you asked if you wanted to be turned into a vampire?"

Silence, then ,"What do you fuckin' think? Of course I wasn't!"

"Ok," Alex continued. "If you weren't asked, then that means you wouldn't have answered. Right?"

"Yeah, no shit."

"Well, you know how you didn't realise that sunlight killed vampires? There's another thing you wouldn't know. And that is that if someone does a favour for a vampire then that vampire has to do a favour back. Did you know that?"

"No,"

"So, if Uncle Les made you that means that he owns you, and if he decides to let you go then you have to do a favour for him. And I reckon that a good favour would be for you all to leave town."

Silence behind the door mirrored the disbelief on Alex's side. His finger was still up to his lips.

"How do you know all this?" Andrew asked.

"I'm a huge vampire nut. I've read everything about them." Les, Judy and Hailey gaped at Alex.

"It's not just me, here." Andrew was trying to sound threatening but he just sounded nervous.

"I know. But didn't Uncle Les make all of you?" Alex looked at Les who was shaking his head. "Well," Alex said. "Except for the first one. Where are they?"

"We ate it," the voice through the door was insipid so Alex knew it was working.

"Well, that's it," Alex said. "If we let you go then you have to leave town." Alex was looking excitedly at his family.

"What does Les think?" Andrew sounded defiant yet scared.

"I think you have to leave town, mate," Les said, smiling. "It's the rules."

"What if we come back later on? I know you don't live here, kiddo. Who's gonna stop us coming back?"

"You could come back but do you remember what happened when your friends went out in the sun? Times that by a hundred."

Once again, there was silence behind the door. Then "You better not be lying to us, kiddo."

"I'm not!" Alex said. Then more silence.

"Ok, we're going," Andrew said. "But, remember. We know where you live, Les. If we get bored out in butt-fuck nowhere then we'll come looking for you. We'll come looking for all of you!" And with that, the family listened as the vampires rounded themselves up then disappeared down the street. Inside the bedroom, Les gave an audible sigh and looked at Alex.

"How did you know all that?"

"I don't," Alex said, still wide-eyed and shaking. "I made it up."

The family stared at Alex. "What if he finds out you were lying?" Judy asked. Alex answered with a shrug, then "I don't know how he could. I mean, I don't know where you'd find out about vampires, so how would he? It got rid of them, though."

"Come 'ere, mate," said Les, grabbing Alex and hugging him. "That was pretty quick. You can come down here any time and be our security."

When Alex and Hailey arrived at their local train station, their parents were there waiting with the expected hugs and questions that revolved around the usual. How was their stay? What did they get up to? How was the food? Alex answered this in what felt like an unintentional monotone while Hailey was as animated as ever. Nothing was asked about their early homecoming.

That night, after dinner and after Hailey had worn herself out with her endless talking, Alex's dad entered the bathroom while Alex was brushing his teeth.

"There was no problem with you two staying at your aunt and uncle's, was there?" Alex's father was a tall, skinny man who looked uncomfortable with yet suited to his work with computers.

Alex spat a gob of toothpaste into the basin and looked at his father in the bathroom mirror. "Nup." Alex bent down to the tap and filled his mouth with water. He spat, and then looked up at his father. "I just didn't realise how buggered I was going to be after school was over. I feel like I need a week's worth of sleep." He laughed when he said this last part and, thankfully, so did his dad.

"Yeah," his dad said. "Two weeks' holiday just isn't enough when you're in high school." He ruffled Alex's hair as he said this. "'Night, son."

"'Night, dad." He put his toothbrush back into its holder and watched his fathers' reflection leave. Alex felt stronger somehow, like he had achieved something important. Saving his aunt, uncle and sister from the hoard of vampires that had threatened them made Alex feel accomplished and down-right clever. It made him feel a step closer to being a man. He stood in front of the bathroom mirror looking, marvelling, at himself when movement behind him caused distraction. "Dad?" Alex asked the reflected darkness behind him. Something in the darkness moved. "Hailey?" he asked as he turned to face whoever it was.

"Alex," the shape said, and he immediately recognised the voice as Andrew. It stayed concealed in shadow as it quietly spoke. "You have to help us, mate."

Andrew stepped forward into the bathroom and into the light therein. Alex instinctively flinched away from Andrews' advancement. His appearance not only made Alex want to run screaming, it also made him want to retch from misunderstanding. The only parts of Andrew that were at all recognisable as being a human body were his hands, feet and face. All the other parts were, as far as Alex could make out, growing back. Or covered by a blood-smeared t-shirt that hung from Andrews' shoulders and a grimy pair of sweat-pants that clung, sticking with blood, to his hips. Alex swallowed, making an audible clicking sound.

"Andrew, I . . . what . . ."

"You have to help us, Alex!" Andrew came closer, making Alex press hard against the basin and vanity. "Most of us are dead. We've got no-where to go. We can't stay in the bush cause we get attacked by animals and we can't stay in the city cause we get attacked by people. We don't know how to defend ourselves."

Andrew was now standing directly in front of Alex. There was a smell coming off of Andrew that reminded Alex of something. It was the way an aroma can force a process of reminiscence. It was the same way the smell of his mothers' shampoo, a sickly yet sweet scent of fake berries, would remind Alex of summer when he was young because his favourite icy-pole had the same smell. But the smell coming off of Andrew was more familiar to Alex, as if he had experienced it in the not too distant past.

"Andrew, what are you doing here?" Alex was trying to focus on not letting his bladder go. "What are you . . ."

"I'm here for you!" Andrew whispered gruffly, grabbing Alex by the shoulders. "You know about us, what we are, so we need your help. We've been through the worst shit you can imagine. We just wanna go home."

Alex realised why he knew the stench coming off of Andrew. It was the smell of the town where his Aunt and Uncle lived. That whole place didn't stink the way Andrew did, but the beginning of every gust of wind held what now wafted from Andrew; bile, blood and decay was emanating from his breath and body. But Alex recognised this smell from further back in time that his recent trip down south. He recognised it from when he was a child and visiting Uncle Les and Aunt Judy. So, how long had the town been breeding vampires? And had Uncle Les helped the farmers with their livestock the whole time? No, thought Alex. If Uncle Les had, he would've known how to save his family when the vampires were loose. This thought enticed Alex to do more of what he had done on the night he became an in-house hero. Make shit up.

"Andrew, there was a part of the rules I forgot to tell you. You don't have to stay away from the whole town. Just Les and Judy's place." Alex stared back hard at Andrew, whose eyes widened.

"Do you mean that we can go back there? We can go home?" Andrew looked excited, like he had just won the lottery.

Alex forced a smile in return. "Yeah. I'm sorry I . . . fucked up."

"Oh, man. Forget it. You just told me the best news I ever heard." He said this while backing away from Alex before stopping. "We just gotta stay away from Les and Judy, yeah? Otherwise the shit hits the fan?"

"Yeah." Alex gave his reply quick, too quick; he sounded nervous. Andrew looked confused, but shrugged it off.

"You're the expert, mate. Thanks." And with that, Andrew went out the bathroom door and disappeared.

Alex waited for ten seconds, twenty, thirty, then turned and threw up into the basin. He filled his mouth with water and spat. He splashed water on his face then paused. He looked up at his reflection before turning to face the doorway. "Shit." Andrew had gone out in the direction of Hailey's bedroom.

Alex bolted from the bathroom, turning left down the passage toward her room before skidding to a stop. Hailey's door was open.

Her door was never open. "What have I done?" He forced his legs into motion, walking slowly towards her bedroom. He stood in the doorway a moment.

"Hailey?" No answer.

He felt on the inside wall next to the door for the light switch, found it, but waited before turning it on. He didn't know what he would see in his sisters' bed. What if Andrew had gotten at her? He might not have. He seems like an alright bloke. But still, what if? What if he had done more to her than just drink her blood? Alex didn't know if he wanted to be the one to find his sister violated, to find her drained of blood and who knows what else done to her.

"Get with it, Alex," he whispered through clenched teeth. He was breathing heavily and his hands were in fists so tight that he could feel his fingernails biting into his palms. "Hailey, I'm turning your light on."

The click of Hailey's light switch showed the usual messiness of her room; her floor was a colourful confusion of toys, pencils and Texas. Alex turned his gaze slowly toward Hailey's bed, toward Hailey who was sitting with her back to the wall and her arms wrapped around her legs. Her eyes were shut, her cheeks wet with tears. But her neck is what Alex focused on. Her neck with the two puncture marks and the trickle of blood that had stained the collar of her nightie.

"Hailey," Alex said as tears sprang to and filled his eyes. Hailey opened her own eyes and spoke in a tiny voice.

"My neck hurts."

AFTERWORD TO "SKY IN THE MORNING"

The older relatives in this story are a mixture of both sets of my own grandparents who were and are characters in their own right. I'd like to thank them for their inspiration and hope readers find them interesting and entertaining. The setting is inspired by a mixture of any and all small towns I have ever visited. The story is inspired by the by a want of something new in the vampire genre. No-one, as far as I know, has ever told a story where the humans use the vampires as a food source.

TAKING IT FOR THE TEAM

TRACIE MCBRIDE

"Fuck. Fuck, fuck, fuck . . ." Corey clutched his head in his hands. He had a bastard of a headache, a naked blonde stranger comatose next to him, and a huge hole in his memory.

Situation normal. He looked at the clock. 11.15 pm.

Normally at this time of night he was just getting started. There was a reason why he had been asleep, he had kind-of-sort-of planned it that way, he just had to remember what it was . . .

"Fuuuuck!" His coach Henry had scheduled a special evening training session for midnight, and he was going to tear Corey a new one if he was late again. He nudged the girl next to him.

"Wake up, darling, wake up," he cajoled. No response. He rolled her over onto her back. Drool trickled from one corner of her lipstick-smeared mouth, and she snored loudly.

Still alive. That was always a good sign. He hadn't lost one yet, but the mere thought of the headlines—AFL STAR IN DRUGS DEATH SCANDAL—made him jumpy. He slapped her tentatively about the face in an attempt to rouse her. Didn't want to be too rough—he could hardly afford to add woman bashing to his list of transgressions. Eyes squeezed shut, she threw her arms up over her face, muttered incoherently and burrowed under the blankets.

Corey checked the time again, looked back to the blonde, then back at the clock. He could always just leave her here while he went to training . . . But the last time he'd done that, he'd come home to a ransacked apartment. No, he'd have to get her out of here.

"Shitfuckshitfuckshitfuck . . ." He hopped around the room with one leg in a pair of sweatpants while he searched for something that might contain the girl's ID. He found her handbag out in the lounge.

Bingo. There was a driver's license bearing the name of Kylie Harris, and a photo that looked vaguely like the woman in his bed. He hoped the address on the front was current as he dialled for a taxi. Returning to the bedroom, he levered Kylie into a sitting position and manoeuvred her into the mini dress he found on the floor. There was no way she was going to make it down the stairs in the stilettos she arrived in, so he stuffed them in her handbag. Outside, a taxi horn sounded.

"Money. Shit. Shitfuckshitfuck . . ." He went on a frantic search for his wallet. Miracle of miracles, it was on his night stand, and it contained close to $500.

Corey frowned. He couldn't have had that good a time if he still had that much cash still on him. Unless . . .

He looked sideways at Kylie, who sat swaying on the edge of his bed, and shrugged. He hoisted her to her feet and half carried her down the stairs to the waiting taxi, peeling off $50 for the driver and stuffing the rest into Kylie's handbag. Whatever anyone said about Corey Boyd, he always settled his debts, even if he wasn't always sure if he owed them.

One problem solved for the day. Now to get to training. A quick dash back upstairs, snatch up his keys, thumb the button to open the garage door . . .

The garage was empty.

"Fuuuuuuck!"

† † †

It was past 12.30 by the time Corey arrived at the training field. The rest of the team jogged up and down under floodlights, their breath pluming in the unseasonably cool late summer air. Composing his features into his best approximation of wide eyed innocence, Corey broke into a trot to join them. Tom Bentley sneered as they drew level with each other.

"Christ, Boyd, you reek. What did you have for dinner, half a bottle of tequila?"

The others didn't even deign to acknowledge him. Arseholes. It wasn't as if the rest of them were as pure as the driven snow.

"Nice of you to join us, Mr Boyd." Henry stood on the sidelines clutching his beloved clipboard and bearing a sardonic smile. Christ, he hated it when Henry smiled like that. It could only mean someone was going to suffer. One of these days he was going to take that clipboard and shove it up Henry's . . .

Corey smiled to himself, lost in the fantasy as he jogged around the perimeter of the field. Heedless, he ran into the back of Jason Steele, sending them both tripping and stumbling.

"Watch it, Boyd, ya dozy prick!" Corey dodged the blow lobbed at his head.

A piercing whistle split the air. Corey winced as it set up an agonising counterpoint to the throbbing in his brain. The other players ran as obediently as dogs over to Henry. Corey paused in a micro-moment of defiance before trailing after them. He knew that, after turning up late to training for the fifth time in a row, his best bet was to keep his mouth shut and his head low, yet he found himself asking the question that must have been on everyone else's mind.

"What's up with the Saturday night training session, Coach? You're fu . . . messing with my social life."

"Several reasons," Henry replied. He tucked his clipboard under his armpit and began to count down on his fingers. "Number one— circadian rhythms."

"Circa . . . what?"

"It's an experimental new training technique," Henry continued. "Similar to the principle of training at high altitude or while carrying extra weights. Training late at night puts an extra load on an athlete's system, so when he resumes a normal schedule, his output will be significantly increased." Henry shrugged. "At least, that's the theory. If it doesn't work, then there's always reason number two—the scheduling of this training session for a weekend was deliberate. I reckon that the team's social lives have had a major influence on us finishing bottom of the table last season. This way, I'll have the satisfaction of watching you lot sweating away your Saturday nights on the field instead of being out on the piss or on the pull.

"And if you'd bothered to turn up on time, you'd have been here when I was explaining reason number three. Speak of the devil—here come our special guests now."

Corey's interest sparked in spite of himself. A rival team, perhaps? Or some rugby union pussies? He followed Henry's gaze as he turned to watch the figures emerging from the tunnel.

Whoever their guests were, they were evidently not professional football players. The six people gathered before them in their ill-fitting training strips were an assortment of sizes, builds and ages. One was a woman, and at least two were of an indeterminate gender. The only thing they appeared to have in common was a distinct pallor to their skin. In fact, they were so white, they almost glowed.

"Uh . . . we're training with computer programmers?"

Henry tossed a ball to one of the newcomers, a curvy little redhead who looked like she didn't know one end of a football pitch from the other. She hefted it experimentally in one red-taloned hand. Corey preferred his women a little more tanned, but she had a certain appeal. He had just begun to imagine her naked, when she drew back her arm and threw. It was an awkward, cack handed toss, yet the ball flew through the air faster than his eye could follow and hit him squarely in the chest, knocking him on his arse. He lay on his back, squinted up at the floodlights and gasped for breath while the rest of the squad snickered.

Gingerly, he rose to his feet. No way was he going to let that lily white bitch get the better of him. "Nice chuck, sweetheart, but in this game, a proper pass goes like this." He balled his right hand into a fist and punched the ball back to her.

Coach and the woman exchanged something—a fleeting look, a tiny nod, it was barely noticeable, but Corey was caught it. They were setting him up. For what, he didn't yet know. It was the not knowing that made the hair on the back of his neck stand up.

"OK, gentlemen. Split into two groups. They're the foxes, you're the hounds. Try to catch them. Go!"

Corey looked at Henry incredulously. This was under 14's baby stuff. Why the fuck weren't they running some proper drills? Henry returned his gaze impassively. They locked eyes for several long seconds until Corey looked away.

"This is bullfuckingshit," Corey muttered under his breath as he ran to join his team.

The redhead was a 'fox' in his group. He dearly wanted to run her down, to wrap his arms around her waist, to plough her face first into the turf and claim it an 'accident', but he avoided her for now. She'd keep. He was unused to delaying his gratification, and the decision made him feel both proud of himself and slightly ill at ease. He turned his attention instead to a tall, painfully thin young man with long black hair that flopped across his eyes. The bloke looked as fragile and ungainly as a daddy long-legs. He turned away from the squad and began to run, taking great loping inefficient strides with his bony elbows flapping like wings. Corey didn't even start after him; moving like that, he'd tire in less than two minutes, and Corey could run him down at his leisure.

Something jabbed him in his already tender ribs, and Corey yelped. Samson Tawhai, the assistant coach, prodded him again with the riding crop he carried to all training sessions.

"Coach says 'jump', you say what?" Samson bellowed. Whereas Henry was always experimenting on the team with painful new training techniques, Samson was stuck back in high school with his approach. Still, he was widely tipped to be the next head coach. He'd been a legend on the field in his day, which only made Corey resent him even more. Corey scowled and moved off after the human spider.

Something odd was going on. The rest of the squad pounded down the field, sweat flying and limbs pumping, and Corey had to extend himself to catch up to the stragglers. Yet the 'fox' maintained a two metre distance between himself and the front runners without appearing to even try. Incredibly, he turned around and began to run backwards, taunting the 'hounds' with a 'bring it on' beckoning hand gesture.

And still they could not catch him.

This had to be some kind of trick, some elaborate practical joke staged by the bosses for some obscure publicity purposes. Corey stopped and looked around the field in search of concealed cameras.

"Whassamatter, Boyd, you too good to run with the rest of them?" It was Samson again. He swatted him on the butt for emphasis. Corey's felt the rage build, and forced himself to count backwards from ten; he'd already suffered a three week suspension and hefty fine for punching Samson. One of these days, though, Cory was going to catch him off duty and off guard. Then he'd show him how to really wield that riding crop.

Henry's whistle sounded again, and the squad gathered around for further instruction. Many of the players were bent over and heaving for breath, and they all dripped with perspiration. Their opposition, on the other hand, looked like they'd done nothing more strenuous than finish their lattés. A theory began to form in Corey's head. This lot weren't computer programmers; they were chemists. What they were seeing here was a demonstration of a potent and probably illegal new performance enhancing drug.

"Is that the best you can do?" Henry's voice dripped with scorn. "Swap places. You wimps are now the foxes. Anyone lasting less than five minutes gets two extra hours of training at 6AM on Sunday morning. I'll even give you a twenty metre head start—GO!" With a chorus of grumbles, the team set off.

"What are you doing still standing here, Boyd? Do you want four hours training on Sunday?"

"I'm not doing it, Coach." Corey stood with his arms crossed over his chest and smiled slyly. "You and I both know that it's impossible to beat these guys. Not without whatever they're on." He tipped Henry a conspiratorial wink.

"Corey, Corey, Corey . . ." Coach shook his head. It was the first time he'd heard the coach call him by his first name, and for a moment it rattled his resolve. "You really are the biggest fuckwit on the planet, aren't you? All right. I give up. You win. Join in, sit it out on the bench, I don't care anymore."

Corey sauntered for the sidelines, but it was all an act. Despite Henry's concession of defeat, he had never felt less like a winner.

† † †

Corey hugged himself against the cold. The squad had been running after or away from their training partners for the better part of two hours, and it had exhausted them more thoroughly than the toughest Grand Final game. He had watched the White Guys, as he had mentally nicknamed them, intently. Whatever they were peddling, it was a beautiful drug. They were still going strong with no sign of tiring and no evidence of a messy come-down. He wondered if their extreme paleness was a side effect, then thought—fuck it. Looking like Casper the Friendly Ghost would be a small price to pay for that level of speed, strength and agility. Whatever they were on, he wanted some. Badly.

Henry gave his whistle one long blast, a reedy Last Post to signify the end of the training session.

"Gather round, boys. Before you hit the showers, I'd like to you offer thanks to our friends."

Offer thanks. It was an oddly formal thing to say. Formalities made Corey uncomfortable, which was why he liked to turn up to awards ceremonies half-cut and stumbling. And the way everyone was staring at him made him even more uncomfortable.

"What are you shitheads looking at?"

Aaron Sinclair stepped forward and shoved him in the chest. "We're looking at you. Shithead."

Corey shoved him back. For a moment it looked like it was all on, and Corey relished it, needing some kind of physical conflict to counteract the mental and emotional strangeness of the day. It was either this, or head for a bar and pick a fight with a stranger, which, knowing his luck, would end up splashed all over the papers. Both options would land him in the shit, but he knew which pile would be shallower.

But Aaron merely raised his hands in mock surrender and retreated. The rest of the squad had surrounded them, and now they parted to leave Corey hemmed in on three sides and facing the White Guys on the fourth. Somebody pushed him in the back, and he sprawled forward to fall at their feet. The little redhead put her boot on the back of his neck and pinned him to the ground.

He knew without even trying that it would be pointless to try to escape. He lay on the ground trembling with rage. The squad filed past him prone in the dirt, and they all had something to say.

"You're a liability, Boyd. You're not half as good as you think you are, and you're a disgrace to the profession. You've had this coming for a long time."

"Fun's fun, Corey, but you just take it too far."

"You crashed my car."

"You broke my nose."

"You fucked my wife."

The coach was last. Corey twisted under the redhead's boot so he could look up at him. Henry tsk-tsked at him from a great height.

"You had such promise when we signed you, Corey. I really thought we could knock off those rough edges, turn you into a man instead of the hundred kilo tantrum throwing toddler that you are. But you just wouldn't listen. Do you know I argued on your behalf? I wanted to drop you from the team, cancel your contract, but the bosses wouldn't have it. Said it would cost too much in lawyers' fees."

Henry sighed. "Still . . . I always say that every man has his uses. Looks like you're best employed serving as an example to others if they persist in fucking up."

"I can think of at least one other use for him." This from the redhead as she released the pressure slightly on the back of his neck. Corey flipped onto his back to gaze into her green eyes.

How had he missed those eyes before? It felt as if she were lifting him up by the mere force of her gaze. His cock stiffened in his shorts, and he writhed anew beneath the weight of her boot. She looked hotter and hotter by the second. Christ, he was so horny, even some of the blokes were starting to appeal. Maybe, he thought hungrily, this was a practical joke of an entirely different sort.

The redhead looked away, Henry nodded to her, and the spell was broken. She leaned down, grabbed Corey by the collar, and pulled him up with one hand, lifting him effortlessly off the ground. He dangled in her grip like a chastened puppy caught by the scruff of his neck. He was suddenly, dizzily aware of just how terrifying these computer programmers, or chemists, or whatever-the-fuck-they-were looked up close. Those eyes, so captivating before, had turned as cold as a shark's. They smelled of copper and moist earth, and their skin had no pores, and right now if someone were to tell him that they had no souls to match, he would have believed them.

Then they all smiled.

Ah, thought Corey, so that's what death looks like. His mind quietly slipped off the edge of the Insanity Pool into the deep end.

They took him by the limbs, spreadeagled him, and pressed their fangs to his skin, to wrist and elbow and groin and neck. The redhead's canines grazed his cheek as she murmured in his ear.

"Come on, Corey, don't struggle—sometimes you just gotta take it for the team."

AFTERWORD TO "TAKING IT FOR THE TEAM"

When we moved from New Zealand to Melbourne, Australia in 2008, it seemed like the first question we were asked as we stepped off the plane was "so . . . who do you barrack for?" I thought that New Zealanders were passionate about their Rugby Union, but the Victorian obsession with AFL takes it to another level. The media coverage of AFL players' off field antics continues to bemuse me—if one believes everything one reads or hears in the news, then those sportsmen are very naughty boys indeed.

How naughty is too naughty? How does one punish a 100kg Naughty Boy, insulated as he is in a swaddling of status, money and contract law? And where do the vampires come in? These are a few of the questions I have tried to address in "Taking It For The Team".

ALL THAT GLISTERS

PETE KEMPSHALL

Hanson dug his fingers deep into the seat on either side of his thighs as the Land Rover bumped down the unsealed road. More than once, all four tyres left the ground, sending a jarring shudder through him when—after an eternity—the vehicle reconnected with the earth. The pain was only bearable because it signified Markham hadn't flipped the vehicle off the track and killed them. Yet.

Hanson rated his chances of chundering were about even, and when that happened . . . that kind of stink in this kind of heat, it'd be on for young and old. His stomach flew up into his throat as once again the Rover took to the air.

Markham shot him a look and cackled. "Too rough fer ya? Better hold onter yer lunch, mate: gets worse before it gets better."

"Perhaps if you slowed down a little?" They were maybe halfway down the dirt road which spiralled down the inside of the crater—it was 150 feet straight down if they came off it.

"Nah, mate," Markham grinned. "Better get youse all started down there, right? Time is money."

"Certainly is, Mr Markham." Hanson forced a smile.

Prick.

† † †

Hanson had been spared the call-up to Vietnam. The asthma that ensured he was picked last for every sport and game at school meant he wasn't picked at all when his fitter contemporaries were shipped out. With so many his age getting shot to bits in country, doors had opened for little Geoffrey Hanson. Big business rolled on, regardless of foreign wars, and in a reduced talent pool, Hanson became a good pick, a resource. And the chiefs at Global Mining knew a resource when they saw one . . . before long he had an office, he had a secretary, he had big bucks. He had it made.

Then the troops started withdrawing.

He had seen the way the Vice President had been looking at him, had known it was only a matter of time before the axe fell. So many new workers, so many with a killer instinct Hanson lacked. But if he was in any doubt, Hanson had realised just where he stood in the grand scheme the moment he was allocated Gabe Markham.

Crammed into a collar and unfashionably narrow tie, it wasn't that Markham had been wearing a suit, more that the suit had been wearing him. Constantly reaching up to finger the starched cloth as it rubbed and scraped at his neck, Markham was at once visible as a man more comfortable in a singlet, shorts and broad-brimmed hat, dunking sheep. If nothing else, that made him intriguing: for him to go to such testing lengths to look the part, to make the right impression suggested to Hanson that Markham might need Global more than the other way around.

"So what can I do for you, Mr Markham?"

"Your lucky day, today . . ." Markham had squinted at the nameplate on Hanson's desk in the way of someone who can read it perfectly well but who wants you to know you're an effort. " . . . Geoff. Today, you get first option on my mine."

"Is that so, Mr Markham? And what mine would that be?"

Then Markham had told him, and a future at Global didn't seem so out of reach after all.

† † †

"How's over there grab you?" Markham took one hand from the wheel to point at a clear spot in the rocks, and the Rover slewed towards the edge of the track. Hanson's arsehole clenched.

"Fine."

"Only I reckon it'll be easier to pitch the tents there, right?"

"Right."

With a final lurch, Markham crunched the Rover to a halt. No more than a second later, he screeched open his door and stepped out into the open air.

Hanson stayed in his seat. The small fan on the Rover's dashboard didn't pack much cooling power, but that didn't mean he was ready to leave it just yet. Positioning his face in front of the weak draught, he let the air play over the sweat that had accumulated in his moustache. He didn't get out into the field much, and had dressed for the trip without really thinking about it, just on the smart side of casual. Now his tight shirt was adhered to his skin, and he wasted no time stripping his tie from around his neck. He stuck it in the glove box, and with a sigh of resignation, stepped out of the Rover.

Almost everyone in the business had heard about the Dwyer Crater—a hole in the world made by a meteorite God only knew how long ago—but the superstition surrounding it meant Hanson hadn't been able to find a single man who'd been down there. The look of the place bore that out. Bleak red dust and rock stretched a quarter mile to the other side, the occasional stubborn, scrubby bush or gnarled tree the only things to break the monotony. Yeah, he could easily believe no one had set foot there in 70 years.

Now here he was to dig up the whole damn thing.

A crunching rattle signified the arrival of the second ute, negotiating the seldom-used track with decidedly more caution than Markham had shown. Hanson would have been more comfortable riding with the survey team, but apart from the need to maintain a professional distance from them, he knew full well that Rigden and Bayliss came as a matching pair. Not so long ago he'd gone to the pictures to see the new Bond movie—there'd been a couple of hitmen in it, chasing the same diamonds Connery was after, and every time they'd been on screen, Hanson had thought of the surveyor and his geologist partner.

The taller of the pair, Rigden, opened the passenger side and stepped out. His bear-like other half squeezed out from behind the wheel, but rather than follow his partner, he stuffed his keys in his pocket and walked to the rear of the vehicle. Popping open the tailgate, he started rummaging around.

"He's distracted," Rigden said with a smile. "Meteor hit like this one, unique soil composition, gets him all . . . you know."

Sure enough, when Hanson looked back to Bayliss the big man was on his knees, scooping dirt into a container.

"'Bout time you showed up," Markham chipped in, as if the pair had been a week behind him rather than two minutes. Hanson had suggested the pair because he knew he could trust them, and hadn't given any thought to what Markham would think. But from the second Markham had laid eyes on the couple at the pre-expedition briefing in Perth, it'd been clear what he thought of their proclivities. "Let's get on with it, eh?" He headed off, leaving a trail of shallow footprints in the dust.

Rigden muttered something Hanson didn't catch, and set off after him.

†   †   †

The instant he'd ended that first meeting with Markham, Hanson had been on the phone. The first call confirmed Markham was desperate—he liked the gee-gees, debts into five figures. The second furnished Hanson with all the information about the Dwyer curse he could get.

A bunch of diggers filed claims on the land in 1898 after finding nuggets in the crater, unearthed hundreds of years before by the meteorite, they reckoned. The old boys pitched in together and started digging. Then just as suddenly, they stopped.

The next time anyone saw one of the Dwyer miners was when one turned up in town to announce the pit was closed. The land, he'd said, had killed his mates, every last one. He now had sole rights to the crater, and he was declaring it off limits, in perpetuity.

And that's the way it stayed. From one generation to the next, the man and his family—the Markhams—ran off anyone looking to recommence digging. Until Gabe Markham had the sudden urge to sell up.

"What do you think?" Hanson had asked on their second meeting. "The place really cursed?"

"Bollocks it is," Markham had sneered. "Buncha blokes die in a mine, mysterious causes . . . bloody obvious, mate."

"Is it?"

"Radiation. Ain't just gold down there, that other stuff too. Uranium. Back then, they wouldn't have a flamin' clue what was killin' 'em."

"Could be. Could be radium, could be gas for all we know— mines can be full of it." Hanson had changed tack, decided to play dumb. "May I ask why you've decided to sell? I mean, your family's held onto the land for—"

"My family's dumb as a sack fulla hammers, Geoffie. Superstitious old shit's standin' between me and a fortune. Between *you* and a fortune."

Hanson smiled. *Hit the nail on the head there, mate.*

†   †   †

The hole in the crater wall was partially overgrown, one of the few places where the vegetation had established a solid hold. If not for the half-buried, rusted tracks disappearing into it, you could miss it altogether.

Markham took a large, wicked-looking knife from his belt and started to prune away the undergrowth. As the mine entrance was revealed, a piece at a time, Rigden sauntered forward and cast an eye over it.

Hanson saw Markham's shoulders stiffen at the man's approach.

"Not too shabby," Rigden called out. "Vertical supports look strong enough, horizontal's weaker, but we should be good." He pulled a large torch from the bag of equipment slung over his shoulder. Shining a beam into the hole, he squinted down it.

"So what d'yer reckon?" Markham stood with his arms folded, in what Geoff could only interpret as an attempt to stare Rigden down. "In and out, coupla hours. Bob's yer uncle."

"Doubt it." Rigden nodded towards Bayliss, who was at last ambling over from the ute. "Adrian and I will need to make a proper survey to assess—"

"Crap," Markham spat. "Gold and uranium down there, you see if there ain't."

"I will, mate," Rigden said, ice in his tone. " I will."

"Let's keep the champagne in the bottle for now, Mr Markham," Hanson said. He treated the older man to a disingenuous smile. "I'm sure you understand Global didn't get where it is today by investing blind."

Markham snorted and turned back to the vehicles. "Best get them tents up then."

Hanson relaxed a little. "You heard the man."

†   †   †

Markham drained his drink, a bubble of beery gas rising to pass the last of the liquid on its way down. Pushing himself up on unsteady feet, he tossed the bottle into the darkness beyond the campfire, where it broke with a desultory tinkle.

"Need a piss," he slurred.

Rigden watched the older man grab the rifle he'd leant against the Range Rover earlier that evening and stagger into the night. "What's he think's going to happen? Bunch of possums going to mug him?"

Bayliss chuckled. "He's probably worried you'll go after him, give him a hand."

"Keep it up, maybe I will."

"Better if you back off a bit. Both of you," Hanson chipped in. "If he wants a new survey team instead of you, that's your twenty grand gone."

"You're that sure there's something down there?" Bayliss asked.

"There'll be gold at the very least," Hanson replied. "There were enough witnesses way back when who said the miners were raking it in. Uranium . . . All comes down to what you 'independent assessors' say." He raised his bottle to the couple in salute. "Just file your report, downplay whatever you find down there and you're quids in."

Rigden allowed his smile full rein. "Be a pleasure fleecing that homophobic fuck. I'd almost do it for free."

Out beyond the firelight, the crunch of disturbed earth. The three men tensed, eyes straining into the darkness.

Only after half a minute or so, when Markham failed to appear, did the trio relax.

"Sounds like your possums are watching us, not him," Hanson quipped.

"Course—no point mugging someone who's not got two cents to rub together, is there?" Rigden said.

The fire cracked and popped.

"Does it bother you?" Bayliss asked at last.

"The man's an arsehole, he deserves everything he gets," Hanson said.

"No, this." Bayliss swept an arm around the shadowed vista. "You get your way, the company'll dig the whole lot up. All the things that live here, all the things out there we can't even see—"

"You not happy with your cut?"

"Yes, I—"

Hanson leaned in to fix the large man with a stare that brooked no argument. "If we can't get this land from Markham—and I mean cheap—I'm done at Global. Out on my arse. If avoiding that means digging a bloody great hole where there's already a bloody great hole, that's fine by me." He sucked in a deep breath. "I'm sorry. This time tomorrow it'll be all over and we'll all be a lot richer. Let's just focus on that." He straightened his back, feeling the muscles crunch in his shoulders. "I'm off to bed. Try and control yourselves around Markham."

"He should be so lucky," Bayliss replied. "I wouldn't touch him with someone else's."

† † †

The protective suits may well have been proof against radiation, but they were bloody useless when it came to the sun. Even this early in the morning, Rigden could feel the sweat trickling down his back, past the crack of his arse to run down his legs and pool in the boots of the all-in-one outfit. He shot a look at Bayliss, whose extra bulk would mean he'd feel the heat even more, and wished that he'd thought to get the equipment ready before putting on the rad suit.

Bending down, Rigden picked up the flimsy looking plastic helmet that completed his protective ensemble and pulled it down over his head. At once, the clear face plate started to steam up, the world outside receding into the fog. He could feel Markham's eyes drilling into him, prejudice burning like acid.

"You ready?" Hanson said from off to his left.

"Ready."

"Channel eight, right?"

"Stay tuned."

And hefting his equipment bag over one shoulder, Rigden pushed his way into the mine.

The feeling was like those hot days on the farm, when he and his brother had made the long walk up to the dam, arriving drenched in sweat and not even waiting to take off their clothes before diving in. That instant transition from bright heat to cool, welcoming darkness, that melange of relief and excitement, was exactly what Rigden felt now.

He shuffled forward to make room for Bayliss, the bulky suit inhibiting his movements. Not waiting for his companion, nor for his eyes to adjust to the gloom, he unclipped the heavy-duty torch from his belt and clicked it on. A slim shaft of yellow illumination speared out to be swallowed by the blackness a dozen feet into the tunnel.

The set-up looked solid—surprisingly so, given the mine's history. He panned the torch light over the struts supporting the roof, and liking what he saw, set off deeper into the mine. A trickle of dust fell from the roof, pattering onto his helmet and shoulders in a red drizzle.

"Is it okay?" Bayliss asked, his voice muffled by the helmet.

"Reckon," Rigden replied. He tucked his torch under his arm and reached into his instrument bag. Pulling clear his chunky grey Geiger counter he switched it on, and, after retrieving his torch from his armpit, swept both around the tunnel.

Bayliss held his breath, the better to hear the metronomic ticking of the counter. "So far so good?" he ventured.

"Hmmm."

"Gas?"

Rigden checked another meter. "Nope."

"So we're okay then."

"Uh-huh. Let's make some money."

†   †   †

"Second gallery clear, radiation nominal. Moving on.

Hanson depressed the talk button on the radio handset. "How's the mineral content?"

"Nothing exciting," Bayliss's voice crackled back. "They either worked the place pretty hard or there was nothing here to begin with."

"Any chance of something deeper in?"

"Let you know." Rigden, this time. "Maybe something next level down."

"Check in again in half an hour," Hanson said. "Base out."

Hanson's mouth tightened. Both Rigden and Bayliss had been briefed against the possibility that Markham would eavesdrop on the status reports, and they'd agreed on a code phrase for a big find. Neither had used it.

Which meant they really had found nothing.

He rose from his seat at the folding table and ducked out of the tent. Outside, the light seared his eyes, and he took a moment to adjust. Tinny music issued from the 8-track in Rigden's ute—the Partridge Family. Markham had set to rummaging through the vehicle as soon as the men had entered the mine, and was steadily working through the cassettes. Even by Hanson's low standards, however, this was a nadir.

"So yer poofters haven't found anything?" Markham had another beer in his hand, glugged on it.

"They aren't my anything, Mr Markham," Hanson countered. "They're independents. And there's still a lot of mine to explore."

"Something special down there, mate. You better believe it."

"I do, Mr Markham. I have every faith."

Yet as Markham grunted and wandered away, Hanson couldn't help wonder . . . if that were true, what was he so afraid of?

†   †   †

After another hour of exploring side-tunnels and galleries, taking samples and measurements, they came to the drop off. But if the struts that held the tunnel up were still strong after nearly 80 years' abandonment, the ladder to the next level down was a different story. Peering along his torch beam, Rigden could see fragments of the rudimentary apparatus lying in amongst the loose rocks at the base of the shaft.

"How about that?"

Rigden turned to where Bayliss's torch played on the roof. A pulley had been driven into the stone, threads of rope still caught up in the mechanism. He saw them sometimes in these old mines, rigged to lift heavy baskets of ore to the surface.

"Don't want to chance it," he pronounced, and slipped the straps of his equipment bag from his shoulders. "Best stick with our own."

With practised ease, he took the hammer and a couple of pitons and drove them into the edge of the shaft. Bayliss held a light on the bag while he extricated a rolled-up rope ladder and attached it to the holding points. He tipped the end of the ladder over the edge and it uncoiled into the dark.

"You go first," Bayliss said, removing his own pack and tying a rope to the straps. "I'll lower the gear."

Rigden lay flat on his stomach, edging his legs backwards into the void until they touched one of the wooden rungs. The climb was tough, hampered by the bulky radiation suit, and even in the cool subterranean air he was sopping before he reached the bottom.

At the head of the shaft, he could hear grunting and the slither of rope on soil as the packs descended. The moment the bags reached the ground, he stooped to untie them, and as his gloved fingers struggled with Adrian's knots, his eyes strayed to the fragments of ladder on the ground. From the top of the shaft, he'd assumed they'd rotted. Up close, looking at the splintered remnants, it was clear they'd been smashed.

†   †   †

Markham sat slumped against the side of the Range Rover, the high sun melting his beer buzz into lassitude. He lit up and scowled at the mine entrance. What if those flaming queers *didn't* find anything worthwhile? He pulled on the cigarette, enjoying the crackle of the tobacco. No, they'd find something. All those stories his dad had told him, passed on from his dad before . . . if they were only part right, this place was a licence to print money.

Then again, if they were right about the gold, who's to say they weren't right about—

"Busy then?"

Markham rolled his eyes up at Hanson, cigarette hanging loose from his lips. "Flat chat, mate."

"Any danger of you putting that out? I'm asthmatic."

"No, mate," he said, smirking as Hanson muttered at him and retrieved his medication from his pocket. "No danger of that at all."

†   †   †

"What do you reckon?"

"Reckon it's what we're here for."

"We clear?"

The Geiger counter in Rigden's gloved hand ticked quietly. "We're clear."

Bayliss pulled off his helmet and sucked in lungsful of cool air. It tasted gritty, old. It tasted wonderful. "Better get some samples then." He placed his headgear on the ground, then shucked his heavy gloves and placed them on top of it. Bad enough climbing rope ladders in the things, but some of his collecting equipment was fragile and if he didn't have to wear them he damn well wouldn't.

"Survey team to base, survey team to base, come in." Rigden released the button on his walkie. It hissed at him. "Survey team to base, come in."

"What's that code word again?" Bayliss asked.

"Low-level incidence," Rigden muttered, twisting a knob on the receiver.

"Bugger all low-level about this."

Rigden's radio spat and farted static. "I'll have to climb up a level. Might as well start lifting the gear too."

Bayliss glanced up at him, a sweat-slick tendril of hair hanging in front of his eyes. "No worries. Two minutes and I'll give you a hand."

"Take your time."

Straight away Bayliss bent to his task. He unscrewed the cap on a small glass bottle, then placed it on the ground beside him before

— 326 —

rummaging in his pack for a small hand pick. The noise of Rigden's steps in the soil receded up the tunnel, and all was quiet.

He picked up the bottle and held it against the wall while delicately chipping at the rock with his other hand. The dead air in the tunnel gave the pick a flat, unechoing tone, the silence quick to suck it away. A small chunk fell from the wall and landed neatly in the receptacle. Even in this dim light, Bayliss could see the lump had enough metal content to send Hanson into cartwheels.

He sat back for a second, planting his hands behind him to take his weight, letting them sink into the cool earth as he enjoyed the moment. A find like this gave him twenty thousand reasons to celebrate.

The faint crunch of shifting earth behind him told him Rigden was back.

"Any luck getting through?" he asked, and twisted round to smile at his lover.

†   †   †

Rigden heaved himself over the edge of the shaft, and lay panting for breath. Fuck, he'd be glad to get above ground, heat or no heat. Taking a tight hold of the rope Bayliss had tied off for the equipment, he started to haul it up the shaft, hand over hand, inch by muscle-straining inch.

Even through the helmet, the scream stabbed into Rigden's ears. Startled, he released his grip on the rope, and heard his pack of instruments smash on the rocks below. Without a second thought, he was swaying down the rope ladder, accelerated heartbeat thumping in his ears.

A second scream reverberated around the tunnel and Rigden released his grip on the ladder, letting himself fall the remaining few feet. He landed heavily, the wind knocked from him. The torch, clipped to his belt, strobed madly around the rock walls. Still the shriek sustained, then choked off with abrupt finality.

Rigden tried to stand, and felt pain shoot up his leg. The fall had gashed open the leg of his suit, the small cut on his calf already crusted with dust. Unclipping his light, he waved it down the tunnel, the beam dancing unsteadily. "Adrian?" He tested his weight on his injured leg, found the pain had dulled to a gentle throb, and started down the tunnel, one unsteady foot in front of another.

†   †   †

"Rigden, Bayliss, you receiving? Rigden? Bayliss?"

There'd been no contact for an hour. The pair's last report had been that they were descending into a deeper part of the mine, and Hanson knew that there might be a problem getting a radio signal out, but that didn't stop cold tendrils of panic burrowing deeper into his chest.

"Give 'em another ten," Markham said. "Prob'ly just stopped for some private time."

Hanson bit back his response and concentrated on the radio. Even inside the tent, the temperature was intense and sweat saturated his moustache, leaving damp smears on the receiver as he held it to his mouth. "Rigden, Bayliss, come in."

"Jesus!"

Hanson looked up from the radio to see Markham barrelling out of the tent, the canvas flap fluttering in his wake. Pent-up dread erupting, Hanson raced after him into the glaring light. Squinting, he recognised the white of a radiation suit, crumpled on the red earth, and ran faster.

Rigden lay on his back, pale, eyes sunken and glaring up at the sky. Despite his bulky outfit and the heat of the midday sun, he shivered like a man hypothermic, his breath a shallow, gasped panting. His radiation suit was torn, crusted with red dirt, and there was no sign of his helmet, nor his equipment.

Nor Bayliss.

Markham fumbled around the thin man's neck, loosening the protective suit. His fingers touched the stricken man's skin and he snatched them back as if burned. "Christ, he's cold . . ."

"What is it, shock?" Hanson asked.

"How the fuck'd I know?"

Hanson felt a surge in his head. "I'm calling the flying doctor."

"Yer wasting yer time!" Markham spat. "Yer won't get a signal down here, have to drive up top, use the CB in the Rover."

"Fuck!" Hanson stumbled out of the tent towards the vehicle, threw open the door and piled in. The key was in the ignition—he twisted it and the engine caught first time.

Thank you.

Wrenching the gearstick into first and feeling the clutch bite, he floored the accelerator.

And went nowhere. The tyres spun, spraying dirt in a fountain of red. Swearing, he engaged four-wheel drive and tried again. The vehicle lurched, then seemed to sink even further into the ground. He cut the engine and jumped from the cab.

"Fuck you doing?" Markham screamed in disbelief. "You bogged it!"

Hanson circled the Rover, checking the tyres. Every one was halfway past the hub-cap in dust.

"How the fuck you bog it?" Markham ranted.

"I'll take the ute," Hanson snapped, stepping towards it and stopping short. "Keys."

"Try the ute, smartarse."

"No," Hanson recalled aloud, "Bayliss was driving, he put them in his . . ."

As one, the men turned to look at the mine.

"Shit," Markham hissed.

"Can we boost the walkies?" Hanson asked.

"Ten mile hike to the nearest hill and stand on top . . . maybe." Markham spat into the dirt.

"He last that long?"

"Fucked if I know."

Hanson stood with his hands on his hips, bent double. He needed to get control, even if only a little. "Get him in the tent."

"The hell for?"

"Jesus fucking Christ, just grab his legs!"

Taking the strain, they heaved Rigden to the tent. Via his grip under Rigden's armpits, Hanson could feel the tremors running through him, transferring a chill into Hanson's own body.

Pushing backwards through the tent flaps, Hanson shifted his weight to manoeuvre his end of the burden onto the low camp bed. The whole time, Rigden's body remained stiff as a board, his eyes staring up at nothing.

The second Rigden was in place, Hanson turned and started to root through the camp equipment piled at the rear of the tent. He pulled out the first aid kit and set to work. Taking a pair of scissors he began cutting away the radiation suit. As he spread the material away from Rigden's frame, dust poured out in a dry waterfall.

"His leg's cut," Markham murmured from the other end of the camp bed.

Hanson put down the scissors. Through the open white leg of the radiation suit, he could see the raw, ragged rip of a wound, less cut than torn apart . "He must have fallen, gouged it on something . . ."

Wheels spun in his head, gears meshed. "Maybe it's blood loss. He's pale enough . . ."

But Markham just stared at the wound for another few seconds, then turned and walked out of the tent.

"The hell do you think you're doing?" Hanson called after him. He hadn't placed the hard-bitten bushman as squeamish. The last thing he needed was Markham going into shock, he needed someone to work on the walkie talkies. If Hanson's first aid was barely up to snuff, his technical skills were non-existent.

Reclaiming the scissors he cleared the white material away from Rigden's wound and started to clean it. Grit and earth had packed into the long cut, and he reached over to the folding table for a canteen of water to irrigate it. As far as he could see there were no other injuries, maybe if he could stem the blood loss from here—

Why isn't there any blood on the suit?

The thought ambushed him, knocked his mind flying. Big wound, apparent massive blood loss, and the pants are clean, bar the dust . . .

"Markham! You need to take a look at this!" Hanson ducked out of the tent, hand up like a visor against the sun. Expecting the older man to be halfway up the track to the top of the crater, he was surprised to see him by the mine, hacking at one of the better established trees with his knife. By his feet sat what looked like a parcel, wrapped in brown paper.

"What the fuck are you doing?" Hanson called out as he trotted over to the older man.

"Saving your bastard life!" Markham snapped back, putting his back into chopping. A thick branch fell free and landed on the ground. At once, Markham stooped and started to carve at it.

"It's not my life needs saving—I need you to look at Rigden's leg!"

"Seen it," Markham sneered. Hefting the sharpened stick, he strode back towards the tent, brushing past Hanson like he wasn't there.

"No, you need to look, there's no—"

The blow caught him under the left eye, a snake-swift strike with Markham's full weight behind it. Hanson sprawled to the ground, extending his hands just in time to stop himself landing face first. Propping himself up on all fours, he was dimly aware of Markham striding into the tent before vertiginous nausea took hold.

He crawled towards the ute, used it to drag himself upright. His hands left bloody prints on the paintwork; must have scraped them when he landed.

From inside the tent, a scream.

A moment later, Markham staggered through the hole in the tent's side. Determination shone in his eyes. Determination and something else. Without a second glance at Hanson, he headed towards the Rover.

Woozy, Hanson made his unsteady way to the tent and half fell inside.

Rigden lay on the cot, unmoving, as if the sharpened wood protruding from his chest had nailed him there. The tiniest pool of blood had welled around the wound.

Hanson snatched the scissors from the cot. Legs like water, he stepped back into the sun.

Markham was still rummaging in the back of the Land Rover, oblivious to his approach, or not caring.

"What've you done?" Hanson shouted.

"He had to die. Before it got too late."

"Too late for what?" Hanson thought his head would spin clean off, which was why he only remembered the rifle a second before Markham pulled it out of the Rover.

"Easy there, mate," Hanson said, feeling his breath catch in his throat. He had to slow things down, get close enough to use the scissors tucked up in his palm. "Why don't you just put that down and tell me what's going on?"

"They were right," Markham called out. Cradling the rifle in one arm, he reached into the Rover with his other hand. The brass casing of the bullet sparkled in the sun as he loaded it into the breach. "I thought it was all just bullshit, but they were right."

"Who?"

"Me dad. His dad."

"What do you mean?"

"You see that cut on the poofter? No fucking blood. Not a drop, not on his leg, not on the suit, nothin'." Markham slammed the bolt of the rifle into place. "Weren't radiation killed all those miners."

"What then?"

"Vampires."

Hanson felt the laugh build in his chest, an irrational reaction to an irrational situation. "Fuck off."

"Think about it. Always dark down there, right, no sunlight. Makes sense, yeah?"

"No. Makes no sense at all."

"Why else would my family stop anyone digging there, huh? Fuck me, why couldn't I just listen to them?"

"Listen to yourself, Markham. Think. If you're right . . . it's daylight now. They can't come out in—"

"That other poofter, you see him come out of there?"

"Bayliss? No . . . we have to—"

"Good." Markham took aim at the mine and fired.

The blast wave knocked Hanson off his feet, pounding the air from his lungs. Dust filled his eyes, his mouth, his throat, and his chest felt crushed, useless. Something trickled stickily from his ears, the sound of his heartbeat loud in them, but distorted, like he was underwater.

His mind lurched. The paper parcel Markham had left outside the mine . . . must have taken it from Bayliss's ute. He and Rigden carried a certain amount on jobs . . .

He turned his head, feeling the dirt scrape his cheek. In the settling dust, he saw Markham, the top of his body inside the Rover, legs on the bonnet, surrounded by glittering crystals of glass. Flaming idiot'd had no idea how much he was using.

Hanson choked on the settling dust. He had to get the company here. He didn't care about the gold, only that they come, that they bring machines. That he survive long enough to see them dig the whole fucking place up, expose whatever was under there, even if there *was* nothing under there . . .

He had to move. Breath coming in laborious, uneven gasps, he tried to move his hands towards his pockets, towards his medication.

He couldn't. Focusing on his hands, he saw his fingers clenched into the dirt, locked there. Concentrating, he willed his hand up.

Not clenched.

Held.

The red dirt seethed up over his skin, like water swamping a tidal pool. In seconds his hands were covered, then his bare arms. He could feel the grains rising over the back of his head, pulling, tugging. Sucking.

His skin reddened where it touched the ground, dozens of tiny pinpricks of crimson welling from his pores and into the dirt. The thick trickle from his ears increased and he felt the blood vessels in his chest, his face, his eyes rupturing. His mouth opened in a cry of agony, and the dirt swarmed into it, rushing in, filling the spaces it emptied as the very land sucked him dry.

And for the barest of moments, the earth was truly red.

AFTERWORD TO "ALL THAT GLISTERS"

There's a reason why all that dirt's red, right?

Quite how I arrived at that particular thought escapes me. It just bubbled up from somewhere as I tried to think of an idea for an essentially Australian vampire story. Here was a way for me to write something about haemovores that came at you from out of left field, that encouraged you in your expectations of what a vampire story should contain, then swerved away at the last second.

Of course, I needed a reason why the very ground would attack someone. Thanks then to my day job, for providing me with the simple answer of "self-defence". A story had crossed my desk about a mining company's massive new pit, located slap in the middle of a site of unique natural significance. A thinly veiled recruitment document for the mining sector, the tone of the piece was that this was somehow a good thing . . .

In turn, the idea that the environment is fighting back against those who would bleed its resources sent me in the direction that all the characters in the story should be, in some way, vampires—metaphorical "bloodsuckers" who will drain their principles, their land, even each other if it got them what they wanted. It was an element that was much more "on the nose" in the first draft, so a big thanks to Russell for asking me to rewrite!

And why the 70s? Well, there's not much of a story if the characters have sufficiently high tech to escape the threat, is there? And it just so happened I'd been watching Diamonds Are Forever *with my son . . . if you want true horror, there's always the safari suit.*

THE RIDER

MARTIN LIVINGS

The Rider's body sits opposite me, slumped in its chair as I sit in mine, a strong young man on either side holding it steady by its shoulders, wearing thick gloves for protection. Its mind, though, its jagged, alien mind, that's nestled against mine, searching for a warmth and safety that it will never find. Outside the room, I can hear the thump-thump of music, people dancing to Cold Chisel, drinking too much, slinking off in pairs to quiet corners to feel each other up. I envy them. I *was* them once, young, free. Happy. I can barely remember it now. It's for the best, given the circumstances.

"Emma?" One of the young men speaks to me, his eyes concerned. He's new, Bill I think his name is. This is his first hunt. Victor brought him in, after Nathan was killed during our last outing, swallowed whole and spat out, empty and inert and cold. I don't feel anything, of course, not for Nathan, not for Victor, who I've hunted alongside for two years now, and certainly not for Bill. That's the whole point. It's what makes me useful.

"What?"

"Is he . . . I mean . . . ?"

I nod. "It's here. Trapped."

Trapped. The word echoes in my mind, spoken by two silent voices, my own and the Rider's. Mine has a note of satisfaction in it, but the Rider's holds something darker. Fear, yes, which makes me smile, but also a vicious determination.

"Are you alright?" Bill reaches a trembling hand out towards me, towards my arm, bare besides the bracelet of dark blue beads.

"*Don't touch me!*" I hiss, and he snatches his hand back like he's touched a hot stove plate. I take a deep breath, soften my tone. "It's not safe to touch me. Not while it's here."

"Even with the gloves?" he asks, his voice small and frightened, a child's voice.

I sigh, feeling so very tired and old, barely twenty years of age and already done. "Yes, Bill, even with the gloves."

That's nonsense, you know, child, the Rider whispers in my head, coiled around my core like a snake. *I cannot transfer without either physical or emotional contact, and that boy has neither with you.*

"No shit," I mutter.

"What?" Bill asks.

Victor slaps Bill hard on his upper arm with the barrel of the pistol he holds in his free hand. "Shut it," he grunts, and turns to me. "How's it going in there, Em?"

I look up at him and nod. He's so relaxed, so confident. Another me might once have found this man attractive. But that me is long gone. Now I'm something else entirely. Cold, alone. Safe.

Safe, you say? The voice in my head distracts me from my own thoughts. *But at what cost?*

"Shut the hell up," I say through gritted teeth. This time Bill doesn't respond. He's learning. Good. "I didn't choose this. You did."

Not I, child, the Rider tells me. *Another.*

"You're all the same," I spit at the hollow shell seated before me. "Fucking parasites." It doesn't respond, of course; the Rider has been drawn into me whole, like being sucked out of an airlock into the vacuum of space, or falling down a well. Or into a tiger trap. I smile a little at that thought, a dark, grim kind of humour. That's what I am now, all that's left of me. A human tiger trap.

It was four years ago now, when I first met a Rider. I was on the Gold Coast for schoolies, into my third day of breaking as many of my parents' strict rules as I could manage when it found me, dancing in the street with dozens of other recent high school graduates. I'd taken some ecstasy and was flying, watching my hands over my head dart and weave like birds in the sky. The music was alive, pulsating in my head and gut and, yes, lower still, awakening a warmth there. And then *it* found me, touched me on the shoulder with its host's fingers, kissed my neck with its host's lips, led me aside into an alleyway and . . .

"We are all parasites," I say, but it isn't me speaking this time. "Every living creature in the universe. We all survive by taking from others."

I take back control of my mouth by force. This one is still strong, stronger than I expected. "Bullshit," I mumble, my lips novocaine numb. I look at the Rider's empty host sitting before me. A middle-aged man, salt and peppered hair receding, dressed casually but smartly. He'd called himself Gregory Marshall, in the flyers advertising this B&S Ball and a dozen others before it, offering free entry, a live DJ, cheap booze. Victor had tracked this one down, introduced me to some of its victims. All still alive, a pleasant change, but drained, empty. Cold. The looks in their eyes, young men and women alike, were reflected in my own, but amplified, distorted, like a funhouse mirror. I was them, only more so. I was a possible future. Death was another.

I'd dressed like a slut, of course, like so many other women here. Bait. I danced and pretended to get drunk. I flirted with this man who stayed in the shadows, always watching. I got close. He got close. Too close.

The trap was sprung, the Rider fallen into me, and Victor and Bill had taken Marshall's limp body between them, hurried it and me back here, to this room at the back of the hall. Locked the doors. Waited for the inevitable.

"I never take it all, child." My numb mouth is speaking again. "You have so much, and I so little. Is it so wrong?"

Look at me! I try to yell, but I only manage it inside my head. *This is what you did to me!* My mouth, though, remains obstinately closed. *Shit!*

"Em?" Victor asks, "are you okay?" I try to look up to him, but my eyes are as uncooperative as my lifeless lips, fixed resolutely on the host in front of me. The concern in his voice, though, it strikes a faint chord in my cold heart.

"Ah," the Rider says with my mouth, "there is something inside you after all, yes?"

No, I think, then wrest control back again. "No," I say out loud, and it feels good. I look up at Victor carefully, but feel nothing. Good. "No, there's not."

I should have died that night, in a dark alleyway in Surfers. The Rider that took me there intended to devour me, I knew that as it swallowed my mind, my heart, my soul. Our thoughts were one, and I knew its dark intent. It drained me, took everything I had, everything I felt. All the light and warmth inside me. Then it was over, and it let me fall to the ground, limp and lifeless and unwanted as a broken doll. It walked away in its human skin, refreshed, energised, filled to overflowing with me. Danced into the crowd beyond the alley. I was alone, empty and cold.

I should have died that night, but I didn't. My friends found me there, thought I'd had way too much to drink, took me back to the hotel. I stayed in bed for two full days, silently feeling the hollow spaces inside me where my spirit used to be. Searching the cracked and broken corners for any sign of who I'd once been. There was none.

On the third day, I rose and went back into the crowd, searching for the creature that had emptied and discarded me, a beer can in the gutter, nothing more. I saw the thing's host on a street corner, watching groups of teenagers walk by with a hunger in its eyes, a desire that should have made me shiver but didn't. Anyone else would have seen a toolie, an adult predator in a children's playground, looking for fresh meat. They would have been close, but still dead wrong. I knew better.

I walked up to the Rider, grabbed its face, and kissed it. Its reaction was automatic, instinctive, and catastrophic. It connected with me, ready to drink and drink again of me, but all it found was emptiness, a vacuum. And, unable to pull back, it fell into me. Its body, empty itself now, fell out of my embrace to the ground, and its head hit the street kerb with a wet crunch. Its wide open eyes died as I watched. As *we* watched, both through my own eyes. I felt it raging within me, like an animal caught in a trap, throwing itself against me time and time again in desperation as its hollowed body perished on the street outside, lifeblood pouring from its shattered skull into the gutter. Then its thrashings inside me became weaker, until there was nothing at all. It was dead, outside and in.

And I knew then what I could do, what I had to do.

You would have recovered, you know, child, the Rider's voice purrs in my skull, silent again now, blissfully silent. *The spirit would have regenerated eventually. Had you but allowed it.*

"It tried to kill me," I said coolly.

We are not all alike. That one may well have intended to consume you whole. I, however, did not. You have so much, it repeated, *and I so little. I never take it all. Just enough to survive. I never take it all.*

"Oh no?" I ask. "What about Gregory Marshall? What about your host?"

The Rider is silent in my head for a few telling moments. *It was . . . necessary*, it says at last. *I do what I must to survive, as do you. We are all parasites. We are all energy thieves.* I can sense it working within me, even as it tried to reason with me, looking for anything, a crack, a loophole, some last vestige of affection it can use. There is none, though, I know that. I've spent the last three years making sure of it, in between hunting these monsters down.

"You have a choice," I say at last, speaking to the body sitting before me. "That's more than I had."

A choice? It actually sounds amused. I'm amazed it has the strength left for that. It can't have long, not in the Arctic wasteland inside me. *And what might my choice be?*

"Return to your host," I tell it.

And then your companion will kill me.

"Yes." There's no point lying. Our thoughts are one. There's no fooling it, any more than I could fool myself.

And my second choice?

"Remain inside me," I say. "And die slowly."

These are my choices? the Rider asks. *Neither is very attractive.*

"That's life, buster," I mutter. "Take it or leave it."

I have lived for a thousand of your lifetimes, it says, and the truth of the words strikes me like a hammer, resonates through me. I feel every single one of those thousands of years, all at once. I see men tilling fields with oxen, hunting deer and cowering in the night from the lightning. Stone becomes bronze, bronze becomes iron, iron becomes steel. I see millennia pass before my eyes as if heartbeats. And throughout all of this, I feel myself feeding on the joy of those around me, sometimes by a touch, sometimes just through the emotional connections between his victims, crossing miles in an instant and plunging into the heart of some distant loved one like an arrow. I'm tasting their love, their happiness, their bliss. And, as each host grows old or weak, I take another, and another, and another, draining each utterly and filling it up with myself, leaving the rotting flesh that was once mine behind. So very many times, so very many lives. My head feels like it's going to explode.

I am truly sorry, child, the Rider says through the ancient memories, its voice old and sad, *but I cannot choose death, not anymore. Release me now, allow me safe passage to my host and away from here, and it will be as if nothing happened.*

Despite my disorientation, I actually laugh out loud at the creature's bravado. "Really?" I manage to say. "And if I don't?"

Then I shall do this.

I leap from my chair and hurl myself at the two men standing opposite me, my limbs no longer my own. One hand curls and strikes out at Bill's chin, hitting it sharply, not with a lot of force, but enough to send him staggering back in shock. He stumbles and falls to the floor. The other hand seizes Victor's crotch and squeezes there as hard as it can, my long nails digging deep into the denim. He shrieks and releases the host's shoulder, but his other hand thankfully retains its grip on the pistol. I find myself a prisoner behind my eyes again, as the Rider rides me, an obedient horse under his masterful control. But my mouth is still my own.

"Shoot him!" I scream at Victor, whose eyes are watering with pain now. He grits his teeth, swings the gun around, and fires a single shot into the host's head. There is a spray of blood from the other side, and Gregory Marshall tumbles sideways off his seat and onto Bill, who is kneeling on the other side. He yelps as he and the corpse collapse to the floor in an awkward bloody embrace.

No!

My hand is still embedded in Victor's crotch, a clawed death grip. He drops the gun to the floor and tried to pry me off him with both his hands. One hand finds my wrist, and his fingers entangle in the bracelet I wear there.

"Don't touch that!" I cry, tears suddenly filling my eyes. And then I stop. Everything stops. Victor just looks at me, dumbfounded. Bill still struggles to free himself of the dead host that lies atop him. But the Rider no longer rides. It's as if the reins have been pulled, and I've skidded to a halt.

Well then, it says softly in my mind. It reaches down with my free hand, touches the blue beaded bracelet on my wrist with its fingertips curiously. *What have we here?*

"Nothing," I lie. "Just a stupid bracelet." But it's no use. Our thoughts are one.

No, child, it says, and I can feel the satisfaction in its silent voice in my head, *everything else you wear is just a costume, bright colours to attract your prey, but this . . . this is something else. Something still significant.*

"No . . ."

Show me.

And it reaches deep into me and finds a memory, buried so deep that even I wasn't aware of it. My Auntie Sarah, sitting with me on the veranda of her tiny farmlet in Central Queensland, late in the afternoon, the hot humid air in my nostrils tinged with the smell of an apple pie cooking in the oven inside. Her hand on my shoulder, a gentle touch. *I'll always be here for you,* she tells me, and I smile despite my tears. I feel safe. I feel warm.

I *feel.*

Yes . . .

And the Rider takes that flickering ember of a memory in its cupped hands, and gently blows onto it, bringing the glow back to a flame. It comes alive inside me, filling me up with emotions all but forgotten, burning bright for a long, wonderful moment before, with a single breath, the Rider inhales it, swallows it in a single gulp.

Then they're both gone, the feeling and the Rider.

"No!" I scream. I collapse back into my chair, suddenly freed from the Rider's steel grasp, and my hand finally relaxes and releases Victor's bruised genitals. He staggers backwards, face pale, eyes wide. Bill, covered in blood, is crawling out from beneath Marshall's body, empty now, abandoned, like a boarded up house or a used condom. Someone is pounding on the locked door from outside, yelling at us to open up. I try to ignore the sound, search frantically in my mind for any sign of the Rider, but there is none. It's moved on, used that last fragment of energy to escape me.

And I know where it's gone. May God forgive me.

"Phone!" I bark at Victor, and he doesn't hesitate, even though he has no idea what just happened. He's a good soldier. He reaches into his back pocket and tosses me his mobile. I dial a number I haven't dialled in so many years, a lifetime ago, a number I had no idea I even remembered until now. The digits come to me so naturally, so easily; it fills me with dread. The phone rings there, four times, five.

A click as it's picked up, but no words, just breathing.

"Hello?" I say, cold fear wrapped around my spine. "Sarah?"

"*Hello child,*" the reply hisses in my ear, and I recognise the voice, recognise it twice. It's Auntie Sarah's voice. It's not Auntie Sarah's voice. It's the Rider's voice.

I want to cry, want to scream and rage and wail, but there's nothing left inside me to do so. It's stolen that from me. "No," is all I can manage, my voice flat, dull. Dead. "No," but the connection has been severed, in every possible way. The phone is silent in my hand, my heart in my chest. I look at Victor, and he sees that in my eyes that we've lost, lost everything. Bill just looks confused on the floor, a dead man's blood soaking his clothes.

And, as the door breaks in and half a dozen burly, drunken men charge inside, their eyes widening as they see Gregory Marshall's murdered body on the floor, I close my eyes, lost in the utter emptiness inside myself, and let the darkness finally take me.

AFTERWORD TO "THE RIDER"

When I first heard about Ticonderoga's Dead Red Heart *anthology, I was completely stumped. I'd never written a vampire story before, let alone an Australian vampire story. How could I come up with an idea? I wracked my brain for weeks on end, throwing things around but never finding a decent story. It was hopeless.*

Then, one morning, I woke up with not one, but three ideas, all at once. One of them ended up being way too big, and might end up in a novel one day. The second I approached in a collaborative fashion, and appears elsewhere in this anthology as "The Tide". But the third, well, that one I found myself becoming increasingly excited about. The idea of an emotional vampire, hungry for pleasure, and a scarred victim who'd unwillingly become a human pitcher plant for these creatures. The shades of grey between good and evil, in a simple battle for survival. And how holding onto any humanity whatsoever can sometimes be deadly.

VITALITY

GEORGE IVANOFF

The Hills Hoist creaked eerily as it spun slowly in the hot wind, labouring under the extra weight. It was one of those old-fashioned clotheslines, common in the 1950s, and still in many a suburban backyards today. Although old and rusty, it was strong and sturdy and reliable, and likely to still be there years from now.

I approached through the twilight-darkened yard. The dead grass, baked from green to a dull yellow by the long summer, crunched lightly under my bare feet. I could smell the blood in the humid air long before I saw the bodies. There were two of them, upside down, strung up by their ankles with a thick rope and tied to opposing cross-supports.

As I got closer, I saw a ring of dark red on the concrete beneath the bodies. The stench almost made me gag.

I stood and watched as the corpses went slowly around and around, mesmerised by the grisly carousel, until the hot wind began to subside. It was several minutes before the air finally stilled and the Hills Hoist ground to a creaking halt.

I stared at the body before me. It was a girl, her tank top clinging to her, her skirt falling the wrong way, revealing pale pink knickers. I crouched down to look into her lifeless eyes. Green eyes in a pretty face, flecks of dried blood like freckles across her cheeks, more of it matted into her long blonde hair. Her throat had been torn open, her blood drained. She looked like she was in her mid-teens. I wondered if the house beyond the clothesline was where she had lived, if her parents were inside, unaware that their daughter had been hung out to dry.

I stood up and moved towards the second body. It was a boy—about the same age as the girl, maybe a little older. Her boyfriend, perhaps? He wore only shorts, his chest battered and scratched, the result of a hopeless struggle. He was taller than the girl, his arms hanging down limply, his hands, grazed and bloody from being dragged across the concrete. Dark rivulets wound their way from a bite in his neck, down across his face and into his hair—so thick with sticky red that it was impossible to tell its original colour—and then dribbling to the ground beneath him.

There's only one of them, I realised. If there were more, then both bodies would have been dry. Hunger had been sated, but both had been killed and strung up. Conclusion—it wasn't just a matter of food; this one enjoyed the killing. That made things simpler for me.

Fighting the growing nausea, I crouched again and reached out to touch the boy's arm. His still warm flesh twitched, his eyes fluttered open, his lips parted in a vain attempt to form words, spilling forth only blood. The smell finally overcame me. I staggered back, dropping to my hands and knees, and heaving up a trickle of bile from an otherwise tight and empty stomach.

"If ya can't stand the sight of a little blood, stay out of the effin' abattoir."

The voice grated through the stagnant air, like broken nails on a blackboard.

I looked up to see a shape moving out from the garden shed. The twilight was dwindling, darkness setting in. I caught a glimpse of white singlet.

"They was out 'ere in the shed. Caught 'im with his hand up her skirt. Her old man probably would 'ave killed 'im if I hadn't got to 'im first."

There was a dark chuckle and then silence. I was being scrutinised.

"You been trailing me for a while now, haven't ya?" he said. "Thought it was time to say g'day."

I didn't answer. I stared at him, concentrating on sharpening my night vision. White, stained singlet over a protruding gut, dark stubbies that were way too tight and a pair of old thongs.

"You a copper or somethin'?"

I shook my head and struggled to my feet.

"Whatcha want, then?"

"Let the boy go. He's still alive."

"'Bout as much chance of that happening as a hooker givin' you a freebie."

He walked over to the boy, grabbed an arm and pulled him up at an awkward angle. With his other hand he took hold of the boy's bloody hair and yanked his head to one side. He grinned at me, and a glint of rising moonlight caught his canines. Then he ripped the boy's throat out.

I turned away as the smell intensified, hitting me like a wave. Is there anything worse in this world than the stink of human blood, its vital energies tainted with frailty? My stomach churned, but I held it down, not wanting to show any more weakness.

I forced myself to turn back.

He was grinning at me again, blood dripping down his chin and adding stains to his singlet. He let the boy drop. The Hills Hoist creaked and the boy's knuckles cracked onto the concrete, as the girl was jerked into a ghoulish dance.

"Ya know I'm gonna tear you apart?"

I nodded. "I know you're going to try."

He snorted loudly, like a feral pig ready to strike.

"But first I wanna know who you are. Why you came after me, all alone?"

"I'm all alone because . . . I'm the only one." I faltered. "I want what you have . . . what you've taken. I want your strength . . . your—"

"Oh, for Chrisakes, you're an effin' groupie?"

He leapt forward, knocking me to the ground, crushing the air from my lungs. His body pressed against mine, his hot breath at my throat. He reeked of sweat and human blood and an unnatural, tantalising vitality. He bared his fangs and ran them along my skin, up to my ear.

"Ya want me to turn you?" he whispered, then chuckled. "I feed alone."

"So do I!"

He pulled back and I saw the surprise in his eyes as I grabbed his throat, digging my nails into his soft flesh, pulling it apart like a ripe, sweet mango. I pulled him down on top of me and buried my face in his warmth, taking what he had obtained from so many others. I clung to him as he thrashed about, wondering if this is what it was like when he fed, wondering if my animal lust matched his. The heady scent of his stolen vitality filled my nostrils and overcame my senses—and became mine. He went limp and still I clung to him, desperate for every last drop he could give me.

When I finished feeding, I tossed the body to one side and sat up. I looked towards the boy, now definitely dead, like his girlfriend. I owed my continued existence to them, as much as to their killer. I would never have been able to drink their blood and keep it down. But their killer, the stealer of their blood—that was another matter. His blood was what I craved. The wind started up again, but the heat had left it, signalling the arrival of a cool change, and the bodies swayed in a gruesome slow dance.

I looked back down at my victim. I could feel his vitality, a second-hand vigour, flowing through me like a drug, giving me strength and fuelling my desire to find more of his kind. Of course, I knew that he would recover—slowly, painfully, hungrily—ready to kill again, to take that which he had no right to take. "No!" I breathed, as I shook my head slowly, sadly. And so I reached out to his chest, tore away the fabric, the flesh and the bone, and consumed his dead red heart.

AFTERWORD TO "VITALITY"

"The editor is looking for stories that capture the essence of vampirism and the essence of Australia," said the submission guidelines. What could be more essentially Australian than the iconic, suburban Hills Hoist? When I read the guidelines, an image of a Hills Hoist with bodies hanging from it immediately popped into my mind. I sat down and wrote an opening paragraph. I then got distracted by other projects, and it was several months before I returned to that paragraph and began to craft a story around it, trying to capture what was, for me, the essence of vampirism—the desire and need to feed on human blood. I was struggling through a first draft that wasn't really going anywhere, when I was struck by a thought—What if there was a different type of vampire? A vampire who fed only on the blood of other vampires. Suddenly, I had the story. I hope you enjoy it.

COMING HOME

KATHRYN HORE

She killed the motorbike engine at the top of the hill. For the moment she just sat, one booted foot resting on the ground, stripping off her leather gloves and gazing down the street. It was a dark night, although it took her conscious effort to notice. It was also a warm night, still retaining a hint of the summer day it had been. Heat radiated from the concrete footpaths separating house gardens and nature strips, from the rough black tarmac of the road beneath her. Again, it took a conscious effort to acknowledge this. She wondered why she did. Maybe because the last time she had been in this place it seemed she had noticed such things and they had been then, for whatever reason, important to her.

Around her, houses slept. Nestled in neat rows on not-quite quarter-acre blocks. They had well tended gardens and expensive, mock-luxury cars resting in driveways. Renovations were popular. Every third or fourth house showed some sign of adaptation or restructure, whether it be scaffolding, exposed housing beams, or simply a skip out in front to collect the debris. It was a suburb becoming fashionable, a post-code on the rise; the young income rich were moving in to take over and remodel forgotten elderly homes, with the forgotten elderly moved on elsewhere. All double incomes and hired housekeepers now. She had chosen well, once, back when she had bought into this area, before its remaking and accompanying price rises. Back when she had still cared about such things like real estate.

Once, the house on the corner down the far end of the street had been her own.

Well, the mortgage had been her own. The title had belonged, mostly, to the bank.

The bike's engine ticked as it cooled. She slipped off it and pushed the heavy machine without effort, up onto somebody's well mown nature strip with its browning grass struggling to survive the summer. Kicking down the stand, she laid her gloves over the seat and pulled off her helmet. Her hair was long and fell from beneath it, black like her jacket, like her gloves, like the night about her. Setting off the pale porcelain of her skin, the red of her lips. She hung the helmet from the handlebars. She didn't think twice about doing so. Nobody would steal such things. Not from her.

She unzipped her jacket and glanced over her shoulder back down the hill, towards the house on the corner.

Time to go settle affairs. She could avoid it no longer.

There was a light on somewhere toward the back of the house. She noted the low glow from a side window even before she had stepped into the orderly garden with its low trimmed lawn, hydrangeas failing in the heat, roses thriving against reason. There was a big tree in the corner, a eucalypt that a possum scrambled up as she passed, tail disappearing around a bough. Flitting, flying bugs clustered round street lamps; crickets sounded loud in the warm still. An owl watched, a bat glided overhead; she was aware of all these creatures, alive and active. Life in the night. But all such living things stayed away from her, sensing something they did not want to interfere with. Even the cats slunk back and the dogs, locked behind gates, secured in back yards, did not dare to bark.

She did not go near the front door. She went around the back instead.

Slipping a hand over the catch of the wooden side gate, she let herself through to the secluded back yard. It was large, though a brick surround swimming pool with all weather spa took up a great deal of it, together with the shade-cloth covered patio. It was a familiar place. It felt strange. She thought she should feel more, coming back after all these weeks. She thought she should be more disturbed that she didn't.

She tested the handle of the back door—locked—then turned it with more intent. The lock snapped somewhere inside the mechanism, a sharp crack, and it opened up into a dark, white kitchen. It was a large kitchen leading to a dining room and formal lounge through one door, a hallway through another. The hallway led down past utility rooms, laundry, bathrooms, down some steps, the bedrooms, the rumpus room, the study. It was a spacious four bedroom, two bathroom split level home in a quiet street in a leafy suburb, not far from public transport and less than fifteen kilometres out of the city. The kind of place to make real estate agents and dual-income families who didn't think twice about large debts rather excited, and rising quickly in price in what the media were even now calling a housing bubble ready to burst.

The state of her credit no longer mattered to her. Interest rates no longer mattered to her.

For a moment she stood on the threshold, gazing in with dispassionate grey eyes. Then, with a shrug, she entered, stepping into the kitchen of what used to be her home. Down the end of the longest hallway she could see a light from under the door of the study and, from another doorway, the flickering hues of an ignored television accidently left on, the sound turned low. The rest of the house was dark. She took the hallway, wandered towards the light. It was no use pretending she was just here to reminisce, dwell in the kind of nostalgia she didn't actually feel. She was here for a purpose. She needed to see this through.

He was at his desk in the study, working late. Typical. He always did work long hours. Seventy, eighty hour weeks, sometimes more. Then again, so had she. Once.

"Jackson."

He turned, a sharp, fast movement, and almost fell from his chair in doing so. She had frightened him. That had been inevitable, she supposed.

"Jesus. Anna. What . . ." He dragged off, needing a moment to compose himself. He was still in pressed suit pants from work, though his tie was off and his shirt unbuttoned, and he'd taken off his socks and shoes. The air conditioner would have kept the room cool enough, but he had always been the money conscious one, preferring to remove layers rather than use the aircon, add more clothing instead of heating the place. The fact both of them brought in decent professional incomes meant they could well afford their utility bills, but that hadn't made a difference to his habits. He'd just kept saying it wouldn't be so easy after they had children, they couldn't afford this without two fulltime incomes. They had to save some money. But while he'd fretted about having no savings, she'd simply understood it wasn't his career that having children would bring an end to.

The things which had once concerned her. They seemed so far away now, such distant, irrelevant bothers that no longer made any sense.

"What are you doing here?" Jackson finally managed, and though his face showed concern, his eyes were wary. "Why aren't you at the hospital?"

Ah. The hospital. In the doorway, she offered a languid shrug. "I live here, I believe."

"Yes, but . . ." He dragged off again. For a man who made his living crafting legal arguments, he was sure struggling to find the words he wanted now. "Anna, you're sick. You need to be in the hospital."

"I am perfectly well, Jack. In fact, I don't think I've ever felt so well in all my life. I've never felt so . . . in control."

She stepped forward. He almost instinctively leant back. "You're working late."

"I have to if I want to make Partner next year," he said, as if she should already know it, and she did, it just no longer seemed so important. "Someone's got to pay the mortgage."

Had she really thought like that, before? She must have. She had worked just as hard, chased partnership in her accounting firm just as fervently as he did in his solicitor's office. She glanced down at the papers on his desk. It spurred movement in him and he gathered them quickly, slipping one page deftly behind another. A medical invoice with an all-too-familiar logo. Her eyes narrowed.

"What was that?"

"What? Nothing."

She reached down and plucked the page from his hand. He wasn't quick enough to stop her. He would never be quick enough to stop her. She looked at the accounts upon it, the figures running down in a fine list of itemised medical expenses. The most private of private doctors; expensive and discreet. But the cost he was prepared to pay did nothing to console her.

Her eyes darkened. "You knew."

"Anna . . ."

"You knew where they had me." She threw the paper back at him. It fluttered to the floor between them. "You've been paying their fucking bills."

He stood up and reached out a hand to her. Maybe he meant to lead her to a chair, as if she were an invalid. Maybe he meant to secure her until he could call the doctor. Either way, she backed off a quick step and would not let him touch her.

"Sit down, Jack."

"Anna, please, you know . . . Well, you know." His face contorted. She supposed he really did care. "Have you had . . . you know, medication?"

Medication? That was what they were calling it? It almost made her laugh. That she could appear standing suddenly right behind him, having crossed through doors he had no doubt locked himself, and his primary concern was whether they had already fed her this night.

Her fingers curled, stiff and clawed. To try and manage this, she made them into fists. She could feel her own nails bite into her palms.

"You're worried I'll take you," she said, a dare for him to deny it.

He ignored that. "I'm just worried about you. Dr Johnson says—"

"Doctor fucking Johnson and his fucking *medication*," she snapped. "It's pigs blood, Jack. Pigs blood laced with high grade morphine."

He was silent. His mouth opened as if he wanted to say something, but no words came out and she supposed that was inevitable. What could he say? That he had known they were keeping her drugged senseless as that was the only way to keep her under control? Or that he hadn't cared to investigate just what his wife's very expensive private hospital treatment entailed?

He certainly couldn't claim he didn't know why she was in there. He might comfort himself by reasoning it an illness, but he still knew the facts.

"Morphine?" he finally croaked. So it was the opiate, not the blood, which shocked him; his new friends must have kept him at least partly informed. "Anna, they promised me, you have to understand. They promised—"

Promises. So many promises. She was sick of their promises. The pretence she was merely ill, that what they did was done for her, all hiding that biting reality underneath—they were afraid of her. He, Jack, was afraid of her.

In an instant she moved. Quick and sudden and beyond the ability of his human sight to capture. One minute she was standing across the study from her husband, an argument like all other arguments, late at night and still half dressed from the day's work. The next she was in his face, one hand grabbing his wrist, the other twisted in the back of his hair and pulling back his head.

His neck was bared. Her mouth inches from it. He cried out a sudden shock.

She didn't do anything. She just let him register that she could have, then she let him go. "Don't worry, Jack. You're not my type. I guess you never were."

"Anna . . ."

She turned, stalking back down the hallway, refusing to listen. Why had she even come here? What had she thought to achieve? He saw her the same as his friends did. A predator, a creature to fear. There was nothing here for her now.

Down the hallway, past the big mirror. An empty mirror as she walked in front of it. It made her stop, it made her want to laugh again. She stood directly in front of that mirror and all she could see in it was her own house stretching out behind her. They had kept all mirrors away from her at the hospital. They had thought it might disturb her, agitate their patient. But it wasn't her who was disturbed by such things, they were the one who seemed so worried by it all. The men around her. The doctors, the professors.

Jackson. Her husband.

How could he? How could he let them lock her up like that?

She heard Jack stumbling after her, trying to call out, and everything was suddenly bathed in yellow. He had turned on the overhead lights so he could see, a pulsing current in a bulb throwing out a good seventy watts. In his rush to reach her, turning the corner of the hallway, he knocked a vase from the low hall table. Expensive porcelain crashed against the ground, a splintering of painted china. Thin slivers, large chunks, it shattered everywhere. Insurance would cover it. They had top cover. Accidental breakage was written into their policy.

She turned, cocked her head as he jolted a sudden stop. He stood surrounded by shards of original Meissen, wearing no shoes or socks. It kept him in place as firmly as locks and restraints had once kept her. He was afraid to move, in case he cut himself. Afraid to incur a wound, however small, that might bleed.

But still he stretched toward her, trying to hold out a hand.

"Don't go, Anna," he said and he sounded genuine. "I'm sorry. I'm really sorry."

"For what? Lying to me? Or being so afraid of me that you let them take me?"

"No. I never. I never lied." His face twisted, a sudden dark frown. "And what else could I do? After . . . after what happened?"

He looked so torn. Standing there trapped by porcelain and desperate to explain. But how could he? He still worried about bills and finances. She was in a different place now. There was a gulf between them that stretched beyond a few mere feet of polished floorboards and broken china.

Nonetheless, she was aware he was doing his best to cross it.

After what happened. So what exactly had happened? Her memory was hazy of the actual events, though the outcomes were only too clear.

"I remember . . . arguing," she said suddenly, trying to take her mind back through the fog. "At some work function. There was a woman. You were speaking to her and you were . . . entranced." She paused, trying to think. "She was so . . ." And then she frowned as the memory cleared. "Beautiful."

Jack nodded slowly. His eyes were pained. "You thought I was having an affair, remember? But she was just a client." He swallowed hard. "Well, I thought she was just a client."

"She wanted you."

"She didn't get me, Anna."

Even now, there was pain. Angst at a flash of memory, Jack staring at the woman so beautiful. Hurt. Anger. Determination not to let this happen. She had gone after them, gone to fight for her husband. Then there was fear. She remembered feeling fear.

"I got in the way," she said. "I would not let you go. So she came for me . . . I remember blood, Jack. All I remember is blood."

The fleeting images faded. That was it, there was no more, her memory just a blank until incoherence, screaming, the hospital and the pigs blood. She looked at Jackson, she waited for him to fill in the blanks. He shifted uncomfortably under her gaze and would not meet her eyes.

"They killed her," he said. It sounded a simple thing when he said it. "The others. They came and said they knew what to do. They said they could save you."

"They imprisoned me."

"It didn't work." His face was anguished. "But I couldn't let them kill you too, Anna. I just couldn't."

So he let them lock her up instead, as if that were some kind of compromise, as if that was somehow better. His new friends, driven, experienced. Obsessive. They had seen this kind of thing before. They had dealt with it before. How long must it have taken him to convince them not to kill her? For them to convince him they must then contain her instead? Weeks were a drugged blur in her memory. She could recall locks and restraints and screaming burning hunger, but little else for much of that time. Pigs blood might have kept her alive, but it did nothing to satisfy her hunger.

Only her mind had cleared, eventually. Her thinking, her understanding. Her sense of self. There was only so long they could suppress her growing strength, in the end.

She smiled a dark smile. She was who she was. And they had underestimated her. All of them.

"Come here, Jack."

His face paled. He shook his head only a minute fraction, so she held out a hand, one white, elongated hand with long, perfect fingers topped in nails painted a blood red. She twisted her mouth, parted her lips. Showed him her teeth, as elongated and perfect as her fingers. His breathing quickened, that pulse beating hard inside him speeding up; she could hear it. She could all but smell the blood in him, moving, coursing through him.

She wanted him. That was why she was back here. She understood that suddenly.

He was her husband. He was *hers*.

On her bidding, he stepped forward an unwitting step. A bare foot onto sharp edges of broken porcelain. His weight crunched it down hard, slivers biting into his skin, tiny spikes of pain she sensed as he felt. She drew him further, another step, another beckoning curl of her fingers. *Come to me, Jack*, she thought, and he did, fear in his eyes edging into terror as he struggled in vain to resist her. Interesting. She had thought he might try harder to hold back as she compelled him forward, but he didn't fight near as much as she had thought he might. He came to her almost willingly, in the end.

He took her hand in his when he reached her, his fingers soft. The soles of his feet were bleeding, she was conscious of every drop of blood he left behind him. Human skin was so easy to break. And so warm. His body against hers, she could feel the living heat of it as she lowered her lips, her sharp-toothed smile, to kiss him. He kissed her back. That was his own doing. She made him walk to her, but the rest he gave into of his own accord.

"Anna," he whispered, then kissed her harder. "Anna. Don't leave." He gripped her shoulders with a force that would have left bruises, had she been human.

But she was not human. Not anymore.

The skin at his throat was vulnerable. He all but turned his head to bare his neck for her. She grinned, tracing her tongue down his chin, tasting the sweat from his skin. Scratching playfully at his throat with her teeth so that he stiffened and readied himself, but she didn't break that skin, not yet. It was a tease, a flirt. She wanted to take her time. She wanted to enjoy this. She wanted him to enjoy it too.

"Do you love me, Jack?" she asked and felt him nod. And maybe he did, at that. Maybe it was just the house and the work and the long hours and their finances and everything else, just everything, which had got in between them in the end. Maybe now there was a way around that.

Instead of sinking her teeth into him, she raised one hand to her shirt and undid the top button, pulling it aside. With one fine blood-red fingernail, she cut into her own skin just above the bra line, a slow slice until her blood beaded up in a thick red drop. It slid downwards, sliding by slow millimetres toward her breasts, a line of dark and pure red against flawless white skin.

He resisted when she tried to guide his lips to the wound on her chest. He was frightened. But she was insistent and though he whimpered, he let her do so. His warm lips on her cold skin. His face to her breast. She pushed his head so that his tongue could find the cut. She murmured something gentle.

The thumping at the door was loud and startled them both.

She pulled his head away from her by the hair. He looked up to her with guilt ridden eyes that she read only too easily.

"I'm sorry," he all but whispered.

He'd known. He'd known someone was coming.

"Who? Who is it?" she demanded. He didn't answer, but that was answer enough. She let him drop with an unsubtle shove away. "Your friends have perfect fucking timing for this kind of thing, don't they, Jack?"

She turned her back and walked down into the lounge, leaving him standing alone in the hallway.

"Jesus, Anna. Try and see it from my side for once," he muttered after her.

"They've come to kill me, Jack," she shot back. "So answer the door and make your choice. Tell them I'm here and this gets bloody. Or trust me and keep quiet."

She drew back into the darkened room, watching as he went to the door, his movement hesitant as he kept glancing over his shoulder. But he wouldn't see her in the dark, she had ways of wrapping it about herself, of folding into the shadows so his kind just never could see. Fading back, listening to those who waited impatiently for Jack to let them in. Those who waited with intent.

She wished she had warned him not to trust them.

They all but barged in. Three of them. The first she recognised only too well; the doctor, middle-aged, harried and carrying his case. Did he go nowhere without his needles, his drugs? Or did he always bring them in the possibility of meeting the likes of her? She bared her teeth instinctively at the sight of him. He would use those drugs on her, if she let him; immobilise her long enough to kill her. She had escaped from him once; he wouldn't give her the chance to do so again, should he ever get her back within his clutches.

The second to enter was less familiar. One of Jack's set, rich, young and idle; one of his new friends. She remembered him in only a vague set of impressions. He had come from overseas, America somewhere, and had done this kind of thing before. He was vicious, brutal even, in his taste of entertainments. He was prepared to kill. This one had the taint of blood on him. He was well experienced in the cause to which these men dedicated themselves.

Death and destruction. It was what they did. They were hunters. And what they hunted now was her.

She stood in the dark and considered her options. She could slip away now, while it was safe, before they even knew she was there. Fade back, make her escape. Leave this place.

Leave Jack.

No. Never.

The third to enter set off every warning instinct her heightened senses could provide. Her skin tightened on sight of him, her muscles tensed fast. He entered slowly, pausing in the doorway to take note of his surrounds. He was young. Driven. She remembered this one. She remembered his dark obsessions from the hospital. The charisma to him, the aura of charm matched by the classically handsome face. The lazy way he made threats when she was restrained and struggling in vain to reach him. The pain inflicted on his command. Research, he had called it. Research into the ways of his enemies. He wore a three piece charcoal suit and behind his pale silk tie hung a small silver cross on a chain. And if his American friend was the one most used to dealing out death, it was this one who was shrewd enough to pick and choose their targets.

Hunter. It was both his name and his profession.

And there was Jack, standing lost in their midst, not knowing who to trust.

"We have a problem," the American began, pushing his way through and stepping down into the formal lounge, flicking on the overhead light as he did so. She had already pulled back into the adjoining dining room, watching still from her cloak of darkness. She knew this house better than he. She knew darkness better than he. He'd never find her within it, not if she didn't want him to.

The others followed, Jack last of all. His face was pale, his eyes darting this way and that. "What kind of problem?" he tried, perhaps speaking a little too hesitantly.

"Your wife. She's escaped."

"Anna?"

The American threw him a dark glance. "You have more than one vampire wife?" he pushed. He sounded prepared for a confrontation; he sounded prepared to provoke one. Jack's shoulders pulled back; he wouldn't like that, the brash attitude of this other who had come ready to lay blame.

"What do you mean escaped?"

He sounded more sure of himself now and it was clear the two of them had faced off before. The American wouldn't have liked the idea of keeping her alive; he would have argued to just kill her outright. So he had lost to Jack's will once already, then. She hoped Jack realised that would only make him more dangerous. There was a bulky shape under his jacket. The man had come bearing weapons.

The doctor laid his case on the leather lounge suite, clicked it open. "Jackson, I'm sorry," he said, before stepping up to intervene. "But our friend here is right. Earlier tonight, your wife broke her bonds. She killed two orderlies stationed to guard her and vanished from the hospital."

Jack pulled away from him when he tried to lay a hand on his arm. "Killed two . . . ?"

"She tore their throats out, Jack."

He was silent. Looking at the men who surrounded him, those who claimed to be his allies, his friends. Visibly struggling to find something to say. Raising one hand to his face, rubbing at his eyes. It was late. Midnight, at least. He would have been up since before five thirty that morning, going for a run then getting into work before eight. No wonder he looked so wan.

"Christ," he muttered. "You said you could help her. You said it wouldn't come to this."

The American uttered a dark sound. "I said it was bullshit. Stake the heart, cut off the head. It's what we do. It's what we always do. This time should have been no different."

Jack turned on him. "Anna was sick. She needed help."

"Your Anna was dead. The thing that wore her face needed to be staked."

Jack stepped up to retaliate. Lawyer to the core, he had never been one to let a direct challenge pass unmet. But the doctor moved again to intervene, drawing Jack back, giving the other a warning look. He tried to get Jack to sit down, urging him toward the soft leather couch which had cost her and Jack a fortune. They had maxed-out more than one credit card in the buying of it.

The doctor's case of drugs and needles lay open on that couch. She was glad when Jack shook the doctor off to stand on his own.

"Okay. Okay. Fuck. What do we do now, then?" Jack tried, but even to her ears it sounded like he was buying time, trying to find himself space to think. Too busy looking about him, probably to see if she was there, he didn't catch the glance pass between the doctor and the so far silent Hunter.

She did.

"Jackson, I'm afraid we are entirely out of options."

Hunter spoke almost casually. When he did, he stepped forward, a hand resting in his pocket, an assuring calm about his person. All attention turned to him. He gave the impression of one who knew just what to do. One who allowed no room for doubt. This was a man who was used to being listened to. She had seen as much in the hospital, with the doctors who had never thought to question his little tests. The way they had kept back as she had screamed and let him just stand there calmly and make his notes.

Jack shot him an unfriendly glance. "You gave me precious few options to begin with, Hunter."

"She will come here. She will come to find you. When she does, we must be ready."

The doctor tried again to draw Jack to sit, but Jack stepped forward instead to confront the other man directly. Perhaps he was finally growing suspicious of these men. Perhaps he understood, at last, that they did not mean to help her.

"You're talking about Anna. My wife."

"I'm talking about a vampire, Jackson, who preys on humanity and kills at will." Hunter looked Jack cold in the face. There was not an inch of give in his voice. "You ask what we must do. We must tempt her to us, draw her out of hiding and into the open. Back into our control."

Beside him, the American grinned. "And then we'll do what I said we should've from the start."

Jack faced them, his breathing sharply controlled. There was a bead of sweat across his forehead and he stood on the balls of his feet. A defensive posture. A fighting posture. He looked from Hunter to the doctor to the American. He did not move.

"No," he said, and his voice was clear. "No. I will not let you kill her."

"You don't have a choice in the matter," Hunter answered. His relaxed assurance didn't falter in the face of Jack's refusal. He looked like he had expected it. "She will come for you. We will be ready for her when she does."

They grabbed him. The American on one side, the doctor on the other. He cried out, perhaps even tried to cry her name, but it was a jumble of sounds and movement as they dragged him to the couch and the doctor's waiting set of needles. Hunter stood calm as the other men pinned Jack down. Jack fought. He fought hard. With all his strength, all his will. But the American spent hours working out every day and the doctor was used to fending off agitated patients. Before Jack could stop them, the American was holding out his arm and the doctor prepping a needle to stick into it.

"Get away from my husband."

She appeared before them as if out of nowhere. Stepping forward into their light, she moved so quick they would not have seen her before she spoke. The doctor almost dropped his needle in the shock of her sudden appearance. Even the American pulled back in surprise.

Hunter stood unmoved. It was he she glared at. It was he who led them.

"Johnson—now!" Hunter ordered, staring only at her.

It wasn't the doctor who jumped up. It was the American. If he had come directly for her she would have ripped his head clean off, but he was too experienced for that and threw something her way instead. She moved out of its path, but it spread out, some kind of netting weighted down around the edges with metallic dead weights. She swatted it away, but her hands became tangled in it. She tried to pull her head back, but it covered across her. What was this? She struggled to get the thing off. It cut into her. It seared where it touched. It stank.

It took her a minute to recognise the smell. Garlic. They'd soaked the expanded netting in crushed garlic.

She cried out, an animalistic howl of anger and pain, and tore at the net about her. It couldn't hold her long, but it burned to touch and she hissed a rising rage. Somewhere down deep, where her rational mind was being pushed, she knew there wasn't enough of the herb upon this thing to truly incapacitate her. But it did fire an animal fury deep in her gut and she lashed out at all around. Precious ornaments flew from the nearby mantle. The low coffee table crashed as it was overturned. A lamp smashed against a wall. She could smell her own skin where it burned with the touch of the poisoned net.

It couldn't stop her. But it did slow her down.

As she ripped it from her body something large hit her with force. The American, throwing himself at her with strangling arms and a powerful grip. She twisted, grabbing out at the limbs that tried to engulf her and tearing through the net in simultaneous motion. The sheer momentum of his dive onto her dragged them both down and they stumbled together, but he had underestimated her. Maybe he was used to seeing her drugged out and starved on pig's blood. Maybe he just didn't realise the full extent of her strength when her mind was her own and she was properly fed.

She found her feet within moments, twisting him round and gripping on with her own fingers like claws, punching holes in the soft flesh of his body. He cried out, but managed to keep one hand free. In it he held a long, wooden stake. He tried to bring it slamming down into her chest.

With bared teeth and an animal growl, she caught his wrist, then swung him around, flinging him from her. His body went flying, but she kept hold of his wrist until after she felt the jerk on it and his cries became screams. The shoulder was pulled from the socket, the elbow broken by the force of her throw. He landed in a crumpled heap, crippled and in agony.

She tore away the final shreds of the net and turned to face her remaining foes with bared teeth.

Just in time to see the needle shoved deep into Jackson's arm and the doctor plunging it down fast.

Her husband struggled, but held down by both the doctor and Hunter he had no chance, not on his own. The fight with the American had distracted her and given them enough time. She cried out an unintelligible sound and flew at them, blindingly fast. She caught the doctor first. He had no defences against her, not in the face of her fury. She dragged him off her husband and held him a foot above the floor with one hand, snarling brutal, long-toothed anger into his face.

With her other hand, she lashed out, swiping only once.

Half his head came away. Her hand was red with gore. His body shuddered, convulsing where she held it, blood pumping over her, over the good leather armchair beside her, over the plush carpet about their feet. She just dropped the body in its death throes and turned back with a snarl to find Hunter.

He was dragging the American up, but left him and straightened when he saw her coming for him. Behind him was the hallway and he stepped backwards up the steps toward it, never taking his eyes from her. He had come here to set a trap, but she had surprised him. She had got here first. And she was stronger than he had expected. Even Hunter, it seemed, had underestimated her.

But this one was smart enough to recognise when he was outmatched and needed to regroup.

She stepped forward. He stepped back. He did not panic, but he sought his escape. If she let him get away from her now, he would return, he would come back better prepared and he would not underestimate her again.

If she let him get away from her now, he would haunt her and all that was hers forevermore.

She stalked toward him, covered in blood, teeth bared and growling low in her throat.

"Stay back, bitch," he ordered and raised his hand. In it he held a small wooden crucifix, whipped from the inside pocket of his jacket.

"So fucking old school," she snarled, then moved with a speed he would never see to reach out and grab the cross in his hand. "I'm atheist, Hunter." She shoved her bloodied face suddenly up close to his. "The symbols of your belief mean nothing to me."

She tightened her grip. She could feel the fine bones of his hand begin to break; she could see the first flash of panic creep into those ice blue, ever cool eyes. He uttered a low cry through clenched teeth as she pushed him back, his perfectly styled hair falling loose and across his face. There was something satisfying to finally breach that controlled exterior. To dig down into the obsessions which lay at his core. She could see the hate in his eyes as she crushed his hand, the struggle he was losing, but even now she sensed no fear from him. Detestation, abhorrence, yes. He burned to destroy her. But he did not fear.

She squeezed harder. She would not let him take what was hers.

The American pulled himself up, clutching at his arm, and tried to throw himself at her again. He had not the strength to knock her down, but it did give Hunter chance enough to pull away, even as she yanked the crippled fighter off her with one hand and clutched about his throat with another. The man's eyes had just enough time to look into her own and widen imperceptibly, before she ripped his jugular from his throat with her clawed fingers and sent his blood gushing from him.

She dropped the dead American. Another body on the carpet. She and Jack had spent hours selecting that carpet when they had first bought this house.

Hunter was already at the front door. She turned to chase him. She would not let him get away.

"Anna . . ."

Jack. Jack's voice. It sounded so weak. It stopped her in a moment.

In front of her was her enemy. Her chance at revenge and the target of all her fury, slipping now out the door. But behind her was her husband and his call was one of need. She drew back a hissed breath and fought to regain control of herself, to push down the rage and the desire to kill. To ignore the near overwhelming stench of blood from the carnage about her, that which spurred her to more and drove her on.

For a moment they stood there, frozen and staring at one another. She and Hunter. Each wanting only the other's destruction.

Then she let him go. She turned and ran back to her husband.

"Jack? Jack?" She fell to her knees next to where he lay. Somewhere behind her she heard the bang of the front door swinging shut and that was all.

Sweat covered Jack's skin. His breathing was laboured. He had tried to get up to reach her, but hadn't the strength and now was half lying on the couch, gripping on to the leather. She helped him back up upon it, reaching out to brush hair from his clammy face. She left a streak of blood across his forehead as she did.

"I'm sorry, Anna," he whispered and she saw how much of a struggle it was for him to speak. What had they done? What had they given him? She could hear his heart in his chest. Just like before when its beat had called to her, only now it was struggling. He was fighting to keep breathing, fighting to stay alive. His pulse, that beating, pumping pulse, was sluggish.

They hadn't been merely trying to knock him out so as to lure her to them. They had been trying to kill him. To trap her with his carcass, as if a dead-bait trap was the only one she'd fall into.

"Those bastards, those bastards," she muttered as she clutched at him. "They didn't need to do this. They had no need."

"They wanted to use me," he tried and if she had been human she doubted she would have heard him, his voice was that soft. "To get to you."

"They didn't need to do this. This was just spite. Anger. Hatred. I would have come for you no matter what. He knew that. That bastard Hunter knew that."

She heard the pain in her own voice. Saw the shaking of her own hands as she tried to find a way to make him comfortable. He was gasping back breaths. His eyes strayed momentarily to take in the state of the room behind her, then the state of her as well. She was aware he would see her sharpened teeth, her black pinprick pupils, that she did not resemble anything human right now. When she had first come here she had made an effort to appear as ordinary as possible, so as not to frighten him off. But in the fight she had forgotten to maintain such a control and the creature she was now, the vampire as those men called her, was all at the fore.

He didn't seem to mind. It seemed he was no longer scared of her.

He tried to smile, a faltering expression. "The house is ruined," he said and she thought he even tried to laugh. She leant her forehead against his. There were tears in his eyes.

"Fuck the house, Jack. It doesn't matter. It never mattered."

"I . . . I wanted there to be somewhere for you to come home to."

He coughed. Blood came up as he did so. Whatever they had pumped him full of, it was attacking his lungs. She gripped his hands as he fought back the fit, but his fingers were weak in her own and he leant against her because he had not the strength to support himself any longer.

"I didn't come back for the house," she told him, her voice gentle. "I came back for you."

"Then I'm sorry, Anna," he whispered, almost inaudible.

"What for this time?"

"Sorry I must leave you. I am sorry to die."

He lay in her arms, looking up at her through falling lids. He knew what she was. Blood covered the room. She was drenched in it. Her hands, her face, making sticky tendrils of her hair. It had soaked into their carpet, their furniture. Only a few feet away lay the bodies of two men he had once trusted and who he had just watched her kill with only her bare hands. Yes, he knew exactly what she was.

And still he worried about death?

She leant forward and kissed him, a soft brush of her lips against his. "Jack, if you think I'm going to let you die now, you are more credulous than even I gave you credit for."

She pulled aside her blood soaked blouse. The cut she had made in her own skin earlier had already healed, but it took her a mere moment to wipe another man's gore from her skin and remake the wound. One sharpened fingernail pulled through her skin, so that it opened up and oozed its own blood.

Before, in the hall, she had compelled him to come to her. She had presented a beautiful glamour, an attraction to tempt him towards the darkness and he tried to resist, though he had wanted her anyway. Now she merely knelt next to him drenched in the evidence of what she was and helped him sit up so he could reach her. This time, he did not resist. This time, when she put his head to her chest, his lips found the cut that released her blood without hesitation.

It would not be easy, the next little while. Jack would be weakened and confused at first. Hunter would come for them and his was a hatred that would not die. They could not stay here. They would have nowhere to live. They would have nothing. But it didn't matter, none of it mattered. They would be together. And perhaps once, back when they were human and exhausted and caught in a cycle of long hours and credit cards, they had forgotten that truth, but in the end it was the only thing that mattered.

They would have each other.

She held his head where it bent to her breast and kissed his hair while he drank.

AFTERWORD TO "COMING HOME"

I grew up loving vampires. Classic, literary ones, like Carmilla and Dracula. Modern, self-aware ones like Lestat or Spike. My teenage years were spent consuming Hollywood flicks, the well-made and decidedly B-grade, featuring good looking bad-boy vamps smouldering up the screen. They in turn led me to the Nosferatu of Herzog, then Murnau. To Bela Lugosi. To Christopher Lee. To me, vampires were about sex and death, blood and allure. About society and its hidden fears; about the unspoken horror behind the innocuous facade. And about good, dark scary stories.

For this story, though, it wasn't the vampires, but their "Australianness" I was most interested in. I enjoy classic Australian imagery of the laid-back outback or beach-bronzed larrikins, but I wanted to write an Australia I could recognise from my own life—a suburban Australia. At least since European settlement we've been an urban, and particularly, suburban culture, our population clinging to the edges of the continent. This was the world I wanted to explore: modern, hard-working and aspirational.

I thought, if vampires are a horror which hides under a normal, if alluring, appearance, then in post-Global Financial Crisis modern Australia, the problems of credit debt and mortgage stress are a lurking darkness behind our pretty suburban fences. These suck us dry and drain our energies as well as any vampires might.

Mostly, though, after watching recent popular vampire tales put the emphasis on love not death, I was itching to return to the vampires of my youth—the bloody, nasty, sometimes campy, always sexed-up vampires I grew up with. Writing "Coming Home" was, for me, about putting the blood and darkness back into the vampire tale. But not necessarily losing all the romance, either.

THE LITTLE RED MAN

RAYMOND GATES

"Have a look at that!"

Mark directed Karen's gaze towards the massive Moreton Bay Fig that dominated the view through the windscreen of her Toyota SUV. Its broad trunk and extensive twisted roots clutched the ground, bracing itself to support its enormous canopy. "It looks like a giant piece of broccoli," she said, earning a mock reproachful look.

"Baby, that is *Ficus macrophylla* at its most glorious," he said with enthusiasm and the boyish wonder she found so endearing. "I mean, I've seen some impressive ones in the botanic gardens, but this is just . . ."

"Big?"

He gave her a lop-sided smile. "Yeah, baby. Big."

She countered with a cheeky grin. "See? You studied botany for years to describe things like that."

"Yeah, well. We can't all have the education of a nurse, now can we?"

She replied with a firm pinch of his thigh.

Though not one of the official campsites listed on the park's maps, well worn ruts in the ground suggested they weren't the first to discover the place. Karen stopped the car just short of the tree's overhanging branches. They got out and stretched two hours solid driving from their bodies.

The air was so fresh; a deep breath was like a draught of clear spring water on a hot day. Standing before the tree, such an impressive specimen of nature, it was clear to her why he was so passionate about his work.

Mark approached the tree, his gaze drawn up into its core. "This has got to be close to fifty, fifty-five metres. Maybe more." He moved as near to the trunk as the complex roots would allow, spreading his arms out sideways. "That's nearly three metres wide." In awe, he reached out to touch it, caressing its rough, grey surface.

"Careful," Karen said. "A girl could get jealous." Mark smiled but said nothing. She left him to his fun, moving to unpack the car.

Colour was fading from the sky, the bright blue of the day darkening to shades of purple. With only a little nagging, Mark broke away from the tree to help Karen unpack and set up. By the time Venus opened its bright eye, water was bubbling away in his trusty billycan, harmonising with sausages sizzling in the skillet over the fire.

They ate, and talked, and laughed, letting their day-to-day strains drift away into the star-speckled night. Karen marvelled at how the temperature plummeted, grateful for the cosy fire, and the even cosier company. Huddled against Mark under the protective canopy of the tree, watching the flames dance, she believed if time were to stop, she could remain in this moment, happy, content, forever.

A coal popped in the fire. Karen jumped, and Mark tightened his arms around her as she giggled at her reaction..

"So?" His voice was low. "How do you like this?"

"This," she tightened her hold on him. "I love."

"Well, that's good, but you know what I mean."

She considered for a moment. "It's really something. Quiet. Serene. It's beautiful." She shuddered as a chill ran through her. "But does it have to be so damn cold?"

"Of course it does." He kissed the top of her head and turned to kiss the curve of her ear. "It gives us good reason to get warm."

"Oh, really?" Karen smiled, tilting her head to accept more of his kisses. "And since when have you ever needed a reason?" She felt his smile against her cheek and the flush of her body as her pulse quickened.

A loud rustling came from above. Several leaves fluttered through the space between them and the canopy. Only darkness could be discerned amongst the foliage.

Mark hushed Karen before she could speak. She stared into the foliage, trying to pretend her racing heart was a result of Mark's affections, not from fear of some unknown visitor.

"It's just a bird," Mark broke the tension, and Karen gasped, realising she'd been holding her breath. "Or maybe a possum. There's all sorts of critters live in the trees here."

Karen's eyes scanned the tree. "Are they all planning on scaring the shit out of me?"

"Babe, you only notice them because it's so quiet out here," he said, his warm breath close to her ear, his warm hands under her jumper. "You'd hear the same thing at home if it weren't for all the street noise."

Karen wasn't convinced, though his lips, soft against her neck, were a pleasant distraction.

"Besides," he said. "You know what they say about the bush."

She smiled, feeling her fear melt away. "What's that?"

His hands travelled upwards. "In the bush," he whispered, the words hot against her skin. "No one can hear you scream."

Karen chuckled, a deep, throaty sound. "You think you can make me scream, bush man?"

Mark carried her off to their tent.

†   †   †

Karen awoke shivering, a cold breeze having found its way inside the tent. Searching for the body that had warmed her earlier, she burrowed herself deeper into the sleeping bag. When her hands found nothing, she opened her eyes. Mark wasn't with her. The tent flap had been left open.

"Mark?" In her half-asleep state, it came out *Muhg?* She shifted, propping herself up on an elbow. "Mark?" Clearer. Louder. Still no answer. She sat up. "Mark? You out there?" She pulled the sleeping bag over her, conscious of her nakedness despite their isolation.

Her ears strained for a clue to his whereabouts. No crunch of grass being trodden underfoot. No splashing to suggest he might be relieving himself. Just the slight rustle of leaves caught in the breeze.

Karen leaned forward and peered outside. She could make out the dark shape of the car, but little else. Butterflies danced inside her as she groped for the torch. "Mark!" she called through clenched teeth. Still no answer.

Her fingers touched upon cold metal and she seized the long, heavy Maglite. She pointed it into the night and clicked it on.

A ghostly, haggard face lit up in front of her.

Karen shrieked as the thing raised a hand to shield itself.

"Jesus! Get that outta my face, will ya?"

She lowered the torch but kept it trained forward.

Still naked, Mark crawled back into the tent and zipped the flap closed behind him. "Bloody hell, what's got into you?"

"Where the hell were you?"

"I was taking a leak." He wriggled his way into the sleeping bag with her. "Where'd you think I'd be?"

"I called out to you. You didn't answer me."

"Babe, I didn't hear you."

Her anxiety turned into annoyance. "You scared me."

"I'm sorry." He moved closer to her.

Warmth radiated from him, and despite herself, she allowed him to put his arms around her.

"You're warm." She hoped she still sounded angry.

"Good circulation." He held her closer.

"You suck." She leaned her face against his chest.

"I know, but you love me anyway."

She exaggerated a sigh in response, knowing full well he was right.

"Go back to sleep babe," he said.

Karen spent a long time listening to his rhythmic breathing before sleep reclaimed her.

†   †   †

Blazing sunlight and bright blue skies banished any residual fears from the previous night. They spent the day exploring one of the numerous walking trails that ringed their campsite, winding their way down into the rainforest valley. Mark was in his element, bounding from tree to shrub, vine to wildflower, rattling off Latin names as if they were old friends. Karen snapped away with her camera, feigning apathy at Mark's exuberance as punishment for bringing her out here. In truth, she was enraptured with the beauty of the forest. From the giant Red Cedars, whose wide, powerful rust-coloured trunks thrust forth from the earth in a beautiful display of Nature's power, to the occasional finch, scrub turkey, or bearded dragon that chose to reveal itself.

The sun had already disappeared by the time they'd returned to camp; the fading pinks and oranges in the western sky the only evidence of its existence. Mark again took on the role of head chef while Karen put together a salad from their supplies, thanking the gods of technology for inventing battery powered iceboxes.

"I'll take you through the Cave Circuit tomorrow," Mark said. "We can do a little spelunking."

Karen raised her eyebrows. "Is that what they call it these days?"

He flashed a lopsided grin. "Caving, dear. Caving."

"Oh." She pretended to focus on her food. "For a moment, I thought I was getting lucky."

Mark rolled his eyes and chuckled. She stared at him, admiring the way the firelight caressed his features. For the first time that day, she noticed his skin had taken on a pinkish hue, a contrast to his usual tanned complexion.

"You got a touch of the sun, babe."

He frowned. "I did?"

"Mmm-hmm. You're bright pink."

He looked at his arms. "Huh." Touched his face. "It doesn't sting or anything." He shrugged. "It'll be tan by morning."

"Uh huh. Well, either way, sunscreen for you tomorrow." She rose, moved to stand behind him, and placed her hands on his shoulders. He slumped, arching his neck back to look at her, pouting. Her lips dissolved the pout away.

"If you're a good boy, I might just rub aloe all over you," she whispered.

With comical flair, Mark bolted for the tent as Karen's laughter rang through the bush.

†   †   †

An awful sound roused her from her sleep. A sound she associated with sickness and disgust. She realised Mark was again absent. *Oh shit*, she thought. *He's being sick.* She scrabbled for her undies and a t-shirt before going outside.

"Babe, you okay?" Her eyes scanned the darkness. The slivered moon was still high, the little light it bestowed filtered by the thick canopy of the fig tree. "Mark, where are you?"

Rustling branches spun her around. Though the air was still, leaves stirred as though dancing in the wind.

"Mark?" She was annoyed at the tremble in her voice. "Seriously babe, you better not be mucking around."

A groan drew her attention towards the car. A dark shape rose and leaned against the car for support. Having found its legs, it took a tentative step forward.

"Mark!" Karen raced over and embraced him. His skin was warm and wet as if he'd just had a hot shower. She ushered him back inside the tent.

"What's the matter?" He sounded groggy.

"You're sick." She found a blanket, wrapped it around him and rubbed him vigorously. "You've got a fever."

"What? No I don't."

"You're sweating." She removed the blanket and tossed it through the tent flap. "You've got to keep warm." She opened the sleeping bag wide, expecting him to climb in.

"I'm fine." He was sounding more like himself. "Just doing what the bears do in the forest."

Karen snorted. "Mark, I heard you throwing your guts up. You were dripping with sweat."

"I wasn't throwing up. Maybe you heard me taking the strain? It was a pretty big one you know."

Karen slapped his shoulder hard. "This isn't bloody funny! What if you're really sick? It's hours to the nearest bloody hospital."

"Babe." He placed his hands on her shoulders. "I'm fine. I promise you, I'm fine."

She resisted his attempt to draw her close. "I know what I heard."

"I don't doubt it, hon, but whatever it was, it wasn't me."

"Oh, really? Then what the bloody hell was it?"

Mark shrugged. "I don't know. It could've been a lot of things. It could've been anything if you were half asleep." He rubbed her shoulders. "But I do know it wasn't me."

The ensuing silence was palpable. Karen fought the urge to yell at him, and it made her angry. Angry at him, angry at being here, but mostly angry at being so scared.

"Okay, look." Mark moved to get into the sleeping bag. "I'll rest up. We'll get some sleep, and if I'm no good in the morning, we'll head back."

Karen cleared her throat. "You promise we'll go back?"

"*If* I'm sick, then yeah." He paused. "But if I'm ok, then we're going to enjoy the rest of this trip. Deal?"

She joined him in the sleeping bag without answering. His heavy breathing descended into a light snore.

Her eyes closed, but the confusion that tumbled through her mind ensured sleep did not return.

† † †

By the time Mark emerged, the sun had positioned itself directly above the fig tree and Karen had decided the chances of continuing their explorations were the same as Buckley's. The sight of him was enough to convince her they had to leave immediately.

"Morning." He sounded in good cheer. "Got any breakfast on?"

She stared at him, wide-eyed and open mouthed.

"What's up with you?"

Karen gasped. "Are you kidding me?"

"No." He frowned. "What's the matter?"

"Have a look at your arms."

Mark cocked his elbows out and examined himself. "Oh yeah, I really did get sunburnt, huh?"

"Babe, you're glowing like a friggin' radioactive tomato!" She strode over to him. Every exposed bit of skin had taken on a dark pink tinge; he looked as though he was covered in cheap nail polish.

"Bullshit." He laughed. "It's not that bad."

"Not that bad?" Her stare dared him to argue. "Look at you!"

"So, I'll put sunscreen on."

"You're not well."

Mark rolled his eyes. "Ah Kaz, not that shit again."

"I'm taking you to the hospital."

"You're overreacting."

"Overreacting?" She directed an incredulous look towards him. "How can you say that? Look at yourself!" She reached out to touch his forehead. "You've got a virus or—" Her hand stopped short. Her eyes blinked, her mind convinced it was being deceived.

"Are you shorter than me?"

"What?" His brow furrowed and he stared at her. "Of course not. You've got boots on, and you're standing on higher ground."

His feet were bare. The ground, however, was quite level. She stood closer and for the first time noticed an odour about him, a mild, sickly-sweet smell, like overripe fruit.

"You're like . . . two inches shorter than me."

"Babe. It's the boots."

"I'm not wearing *stiletto* hiking boots, Mark!"

"So, what are you saying?" His voice was rising. "That suddenly I've lost six inches in height? That I've caught some mystery virus that's turning me into the incredible shrinking man?"

Karen bit down on her instinctual response. "Something is going on," she said through clenched teeth. "You need to see a doctor."

Without warning, Mark grabbed her wrist, hard enough to make her wince, and forced her hand against his forehead.

"Am I warm?"

"You're hurting me."

"Am I *warm*?"

If anything, his skin was cool to touch. Dry, but soft, as if it had been well moisturised.

"No," she said, unable to meet his burning stare. She snatched her hand away.

"Right." He stepped past her. "There's still enough of the day left for us to check out some of the caves. We might miss out on the falls though. They're further down in the valley." He glanced upwards, searching for the sun through the overhanging branches. "I don't think we'd make it out before dark."

Karen stood with her arms folded. "You still want to go walking?"

"Damn right." He made his way back into the tent, and donned clothes and boots more appropriate for the journey. He came out with his pack on, holding hers out to be taken. "Ready?"

He looked as if the conversation hadn't happened, as if he expected her to step into line and follow him along the yellow brick road. An image of him jiving through the bush like an oversized pink pixie flashed into her mind. She didn't want to go, but something told her he wouldn't take no for an answer.

"Can we just make it a short one today, babe?" She attempted a smile. "Maybe just go have a look around, come back and spend a little quality time together?" Now the smile felt more convincing, more natural.

Something flashed through his eyes, something not Mark, and then it was gone. "Sure babe." He wore that lopsided smile she'd fallen in love with, but it failed to extend to the rest of his face. "Let's go." He strode off towards the waiting bushland.

With apprehension, Karen shouldered her pack and followed.

†   †   †

Dusk had drained colour from the world by the time they returned. The fig tree had taken on a sinister appearance, like the old house at the end of the street that goads children into daring one another to knock at its door.

"That was a good walk." Mark dropped the pack from his shoulders and prepared to light their campfire.

"Hon? Why don't we just pack up and head off?" She hesitated, gauging his reaction. "We're leaving in the morning anyway."

He turned towards her, his face blank.

"Wouldn't it be good to get back to a real bed? We could sleep in." She attempted a coy smile. "Or other things."

His regarded her with an impassive stare for several moments. "Don't be silly babe." A smile flashed across his face, reanimating him. His attention remained focussed upon the growing fire. "It's too dangerous to drive through the bush at night." The flickering flames lit up his pink face; he looked like he belonged in Goethe's *Faust*.

Karen shivered. "Why? We just go back the way we came in."

"Because." His voice was that of a parent losing patience with a child. "We didn't exactly follow a road in here, did we? There aren't exactly street lights, are there? You really want to be driving blindly through the bush, at night, out *here*, trying not to careen down the side of the bloody mountain."

Karen pressed her lips together. "No. I suppose not."

He whispered something she swore sounded like *good girl*, and busied himself pulling together the remnants of their supplies. Karen marched off towards the tent.

"Don't you want dinner?" he called after her.

"I'm not hungry." She threw open the tent flap, hustled inside, and drew the zipper back around.

He's sick. He's unwell. He's not himself. She palmed the tears from her eyes.

† † †

When Mark finally joined her, Karen forced herself to relax and breathe in a sub-audible snore. She felt his body against hers and was surprised by her impulse to recoil. Within minutes, Mark's breathing signalled the onset of deep slumber.

Karen closed her eyes but remained awake, aware. As minutes turned to hours, she wondered at how the bush at night could be so quiet. Weren't most bush critters nocturnal? Surely she should be able to hear something besides Mark's rasping ode to the night. A possum. A fruit bat. Something.

Mark stirred and became restless. With a snort, he rose and exited the tent. She illuminated the display on her watch. Five minutes to one.

Time passed, and Mark didn't return.

Karen chewed her lip in thought. *What if he's been sick again? What if he's collapsed somewhere?*

What if he's waiting for me?

She glanced at the watch again: quarter past one. She closed her eyes and counted to thirty.

No sounds. No Mark.

Taking care to be quiet, she dressed and went outside. The clearing was still shrouded in dark gloom. Objects revealed themselves in vague shapes, their identity only discerned by their familiarity. She could see the car, the remnants of their campfire, and a portion of the clearing to the tree line. But no Mark.

She opened her mouth to call out, then closed it again. Retreating back inside, she found the Maglite and held it the way she'd seen on those reality cop shows. Its weight was very reassuring. She checked it was working, took a deep breath, and crept outside.

Aware of the cool earth on her bare feet, she took small, cautious steps, searching for any Mark-shaped silhouettes in the gloom. Using the tree as a reference point, she walked in a slow, expanding circle.

She whirled around, thinking she'd heard something. Her finger tapped a rhythm against the torch button but did not turn it on. She strained her eyes and ears.

There it was. A soft, stuttering hiss like a sharp intake of breath through chattering teeth. It seemed to be coming from the tree. Karen scanned the branches, her pupils dilating, trying to suck in all available light.

It came again. Not from the tree. Behind it.

Willing her legs to move, Karen stepped in an arc around the twisted trunk. As she moved, a form revealed itself against the dark background. A human outline, it looked to be squatting on top of something; something whose shape suggested that it was also human. The sound came again, an almost slurping sound, and the form seemed to quiver.

Knuckles aching from her tight grip, Karen bathed both shapes in light.

Mark's unclothed form lay prone on the ground, unmoving. Perched on his rear appeared to be a small man, naked and hairless, with bright red skin. Its face was turned up to the sky, eyes closed, thin lips drawn back over wicked teeth in a grimace that was grotesque in its ecstasy. Any resemblance to a man ended at its hands and feet. Its fingers and toes were short, fat tentacles. They gripped Mark's body by their tips, a rhythmic ripple pulsing through each individual digit at regular intervals.

Karen tried to stifle her cry with the back of her free hand and failed. The thing turned towards her, the light catching eyes like oversized blood blisters before forcing it to look away. Sound issued from it, unlike anything she'd ever heard, as it detached one hand with an audible popping sound and shielded itself from the light.

Her mind screamed, *car, thecar, gettothecar*! She forced her body forward, keeping the thing and Mark in the light. It averted its face, covering it as best as it could with its free hand.

"Get off him!" She took another step. "Get *off him*!" Another step, and another to bring her within reach. She raised the torch high, feeling a surge of adrenaline course through her.

The thing turned to face her, shielding its horrible eyes. For a brief moment, it stared at her with a vicious snarl on its lips. Then, with a sound like suction caps being pulled off a wall, it detached itself from Mark and leapt from his body to the trunk of the tree.

Karen swept the beam after it, catching its legs as they propelled it into the canopy. She scanned the foliage, her trembling hand causing the light to dance amongst the branches. There was no sign, no trace that the little red man had ever been there.

She turned back to Mark. Coin sized spots of blood ran along either side of his back. He wasn't moving, didn't seem to be breathing. She crouched beside him, removed her t-shirt and covered his wounds as best as she could. Blood seeped through the material. "Mark!" She shook him gently. No response.

She reached forward with her torch hand and pressed her fingers to his neck. She felt around, finding nothing. In panic, she pushed deeper and was rewarded with a faint *thrum-thrum-thrum* against her fingertips.

Rustling above her made her spin. She dropped onto her backside and shoved the torch upwards. Several branches swayed but nothing could be seen among them. "Fuck off! Leave us alone!"

Gotta go now, her mind pleaded. She checked the wounds. The skin was unbroken. Red welts, like oversized mosquito bites, were the only evidence that anything had been there at all.

She shook him again, harder. "Mark!" She tapped his cheeks, thumped his shoulder, pinched the skin along his side. Nothing roused him. *Shit!* She considered dragging him to the car, then dismissed it.

She shone light up into the tree again. Nothing moved, nothing could be seen. But it was there. She knew it was there.

Staying focussed on the branches, Karen backed towards the tent as fast as she dared. Nothing made a sound save her shuffling feet.

She tried to picture where her keys were and reached inside to grab them.

They weren't there. She went inside and searched through their belongings. "No, no, not now, not now!" She found her pack and rifled through it. *Where are they, where ARE they?* Her fingers closed around something jagged and metallic. She ripped the keys out of the pack and burst back through the tent opening.

Karen froze, her breath caught, and her heart seemed to stop.

The creature was on all fours, its mouth open to an impossible size. Mark's legs protruded from between its teeth. Its throat and body were grossly distorted, as if its skin, its very structure, were made of latex. Its mouth opened even further. Using all four limbs, it lurched forward and drew Mark's legs further down its gullet. Its teeth now clamped around his knees.

Karen thought she was screaming but couldn't be sure. It sounded distant as if coming from behind a thick wall. The thing had reached Mark's ankles, and now stood, tilting its head backwards. A final gulp, and the last part of Mark disappeared.

"No!" Karen raised the Maglite and charged her lover's devourer. "You fuck!" she cried as she swung with adrenalized, lethal intent.

The creature sidestepped the blow with agility that belied its comically misshapen form. Its lips twisted into a sardonic grin as it regarded her with crimson eyes.

She cocked her arm, ready to strike again. "You mother—"

Her curse cut short as the thing spat a foul gob at her face. It reeked, like fruit long rotten. It stung her face and eyes, the pain intensifying as she attempted to wipe it away. She stumbled backwards. A prickling numbness raced through her face and up her arms, spreading like quicksilver throughout her body.

Through tearing eyes she saw it watching her with amusement. Her legs buckled, and she flopped to the ground. It turned away from her, and started to jig and hop around, bending itself in all directions. After each pause it resembled a little more of its original self.

Her world started spinning, becoming fluid. With a final shuffling jump, the last distorted angle in its body disappeared. It reached for a low branch, and without hesitation, swung itself up into the canopy.

A dark curtain shrouded her vision. As she slumped into unconsciousness, Karen thought she heard it laughing.

† † †

Karen opened her eyes to discover the colours of the world were returning. Dawn wouldn't be too far away.

She touched her face. It was dry, and painless. Her body felt sore, like she'd slept in the same position for too long, but the pins-and-needles feeling had gone.

She scrambled to her feet. The torch had rolled from where she'd dropped it, its beam still cutting a bright line across the ground. She snatched it up and held it with both hands like a baseball bat. She up into the maze of branches. There was no sign of the creature.

She made to call for Mark but stopped as it triggered her memory. *I didn't really see that*, she told herself. *I didn't see that thing eat him.*

Making sure she had the car keys, she ran back to find her mobile phone. She was already moving towards the car as it came to life. No signal, but the battery was strong. She climbed into the car and tried to start it. There was a whine, then the engine kicked into life. Karen revved the motor for good measure before allowing herself to breathe again.

A mass dropped onto the bonnet with a metallic *whump*. The little red man squatted there with its sucker-like toes, and stared at her through the windshield.

Karen shrieked and slammed the lock button; the locks on the other doors followed suit. She pushed back into her seat, trying to put as much distance between her and the creature as she could.

Its body convulsed, a rolling movement that started at its belly and travelled all the way to its cheeks. Its mouth jerked open, yawning like a dark fleshy chasm. Another convulsion seemed to make its jaw unhinge. It made a retching sound, like a cat clearing a hairball. Its whole body was tense, and shaking with the effort.

Karen's eyes and mouth opened to almost equal sizes. The creature convulsed again. Something appeared from the dark depths of its throat. Something smooth, red, and fleshy.

There was a final, violent heave and it disgorged the thing in its mouth onto the windshield with a wet *smack!* It glistened from the coating of clear fluid all over it; saliva or gastric juices or both. The thing moved, rolled itself over, and rose up on its own spindly limbs.

"No!" Karen's stomach twisted, threatening to purge itself. "Oh God, no, please no, please God, no!"

From its red skin to its stature, its hairless body to its tentacled fingers and toes, it resembled the other in every detail. Except its face.

Though now bald, and sporting its own bulging crimson eyes, its facial features were still very much Mark's.

"Oh God, baby no, please no. No! NO!"

The little red Mark turned towards the thing that spawned it. The other raised its arm and pointed towards the windshield. Towards Karen. The Mark thing considered her through the glass barrier. It smiled. A lop-sided smile.

The engine screamed as Karen pushed the accelerator flat to the floor. The tachometer leapt into the red zone, but the car remained stationary. Both creatures started, alarmed by the sudden noise, their arms shot out to their sides to steady themselves. Karen paused in bewilderment before realising the problem.

She slammed the automatic shift into drive and trod on the accelerator.

The car bolted forward, spewing dust and dirt in its wake. The Mark-thing gripped the bonnet with its sucker fingers and toes. The other rolled over the faring and struck the ground. In the side mirror, Karen caught a brief glimpse of it tumbling in the dirt like a bright red ball. She brought her attention forward.

A red hand plucked itself off the bonnet and stretched towards her. Its suckered fingertips puckered liked gasping fish. They rippled as they attached themselves, an audible clunk as their suction pulled against the sheet metal. It pulled itself closer.

They reached the tree line and plunged into dense bushland. Karen squealed as small branches whipped against the car, intermittently striking the Mark-thing. She dodged and weaved her way as best as she could, terrified to look at the thing that was once her boyfriend but forced to guide the car along the narrow trail.

Red suckers grasped the windshield and the thing knelt in front of her. It balled its other hand into a meaty fist. Karen screamed as it struck the windshield, a spider-web of cracks jagging the glass. It pounded again, and a small hole appeared at the epicentre of its blow. It bared its teeth in a snarl, punching forward to drive its fist into the car's cabin.

"No! No!" Karen strained away from the groping, slurping fingers.

A dark, hairy lump stumbled suicidally onto the road. It crunched under the wheels, jolting the car violently. Karen's head thudded against the roof and sparkling spots danced in her vision. The creature's clutching hand wrenched out of the hole, tearing long gouges in its arm. The thing howled and clutched its arm to its chest.

Karen saw her chance. She stomped on the brake, the seatbelt biting into her chest as she was thrown forward. The creature pitched forward over the bonnet and sailed through the air. One of its knees twisted at an impossible angle as it tumbled and slid along the road.

Karen caught her breath and opened her eyes. Her head pounded, and her neck felt like it was wrapped in an iron collar. She gazed through the shattered windscreen at the still, red lump lying in the middle of the trail.

Is it dead?

The Mark-creature twitched. It pushed itself upright with one hand and raised its head. Flesh had scraped free from the side of its face as it skid along the ground. In obvious agony, the thing dragged itself across the ground. Towards the car. Towards her.

Its mangled face split into a lop-sided smile.

Karen pressed the accelerator to the floor.

It kept coming. There was a sickening thump and a sound similar to the snapping of old twigs as the car rolled over the thing that was once Mark. Karen cried out as the rear wheel jounced over it.

She kept her foot down. Her eyes drifted back to the mirror, expecting at any moment to see those crimson eyes, that smile. Only dust pursued her.

†   †   †

The dirt road gave way to bitumen. Karen focussed on the white lines zipping past her until signal bars appeared on her phone's screen.

She pulled over to the shoulder, snatched up the phone and dialled the emergency number.

"Emergency, do you require police, fire, or ambulance?" a polite but authoritative female voice enquired.

Karen mouthed words but nothing came out. The phone shook in her trembling hand.

"Which service do you require? Police, fire, or ambulance?"

"Help me," she whispered.

"I'm sorry, could you repeat that."

She cleared her throat. "Help me."

"I'd like to help you, miss, but I need to know which service you require. Are you hurt? Are you in trouble?"

"Help me!" She clutched the phone to the side of her face. "Help me!" She held it in front of her face, shook it, willing it to understand what had happened. *"Help me!"* She dropped the phone, the voice on the other end buzzing something unintelligible.

Karen collapsed against the steering wheel, her body racked with shudders, as she alternated between crying and screaming.

AFTERWORD TO "THE LITTLE RED MAN"

"The Little Red Man" came to me at a time when I was just starting to send my imagination out into the world, and experimenting with different approaches to writing. Feedback that I'd received from a critique group I was involved with, coupled with concepts in horror writing I'd researched, got me thinking about the way stories are told, and particularly how they end. I wanted to experiment with the absence of direct closure; to leave something for the reader's imagination to play with; to dwell on what's next? *In doing so, I hoped to give the reader a little more sense of truth: we all love a happy ending, we know that's not how it always goes.*

My opportunity came when I chanced upon what is reputed to be Australia's own vampire legend, Yara-ma-yha-who. *I loved that this creature was so far removed from the creature of the night most of us know. Here was a vampire that was neither oversexed sociopath, nor emotional teenager. A creature that seemed so unique, yet somehow so apt for the Australian bush, it begs the question: What is a vampire? We think we know: we've read the books, seen the movies, and, for some of us, even dress up and don the fangs. But what if there was something else out there? Something vampiric, that doesn't fit into the stereotypical mould?*

And what if it could be in our own back yard?

Have I got you wondering?

If you're enjoying the cool shade of a rather large tree, and find yourself continually looking amongst the branches for . . . Something. Then maybe I have.

DEATHBORN LIGHT

HELEN STUBBS

Mud was smeared in dry streaks on my skin, cracking, pulling at the fine hairs. I could smell the rainforest: leaves and orchid flowers over a base scent of creek water creating humidity, even on the dawn air. I woke a little more, listening to the percussion of forest life. Heartbeats of mammals, birds and snakes wove a matrix of living fabric around the black stump at the forest's heart.

I had slept a day and a night in the shallow dirt-bowl beneath the dead tree. I woke a little further from more than sleep, from the other thing that I had become, the one that drank the blood of bandicoots and sucked the life from goannas, cattle and . . . people.

On the dry dirt I rose to my hands and knees, arched my back and hung my head. In my mind I sought out my name . . . Demi. It was not quite lost.

Traces of human shame and pity stirred as I remembered the screams from my kills. I recalled the glinting eyes of the woman who emerged from her tent to squat over a hot stream of urine. Her death had marked the beginning of my feast along the Border Track between O'Reilly's and Binna Burra, far enough from my forest home that no-one would hunt for me here.

I sat up and arched my spine sharply, thrusting out my breasts. My knotted hair tumbled down my back. My hands caressed my swollen belly. The baby was the reason for the human massacre. It needed nutrients from the blood of its own kind.

The black roots rose like columns around my nest. I forced my shoulders out through the arches and pushed through the sharp grass. Giant trees surrounded me, cloaking the undergrowth in shadow.

I squinted and covered my arms with my hands, afraid. I'd never woken in the day, not since Hugh had bitten me and changed me, many months ago. Within my abdomen the foetus's heart beat like the sun, its solar flares urging me to stand. Its rhythm drove me toward the river like rapid music.

Leaves rustled as I brushed past low branches. I frowned and dodged a dancing sunray that penetrated the canopy. I misjudged the beam's jig and it burned a streak onto my arm: *hiss*, sting.

"Ah!" I cried, swinging away, but another ray struck my shoulder, leaving a black line that emanated smoke and the stink of cooking meat.

I slipped through the undergrowth more cautiously. The trees were sparser around the grey rocks of the creek. Pinpricks of light, like dangerous lasers, reflected off the trickling water so I stayed behind the line of trees and followed the river upstream toward the deep waterhole that lay in thick shadow.

Hugh had loved water. We had loved in it together, in forests and on stretches of beach. White waves had fizzed on my naked skin. Then he'd changed. We'd restricted our water loving to night time, until the monster within had taken him over entirely. Then the water had turned red with his betrayal and my blood.

The waterhole came into view, wide and black. An old fig cast a solid shadow over the other side of the pool, but I'd have to survive crossing a metre of strong sunlight to reach its sanctuary.

I ran and dived through the air, skin sizzling as I flashed through the burning sun. The pain awoke my anger and I wished it was Hugh burning, not me.

A moment later my fingertips broke the still water and I shot down into the cold clear liquid. I swam to the very bottom of the pool, three metres deep.

I glanced at the sunlight's fingers shuffling the ripples above then blinked and turned away, to the rock wall behind me. A vertical cave promised safety and I swam into its shadow. Inside, the cold water was entirely dark, so I reached out my arms, seeking the back wall of the cave. My hands found a spear of stone extending out from the rock. Dangerous. It could kill someone.

I moved away from it and closed my eyes. The cold water had soothed my sunburn and I wished I could stay down here forever, but my living passenger would die in this cold. Hugh would win, it would be *got rid of*, as he desired. The darkness cloaked me, invaded my ears and nostrils. It convinced me the living pulse did not matter . . . almost.

But the bright light above was strong. It reminded me I wanted the baby to live, so I must go back up there, soon. I promised myself to return when it was gone.

I washed quickly, running my hands and fingernails over my slippery skin and through my hair, scraping off all the muck and dried blood. When I was clean I bent down and swam, running my hands over the smooth rock. I dug my fingers into the spaces between the rocks, clawing my way out along the river floor and up through the shallows. My face broke the surface and I moved over the granular sand, then stood in the dense shade.

A chill ran from my toes up to my neck as the water evaporated from my skin. Warmth rushed into my swollen body, massaging the life inside. Its heartbeat sped faster, turning orange then red again.

Sharp pain struck. The cramp made me grab my belly and I bent over, staggering deeper into the forest's shade. I could not make it all the way back to my burned stump, so I trudged further into the forest, seeking . . . somewhere.

Here—a fallen tree above a thick bush. A passage underneath it had been worn down by some animal. The trunk was as thick as my embrace and staghorns hung from its girth like webbed curtains. I pushed the leaves apart and crawled through the tunnel. A bed of pressed dry grass crackled under my knees.

I crouched, waiting for the living thing to come—not the animal that lived here. It would stay away while it smelled the hungry dead. I waited for the pulsing sun inside me to emerge. Its light stung my darkness as it brightened, descended, breaking from the miracle that had kept it alive.

Lifeless tissue within my abdomen made way and membranes parted. These changes meant nothing to me as I watched the ball of light emerge from a cloak of death.

"Wuh. Wuuuh," said the little thing as it slipped onto the dried grass.

I reached for it, raised it up in my hands. My fingers were white over its red body. It was hot, human and . . . female. I gasped a shaky breath—an old habit of emotion.

Her face screwed up and she howled through an angry mouth. I looked down her throat into a pure alluring darkness.

I pulled her in against my breast. She cried louder, finding my flesh like stone, too cold. Even the womb that had kept her warm inside me was cooling. The cord that had carried living blood lay shrivelled on the ground. My last shred of humanity was dying with it. The monster within whispered that this infant was an instant snack.

The baby howled for warmth.

I'd kept and dried animal skins for this day but they were far away, draped over a sunlit rock. I crawled from the nest with the baby bawling in one hand. With the other hand, I tore banana leaves down from nearby trees. I scraped soft leaf-litter from the forest floor and covered the large leaves with it, for warmth. I ran my hand over the litter, ensuring no other parasites would bite my daughter. Bundled in the leaves, the newborn became silent. I touched her cheek, cupped her head in my hand.

I held her to my chest and wove through the deep forest, ignoring the call to feed and the need to sleep. A stick broke beneath my foot. I did not belong in the day. Even the filtered light threatened me, yet I pushed forward to find the furs I'd prepared.

As I moved my hunger grew. Fresh blood would heal my burns and give me energy to return to my nest. This living thing in my arms would taste hot and fresh.

"No," I hissed, "You cannot kill her!"

She heard me. She opened her blue eyes and looked at me hard. *No, mother, you should not kill me. Is it not enough that father will likely try?* She did not cry, but closed her eyes again and slept.

I reached the rock where the grey skins lay in a spotlight of midday sun. I thrust my arm through that fire to snatch them out, then wrapped the baby in a foetid, but warm, cocoon. I tied the paws of the animal to wrap her tight. She was well cushioned and insulated.

Beyond the rhythm of heartbeats a smoother sound moved: a car engine humming, its tyres rolling. The road was behind me and I turned and stalked towards it, one arm burned black from the sun, the other carrying the child.

I stopped when I reached the roadside and held the little thing up to my face, placed my nose against its scalp. It smelled sweet, sugary. I pulled her to my chest, lay her head against my shoulder. I loved her, but I had no choice.

"Goodbye . . . Stephanie. I will, come for you, one day."

The canopy above shaded the road that wound up the mountain. I stepped onto the gravelly edge. I looked up and the birds fell silent. Evil had arrived.

I turned my head and Hugh shoved his shoulder against my back with such a powerful jolt that it threw Stephanie out of my hold. The thick package thudded onto the road and rolled. The baby inside screamed.

Staggering forward, I regained my balance and turned. Hugh was burned black, his skin hung in strings of charcoal. His corneas had been burned down through their layers and were stained with smoke. He dived past me, aiming for Stephanie. I threw my weight against him and we tumbled onto the road. He shoved me off and scrambled away.

"Leave it," I said, standing tall. "Come with me, Hugh. There's deep cool water near. It will sooth your burns. Forget the runt."

He looked at the wailing bundle again. I fought the urge to step closer in her defence.

"It'll die, left on the road," I said, "Your job is done. Come with me. Your pain's terrible, you're burning."

He nodded. "It was a long way."

I could hear the car coming. My body swayed, my legs suddenly weak as it rounded the corner.

The driver's eyes widened as she saw me, emaciated body with one charred arm, and the black beast behind me. The tyres squealed on the asphalt as the back of the car swung to and fro, and it skidded to a halt at our knees.

"Now!" I whispered to Hugh and clamped my hand around his wrist. "To the water."

I dragged him into the forest as fast as the wind, trusting the water to seduce him. Far away, the car door clicked open. The baby ceased her cry and the door slammed shut.

"Come down into the river," I said to Hugh as we crossed the river-sand. The cold water covered our toes. We walked deeper in and it covered our ankles and knees.

"It's not over," he said, eyes narrow. "It's my child. It must die. I will not allow a human born of me."

I slipped my hands up his arms, around his shoulders. "Isn't the water cool," I said. "Let it be, for now. Worry later."

His muscles tensed beneath his burned skin.

"Come down," I said, "It goes deep. There's a cave. Let me show you."

I clutched his fingers and led him deep into the water, then pulled him down to the bottom. The cave was less defined as the evening was nearing, but I remembered where it was and pulled him in behind me.

Inside the cave I stepped around in front of him and took each of his hands. I kissed him, urging him backward gently.

When I guessed he was close to stone spear I pushed him backwards. I felt his flesh give as the stake pierced his back. He jerked and kicked, but I pressed my feet against the floor and pushed him further on. I ducked as the skewer erupted from his chest.

His fight intensified but failed. His flesh turned to oil in my hands, then the liquid exploded into white flame. The fire caught onto my fingertips and my nails burned like candles, trailing through the water, terrifying but tempting. I should burn, too, make this tragedy be over, like putting an end to a curse.

I shook my hands fast and the ten fires went out. By the time I looked up again Hugh was gone.

I waded up through the river, shook the water from my hair and ran back to the road in the fading light. The car was gone. The driver had taken Stephanie.

I closed my eyes, imagining the vehicle swerving away after saving the baby from the two monsters glimpsed.

Bloody tears ran from my eyes as I looked far into the distance. Their heartbeats blazed like meteor trails, winding along the mountain road, making tighter curls far away.

Stephanie's heart shone redder and hotter than all others in the world, so I knew I would find her when the years had passed. But for now I was finally free of her burden. Her light inside me was gone and I'd dealt her father the end he deserved.

My eyes shined silver as I put my head back, seeking night's sky, to hunt. I existed only for me now: a monster pure.

AFTERWORD TO "DEATHBORN LIGHT"

"Deathborn Light" was created from some delicious contradictions: the viciousness of mother instinct; a live child born of a dead woman; and a setting of beautiful but dangerous rainforest.

The story is set in the Gold Coast hinterland, a wild yet nurturing environment. South East Queensland's mountains are cloaked in lush ancient growth.

I've walked along the ridge from Numinbah to Binna Burra, and it was so detached from the Coast that dinosaurs could have been herding through the valleys below. You never know what you'll find in that forest. A huge snake; a black panther. (I have seen the panther.)

In "Deathborn Light" Demi is a pale dirt-streaked monster. Her gentility is compromised because she's as cold as stone yet she defends Stephanie violently. I think it gives her great satisfaction to skewer Hugh onto that stake.

Demi's toughness feels very Australian, to me. We don't mind getting wet or dirty to do what we have to do.

I can envisage a sequel for "Deathborn Light". Demi finds the fully grown Stephanie, who is horrified to discover that her mother is a monster. Alternatively, Stephanie could force her foster mother to tell her where she was found, then she would search for Demi in the forest.

Maybe Demi and Stephanie will have to take on Hugh together. He died in "Deathborn Light", but will he stay dead? You never know what's hiding in a deep cold creek. And with a vampire, you can never be sure.

THE LIFE STEALER

DONNA MAREE HANSON

A cool breeze stroked Jake's neck as he gazed out over the Queanbeyan River from the veranda. He didn't mind the crispness in the air as it was a welcome reprieve from a series of long, hot nights.

The morning quiet cocooned him as he took in the bush clad hills looming over the near stagnant river and the housing estate surrounding it. Very soon the sounds of insects, bird calls and the yipping and bark of dogs intruded. Even with that background noise, he still felt it was quiet, so quiet and calm.

The scenery changed every day and yet it was so easy to take it for granted, to get up for work each day and not see it, not see the surrounding beauty. He remembered that from his childhood, living with a family that never understood his need to be close to growing things. Lucky for him, there had been a school teacher that took an interest and put him on a path to the ideal job—a park ranger. You would think with looking out over the forest canopy on bushfire watch would have cured him of looking at trees. Yet the canopy was always changing too, shifting colour and shape, just as a tree was different from the next one, in its posture, its texture and its character.

Jake laughed aloud, picturing a copse of cranky trees. My, he was fanciful this morning, he thought to himself.

The screen door opened and Rick leaned out, hair on end, eyes puffy with sleep. "You're up early man. You goin' to work?"

It wasn't quite bushfire season, so no lookout for him today. It was time to plough through the papers on his desk.

"Soon. Just enjoying the view."

"At seven thirty in the morning? Right. See ya, later, mate." The door clanged shut. Jake sighed. His housemates didn't quite get him. The house appealed because of the view of the river and the bush.

He dashed inside and put on his work shirt, hooked his phone to his belt, and stuffed his bag with his gear. Back out on the veranda, the sun brightened suddenly. He paused there on the stoop, looking out at the light as it played over the hills, seeing the dark clefts nestled between them, making him think of the secret shadow between a pair of breasts. The shadows moved quickly, dodging from one spot to the next. Some contracted and others darted to safe spots in a gully or under a rocky outcrop. Looking up, he saw scudding clouds, a large, slow one casting a sizable dark smudge beneath it. The shadows kept moving. His eyes danced as he following them, liking how the light changed the colours, until he felt it.

One shadow was not like the rest. Jake closed his eyes and felt it there like a hard dark nut of something. There was something similar inside him; anger, resentment, a feeling of being lost. This dark spot was not his feelings. It was separate, alive, hungry.

Jake sent a text to the office to let them know where he was, then he secured his pack to his lower back and headed towards the riverbank. He had to get closer, had to see for himself. Cars exiting driveways filled up the roads. The place was waking up around him. He dodged a few cars and continued. The ridge of hills rose up over him as he neared the river.

After climbing over the fence rail, he stood there, taking in the mallards waddling in the long grass as he contemplated the hill in front of him. Shifting his gaze left and right, he searched for that dark spot. Morning sunlight glittered oily on the surface of the sluggish water. The houses ran up close to the edge of the river in places. People talking, doors slamming and engines idling reached him. He had lost it. Temporarily frustrated, he lowered himself to the ground, rethinking its position in relation to home, while he ripped off the tops of the long grass, pulled them apart, shredded them, inhaling the sweet smell.

Alone with his thoughts, he could reach out to the world around him with his spirit. Since puberty, an awareness that was both fleeting and powerful had been growing in him. It came to him near water or the bush. He could spot wombats on the riverbank before others. Find lost things in the bush, whether it was a handbag or a lost shoe.

The sunlight brightened as the clouds shifted again. The green of the grass and the darker green of the trees faded in the harsh light. Day was here, washing away the sticky cobwebs of night, and revealing everything. He would have to move up the bank to locate that spot of darkness, that kernel of menace he had sensed earlier. It was there, he was sure, just not visible from where he was. He could taste its pain, as if sunlight hurt it.

A rudimentary weir down the banks of the slow moving river allowed for an easy crossing. Many locals walked their dogs or jogged there. The tracks cut into the bush rough, faded pink clay paths, held together by grasping tree roots. Dry, they were easy to walk along. He took a left and headed up the hill to the cleft where he felt the shadow lay.

The trees rustled around him as he climbed the path. Here and there, shafts of yellow sunlight filtered through the branches. A magpie flapped away. A couple of doves coo cooed as they launched from a branch. A trio of roos bounded away at his approach. He liked the feel of the bush around him, the life, the energy. He threw his concentration forward to the place where the dark spot of hunger dwelled.

It was as if the darkness was drawing him in, stuck like a pin in the map of his mind. The track was well worn. Water had washed the clay, leaving gouges and revealing large stones and thick tree roots. His toes gripped the soil as he pushed his way up the hill, dodging low-lying branches and bushes. He angled right and up following a twist in the track.

Sun filtered spots hit the leaves and the scent of eucalypt eased into the air as the day heated up. He drew near the spot, the base of one of the small hills, where the land rose up again, making a cleft where the sun rarely shone.

At his feet, he saw small dead things: dried corpses of possums, the dried hide of a wombat and the rotting frame of a young joey. He kneeled down and touched the ground, sweeping the dirt with his fingers. Tiny skeletons littered the soil; desiccated bodies of ants, millipedes, redback and huntsmen spiders. Lifting his head to take in his surroundings, he saw that it was a dead space, nothing remained alive in that spot. At the base of the bushes along the path, he could see tiny white bones of ribcages, some with feathers clinging to patches of dried skin. Even the foliage on the trees and scrub was dry, dead and brown.

Voices on the ridge above him filtered down to where he crouched. He squatted down and ran his hands over the dirt. He wanted to feel what that thing felt. It was a live thing, he was sure—a spot of dead that had a mind, a will and a hunger.

A sliver of fear entered his mind. Could he trust this knowing he had or was he losing his mind? They said his mother was so crazy she couldn't look after him, which was why he had ended up in foster care as a child. The memory of her was dim, faded. They say insanity runs in the blood.

Shaking off the doubt, Jake closed his eyes and inhaled, sending his other senses around him. A leaf jostled by the light breeze. A blow fly landing on the kangaroo carcass laying eggs. Already maggots were squirming in the dead flesh but there wasn't much left for the newly hatched ones to eat. He pictured the peeling bark on the gum tree behind him and the slow ooze of sap hardening on one side and the trail of dried, dead ants stuck to its trunk.

Below him, he sensed the carcasses of the dead earthworms, silverfish and cockroaches and even the death of the deep roots of more distant trees. The soil was dying. The trees here would die too eventually. They were starved of life. The whole area had the life sucked out of it.

The thing must have been trapped for a while considering how deeply the death went and how wide. It was gone now. Left this spot. Took its chance when the cloud blocked the sun and shifted in the shade. He wondered where it went.

From the ridge above him, the voices came again, suddenly clear. He could detect fear in their voices. Something was wrong. Taking an upward path, he walked under shafts of light, to where he thought the voices came from.

A smell of stale smoke teased his nostrils. It wasn't good that they had had a fire away from the approved camping grounds. He wondered if he should call it in. He frowned as he entered the small clearing where a small campsite had been set up.

A group of people huddled there and he saw that they were indigenous. They didn't start with surprise when they saw him but they stopped talking. It was an old woman with white hair and large sagging breasts, who came toward him. Her eyes rested briefly on his uniform and nametag. Trailing behind her were two young men, probably twenty or so, and a snotty nosed kid about seven years old. One of the young men, shorter than the other with a scar on his chest, nodded and said, "Bro . . ."

Jake nodded back but didn't speak. He found it hard to speak to indigenous people. The old woman moved toward him with an uneven gait, her dark eyes under white brows staring at him. She nodded as she moved closer.

"Who are your people,'" she asked Jake.

"I don't know," he answered. Can they tell his blood? Do they know if he is kin? Just then he realised why he felt uncomfortable. He was not part of them, didn't know them, their ways, their language. His father had been stolen from his family out bush somewhere and he had been too gone with drink to tell Jake what he needed to know. It was so long ago now and it didn't matter anymore.

"Why don't you know?" she asked him, still nodding as she sized him up.

Jake shrugged. He hated answering that question.

"I'm Pat. My people are the Ngunnawal people." The taller man came forward and offered his hand. Jake took it, surprised at the acceptance. "I'm Birdie and that's Arlo, my cous and that's little Bess."

Jake nodded. Pat stared at him. He coughed to cover his embarrassment, and stepped into his role as park ranger. "I'm sorry, you shouldn't have a fire here, shouldn't camp here either. If you have a map I can show you were the designated camps are . . ."

The old lady nodded but she wasn't listening. Her gaze moved to the bush around them, searching, waiting, hoping. On top of the hill, they stood together while she sniffed the air and then her gaze returned to him.

"Is there something wrong?" he asked her.

Her eyes lowered. "We're looking for someone."

Jake lifted his chin. "I'm looking for something."

Her left eyebrow lifted and the taller boy moved forward and whispered to her. She nodded as he poured words into her ears.

"What do you know?" she asked him again, her gaze now travelling over him and behind him as if he had brought more people with him.

Jake hunched his shoulders, feeling uncomfortable with her scrutiny. They were all looking at him, even the snot nosed kid. He didn't want to talk about the feeling. He didn't want to hear their laughter and their scorn.

Then the little kid, Bess, said, "Please."

Jake struggled, trying to frame the words, logically and well reasoned, and then realised that he couldn't. Not like that. He'd have to speak from his heart, from his true self.

"I felt something, something hungry, something that leaves bones behind."

The old woman nods. None of them was laughing.

"What are you looking for?" Jake asked her.

"My grandson, Lee. Went missing during the night. I think he strayed from his bed. We were camped, just for the weekend. We live in Canberra but we like to come here and be on the land sometimes."

"He's lost in the bush? You check the river?" Jake asked.

"Yeah. We did," said Arlo.

"Aunty, why are you wasting time talking to him? We should go looking again." Birdie added.

Pat kept her eyes on Jake, assessing, measuring. "He knows somethin'," she said at last.

Jake stepped back as the young men bristled, gathering their muscles, transforming from friendly to aggressive with a breath. "Tell us."

Pat shook her head. "Not about Lee, about what is out there, what might be dangerous to him. How to track it . . ."

"I'll call in the police."

"Wait," she said. "You can help us."

Jake was not sure what to do. Then he felt it, felt the presence shifting around him, away then closer. Above stray clouds cast running shadows. The thing was moving again. Jake wished he was a bird so he could look down, pin point it in the trees, in the shadows. He had a stray thought that if he stayed in the sun he'd be safe. But safe was not on his mind. He wanted to help find the little boy, keep him from the thing.

A shiver passed through him. It wasn't some thing, some oddity, it was a threat to him, to the missing kid. "I should get help."

"If you don't find him then call for help, but later. Go now. I have a feeling there is not much time."

He nodded. His phone had a satellite connection. He could call it in. "Do you men have a light, a torch or something?"

Birdie nodded and went to the pile of belongings and brought over a couple of torches, checking that they worked as he did so.

Jake undid his pack and drew out his own. "Keep them with you."

Birdie wrinkled his brow. "But it's daylight and fully sunny. What do I want a torch for?"

"The search may take a while, until night even. Or you may go into a canyon, into shadow, and then you'll need it."

In the dirt, Jake drew a rough map of their position. "Birdie you go into that section, search closely, look for anything. Arlo do the same thing but here. Do you know the rocky outcrop? Good. We'll meet there in three hours or so. I'll take this section?"

The young men nodded. "What about aunty?" asked Birdie.

Jake saw how difficult the old woman found it to walk and knew she couldn't go down the ridge face.

Pat picked up on his hesitation. "I'll keep calling out to him so he knows where we are. Go," she said. "Follow your feeling. Keep looking."

Jake darted into the scrub trying to escape the rocking emotions the encounter caused. Meeting them opened up a part of him, he thought he had put away forever. He breathed slow and deep, trying to immerse himself in the bush once more. He needed to stay focussed because a child was in danger.

He heard Pat calling instructions to her nephews. They made a noise as they pushed into the bush clump, clumping and snapping branches. The sounds put Jake's teeth on edge. Jake glided through the bush, carefully shifting branches and passing over fallen ones without snapping them. Not far in, he found signs of the boy's passing. There was a sock, dirty and covered in dried leaves and small twigs. There was also a broken branch, low down, like where a child would be.

There was a smell, familiar and rank. Death. Old death. He widened his search and then centred on the spot where the stench emanated. He drew nearer, his heart beating hard in his chest. He saw the khaki walking boot first. At an angle, the naked ankle bones protruded. The corpse was dried and shrivelled. A lost bushwalker maybe. The clothes were fairly clean and dry and there was a backpack nearby, covered in leaf fall.

Jake pulled out his phone and dialled the office. "Yeah, it's me, Jake. Look I'm out here at ridge on back of Queanbeyan River."

"Aren't you on duty?" the receptionist asked.

"Yes, kind of. Look I have a situation out here. I need to report a body. I'm going to message you the coordinates. I'm searching for a lost kid right now, but let the cops know and I'll guide them in. Okay?"

The receptionist rang off, promising to let all those who needed to know what was going on. Jake checked the coordinates on his GPS and then texted them to the office. Jake finished up examining the site and then moved on.

Signs of small deaths, of the little lives stolen, baby possums, a cockatoo, a brown snake littered the area in a narrow line. As if a tendril of dark, sucking death had reached out to snatch at passing life. He realised it was not an old body, long forgotten, unknown. It was new, the clothes weren't weathered. The thing had taken it, taken the life from the man. When someone found the body, they'd think he died of thirst and hunger all shrivelled up like that. He thought of the little boy and the old lady who loved him, cared for him, who was family to him. He did not want that child's life stolen.

The light around him faded. Looking up he could see the clouds closed over and darkness formed around him. He wondered then, could the creature jump between pools of shadow or did it need a continuous channel of dark? Despite the questions, the logic, he felt the threat. The creature was close, hunger and darkness driving it. He flicked on the torch and shined it around him. It barely made a difference so he flicked it off.

Jake didn't know what to do as the afternoon came and the shadows lengthened. Jake liked the night. The thing that threatened him was not the dark itself but something that waited in the dark to steal life. He patted the torch, hoping it would be enough. He met Arlo and Birdie in the shadow of the outcrop. They shook their heads when he approached them.

"I found this," Jake said as he held up the sock. Birdie's sharp intake of breath was enough confirmation.

"It's getting late, so keep your torches handy. I want you to come down through this section here, spread out but stay within shouting range. I'll keep my back to the outcrop so you should be able to locate me at short notice."

Jake glided between the low-lying scrub and carefully stepped over fallen branches. He gritted his teeth at the sound of Birdie and Arlo crunching through the bush.

"Lee!" he called out.

When he found a small sandshoe, he called out again, certain that he was close. He could feel that mind, that hunger so the creature was close as well.

A whimper sounded close by and he knew it was the boy. "Lee? Lee. I'm coming to get you," he called out. There was an answering wail.

The muffled sounds of voices reached him. It was Birdie and Arlo not too far away. "I found him!"

He jogged, pushing a branch out of his way, then pulled up short. The boy was up a tree about one hundred metres away. Not a very convenient spot for rescue and not a safe place to hide from the creature.

He sensed the mind behind the spot he'd been following and his gaze riveted to the dark patch of shadow at the base of the tree. It was alive, hungry, desperate. The clouds moved again. The light arrowed down through the trees and a shaft fell on the tree trunk where the boy was clinging. The slavering spot of dark pulled back, fearing the light.

A sound of leaves crunching drew Jake's attention. A couple of kangaroos bounded through the bush, followed closely by Birdie and Arlo. The boy, Lee, saw them and cried louder.

Birdie went to walk over to get him.

"No wait. See that?" Jake said pointing.

Birdie paused. Both he and Arlo shared a look and turned their gaze to the shady spot on the ground. The creature was featureless and formless. Its shadowed form rose up like a blob of liquid tar on the boil.

Two pairs of rounded eyes stared back at him. "That's it?" Arlo choked out.

Jake nodded.

Already the ground was dry and brown. In the surrounding area, the leaves fluttered down already dead and a trail of bull ants, slowly filling up with casualties.

The creature was between them. This close Jake could feel its thoughts, feelings. It was hungry, afraid, angry, alone. It did not want to die. The light shifted again and the thing silently shrieked, sending a wave of emotion over Jake. Perhaps it didn't need to hear to track its prey. Maybe it could feel him, sense life, as he could sense it.

It was growing darker beneath the canopy of the trees. It would be dark there before the fall of night. They had to use the light while they could.

He pulled out is torch and switched on. With a nod to the others they did the same. "Be ready," he said.

A shaft of sunlight speared down, clearing a path to the tree. Jake saw his chance and darted across the space between them. He jumped at the trunk to where the boy clung. After a little bit of convincing,

Lee let go the tree and clutched him tight. His little body shook. Jake clutched him awkwardly, checking the ground to make sure there was still a patch of light to land on.

He shone the torch at the base of the tree to make certain. "Here focus your torches here." Arlo and Birdie turned their lights to the base of the tree, even though it was still bathed in sunlight. Jake dropped, clutching the boy to him.

With his feet on the ground, he sensed the creature all around him, waiting to suck out their lives. They were food, nothing more. The shadows lurched again and light and dark shifted like disco lights along the leaf litter. Jake ran quickly to follow the sunlit path. Arlo and Birdie kept their torches focussed on them. Lee boy screamed as the shadow lunged. Turning back, Jake fumbled for the torch and shone it straight into the dark centre. The creature recoiled a fraction, enough to give Jake space.

Jake took a dive with the boy and landed in a clearing where the sun beat down. The boy, Lee, whimpered and Jake thought he might have been hurt. "Let me see," he said to the boy.

Arlo and Birdie retreated, stepping close to huddle with them. Their torches shone outward, bathing them in a ball of safe life.

Jake reeled from the sight. The toes on Lee's right foot were shrivelled, dead. They had not saved the boy completely, some of him was sacrificed to the creature. A wind came and shook the trees and darkness grew around them. He patted the boy on the head. Snot and tears covered the boy's dark face. "I'll take you back to your grandmother, okay?" The boy nodded, his tears slowing.

To the others he said, "I'll call an ambulance and have them meet us at the gate near the oval. You know it?"

"Yep we came in that way," Birdie said.

Jake bent down and hoisted the boy on his back. They ran the distance, puffing and wheezing with the exertion of climbing the ridge and having that thing chasing them. Once full darkness was on them, the creature would have no restraint.

As they neared the clearing he called out. "We've found him. We have him."

Pat climbed down the slope part way to meet them. "My boy. My little boy. You are safe."

They met and she clutched the boy to her chest, running her hands over him and checking everywhere to make sure he was whole. Her hands paused on his bare feet.

"I'm sorry. His toes. It got his toes."

Pat held the boy's foot and cried. Wiping her tears, she said, "He lost his toes. He could have lost his life."

"I've called an ambulance. Best get him seen to."

Pat nodded and Birdie and Arlo went to their belongs to pack up. Jake's phone beeped. He glanced at the screen quickly. The police were waiting for him and an ambulance had arrived at the same location.

The afternoon sun slid behind the hills. The colours around them darkened and the smells changed with the dew. Jake felt a shiver. He could still feel the creature, feel its hunger. It was still there, maybe it would always be there, loitering, waiting in the bush, in the dark clefts between the hills and in the crevices of valleys.

"It's not safe here. Not in the dark," he said.

"Yes, I agree. You come with me, yes?" said Pat, clinging to her grandson while she walked with her rocking gate and part limped toward the car.

Jake thanked her. "I have things I must do now."

"You don't have to stay lost, you know."

"What?" He stopped dead and gaped at her. How did she . . .

"You don't have to have your life stolen like your father's was. You can find your life, your heritage."

Jake swallowed. He tried to forget that stuff, tried to make it seem like it didn't matter.

"I . . . er . . ."

After placing the boy in the car, she touched his hand. "Look for me and I'll help you okay. I'll help you get your life back."

Nodding dumbly, Jake watched them pull out. He'd check with the hospital when he finished up here. There was a warm spot inside of him. Pat had kindled something, a hope, a possibility that there was more to who he was. The close encounter with the life stealer made him think it was time for him to find that which was stolen.

† † †

The police brought lots of equipment with them in a van. Harsh, powerful spotlights attached to a generator. Jake grinned at the sight of them. By night the body of the bushwalker was fully illuminated. He felt the creature out there still, circling, prowling. The darkness allowed it to roam freely, supping on little lives, letting them plop to the ground. Where did such a thing come from? How was it held in check? Fire, he thought to himself. A bushfire could run faster than it, could trap it in a swift change of wind. Nature kept it under control.

The creature came closer, held at bay by the bright lights. Jake stood watching silently, listening the chatter as the police and forensics examined the corpse and the scene, looking for signs of foul play.

A lone technician left the others, went out into the darkness beyond the closer trees to piss. Jake felt the creature move. Without thinking, Jake leaped up to the nearest stand holding the searchlight and swung it around.

The technician started in fright. "Stupid pervert bastard!" he yelled as he tugged up his fly. "Nearly pissed all over myself."

"Sorry, thought I saw something." Jake kept the light on the creature, heard it scream, felt it shrink, felt it skulk away, far away.

AFTERWORD TO "THE LIFE STEALER"

The idea for the creature in "The Life Stealer" came to me when I was walking down to the Queanbeyan River in Karabar, New South Wales, not far from home. The sun was setting, the green of the trees and the shrubs altered, grew richer, darker and the shadows in the clefts of the hills moved slowly. There always seemed to be a dark place where the sun never shone and I thought what if . . .

It took a while for the story to grow, to find the right character to carry it through. It was then I thought of the stolen generation, of the culture denied and the struggle for its return and of Jake, a man even further removed from his heritage. The life stealer teaches him that it is not too late to get back that which has been stolen.

BEHIND THE BLACK MASK

JACOB EDWARDS

15TH FEBRUARY 1879

A telegram has arrived via Mr Seymour from the Chief Commissioner of Police, a Captain Standish. The fellow is renowned, Seymour informs me, as an obdurate man but at last has consented to seek out our assistance. Which is just as well. We set out two days ago.

Corporal Charlie is in a bad way and from the demeanour of the others I cannot imagine that he will pull through. I came across Billy staring off into the distance, as they do, and tried to broach the subject with him; but before I could utter a word he gave a terse shake of his head and told me, "Yarama'yhawho strong, Mr O'Connor. Charlie strong too. Hold Yarama'yhawho, but Yarama'yhawho not let go. Them both for the never-never."

Billy speaks with matter-of-factness but over these last few months I have come also to recognise just the faintest brushstrokes of anger; sorrow; pride; purpose. My teachers might appear as impassive as the country they bestride yet they are tied to this dry, austere land and comport themselves as befits men of responsibility.

Captain Standish has sanctioned our involvement. We would have come even had he forbidden it: Billy, Harry and Tommy; Jimmy; Dick; Corporal Charlie, whose insides still writhe; and me, a white man sharing their burden.

We head south to where it lurks.

† † †

3RD MARCH 1879

The *Alexandra* has arrived in Sydney: two weeks from Cooktown via Brisbane and we all of us hope never to set foot on a steamship again. The journey has been particularly harsh on Corporal Charlie, who is feverish from the Yarama'yhawho and suffered even more than the others on occasion of being cut off from the land.

We travel now by train to Wagga Wagga and then Albury, where Captain Standish waits to accompany us on to Benalla. This town will serve for our base as we attempt to track down the scourge.

Autumn is upon us and frowns coldly as we move further from the coast: south and west, far from the tropics of Cape York Peninsula. The trackers shiver in their blue uniforms and gaze restlessly out the window, yearning for the bush.

Somewhere out there the Yarama'yhawho waits.

†   †   †

18TH MARCH 1879

Our first expedition has proven a disaster. Standish—who is indeed a brash and stubborn man—insisted that we take white officers and pack horses enough to seek out the Holy Grail itself; and for consequence of this we proceeded but slowly, and with much noise. Having caught thus not a whiff of our quarry, Captain Standish then thought to place the blame not where it belongs but instead upon the trackers, whom he perceives in some way as having retarded our progress!

Even when Corporal Charlie died and, in Billy's words, "took him Yarama'yhawho never-never", Standish saw this not as an act of strength or courage but rather as weakness. He knows not what we do nor even what we hunt. Bushrangers, he thinks; men of horse and pistol living as fugitives in the vast tangle beyond civilisation. But our presence in Benalla is too readily apparent and wherever we set foot we find that sympathetic mouths have forewarned these so-called outlaws. No longer do they travel by horse—such animals being too easy to track—nor do they rely on anything so ineffective as mere pistols. The Yarama'yhawho is an insidious foe. It bides its time. It sticks close to the trees.

And so we must leave: up into the Wombat Ranges where we know there to have been bloodshed. "Yarama'yhawho, him live for blood," says Harry. "Start with blood, Mr O'Connor, then we find him bloodsucker."

† † †

21 MARCH 1879

We camp tonight at Stringybark Creek, having spent much of the day riding through thick, dreary forest. It is cold up here in the ranges; wet and dark. Imperious blue gum trees rise alongside mountain swampies to form a canopy far above our heads. They blot out nearly all the sunlight, yet beneath them there still thrives a wild tussle of wattles and dogwood; bracken and mongrel shrubs and wildflowers whose names I can only guess at. The bush rustles and bristles with life: from the steady passage of wallabies, echidnas and lizards to the flittering transience of currawongs and bowerbirds. Wonga pigeons let forth operatic *coos!* from above while at ground level a sinister posse of lyrebirds surrounds us. So acutely do these birds mimic the scraping of pans, the whinnying of horses—even the sound of gunfire!—that I am posed no great difficulty in imagining the events that Billy has described for me.

Harry, Dick, Tommy and Jimmy are out patrolling a half-mile circle around the campsite, checking for signs of the Yarama'yhawho and hunting for dinner as they go. Their eyesight is incredible. I have seen them spot horses more than a mile away and tell accurately as to whether or not these animals are saddled. They can discern from the faintest of tracks not only what creature has passed but also how long ago and often its age and size. A scratch; a broken twig; a discolouration caused by sweat: to outsiders it seems impossible but even after five months Billy was able to read to me the bush at Stringybark Creek.

"Man him shoot at parrots." Billy handed me a blue tail-feather. "Yarama'yhawho, him quiet, him hunt, but man him shoot." He ran one finger over a sap-cauterised nick in the nearby wattle tree. "Him miss." A flare of the nostrils and then: "Man him camp here, him make fire. Yarama'yhawho come hunt man but Yarama'yhawho fear fire, him stay back. Others—" Crouching down. "With Yarama'yhawho but not Yarama'yhawho, walk like men, shoot like men. Spill blood here, and here, and here . . ."

On he went, telling it just the same as it's written in the police report; only better, because the authorities do not know of the Yarama'yhawho or what role it played in the massacre. Even the surviving Constable—McIntyre, I believe his name is—knew only the details of what had taken place, his ignorance prompting him to overlook the devil within.

But where to next?

The trackers have just returned, Jimmy carrying carrot-shaped tubers in one hand; Tommy a small snake; and Dick what looks to be a wild pig. Harry shrugs one shoulder as if to say, "No wombat, Mr O'Connor"; but even so, we shall eat well this evening, sobered only by thoughts of what less palatable offerings may have been devoured upon this very spot.

With night comes a deepening of the forest's natural darkness. The first, insomnious possums set off across branches high above us and somewhere off to my right a lyrebird lets loose with an all-too-human cry of anguish. The bush echoes with its eerie refrains. I find myself shivering, for this is a place of restless dreams; of turning in one's sleep.

Billy will keep the fire alight. Come morning the trackers will round up our horses and we shall see if anything remains of the Yarama'yhawho's trail.

†   †   †

24TH MAY 1879

Our time here is becoming ever more frustrating. Benalla is a cold, miserable place and the surrounding land is bestrewn with miscreants and misinformation. Adding to our difficulties, Captain Standish has now proven himself thoroughly intractable.

We returned to the hotel this evening and found everyone in a state of great excitement, there being much movement over at the barracks. I inquired of Superintendent Hare as to what news had been received but he had been sworn to secrecy by Standish and felt duty-bound to play dumb through his embarrassment. Tommy has talked to Moses, a fellow tracker, and learned of a sighting made just east of John Patterson's; Cleary's place, he said, on the road to Tom Smith's. I confronted Standish immediately and berated him over the folly of withholding this information from us, but he was unrepentant and indeed positively forbade us from joining the party under Hare's command, boasting: "I will endeavour to get at them without your assistance!"

Trumped-up ignoramus. I told him to go sit under a fig tree.

Superintendent Hare at least seems a good enough sort and if not for Standish's reprobation would, I imagine, be rather more favourably disposed towards us. Still, our position is galling.

"Bloodsucker," said Billy to Captain Standish, a squirming leech held between thumb and forefinger. "This one him small. Yarama'yhawho big. This one him stupid. Yarama'yhawho clever." He pointed one arm towards the bush: the wild country through which ride outlaws, stirring up their hue and cry. Outlaws, and other things.

"Blackfellas, we hunt Yarama'yhawho," Billy continued. "Whitefella—" He dropped the leech contemptuously at Standish's feet. "Whitefella, him just blood walking."

Then he turned his back and stalked off into the darkness.

†   †   †

27TH JUNE 1879

Just this night we've heard tale of the murder of one Aaron Sherritt: identified as a police informer and shot dead in his hut up at Woolshed. Joe Byrne is the man responsible, or so says the market gardener whom the murderer and an accomplice obliged to knock on Sherritt's door. A telegraph from Superintendent Hare requests we join him on the train to Beechworth and thence in pursuit of the murderers.

"Yarama'yhawho wants trap us," opines Harry. "Knows what Charlie done other bloodsucker. Afraid us blackfellas."

"We go," Billy decides. "Yarama'yhawho hunt night. Sun him come, him go. Sherritt blood cold. Go now, sun him come again. Yarama'yhawho think us afraid, think us not go."

But my teachers do not recognise fear, preferring instead to see only what is and what needs to be; and so we hunt. A special train from Melbourne yard is due soon.

†   †   †

28TH JUNE 1879

We left Essendon shortly after ten o'clock last night and pulled into Benalla this morning at half past one. Superintendent Hare and his seven troopers having embarked, we continued on towards Beechworth, a pilot engine now preceding us in case the lines ahead had been torn up or laid over with logs. Steam billowed from both engines and the wheeze of the pistons was unnaturally eerie, coming as it did from two trains in convoy and accompanied by the distinctive *choo-choo* of the pressure valves opening, sometimes separately, at other times in unison. We proceeded cautiously along our metal snake-path through the bush, slowing then stopping at an out-of-the-way town by name of Glenrowan.

"Here," said Dick. He had his head stuck out the window and his nostrils flared open. "Yarama'yhawho close."

At my nod Superintendent Hare ordered the horses be taken from the train. Adding to the urgent whispers and quiet whinnying, the metal clomp of horseshoe on wood, there came the sound of someone approaching: ragged, breathless gasps; the heavy tumble of booted feet. Police Constable Bracken (as we later learned his name to be) staggered onto the platform and grasped Hare by the arm, pointing back toward the township.

"Over there—" he urged. "Not five minutes ago—stuck us all up—the four of them—quick, quick!"

I started to rise but hesitated when Tommy and Jimmy remained seated beside me. I looked to Harry who sat squinting down the uncocked barrel of his revolver. Next to him Billy stared back at me and shook his head. "Sun him not come, Mr O'Connor. Yarama'yhawho strong now. Want us come. Think us run never-never." Dick pulled his head back in and closed his eyes. "Old spirit, evil spirit. Yarama'yhawho strong when sun him not come. Us wait, Mr O'Connor, then sun him come with us."

Superintendent Hare was not privy to this conversation and would not likely have taken heed even had he been; instead, he grabbed up a rifle and dashed off towards the Glenrowan Inn, some 200 yards distant, shouting, "Come along, boys!" Believing themselves to be in pursuit of ordinary bushrangers, the seven troopers rushed pell-mell after him while their horses galloped off in the other direction and hid themselves in a nearby paddock.

Shortly thereafter the first shot rang out, its powdery discharge segueing at once into a splintering ricochet off rotten wood. Further shots followed and before long the crisp predawn resounded with urgent entreaties and the smattered, pinpointed *crack!* of rifle fire. It was all I could do to stay put at first. The impromptu siege called to me, pulling at my resolve; but Jimmy, perhaps sensing my unease, began to tap his rifle against the window of our carriage. Tommy joined in, striking up a rhythm in counterpart while Billy and Harry closed their eyes and let forth a low, rumbling chant. Then Dick sang.

He sang the story of Yarama'yhawho: of his birth amidst the murky waters of a billabong near the Murrumbidgee; of his growth and emergence and of how he took shelter beneath the rough leaves of a sandpaper fig; of his patience, his thirst; of how he dropped down upon his first victim and drank of the animal in its sleep, the two of them slowly merging into one creature; of Yarama'yhawho's transcendence; of how he spat his host out, smaller and redder, and took his own, newly engorged body back up into the fig tree, thence to drop down again upon a bigger, meatier animal . . . I had heard the tale before—or as much of it as I can make out with my smattering of the Murri language—yet as ever it entranced me, soothing my nerves even as it chilled the bones upon which rests my blood-soaked and vulnerable flesh. Gunfire continued to sound from inside and around the inn but against the backdrop of chanting it seemed muffled, like the crackling of burning wood as one stares entranced at a campfire. "Then Yarama'yhawho, him stand up," Dick concluded. "Him spit out man come never-never. Him walk like us." Abruptly, Jimmy and Tommy stopped tapping. Billy and Harry let their chant drop away, like the last rumbling echo of a bullroarer. Dick whispered: "Yarama'yhawho, him hunt now."

It was cold in the carriage. White smoke drifted over from the inn, looking for all the world like the frosted breath of some angry giant. A bullet struck our engine with a fulminous *ping!* and shortly thereafter Superintendent Hare reappeared, his wrist held awkwardly and his boots crunching the gravel path as he staggered towards us. "I'm hit," he proclaimed; and indeed the blood ran freely from his wound. We patched him up as best we could and sent him off on the train back to Benalla.

When finally the dawn approached, a foreboding silence fell down upon the town of Glenrowan. It was as if the combatants had paused to take stock; to check their weapons and ammunition; to see indeed whether their own persons had made it unscathed through to the breaking of this new day. The horses agitated in the nearby paddock but all else was still. White man in tow, my teachers crept from the train station and spread out in a circle around the inn, vanishing into the darkness with an ease scarcely credible. Black Devils, according to the Yarama'yhawho. Angels, more like, though certainly they meant to bedevil those holed up within the inn.

Patchiness and confusion here taint my recollections; it is so soon after the events in question and yet still I find myself as muddled as the next man! I remember the firing starting up again. I recall taking cover in a nearby drain-way while Jimmy, Tommy, Billy, Harry and Dick sought a reckoning with those vile creatures, one the likes of whom had taken Corporal Charlie with it into the never-never. Guns popped and bullets flew in all directions; disappearing into the bush, clanging off the inn's iron roof. A woman tore out her soul, shrieking, "They've killed my child, they've killed my child!" over and over again. Blood flowed and in the coldness of that fateful morning I thought I might see Yarama'yhawho's last stand.

Of the three accomplices Joe Byrne was first to fall, a shot from Harry piercing his groin even as he raised a drink to the gang's bloody new way of life. Harry once told me: "Yarama'yhawho, him suck blood, Mr O'Connor. Don't mean him not need blood." And it was true. Byrne fell to the floor and bled out through his femoral artery; a witness later confirmed that he died within seconds.

Steve Hart and Dan Kelly went next and from the manner of their passing I can only conclude that they had not yet been fully subsumed. In Billy's words: "Yarama'yhawho, him need blood. Man him need alcohol. When them fight them drink both. Big drink, big mix." Which explained why Hart and Kelly had drunk the bar almost dry and why the Glenrowan Inn then burst up into an unholy conflagration. I shan't ever forget the sight of Billy dropping cartridges into his .577 Snider-Enfield. *Bang!* He would fire a shot; upend the rifle to release the spent shell; then *Bang!* Ten shots in one minute, I counted, each wooden bullet set alight in the small fire by his feet before being loaded up and sent flying into the inn. How he avoided burning himself I shall never know but the proof of his work was beyond dispute: decrepit weatherboards caught light wherever struck and Steve Hart and Dan Kelly did likewise; the alcohol in their blood ignited and the erstwhile bushrangers went up like haystacks. They screamed—that small part of them that was yet to succumb—while the Yarama'yhawho let forth a screeching that ripped and tore at the eardrums of all present. Both creatures blazed into the never-never.

It was about then that Dick crouched down at my side and said, "Look close, Mr O'Connor. Yarama'yhawho, him scared now. Him run back bush, find fig tree."

Yarama'yhawho afraid? I opened my mouth to question the wisdom of this assertion but Dick stood and was gone, just one more shadow in the all-embracing gloom. Barely a minute passed before he was proven wrong.

Wood crackled as the Glenrowan Inn burned. Yells and wails issued from within and forthwith there came an exodus of hostages no longer held prisoner. At last the sun popped up for a cautious look over the tops of the gum trees and as I rose similarly from the cover of the drain, that is when the Yarama'yhawho appeared.

The first I knew of it was when the sporadic gunfire changed direction and became more focussed. I turned, as did many a white man, to see five black figures converging on what appeared to be a tall, pale ghost, and peppering it with rifle shot. Their target had no head—only a neck—and bullets bounced off it to no effect. *Ping! Clang! Ding! Tonk!* The apparition advanced in turn, its movements slow beneath a long, cotton coat. Dark boots scrunched the ground underfoot. It held a revolver in one hand.

Ding! Clang! The headless bushman ploughed on. *Ping! Tonk!* "*You can't hurt me!*"

This seemed to me to be more than just an idle boast and so I sank a little deeper into the recesses of the drain in which I huddled. But the trackers quickly saw what others might have failed to: that the monstrosity before them was not headless at all, merely helmeted; and that its long coat concealed boiler plate armour that extended no further than the upper leg.

The metal-sheathed creature raised its revolver and turned its bucket head in search of a target. As it rested one booted foot up upon a log, Billy crouched down and sighted along the barrel of his .577 Snider.

"*You can't hurt me!*" taunted the bushranger once more.

Billy shot him in the legs at thirty paces.

I doubt if anyone else saw the entirety of what happened next; but from my vantage point I took in the whole ghastly spectacle. Tommy and Jimmy fired further shots and the helmeted figure began reeling about, roaring in fury. Dick added a bullet, then Harry, and eventually their target came crashing down to lie broken next to the log upon which it so recently had struck pose. Everyone rushed forward to see what lay underneath the long coat and armour; the face beneath the black helmet. It was a man of course: a small, red-skinned man who seemed now dwarfed by his outlandish accoutrements. The reason for this—and it was only I who knew it—was that the Yarama'yhawho had spat him out shortly after being shot and now was humping its bloated, corpulent body over towards the shelter of the bush.

"Billy!" I yelled out. "It's getting away!"

The creature cut a nauseating sight: all sagging bits of skin yet strangely engorged and dripping with blood. It moved in a lurching progression of desperate surges, like cow udders cut loose and bequeathed life, yet despite this urgency it should never have gotten far. But there was too much smoke from the gunfight; too much commotion around the bushranger's fallen body. Billy and Harry, Tommy, Jimmy and Dick, they all took off in pursuit; but before they could close in upon it the bloodsucker had squirmed away and lost itself in the dense undergrowth. Boneless, formless, it fled through the scrub and disappeared.

And so the siege ended in Pyrrhic victory. Word spread of the gang's defeat and those who had been held captive inside now formed a bucket line to save Glenrowan's burning inn. Joe Byrne's body was strung up for the photographers. The surviving bushranger had his wounds tended. There would be a trial; execution; celebration . . . but not for everyone. The trackers stood with their backs to it all; heedless of the commotion; sombre and still in their contemplation of the bush that lies ahead.

Black mask notwithstanding, the Yarama'yhawho has escaped.

† † †

11 NOVEMBER 1880

Ned Kelly was executed this morning: hanged at Melbourne Gaol despite a petition for clemency that ran to some 30,000 signatures. He looked dazed and to me appeared ill-at-ease, more so even than one might expect given his impending death. Circumstances drove Kelly into the bush. Something else entirely brought him back out. Seemingly, he had no more idea than anybody else as to what precisely had happened.

"Such is life," Ned Kelly is said to have mumbled by way of final words—which I suppose would be apt enough, although I did not myself hear him speak. I was too busy appraising his shrunken red skin, seeking a glimpse of the creature that for a time had swallowed up and consumed him. None was to be found. Ned Kelly looked no more threatening than a raspberry shaken loose and fallen from the bramble.

They'll take his body away, I suppose, and cut off his head, examining its contours for any lumps and bumps that could explain the young man's ascent into ignominy. The Yarama'yhawho being what it is, they might even find something. But anything they do uncover will be the result of effect, not cause. Ned Kelly's mortal remains will yield nothing by way of the truth; for truth is a commodity reserved for the land's guardians and shared but rarely with white men such as myself.

"Whitefella come live, Mr O'Connor. Come live but him not here," Billy told me soon after we met. He stood motionless and black as a burnt-out wattle, one arm held in front of him, finger pointing to the dry bushland that we Europeans find so alien. "See fig tree, think fig tree. See billabong, think billabong. Whitefella, him not look what them carry. Us blackfellas careful, Mr O'Connor. See land, feel land, walk land. But you whitefellas—" I've never forgotten how he turned his head ever so slightly towards me, as if my presence were, *ipso facto*, enough to justify his verdict "—you all for the never-never."

Looking back at what's happened I find it hard now to argue. Ned Kelly is dead, and Dan Kelly and Steve Hart and Joe Byrne as well; but as men rejoice throughout the six colonies—rejoice or mourn, each according to his disposition—even now the scourge lurks with baleful eyes upon us: from egg to mosquito to bilby to wombat and now, with our arrival, into something else entirely . . .

Wherever there is blood, Yarama'yhawho lies waiting.

AFTERWORD TO "BEHIND THE BLACK MASK"

A history of bad blood: there are few more striking images in Australia's wild, colonial history than that of Ned Kelly's helmeted figure surging forward against a hail of bullets at Glenrowan, his own pistols firing defiantly. Australians acknowledge—and often celebrate—our outlaw heritage, and Ned Kelly's iconic rise to infamy reflects many aspects of Australia's frontier evolution from convict colony through early settlement to an increasingly free and independent nation. When the Kelly Gang took to the bush, they stood on the one hand as anathema to the governing upper class but on the other as a rallying inspiration for poor and downtrodden migrants. Ned Kelly was himself mistreated by the authorities and, though violent and coarse in his behaviour, must nevertheless be acknowledged as having sought out both social and libertarian reform. The shoot-out at Glenrowan constitutes a preserved moment in our historical development from "English" to "Australian".

Consigned to the background throughout much of this struggle were the Aboriginal people upon whose land it played out; yet even from the pages of an overwhelmingly white historical record it seems clear that black trackers played a significant part in the Ned Kelly saga. The names of Stanhope O'Connor's native troopers are recorded—albeit mostly in arbitrary, Anglicised form, with little consistency—and in recent times the descendants of two of the trackers have taken legal action over the non-payment of £50 rewards that had been promised to and then withheld from their ancestors. O'Connor himself clearly saw an injustice, refusing on principle to accept his own reward. Here, as elsewhere, the unwritten Aboriginal history of Australia invites further investigation.

The Yarama'yhawho—for those who may not recognise its sketchy appropriation from Aboriginal legend—is Australia's first vampire, and remains no less frightening through dint of colonisation and the written ascendancy of Bram Stoker's progeny.

INTERVIEW WITH THE JIANGSHI

ANNE MOK

"I shouldn't even be here," I griped at April, as we stood in line for registration. "I don't know how you convinced me, but your whammy is wearing off."

She punched me lightly in the shoulder. "Don't chicken out now, Jackson. It won't be as bad as you think."

"Really?" The line moved forward, and the giant banner above the registration desk glittered into view, silver thread on black velvet:

TENTH ANNUAL INTERNATIONAL VAMPIRE CONVENTION
FANGS FOR THE MEMORIES

"Come on," April said. "Everyone likes a good pun."

I could have disputed whether any pun deserved to be called good, but that wasn't the real problem.

The line moved forward again, and we were standing in front of the desk. A pale blonde woman in a black dress smiled toothily at us. "Names?"

"April Sullivan," April said, smiling toothily back. "And Jackson Cheng."

"Sullivan, Cheng." She ticked off our names, but her pen continued to hover over mine. "Mr Cheng, you're listed here as a full member, not an associate member . . ." She trailed off, eyeing me up and down: my lack of a toothy smile; my long white hair and pointed black nails; and, of course, the obvious unlikelihood of anyone named Vlad in my ancestry.

"He is a full member," April assured her. "He's a Chinese vampire."

"I'm sorry, I didn't realise." She sounded as uncertain as I felt, covering it with an awkward smile.

"No problem. I get that a lot."

"Here are your programs and badges. Enjoy the convention!"

We shuffled off to the side of the foyer, April scanning the program avidly while I tried to look unobtrusive. It wasn't hard. The Melbourne International Convention Centre was built on an ostentatious scale, lined with towering columns, and walled with long panels of glass. All the windows, floor to ceiling, were draped in thick black velvet, screening out the sun. You couldn't tell it was dusk over the Yarra.

"All this glass seems kind of hazardous," I remarked. "Wouldn't it be better to book somewhere more shielded? Then you wouldn't have to bother with all these blackout curtains."

"This is a world class convention," April said absently, "and it deserves to be at a world class convention centre. We're not going to huddle in some concrete bunker like second class citizens."

"You sound like Richard Wells," I said.

"Oh no!" She thrust her program in front of my face. "His keynote address started five minutes ago."

"All right," I sighed. She probably meant to get his autograph too.

† † †

Richard Wells didn't look particularly vampiric, with his red hair and craggy features, and broad shoulders filling out his grey suit. But he was probably the closest to an unofficial spokesman we had down under. He had campaigned tirelessly for the Undead Rights Act, pushed discrimination test cases through the High Court, and even run for Federal Parliament. And whenever Pamela Hayward appeared in the news, putting forward the honey poison of the Humanity Alliance, Richard Wells would be there too, with his reasoned rebuttals and impassioned arguments.

I had heard him speak before, so I let my attention drift to the audience instead. Men and women, mostly in black; the majority seemed to be Europeans, although there was a sizeable American contingent, and a fair representation of locals. I've organised enough conferences to expect speeches to bring on fidgeting and distraction, but today, no one was checking their email while Richard was talking. The energy in the atmosphere was palpable.

"We've come a long way," he was saying, "but we've still got a long way to go. Right now, Parliament is debating the Undead Registration Act, which would force us to be tracked like criminals. We must let the world know that we will not stand for our freedoms to be curtailed in the name of fear! This isn't just a convention: this is a meeting of minds, where together we can tackle the great problems of our age."

Thunderous applause, as he stepped back from the spotlight. The qi levels surged, making me dizzy, and I had to grip my armrests to keep myself upright, to restrain the impulse to breathe it all in like oxygen.

When I could focus again, I was sitting alone in the row. Everyone else was filing out, a few casting me odd looks. I searched for April; she stood in the knot of people who were clustered around Richard. She waved me down.

Richard seemed keen to talk to everyone. When it was our turn, April introduced us, and he signed her copy of *A Bloody Injustice*.

"So, Jackson," he said, "where are you from?"

"Melbourne," I said. "I came in on the tram."

"I meant originally."

Of course he did. I've been here since the damn gold rush, but I'll get asked that question till the day I die again, while some Transylvanian who unloaded his coffin from the plane yesterday will never have to face it.

"China," I said, pleasantly. "But I've lived here for a while now."

Sensing the tension, April broke in with, "I liked your speech. Especially the part about how we're all brothers and sisters under the skin."

"Thanks," Richard said. "I believe we all share a bond, and we all have a responsibility to look out for each other. That's why this convention is so important—to connect us and show we don't stand alone."

Exactly who doesn't stand alone, I wondered, but did not say aloud. Instead, I said, "Fair enough, but why Australia? It's a trek, and for what? 'Come see our beautiful beaches?' Kind of the wrong crowd."

Richard remained unfazed. "We can walk the beaches at night. We can still enjoy the surf and the sand."

"Oh yes," April chimed. "And watch the stars."

"That's right," Richard said, smiling. "Even the stars are different, under the southern skies."

He nodded and moved on to talk to the next group that was hovering near him. April sighed.

"Well, obviously the stars are different," I said.

She gave me a look.

†   †   †

I sat in the darkest corner of the convention centre bar, elbow propped on the table, leafing idly through the program book again. April was at the 'Sunproofing Your Home' panel, which I had excused myself from. None of the others caught my interest either: 'Family Matters: Sire and Childe Relations', 'Recent Developments in Synthetic Blood Research', 'Inheritance Laws and You'.

"Buy you a drink?"

The blonde woman from registration extended a hand towards me. "Monique Dubois."

We shook. "Thanks for the offer," I said. "But I don't drink blood."

"It's all animal blood, you know."

I shook my head.

She raised an eyebrow. "You're not an Aetheran, are you?"

"A what?"

"One of those vampires who claims to have discovered how to live off meditation."

"No, nothing like that." I traced a circle on the bar. "I'm a jiangshi. We don't drink blood. Or meditate."

"Then what do you live off?" She seemed genuinely curious.

"Uh, energy. I absorb energy from the environment." If by 'environment', you meant 'people'.

"That's remarkable. I've never met anyone like that before."

"There are a few of us around. Like Christina Lee, who writes for the *New York Times*."

"Oh, her? I had no idea."

It turned out that Monique worked in finance. "And what do you do?"

"I'm in event management. Concerts, mostly." I drifted into reminiscence. "The vibe is incredible. I could live off it forever."

Wheels turned behind her eyes. "Oh, so you're a psychic vampire!"

I smiled weakly.

†   †   †

"Are you sure we're not late?" I asked April, in the taxi. "It *is* the Dusk to Dawn Ball."

"Relax," April said. She was busy touching up her makeup. "This kind of party, no one will be there till midnight." She bared her teeth at me. "Do I have lipstick on my fangs?"

I was used to being her mirror substitute. "It's fine. No spinach either."

The driver dropped us off outside the convention centre. A sea of candles floated in the forecourt, held aloft by dozens and dozens of people. At first I thought they were part of the arrangements for the ball, until I saw the placards and heard the megaphone.

"This midnight vigil is our message!" Pamela Hayward, in an elegant pantsuit, talking to—oh god—the news cameras. "We ask the government to take action to protect our sons and daughters. We have the right to know who lives in our neighbourhoods and works in our workplaces. As these people feast and celebrate, we remember those slain by rogue vampires."

Those next to her held up photos of family and friends, loved ones who were gone, faces stark. I had to look away. I'd never hurt anyone, but it made me feel complicit.

The cameras caught it all, vampires in tuxedos and gowns hurrying past, as the crowd looked on in simmering outrage. I could imagine how it would play on the news.

"Come on," I said, throat dry. "Let's find the back entrance."

We slipped inside, and walked down the corridor to the double doors. They swung open; April and I entered arm in arm.

For this one night, the auditorium had been transformed into a ballroom, with red drapery, gilt mirrors, and brass candelabra. I had expected it to be cheesy: men swaggering around in opera capes; women flitting about in lace corsets. But somehow, the mood was sombre; even though nothing could be seen of the outside, we all knew what lay beyond, and what they thought of us.

Still, the music played, a slow waltz, and couples moved across the polished floor like constellations across the sky. Dancing against darkness, and I began to understand why Richard Wells had wanted to bring this event here: to say, this is who we are, and we are not alone.

He was here now, circulating through the ballroom, stopping every few moments to exchange words with someone else. He paused by Monique, who chatted to him with animation. He glanced over at me once. I waved back.

Eventually, I found a place against the wall, where I stood sipping my chilled water, while April went to powder her nose. A woman sagged against the wall next to me.

"Are you okay?" I asked, steadying her.

"These damn corsets," she said, tugging at the waist of her dress. "You'd think they wouldn't be so uncomfortable if you don't have to breathe."

I nodded in polite sympathy. "Take it easy."

She leaned her head back and closed her eyes. "The things we do, eh?"

It surprised me to see Richard approaching me. Noticing even the wallflowers.

"Hey," I said, but his expression was serious.

"It's Jackson, right?" he said. "I have to ask you something."

"Sure—"

"Are you draining energy from anyone?"

My smile froze. "What?"

"I've been told about what you do." His level gaze met mine, not looking at anyone else.

I went cold all over. "That's not why I'm here."

"That's not what I asked."

A circle had opened around us, as people stopped dancing and drinking to stare.

"No," I said, face burning. "I'm not. You think I'd—"

"Look, we're responsible for the safety of our guests. Any hazards—"

"I was just taking a rest," said the woman leaning against the wall. She rocked upright, swaying on spike-heeled boots.

Richard glanced between us, then nodded briskly. "Sorry to have troubled you." Aware of the gathered crowd, he called, "Please enjoy the rest of your evening."

Monique was pushing her way through the crowd towards me. I turned and exited, not meeting anyone's eyes.

At the double doors, I collided with April, returning.

"Hey, watch your—Jackson?"

"I'm going home." Ignoring her shouted questions, I strode down the corridor, hung with velvet black as my vision, as the protesters began to chant.

† † †

It was drizzling in Chinatown, the black asphalt slick with rain, reflecting the red and green neon. Passers-by hunched into their jackets or huddled under umbrellas, casting me wary looks, voices whispering to each other in Cantonese.

I walked on, past shop windows displaying roasted duck and mournful fish, fat buddhas and beckoning cats. I walked past them all, to the Facing Heaven Archway, and the rock garden beyond. White stone lions guarded the gates.

I sank down onto one of the rocks, and lowered my face into my hands.

After a long time, footsteps crunched on the gravel.

"I already told you," I said wearily, "I'm going—"

"I'm sorry," Monique said.

I raised my head. She stood there, wrapped in a black coat, rain speckling her blonde hair.

"It was idle chatter," she said. "I didn't mean for anything like that to happen."

"I'm not into ballroom dancing anyway." I undid my tie, crumpling it in my hand.

Monique settled onto a neighbouring rock, watching me carefully. "I know so little about you."

"You want to know about me?" I flickered her a ghost smile. "I never had a sire. I was murdered, and the priests brought me back."

It was still vivid in my mind, even though Buckland was a hundred miles and as many years away. The fires, and the rioters, and finally, the cold clammy pull of the river. They had torn apart the tents and clubbed down those who were slow to flee, and screamed names I needed no translation to comprehend.

"Who killed you?" Monique said quietly.

"People who didn't think I was human."

The rain paused. Hissing was replaced by silence, then filled by the soft roar of traffic, and a distant radio, playing a song about a green island, far away.

"Have you ever thought about going back home?" Monique asked.

And what a loaded word that was. *Home.* Was it the plane to Guangzhou, or was it the tram to Fitzroy?

"I don't think I would fit in there anymore," I said. "We've grown in different directions. Besides, China is no more fond of vampires than Australia. At least here, you have a Richard Wells."

It had to mean something, that I had died here and been reborn here. This place was in my bones now, seeping in like a slow tide, drawing me into its treacherous current. Forcing me to learn to breathe underwater.

"I suppose that's why I feel drawn to you people," I said. Monique watched me, green eyes luminous in the dark. "Because you face the same things I do. Being dead. Being different. Being feared."

"Being an outsider," Monique said.

I nodded. But there were different layers of outside.

"I haven't seen my children in six years," Monique said.

"I didn't know you had children."

"A boy and a girl. My former husband has custody. I'm not allowed to contact them."

"I'm sorry," I said.

"I tell myself, one day, they'll be adults, and the court orders will lapse. And maybe they won't care what their mother is."

I reached out and covered her hand with my own. We sat in silence for several minutes.

"There's still an hour till dawn," Monique said at last. "Come back for one last dance?"

I hesitated. "Well, why not?"

† † †

The sky was already lightening as we returned to the convention centre, the clouds clearing in the promise of a beautiful day.

"Maybe you should skip the ball," I said, calculating sunrise, "and go straight home."

"Don't worry. I have a sunproof car."

Candle stubs and broken placards littered the forecourt, like the remnants of a disturbing dream. I was relieved that we didn't have to run the gauntlet of accusing stares, but surprised that the protestors hadn't stuck out their vigil.

As we entered the foyer, a distant roar sent unease crawling down my spine.

"What *is* that?" I asked.

But Monique was already running for the ballroom.

The double doors were flung wide, and a thin line of grey security stood between them and the seething mass of people who pushed and shoved.

"We want justice!" they chanted, over and over.

The vampires inside were no longer dancing, but stood in apprehensive clusters, at a loss for what to do. There were only a dozen left, outnumbered and dismayed.

Richard stepped forward, clicking shut his phone. "Listen!" he shouted above the crowd. "The police are on the way. Go home, before things get any worse."

"We're not scared of you!" a man shouted. His shirt was emblazoned with BLOODSUCKERS OUT. He launched himself at the cordon and broke through. The crowd followed, as though he had been a spearhead.

They surged through security in a whooping rush, overturning tables and smashing glasses, while the vampires backed away into the furthest corner. Richard stood in front of them, arms outstretched in a barrier, but his face was taut. The protesters closed in.

"Hey!" I called, and they swung towards me. "That's enough. You've made your point."

"What do you care?" the Bloodsuckers Out man said. He looked me up and down, and his mouth twisted. "Don't tell me you're one of these freaks."

"I don't know anymore," I said. "*Am* I one of these freaks?" I spread my hands. "Maybe you should get out of here before I make up my mind."

"Fucking creep. You can burn with them!" He yanked on the nearest curtain. It collapsed in ponderous folds, like a vast sail, exposing the glass beyond. Morning sun blazed through.

I stood, blinking, enveloped in the light.

Then I smiled.

"You should research your vampire lore," I said, advancing. "Stakes won't hurt me. Crosses don't scare me. I can stand in full sun. What do you think you can do to me?"

He rushed me then, seizing one of the heavy candelabra. I dodged sideways, and collided with someone else, who grabbed my arm. The other protestors were closing on me now.

I opened my mouth and inhaled. Their qi swirled from their bodies and into my lungs, filling me with strength and power. And they wavered, and fell, like cut flowers, stirring feebly.

I stood in the single pane of sunlight in the shadowed ballroom, as the vampires stood staring and silent.

When the police arrived, they arrested me.

But you already know that part, right, officer?

†   †   †

"Sign here," the sergeant said, after I had finished reading over my statement.

I signed the illegible scrawl I used for my credit card. Beneath that, in careful calligraphy, I wrote 'Cheng Kai Gong', and next to that, 'Jackson Cheng'. Because they were both my name.

April was waiting in the foyer of the police station with Richard and Monique. She leapt out of the plastic chair when I entered. "What were they doing, taking down your life story?"

"I'm fine, thanks for asking." We hugged. Then I turned to Richard.

"Thanks for putting up my bail."

He shook his head. "Don't worry about it. Our best lawyers are already on it. It's a clear case of self-defence."

"The nerve of Hayward," April said, "to press charges!"

"So will we," Richard said grimly. "It could have been very bad." He sighed. "It's hard to believe that it's the twenty-first century, and people still harbour prejudice against those who are different."

"Yeah," I said, after a moment. "Hard to believe."

As we left the police station, April and Richard fell into discussion about making the theme of the next convention 'Tolerance', while Monique and I walked on ahead.

"I'm sorry you had to go through this, after what you did," she said.

"At least now, we're fighting in the courts, not on the streets." This time, no one had died in the river, no one had burned up in the sun. But who knew about next time? Prejudice was a monster that rose from the dead no matter how many times you thought you had buried it.

But we who had witnessed it before would not stand by and witness it again. No matter who the target.

"I shouldn't even be here," I said. "But I'm not sorry I am."

AFTERWORD TO "INTERVIEW WITH THE JIANGSHI"

Australia is a nation with a unique mixed heritage, so it seemed only natural to include a jiangshi among the vampires who call it home.

I am indebted to Kathryn Cronin's book, Colonial Casualties: Chinese in Early Victoria, *for valuable background research. It gave me chills to read that the other colonists had actually used the term "evil vampires" to describe the Chinese.*

While the attitudes that drove the Buckland riots have retreated into history, I hear similar rhetoric bandied about today, only about different groups of people. I have no doubt that if vampires emerged in Australia, they would face the same challenges that confront each wave of newcomers to these shores.

WHITE AND RED IN THE BLACK

LISA L. HANNETT

The shit-stench of fear stings DJ's nostrils, pungent in the midsummer heat. Scattered across the pen, a dozen sheep lie heavy on their sides, heads twisted at unnatural angles. Dust-grey fleece clumps around their necks with a red so dark it looks black in the moonlight. Deep gashes shear their flanks, faces, legs: finger-wide and bloody, evidence the animals managed to break their attackers' grip at least once.

Dingoes, thinks Daniel Shenk Jr, a sour taste in his mouth. *Three, maybe four.*

High-pitched bleats still yodel into the night, no less frantic now than when they'd called the farmer's son from his tea. Eager to put as much distance between themselves and their mangled mates, the surviving sheep press against DJ's legs, tripping him up as he walks across the enclosure. His knees crack as he crouches beside one body. Death clouds the ram's eyes. Wet irises roll far back in the sockets; its sightless stare almost completely white.

DJ's voice breaks as he bellows for his father.

He scans the pen, looks for any sign of how the culprits got in. Panicked hooves have churned the packed ground into a mess of pits and furrows; there are no tracks inside or around the perimeter, no ochre tufts of canine hair caught on the fence. But for weeks he's heard those wild dogs howling as the distant crackle of bushfire smoulders up the peninsula from Wangary all the way to Poochera. Shaking his head, he swats flies away from his ears and brushes them off the carcass. He traces a finger along its velvet muzzle, rests a hand on its flank. The wool is greasy and still warm beneath his touch. His palm comes away wet.

The dead sheep convulses. Tremors run from rump to shoulder and its body jerks as though possessed. Scrambling to stand, DJ trips on a rut and falls on his arse. The corpse inches towards him, moving across the dirt in erratic bumps and jolts.

"What the fuck?" Halfway to pushing himself up, DJ freezes. The ram's head lifts and turns to look at him with vacant eyes. Black wings stretch behind its ears, stealing the boy's breath—but only for a second. He springs to his feet as the sheep's snout lolls forward. As the bat heaves and wriggles free.

Bloated from feasting, the thing flops on its stomach and stays there until it has gathered enough energy to stand. Leather wings flex and contract, slick and shiny with blood. DJ chuckles as his pulse slows, glad Lizzie hasn't seen him make a dick of himself over a ruddy bat—but as the rodent takes flight, the laugh catches in his throat.

It has a face.

Not the squashed pug nose and wrinkled skin he's seen on a thousand other bats; this one's a red-lipped, long-toothed, pink-eyed face. A baby's old man face. Shrunken and unmistakeably human; fierce and undeniably animal. Its flesh looks soft, and cheeks plump. Arms detached from the black wings, legs long and muscular; hands and feet tipped with ten fingers and ten toes, covered in a pelt so pale it must never see the sun.

Yelling for his dad again, DJ bolts from the pen. He's seen that kind of visage before, seen what it grows into, sketched in harsh black and white. *A gift from Mother England*, the antique poster explains. *For all Hunting enthusiasts in Her newest colony.* A hundred and fifty years ago, every farmer in the state had a copy nailed to their barn doors, courtesy of one Thomas Austin Shenk. Daniel Snr keeps theirs framed and hung on the dining room wall. A reminder and a constant warning.

Thinking of the stories he's heard—of blood-plague sweeping the country after the pests spawned like rabbits; farmsteads ravaged, whole families butchered in their homes, strung up like sides of beef from their Hills Hoists; decades of hunting, and being hunted by, Shenk's *gifts*—DJ sprints for his rifle.

They're all dead, he thinks. The last killed off when Pops was a boy, a public holiday celebrated each year. *They're all supposed to be dead.*

But every stockman worth his salt knows you can't get lambs without ewes and a ram. Legs pumping and lungs charged with charcoal air, DJ looks skyward and prays to God for dingoes.

† † †

DJ checks the first spotlight. Its glare makes him squint, so the batteries mustn't be too old. The second one, on the other hand, is no brighter than a fairy bulb.

"Hey, Pops!" After half a dozen stubbies, Mick's shout is loud enough to split wood. Five years younger, he's nearly twice his brother's height and half as stocky; the spitting image of their father at seventeen. DJ moves over to give him room in the back of the ute, then continues strapping down nets, guns, and the spare cans of petrol they'll need for the hunt. "We got any more juice for the spotties?"

"Reckon I got some in the shed." Their old man has the driver's side window rolled down, but speaks through the broken glass panel behind his head. His thick-knuckled fingers fumble with the door's rusted handle.

"No time," DJ says. "If those things come back . . ."

"Mate." Mick's expression is stern but his voice wavers. He rattles the framework of chrome rails sprouting from the ute's tray, pushes his weight against the waist-high bars, checks for loose rivets. "You sure you saw what you saw?"

DJ pictures the sheep's mashed throat, its blank gaze. Imagines the bloodsucker's plump red mouth. He blinks and in his mind Lizzie's lying there in the filth of the pen, blonde hair and tanned skin shredded and covered in gore. Adrenaline surges through his veins. He slaps the roof of the cab, a couple of solid hits. "Let's go, Pops."

"Bring us back some meat for the pups." Betty Shenk sways in the back doorway as the men clip ropes to their belts, securing themselves to the bars. One hand outstretched props the screen door open; the other clutches a glass, clinking ice cubes in time with a pair of guitars twanging on the radio. As the truck roars to life she raises her drink, finds it empty. She bends over to chip some fresh ice from the esky they keep by the stoop.

"Get inside," DJ calls. "Ma—"

"I'll mind Lizzie," Betty says, shooing him with a flick of her wrist. "In case she decides to pop while you're out." Brushing her long fringe to the side, she gives DJ a wink; the uneven crimson in her hair and the whites of her eyes both products of nine-dollar bottles she regularly buys at the shops. "Your girl will be just fine—and first babies are always late. Go'on now." Turning her back, she gets to work with the ice pick. Between each jab her thready voice warbles, '*I will know my Saviour when I come to him . . .*"

Stomach churning, DJ shouts at her to get back in the house; to lock the windows and doors. His mother's voice diminishes as the truck pulls away. Within a hundred metres, burning oil and road dust replace the familiar scents of manure, feed, and lanolin-rich fleece. Another fifty and darkness swallows the welcoming light spilling from the farmhouse windows. They race beyond property lines, away from settled land, aiming for a smudge of orange on the horizon. Around them, the world is navy frosted with silver; a star-speckled sky floats on heat still rising from the sunbaked earth. Hot wind scorches all feeling from DJ's skin and makes his eyes water. He wishes he'd given Lizzie a kiss goodbye before they left.

Flicking on the spotlight with shaking hands, he tries to steady his nerves. Breathes in, exhales, and struggles to get Betty's song out of his head.

†   †   †

A half-hour out, DJ hears a bass vibration. A *thump, thump, thumping* in the darkness. Consistent, but not regular; a car stereo without the car. An insidious sound that punches him in the guts and twists his balls until he squirms.

"Hold it steady! Higher—I can't see a goddamn thing!" Mick hefts his crossbow, scowls at his brother. From where they're standing, the ute's headlights are as useful as a couple of candles thrown into an abyss. DJ wipes the sweat from his palms, adjusts his grip on the light's plastic handle. The noise gets louder. He points a single yellow beam through the darkness; it bumps along the earth in circular patches as they speed across rough terrain. Black smudges pockmark the ground, evidence of the burrows Shenk's pests used to dig to hide from the sun, and abandon nightly to forage for victims. They've been empty for years. When they were little, Lizzie used to visit from next door so the two of them could exhume skeletons the monsters had left in their dens: possum and sheep mostly, but once DJ swore she'd found a human skull. The memory makes his hands shake; he braces the spotlight against the truck's cab to keep Mick from yelling.

Thump, thump, thump.

Closer now.

His heart revs along with the truck's engine. Gaze skimming left-right, flicking up-down, he stares so hard it makes his head hurt. The burrows gape like open mouths. Over the past year or so, Lizzie had led him back into those warrens so many times he'd lost track.

Thump, thump.

He shivers, grateful that getting his girl up the duff was the worst trouble they'd found down there.

Sweeping the spotlight in metronome arcs, DJ's pulse jumps every time the beam reflects off retinas crouching close to the ruts. Either their prey is too fast, or he's too slow: right and left, he finds nothing but foxes and hares. Rosellas. The occasional bluetongue or snake. Still no sign of the thumpers, just the reverberations of their swift-moving feet.

Closer.

And closer.

Mick whistles, a short sharp burst he uses to herd sheep. DJ's head snaps up. He can hear their footfalls so clearly now; pounding the frantic rhythm of a heart on the verge of attack.

"Where?" DJ asks. "Where?"

Mick looks to the sky, the air thrumming with the sound of wings. He shoulders his weapon and points it where the noise seems loudest. A bolt shoots from his bow, sharp grey streaking into the dark.

"Don't fucking waste ammo," Daniel Snr hollers from the front seat.

DJ brings the spotlight back around to the left while Mick reloads. Eyes locked on the horizon, he fumbles for his rifle.

A flash to the right: white and red in the black.

"There! Down, over—"

His throat constricts. Dozens of eyes shine from pale faces surging over the ridge of a depleted riverbed. Like aerial scouts, a cloud of bats circles their heads, giving directions while dropping in and out of the pack. They lope toward the truck, bobbing and weaving across uneven scrub. Naked, they cover too much ground too quickly. Huffing like lions as their arms and legs flail for speed.

They're not real. DJ can't look away. *There's so many.*

"Take aim, boys!" Daniel Snr guns the accelerator, volleys orders from the driver-side window: 'There, Deej; the light! Now, Mick—now! Now! Fire now!"

But DJ is paralysed. This morning these creatures were a drawing on the wall. Stories their granddad would tell at Christmas, when he wasn't obsessing about war or the drought. A handful of bones found in museums or at the bottom of cold burrows. Now, even from a distance, he can smell their musk. He can feel their sharp teeth tearing bloody chunks from his jugular. In his left hand, the spotlight illuminates their features, jumping from one figure to the next of its own accord. The rifle butt slams into his right hip; he doesn't remember pulling the trigger. The shot zings away, hits nothing.

Twenty feet, he thinks. *Fifteen. Ten.*

"There's too many." He shoots randomly into the crowd, misses. When the creatures are within arm's reach, legs primed to jump into the tray, DJ pounds on the window behind his father's head. "We can't take them all, Pops—floor it!"

"Steady, you drongo," Mick yells. He knocks another bolt into his bow, shoots. The quarrel vanishes in the throng. "Fuck!" Reaching for another, he swears again and releases a third shot. And a fourth. One more.

The next stake strikes true. A near-human shriek: a body tumbles, taking several others down with it. Mick grabs DJ's rifle, slides new cartridges into the stock, then hands it back.

"Hold on, Pops," he says, readying another bolt. "Give me one more bash."

But ash and dirt spew from the ute's tires as Daniel Snr kicks it into overdrive, turning the wheel hard to the left. The reek of old fires overwhelms as they push away from the patchy grass, away from the racing herd of prey-turned-predators, and onto a charred swathe of land. Bushfires tore through this region almost a week ago—but the fields, tree stumps, and fence posts still bear glowing marks of its passing. DJ takes shallow breaths as the air congests with blowflies, the pong of charcoal and melting rubber clogging his lungs.

Cinders flare and expire as the truck forges ahead. DJ looses a couple of shots, but doesn't fool himself into thinking his marksmanship is what leaves the beasts pacing the boundary between scorched earth and cool dirt.

Thank Christ Thomas-fucking-Shenk never thought to give them shoes.

DJ's guts turn to water. *Shenk.* Dizzy from the close escape, he clings to the guard rail and lets the spotlight fall drunkenly at his feet. He bends over and leans his forehead against the gritty metal. They won't be able to stay out here much longer; it's only been five minutes and already it feels like his eyebrows and nose hair are singed from the fire's residual heat. He squeezes his eyes shut. The refrain of Betty's song lilts through his mind. Blue and white afterimages swim behind his eyelids, frantic swirls made of hollow sockets and long, sharp fangs.

To be sure they've lost the pack, Daniel Snr drives a good ten k through the smoke before finally heading back to firmer ground. The tires are bald by the time he pulls onto the road, which makes for a bumpy, but quiet, ride.

"Hell, yeah!" Hopped up on testosterone and the buzz of a tough hunt, Mick claps his brother on the back hard enough to bruise. Hooting with laughter, he wrangles him into a half-wrestle, half-hug. "Taught those cunts a lesson, didn't we?"

DJ pushes Mick off and, legs rubbery, slumps against a pile of nets. "What fucking ute were you in, mate?"

"Same as you, dickhead."

"You reckon?"

Mick snorts. "Look around, *mate*. See any sign of them now?"

"But that's just it—"

Something fast and heavy thuds into the bonnet. There's a screech of metal before the headlights go out. DJ's head whips forward and back; Mick's teeth clash together as they both slide into the railing. The spotlight whirls a dervish around their feet, and then the whole world follows suit. Safety ropes keep the boys from flying to their deaths as the ute fishtails to a halt on the road's soft shoulder.

For a second, DJ's thoughts are calm, unburdened by time or reality. *I forgot to tell Lizzie about my dream last night.* He laughs and brushes a stray eyelash from her freckled cheek. *Sure do love you, babe.* Sounds emerge and begin to register. *Are you okay?* One at a time they trickle in, shaking him from his stupor: the drill of cicadas; the blare of the horn; the hiss of a crumpled radiator, punctured tires, or both. Mick whispering, shouting, "Are you okay?"

Ten metres away, a white lump of flesh yowls like a scalded cat, loud and shrill, though she has no breath in her lungs for screaming.

Mick scrambles to his knees and grabs his crossbow. "You right, Pops?"

A grunt from the front seat and the door swings open. Daniel Snr emerges, a deep gash livid beneath the wisps of white hair clinging to his scalp. He sucks air through a gap between his front teeth, spits on the ground beside his boots.

"Motherfucker," he says, taking in the extent of the damage. The grille is crushed, two tires are flat, and judging from the bonnet's steep list there's a good chance the front axle has snapped. "How's Deej?"

"Alive." His waist burns from the rope and his head aches from banging it against the truck's metal panelling, but nothing's broken. Peeling free of his restraints, he peers down the road. "What did we hit?"

Mick's crossbow twangs. Twice in quick succession. As if that isn't answer enough, the *thump, thump, thump* of feet confirms it.

Oh, Lord. We got one.

DJ stops and listens to the running. He leans toward the din: the abomination of bloodsuckers is already a decibel nearer. *Bats*, he thinks. *Echolocation.* It doesn't matter where she's taken now; they've homed in to their female's calls of distress and they'll track the sound as long as it takes to find her.

As long as it takes to find them.

† † †

The fuel ignites with a whoosh. Blue and orange tongues lick the road; DJ watches them arc around ute, men, and beast. Right now, the large ring of petrol soaking the ground smells better than Betty's Sunday cooking. Better than Lizzie's skin after they've had a lazy lie-in. As the liquid flames, DJ breathes deep and inhales the strong fumes of safety.

He knows it's counterintuitive: not only lighting a fire in the driest of South Australian summers, but also purposely jumping straight into it. If he knew the right terms, he'd observe the irony of his situation. But he doesn't: know or observe. What he does have is half a book of matches, a few gallons of fuel, a hunch and head full of songs about Jesus. Tonight he relies on all four to save him. Feeding the fire with a few more splashes, he caps the jerry can and steps back from the blaze.

The air, already hot, now stifles. *If the bastards won't even tread on burnt earth*, DJ thinks, *then this ought to keep them at bay.*

He prays.

He doesn't have to look to know the herd has nearly reached them. Their calls pierce the night, growing frenzied at the sight of the beacon. Bare feet slap with increasing pace; black wings thrum overhead. His mouth goes dry as he imagines their breath on the back of his neck.

"We're fucked if this goes out," he says to Mick, placing the spare cans within easy reach.

Mick mumbles something in reply, not really paying attention. He's busy prodding the supine figure with the toe of his boot. "Shut it," he says to hush her moaning, then elicits a thin yelp as he kicks her once in the kidneys.

For the first time, DJ turns and openly stares at the thing. Pinned by the two stakes protruding from her body—once kneecapped, once shot in the belly a hand's width above her bulging pouch—she lies steaming, so close to the fire. Her beige pelt is splotched white and red; uneven pigmentation mixed with gouts of her own dead blood. Sagging dugs, washboard ribs, pink irises, hair so white it's nearly invisible; all skewed from the impact and plastered with muck.

Her overly long fingers still throttle a lamb, its flanks sprayed Shenk blue. From where DJ's standing, the creature's snack could just as well be a child. If they didn't take care of her now, one day it would be.

He'll be damned if he lets her get his.

He takes a step closer without feeling his legs. Up close she's almost as pretty as Lizzie but twice as awful to see naked: high cheekbones coloured in bruises; bites and gashes weeping and rimmed with charcoal; delicate nose off-kilter and twitching. All of her, twitching.

Across her midriff a maw gapes then snaps shut. As she squirms, her pouch droops and contracts as though talking. A tiny hand tongues out of her ballooning belly, followed by the tip of a flimsy black wing. It claws at its mother's breast, feels the heat. Instantly withdraws.

"Jesus Christ."

DJ wants to wake up now. He wants to be home, curled up with Lizzie in bed, with Betty's singing rising up through the floorboards.

Pale faces emerge from the darkness, the tattoo of running frenetic as they catch sight of their goal. "Don't just stand there," Daniel Snr shouts. "Shoot the fuckers!" DJ hesitates, his gun slung over his shoulder. "Jesus Christ," he repeats as he finally sees the bloodsuckers for what they are.

Not the vestiges of a dying species; the founders of a new generation.

Vertigo rushes from DJ's bowels upwards. He looks at the figure writhing away from him, drawing so near to the flames her fine pelt blisters, and thinks: *She's a goddamn breeder.*

Furious bats dive-bomb their heads. Daniel Snr swats them with a tire iron into the flames as Mick gets to work with the crossbow. Projectiles thud into torsos: one beast is felled, another eviscerated. DJ draws his rifle and circles the dam, then grabs a fistful of her greasy hair. Her breath is so rank it's almost sweet; black treacle that drips from her tongue. Around her mouth, fresh blood and old soot. She bares her fangs, sharp as those flashing from her counterparts' chops. Her hiss builds to a growl. Instinctive, impotent threats, much like the circling pack's howls.

He flips her over and forces her to kneel like a dog. The stake in her knee plunges all the way in until its filed tip tears a hole through her calf. Her scream is full-throated, a mixture of pain and rage. DJ yanks her head back, thinks better of it; pushes her face down and away so he won't have to look at her eyes.

Mick replenishes the fire, tosses the empty can to the ground with a plastic thud. "Stop feeling her up and smash her already!" He rips the stake from her leg, reloads his weapon, and fires. "While you're standing there gawking, she's healing." DJ forces her onto her side: the bloodsucker's nose is straight now; the bolt in her abdomen dangles, almost expelled from the shrinking wound. "We can't fight them from both sides, mate."

"Give me a hand, Pops," DJ says.

There's nothing human about her, he thinks as he trades places with his father. The old man kneels down, uses his size and weight to restrain the creature while DJ puts the barrel of his rifle to her temple. Planting his feet wide, he cocks the hammer. *She's a killer, pure and simple. An animal who'll feed on children to survive.*

Blood and brains spatter. Muscles slacken. Piss streams between her legs, pools around DJ's shoes, then seeps into the dry ground.

A little round head with sharp ears, a thatch of white hair, and a perfect red mouth pops out of its mother's gut pocket. Its eyes are pink, like hers. It blinks, pupils contracting in the light. From its back, two midnight wings stretch, transparent as wet tissues. Tentatively, it hops toward DJ.

It's a boy, he thinks. Then, out of nowhere: *God, I hope we have a boy.*

Mick runs to the ute. "Almost out of ammo," he shouts, chucking bags and boxes from the tray.

The joey flinches at the sound of Mick's voice, tries to fly away. After a rough start it lifts off, wobbles to shoulder level. DJ watches its progress in a trance, reaches out as though to catch it—until Mick snatches the rifle from his hands, flips it, and bludgeons the bat into the flames. Its wings sizzle. Disintegrating, it squeals like a lobster on the boil. The crowd seethes, its parents heedlessly rushing into the fire to rescue their offspring. Mick hammers burning arms, snapping jaws, outstretched hands until the pack retreats. Then he turns the weapon on the beast at his feet. With full-armed whacks, he chops over and over, pulping her neck. Shearing the head from her body.

"Catch!" Out of bullets, Mick regains his crossbow and launches the rifle back to his brother. Clattering, it lands uncaught.

Daniel Snr stokes the fire, emptying their second-last can of fuel. He shouldn't have bothered: the bloodsuckers have gone quiet. They pull back. Reaching some tacit agreement, they regroup. Shuffle into a jog. Spring into a run. It's a full retreat, all casualties left behind.

"That's right," Mick says, laughing and throwing stones at their backs.

One last creature lingers. Scrawny and adolescent, he's much too large to be a bat, but the presence of shrivelled wings shows he's not yet an adult. He sniffs the air and barks a threat, a challenge, an admission of defeat. DJ isn't sure which. Then the creature turns and meets his eyes. Chin lifted defiantly, the young vampire withdraws, sparing one last glance at his dam.

It means nothing.

The illusion of safety adds life to his brother's taunts: behind a high wall of fire, facing empty night, he snarls and growls like a bear.

"Shut up," DJ snaps, trying to think. *They're nothing but animals. All they do is eat, sleep, fuck, hunt.* Blood drains from his face and sweat runs cold on his body. *And attack those who threaten their young.*

He swallows his fear.

"They're heading for the farm."

Mick stops laughing. "What?"

Oh, God. DJ runs to the truck, hauls a blanket from the back, uses it to smother an exit through the flames. *They've been there before; they know where it is.*

They know the girls are alone.

"Pops," he says, not looking at the empty petrol cans littering their burnt oasis.

His old man nods. "There's enough, Deej. Go'on. I'll be right until dawn."

They both know it's a lie. Silently, DJ examines his father's rugged face, its familiar crags and well-earned lines. Forty years on the farm and in it for life.

The stockman's crook knees would collapse before he could run to the other side of the road.

"Pull the rug away soon as we're gone. Then lock yourself in the ute."

"I have got some sense, boy." Daniel Snr's legs quiver as he crouches to take a corner of the blanket. "Now go give that grandkid of mine half a chance."

Wearing a sober expression, Mick slings the last bag of ammunition over his shoulder then passes DJ the spotlight. He takes it and the rifle, to wield as a cudgel until they can restock at the farm. And they will, he tells himself, gather supplies before the assault. A few minutes is all the advantage they'll need; there's too much at stake for them to fail. *Pops. Ma's hymns. Lizzie's smile. All the years of our son's life.*

They sprint through the opening before the blanket is consumed. Neither looks back, neither speaks; both save their breath for running. Beyond the circle of fire, thirty degree air hits DJ in the face like an arctic breeze. He fills his lungs, sets a gasping pace, and hopes the acid in his muscles will help burn the young vampire from his mind.

It must have meant nothing.

But his stride is thrown. He wonders if revenge is an instinct all animals share. If it's something that runs in the blood. Desperation propels him forward as he prays never to learn the answer.

We're coming, he thinks, legs cramping. *We're coming.*

Two kilometres from home, he hears dingoes howling.

AFTERWORD TO "WHITE AND RED IN THE BLACK"

On their first visit to Australia, my friends and family from overseas ask a series of (now-predictable) questions: "Does water really go down the drain counter-clockwise here?" or, "Uluru is how far away?" or, as they're thinking of other things to ask, "Can I have another glass of that lovely wine, please?" And once they've practised the accent (and realised they can't imitate it) and the giggles following their attempts have subsided, conversations inevitably turn to one thing: this country's deadliest wildlife. Admittedly, Australia's reputation for dangerous creatures is not unwarranted— so it seems that its vampires should be equally threatening and frightening. In a way, fear comes from not being able to rationalise with something: sharks are scary because they have razor-sharp teeth, but also because we can't talk them out of eating us. In this story, I wanted to emphasise that irrational side of vampires. The side that is animalistic and uncontrollable. The monstrous, non-sparkly, shark side: eat first, no questions later.

LADY YANG'S LAMENT

PENELOPE LOVE

"We are always portraying ghosts and demons in our operas, therefore we must be especially respectful to them."
— Hocus Pocus

SANDHURST GOLD FIELDS, 90 MILES NORTH OF MELBOURNE.
1854.

The stage was bare, as custom dictated. All actions were indicated by gesture, galloping by a flourish of a whip, travelling a thousand leagues by walking in a wide circle. The actors' faces were painted in brilliant colours. The silk costumes were worn, darned and patched, but they looked effective in the glare of the stage lights, with their exaggerated flowing sleeves, the gaudy pennants worn on the backs of the heroes, and the pheasant feathers nodding from their elaborate head pieces. The chorus were adept at their acrobatics in the battle scenes. The orchestra played valiantly, the clappers beat, the cymbals clashed, the jinghu players plucked and the erhu players bowed furiously.

Da Shan could see why the troupe were going cheap as soon as the leads opened their mouths. The actors were supposed to perfectly embody their parts, the painted face monster, the clown, the young hero and the heroine. These didn't. The monster's voice was a reedy squeak. The clown wasn't funny. The 'young hero' was old. Da Shan slumped in his chair and whiled away the time by looking over their contracts. They were watertight, and very cheap.

Then Ah Jin entered. He played the heroine. He stood, gathering all eyes, then made two delicate, sweeping, pitiful gestures of his hands and sleeves.

Da Shan was a swaggering, bull necked Guangdong merchant. Like all Han he shaved his forehead and wore a long queue plaited down his back. He had fought his way up from the roughest quarter of the Four Districts, and never had time to cultivate more than a thin veneer of civilization. But even Da Shan knew he was looking at the ghost of Lady Yang, the doomed and beloved concubine of Emperor Ming Huang. He sat up and paid attention.

Ah Jin sang:
Amid confusion and uproar my life was ended,
And here I drift, a wandering spirit,
With my white belt fastened around my throat.
All pleasure is gone, our pledge is at an end.
And my body is no more;
But my love remains unchanged.

The song was divine. Every note, every gesture, every step was exquisite. The wretched orchestra rose to unguessed heights. At the plaintive tones, Da Shan thought of his own home town, where he might as well be a ghost, and tears ran down his cheeks.

Such perfection demanded immediate response. He put his personal seal to the contract as soon as the song finished. He knew Ah Jin would make him rich.

Da Shan hadn't wanted the deal at first. It seemed too good to be true. But the other man was desperate. "You'll make a fortune. "Every true Han loves opera"," the merchant quoted. He was right.

"Return home with wealth and glory!" Da Shan chanted to himself, joyfully, as he made arrangements for the troupe to accompany him back to the goldfields.

† † †

Now, once again, the nightly performance was over. Da Shan finished counting the take, and locked his strong box. Fatty Sam stuck his head into the tent. Fatty was the company cook. His jolly, creased face was fiery red from drink and heat. He was wet with rain and clutching a round wax paper lantern and a greased umbrella.

"The Protector wants to see you, boss," he said.

"At this hour?" It was almost one in the morning.

"He probably wants to complain about the noise."

"Again." Da Shan had learned the hard way not to perform operas after midnight or on Sundays. Apparently the first disturbed the Protector's rest, and the last was disrespectful to the local god, Ye-su, a god that Da Shan personally had little time for since learning he was a god of the poor. But the Protector could cancel Da Shan's opera license with one pen stroke.

"Come with me," he said, stepping outside. Fatty had spent a few years in Malay and picked up a smattering of pidgin. Fatty was curious to death, and all too eager to come along. He opened his umbrella to protect Da Shan from the rain.

Da Jin shot a watchful glance around his camp, the huge bulk of the opera tent dominating the rest. He scowled at Ah Jin's tent, and the lights shining within. Ah Jin was being feted by admirers and smoking opium, neither of which were good for him. "Bring the kid along," he said.

"Are you sure that's a good idea, boss?" Fatty asked.

"I'm sure." Da Shan grunted. The only way to keep Ah Jin out of trouble was to keep both eyes on him.

Fatty ducked over to Ah Jin's tent and a slim figure followed him out. Out of costume Ah Jin was a too-handsome youth with high cheek bones, large eyes and a disdainful expression.

Rain pissed down over the diggings. A strong wind tore at the clouds covering the moon, revealing a dismal scene. The trees had been cut for miles in all directions leaving the rolling hills bare. Along the valleys the slick, muddy earth was dug into shafts, some oval, some square like giant graves, while huge mullock heaps of yellow clay, gravel and white quartz towered overhead. The ground was riddled with shafts, and the wind howled through the mines like a madman.

Scattered lights showed where the foreign devil miners' tents were pitched beside the claims. Han miners were herded into ranks of tents within the Chinese Protectorate camp; "for their own good" the foreign devils said.

Da Shan pondered his troublesome star as they picked their way to the Protector's office. Now he knew why the other merchant was so desperate to sell. Sure, Ah Jin coined money. Every night, they built up to Lady Yang's lament, and every night there wasn't a dry eye in the house. The audience threw bags of gold dust at his feet. It was their own exile from their beloved homeland that he sang. Offstage, the kid was a handful. He was an orphan and never had any family to instil respect in him. He smoked opium, drank rice wine and chased girls. Da Shan couldn't entirely blame him. If he spent his working life pretending to be a woman he'd be after girls to prove his virility too.

Problem was, the foreign devils hated the Han chasing their women. Time and again, Da Shan was forced to move from a lucrative diggings because a local miner caught Ah Jin at it again. Ah Jin was lucky to escape murderous beatings, but they could never catch him. His actor's kung fu training made him nimble, flexible and extremely fast on his feet.

"Please Guan Yu, Goddess of Mercy, let Ah Jin not get caught this time," Da Shan prayed.

† † †

After a short trudge they arrived at the Protector's office, a large tent with a tree outside on which were hammered official notices, now sodden and illegible with the rain. A horse and cart stood tethered to the tree. Within the cart was a long box covered with a wet blanket.

The Protector was seated on a camp chair with a plank table before him. The Protector was a burly devil with a black beard down to his waist. His face bulged red and his blue eyes were bloodshot. He had hair all over his body, like a beast. It poked in tufts from the neck and wrists of his Western suit. The sensitive Ah Jin could not drag his eyes from it.

"Long time no see," Fatty bowed to the Protector and spoke pidgin, politely.

"What, no tea," Ah Jin said, blandly. He spoke Cantonese so there was no chance the Protector could understand him, but Fatty Sam nudged him, hastily. Greasy Wang was sitting to one side. Wang glanced at them sharply. Greasy Wang was an unctuous Guangzhou man, a big city guy, who'd seen which way the wind was blowing and converted to Christianity. Every loyal Han in camp hated him.

The Protector pulled a piece of paper across his desk, without looking at them directly. He spoke, and Greasy Wang translated for him.

"Da Shan, circus owner," the Protector flicked the paper disdainfully. "I've had complaints."

Da Shan started to answer respectfully, but the Protector broke in without waiting for him to finish. "Strange thing happened this morning, horse and cart came wandering in. Got them tied up outside." They were nonsense words with Greasy Wang's translation as a meaningful echo. "Not a living soul with them," the Protector continued. "What's in the cart? One of your Celestial coffins with a dead Celestial inside. Damndest thing."

The echo caught up too late, and Da Shan's protest was drowned out by the Protector resuming his speech. Da Shan didn't know why the Protector was talking to him about a corpse. But as the translation continued, the dim horror firmed.

"I don't have time to worry about dead Celestials with you living ones causing me so much trouble. You're a local business man, respectable character. I can trust you. Look after your dead countryman while my secretary here looks into the matter."

This was a disaster.

"No savee, no savee," Fatty Sam tried, frantically.

The Protector came to his real point. "You Celestials respect your dead, don't you? You'll have to quit that unholy racket until you've given him a decent service. So, we might get some peace and quiet for a few days, eh?" He sat back pleased, and spoke to Greasy Wang. "Remind them I can cancel their license any time if I think they're disturbing the peace. Good night and sweet dreams. I shall have sweet dreams indeed," he laughed.

†   †   †

As Da Shan headed out he gestured Fatty to take the reins of the waiting horse. Fatty refused. A nameless corpse. Unlucky to death! Fortunately Ah Jin kept his head. He untied the beast. Da Shan grabbed the reins from him, his instinctive horror of the dead killed by the far stronger emotion of commercial common sense.

"Watch out for your hands!" he hissed. Any singer had to be the physical embodiment of his role. A heroine could not have soiled or callused fingers.

He re-arranged the blanket which had fallen off the coffin. "These foreign devils show no respect," he muttered, as he dragged the sullen, tired nag along. The rain pelted down. His umbrella was sodden and cold trickles wriggled down the back of his neck. "What bad luck!" he cursed. No one would share an opera tent with an uninvited corpse. And actors were a superstitious bunch. The stage baby had to face up during performance, but was always packed facing down, otherwise the spirit of the child it represented would haunt them. The actor playing the war god, Lord Guan, had to deliberately leave his make up incomplete, or the god would be angry at the resemblance. The Goddess of Mercy alone knew what they would think of the coffin and its unwelcome inhabitant.

"It's not so bad," Ah Jin stepped up beside Da Shan, glancing back at Fatty who trailed sullenly behind. "Praise Guan Yu for this foul weather. We get this back to camp and bury it. No one will see it. When the Protector wants it back we just dig it up again."

Da Shan's spirits rose at Ah Jin's cool suggestion. "Great idea!"

"I'll keep quiet. But you need to shut Fatty up."

"He's loyal," Da Shan asserted. "Hey Fatty, join us here," he called. Fatty loitered up reluctantly, giving the cart and its unlucky burden a wide berth. The wind gave a strong gust as he arrived. The blanket flapped, showing the two rounded peaks of the lid. Fatty started.

"This is all wrong, boss," Fatty hissed. "Who would send him home in a coffin?"

Da Shan was at loss himself. Normal practice was to cremate the corpse and send an urn home. "He must be rich," he guessed, trying to sound encouraging.

Fatty wasn't appeased. "Where's the cart driver? I bet he's dead somewhere in this rotten wilderness. This corpse is lost and angry. A hungry ghost!" A fresh blast of wind snuffed out their lantern. Fatty shrieked. Da Shan grabbed his arm.

"I don't have any time for this Taoist nonsense," Da Shan said, stern. He was a stout Confucian. The dead were dead, to be judged by the Yama Kings in Hell where they belonged. Talk of ghosts was spread by Taoist priests to extort money from the credulous. He had no time for those charlatans, attacking invisible demons with swords made of melted coins. "A corpse is nothing to be scared of. Keep quiet and I'll reward you. But if word of this gets out, no reward!" he said.

Fatty gulped, fell silent and followed. Da Shan was relieved by Ah Jin's calm. Perhaps playing a ghost for all those performances had made him immune to fear of them.

Now Da Shan remembered his high hopes when he first signed the contract: "Return home with wealth and glory!" There seemed precious hope of that now, he reflected, bitterly, as they arrived back in the opera camp with their loathsome burden. They stole behind the opera tent to a patch of waste ground where the company horses were tethered. Fatty fetched some mattocks. Da Shan hefted one.

"I can't let you dig, boss," Fatty said, concerned.

"I'm a Guangdong man. I can do whatever it takes," Da Shan took out his frustrations on the hard earth.

"What if anyone sees us?" Fatty asked.

"We'll tell them we're digging for gold," Da Shan joked.

Neither of the others laughed.

The earth was red and yellow clay, mixed with gravel and studded with fist sized chunks of quartz. Digging even a shallow grave was hard work. Eventually the earth was tossed high on either side. Fatty and Da Shan refused to let Ah Jin help manhandle the coffin. Da Shan stood in the cart and heaved at the base, while Fatty pulled from the front.

"How heavy this is!" Da Shan gasped.

"He must be rich and fat. Heavy to death," Fatty joked.

Da Shan laughed just as the coffin finally moved. He lost his grip on the slippery surface. It slid forwards with irresistible force. "Watch out!" he shouted.

Fatty leaped clear just in time to avoid being crushed in the grave. The lid fell off. All three gasped and averted their eyes. The disrespectful handling of the coffin promised the most horrible bad luck. Da Shan was the first to peep. He cursed, first with surprise and then with anger. The other two gathered courage and peeped themselves.

It was one thing to have a coffin with a corpse on your hands, another thing entirely to have a coffin with no corpse.

"The foreign devils haven't—eaten him, have they," whimpered Fatty.

"This is a trick," Da Shan snapped. "Fatty, go back to the Protector at once and tell him the body is missing."

"Now?" It was almost three o'clock.

"Yes now. No, not to the Protector. Tell Wang. Make sure he knows we've seen right through him."

Fatty ran.

Da Shan still wouldn't let Ah Jin help. He put his back to the coffin, took a deep breath and shoved. All his muscles writhed, and his shirt burst before he got the inert mass of timber to budge. At last the coffin dropped into the grave, and he dragged the lid over it.

He covered the grave with the sodden blanket, then piled quartz rocks around the edges to pin the blanket down. He tied the nag with the company horses. He scattered earth over the blanket then overturned the cart on top of it. "That will keep it safe for now," he grunted.

Fatty came back. "Wang said he'd come over in the morning," he reported.

A dirty dawn was breaking in a sodden sky. Ah Jin retired. Fatty headed off to stoke the breakfast fires. Da Shan went to his tent but did not sleep, which was fortunate because Greasy Wang was over early. Ah Jin was keeping a watch for he turned up, uninvited, curious to witness the scene.

Greasy Wang refused offers of refreshment, so they took him to the grave. It was a raw morning and most of the company were at breakfast or rehearsing.

"You took your time," said Da Shan.

"Three men were murdered last night. I was busy," Wang said, shortly. They all silently hated him for not bothering to think up a more convincing reason. They couldn't have been Han deaths or they would have heard about them already, so they were foreign devil deaths and had nothing to do with Wang.

Fatty and Da Shan lifted the cart, turning it so as to shield the grave from any curious onlookers.

"Now what's the problem?" Wang sniped. "Your cook was incoherent last night. Probably drunk."

Da Shan raised the blanket and gestured. Fatty lifted the lid with a flourish, then screamed and leaped from the grave vertically, an impressive feat given his physique.

The coffin was no longer empty.

Greasy Wang looked down and sniffed. "I gave you one coffin, one corpse. Here is one corpse, one coffin. All tallies."

"It is the—right—corpse?" Da Shan's voice shook.

Greasy Wang stared and sniffed some more. "Of course. I looked him over when he came in. See, his head's all bashed in. Now, how long do you want to keep me waiting?"

"Please don't let us stop you," Da Shan said, sickly. The corpse was bloated and foul, its face grey with blue patches of rot. It was slick with the moisture of the grave. Its nails and hair were long and rank, the dead flesh shrinking back. It stank. It wore a cheap Western suit of blue serge, which killed any notion of it being the remains of a rich man, leaving again the puzzle of why it was being sent home in a coffin.

With Greasy Wang safely gone, the three stared at each other over the grave.

"Vampire!" Fatty hissed. "He was murdered and his last breath got stuck in his throat. Now he's become a hopping corpse, doomed to steal other people's breath." Fatty drew a deep breath and held it. Lacking breath themselves, vampires couldn't see you if you held yours.

Da Shan slapped him hard. Fatty coughed his treasured breath out. "Don't be stupid," Da Shan said, irritated.

"Guan Yu protect us!" The unflappable Ah Jin finally lost his cool. "Those three men were killed by the vampire. The foreign devils can't tell a living Han from a dead one. They'll blame us!"

"This is some trick of Wang's!" Da Shan insisted.

"Why would Wang do such a stupid thing?" Ah Jin said. "We need a Taoist priest. Send to the Melbourne temple at once!"

"We'll all be dead by the time they make it back!" Fatty wailed. "We need sticky rice to stop it from escaping, and chicken blood, lots of chicken blood, to keep it safe," he shouted. He started running for the camp kitchen.

Da Shan tripped him before he had run three paces, then stood glowering at him, fists clenched. "There is no hopping corpse!" he said. "I'll stake my life on this. I'll keep watch on this coffin tonight, myself," he promised. "You'll see. I'll catch Wang and see what his stupid tricks do for him then." He slammed one meaty palm into his thick fist. Ah Jin and Fatty looked impressed. "You two, go about your business. Don't talk to anyone. I'll deal with it."

† † †

His promise was the only thing that held Da Shan to his unpleasant task that night. He took the cart off the grave again, and propped it sideways facing away from the opera tent, to hide the coffin from view. He huddled inside the cart. It was cold and wet again, although at least the wind had died down. His breath puffed silver as he sat under a damp blanket. He didn't have a lantern for fear of someone seeing him. He had to make do with the stray gleams of warm light spilling from the opera tent.

He brooded on his wrongs. Superstitious nonsense on top of everything else! Da Shan knew his troupe hated him, but as long as they showed respect to his face he didn't care. They had signed contracts, and he had a right to enforce them. He didn't know why a genius like Ah Jin had joined such a poor troupe, but it didn't matter. Their country was being torn apart by greedy foreigners and rebellious peasants. Secret societies fomenting revolt were everywhere. There could be many reasons why Ah Jin left China.

He fretted that he should be selling tickets and supervising the front of house. But he could not go back on his word. The only comfort was Fatty, who topped up his tea and brought him snacks. "Gotta keep your strength up, boss." Fatty didn't stay to chat. He hurried off, with a fearful glance at the wet blanket sagging over the coffin.

Still, Da Shan had the satisfaction that he'd kept a lid on things. Over in the opera tent his cast and orchestra were giving their best, and the audience were enjoying themselves, another full house. Calls for steamed buns and dumplings and tea were running Fatty and his assistants off their feet. Crouching by the grave in the hissing rain Da Shan could hear the boisterous tones of Lei the Lute Player from 'the Patriot and the Rebel' scene:

I hate the barbarian who has polluted the throne,
Like the toad in the proverb who tried to eat the swan.

It was good, rousing stuff, delivered with vim. The audience lapped it up, although it was odds on whether they were thinking of the opera, the foreign Manchu Qing dynasty, or the last foreign devil who had beaten them.

Da Shan rose to stretch his legs. Standing, he noticed the blanket was gone. A gust of wind must have lifted it. Damn. He stomped over. Only as he reached the grave did a cold prickle run down his spine.

There was no wind. Besides the blanket had been weighed down.

The tethered horses whinnied and stamped, in sudden fright.

Fear cramped his belly but common sense reasserted itself. Damn Taoist nonsense. The damn blanket had fallen down into the hole.

Nervously, he stretched his hand across the grave, just as there was a muffled clang from within. The lid of the coffin exploded out of the depths and landed sideways on the muddy ground. Da Shan fell over backwards in fright, then gasped and clapped his hand over his mouth, as the smell of rotten mud, rotten flesh and grave gas gusted over him.

A figure shot straight up, in one piece, stiff with rigor mortis. Light from the opera tent illuminated it.

Da Shan saw the corpse. He could not mistake it, the bashed in scalp, the grey and blue face. Its eyes were tight shut and its lips sealed on its last breath. Foul water ran down its bloated features and dripped from its damp Western suit.

One leap propelled it out of the grave, with arms outstretched. Its long nails were claws. Da Shan scrambled backwards. Horror shrieked within. There was no way this could be a trick. The movement was too unnatural, even for a trained acrobat. Besides the stink—!

The horses screamed and reared and hauled at their tethers. Fortunately, a blast of music from the tent drowned out their terror.

His treason is so disgusting
That even if I eat his flesh and sleep on his hide,
I shall never forget my hatred!

The corpse balanced on the lip of the grave, facing Da Shan, swaying. Then it leaped towards him, both legs together, hands outstretched. Da Shan knelt, sick with stench and fear, hands clapped his mouth and nose. He couldn't run. He couldn't breathe. He couldn't do anything except take this horror in. It was not dead, not alive, a spirit caged in rotting flesh and bone. He could feel its malevolence. Active. Alert. Aware. The dead were no longer sole property of the Yama Kings. Nothing would ever be sane or safe or normal again.

The corpse was two feet away, but it came no closer. It turned left, without moving its feet, seeking him. It turned right.

The Taoists were correct. Without breath, it couldn't see him.

Da Shan squeezed his nose even tighter. His lungs were bursting.

The corpse jumped again. It was now alongside him, looking forwards.

"Not the opera tent, not the opera tent, not the opera tent," Da Shan prayed.

Tang Ming Huang was the patron saint of opera. And Tang Ming Huang must have heard him. The corpse turned again and bounded out into the darkness of the diggings.

Da Shan had to breathe or pass out, so he took a huge, grateful gulp, then held it again. He was safe. The vampire did not come back.

Some people have courage. Da Shan had cold commercial common sense. Fear of anything happening to his opera outweighed his fear of the vampire. "Chicken blood and sticky rice," he gasped, and ran towards the kitchen.

But he stopped at the threshold. Fatty and his apprentices were working hard within. Fatty would realize something was wrong if he came in asking for sticky rice. If Fatty panicked, then everyone would panic. The vampire was gone for the night, away from the Han camp. Why cause a fuss?

Da Shan turned away and strode down into the ranks of tents of the Han camp. He went to three different shops, woke the shopkeeper, and bought fifty pounds of sticky rice from each. "Business is booming, we're running short," he blandly agreed with each, hoping they did not swap trade secrets. The ordinary nature of the common commercial transaction steadied him, but at each shop he felt the barrier between this world and the next loom close. It was no longer a reassuring wall, but paper thin. He would never be rude to a Taoist again. He dragged each load back to camp, and stowed it underneath the cart. Chest heaving from the effort, he stood, satisfied. Now he only had to wait for morning, and the vampire to return. He would cover the coffin with sticky rice and trap it within. No one else ever need know a thing.

Standing at the grave, he heard a commotion from the opera tent. He ran over, fearing that the vampire had returned early. The performance was finished for the night, and the audience was gone, but the lights were still burning. There were a dozen foreign devil miners at the entrance, red in the face with rage and drink, shouting gibberish and clutching burning torches. They were—almost—worse than vampires.

The opera tent was sodden canvas but there were plenty of costumes within, delicate, flammable, costly silks. Fatty bravely tried to bar the devils' path, but one of the devils picked Fatty up and flung him aside. Another of them knelt on his back to pin him down, grabbed Fatty's plait, and unsheathed a knife.

Da Shan rushed in, and hauled the man off Fatty's back. Fatty leaped to his feet and bolted into the opera tent. Another two devils jumped Da Shan.

Da Shan laid about with windmill arms, but the devils overcame him. It was his turn to be pinned down, kicking and punching furiously. A roar came from within the opera tent, building louder and louder. Then Fatty burst back through the entrance, screaming with fury. Fatty held one of the audience benches before him like a shield. At his heels ran Ah Jin in full make up and costume.

Fatty's table bulldozed the two devils pinning Da Shan.

Ah Jin kicked a devil in the chest. The devil flailed backwards. Ah Jin kicked a second, then used him as a springboard to kick a third in the head. All three sprawled. Ah Jin vaulted to the ground and faced them, calm and unconcerned, in fighting stance. The devils gaped, wondering who this woman was and how she had thrashed them so soundly.

"What's going on!" Da Shan roared at Fatty, as he scrambled to his feet.

"Another miner has been murdered," Fatty yelled. "They saw a Han jumping away. They think he's a circus acrobat, so they're going to beat us and burn down the opera tent."

Da Shan had not thought of the harm he would cause by allowing the vampire to escape, but the threat to his business stirred every fighting instinct. "Crap yourself to death before you burn down my opera!" he yelled.

The devils howled curses and drew their knives.

Then another devil spoke, in loud, authoritative tones.

The Protector strode between the miners and the smaller group of Han, arms raised, shouting and pointing. Greasy Wang was at his heels. Da Shan had never thought he'd be glad to see him.

"What's going on?" he hissed.

"He's telling them he knows their names, and he'll have them up before the British court," Greasy Wang translated.

The Protector's appearance calmed things down. Arguing, threatening, but sobering up, the devil miners retreated from the Han camp. Da Shan ran to his tent and grabbed a bag of gold dust from his strong box.

"I thought you said they'd stop that damn caterwauling with a coffin around," the Protector grumbled to Greasy Wang.

Ah Jin relaxed his fighting stance, and curtseyed to him.

The Protector eyed Ah Jin, and stiffened. "Is that a girl?" he asked, horrified.

"No sir, he's an actor," Greasy Wang explained.

"Mr Wang," Da Shan called. He bowed and clasped hands before him, holding the gold dust high. "We law abiding citizens in the Han camp are very concerned about the murderous criminal on the loose. Here's some gold to help find him."

"That's why we're here. Two killed tonight. Witnesses say the murderer "jumped away". Are any of your actors missing?" Greasy Wang asked, sharp.

"I personally vouch for all my cast and crew," Da Shan said. "Besides we've been performing for the last three hours to a full house. You can ask anyone. "Every true Han loves opera"," he quoted, virtuously.

Greasy Wang accepted that, reluctantly. He translated Da Shan's speech and passed the gold on to the Protector, who weighed it in his hand, and beamed.

"Excellent. Sticking together you lot, clannish as usual," he confided to Greasy Wang, as if he didn't know. "This will get us another twenty special constables." He brightened. "I'll recruit the trouble makers, give them something to do." He glanced at Da Shan. If Da Shan hadn't been a Celestial, he almost would have said he recognised him. "Thank him, will you."

He strode away, alert for further trouble. Greasy Wang tagged behind him.

"If we can't lay our hands on the murderer there'll be another riot. The whole Protectorate Camp will burn," the Protector told him.

The Protector had been given the job of looking after a bunch of crazy, heathen Celestials. But they were *his* crazy, heathen Celestials and he fought tooth and nail for them, despite being kept perennially low on funds by penny pinching city officials. This murderous spate had him baffled. How could a scrawny little Celestial overcome one brawny miner, let alone five. By strangling, no less. By God, it didn't make any sense.

Da Shan noticed his cast and chorus peeping from the tent entrance. He clapped hands. "Excitement's over," he said. "Let's have a good rest, then work hard tomorrow." He turned to Fatty and Ah Jin, and bowed low. "Thank you for helping me," he said.

"Hey, what's this about a murderer "jumping away"?" Fatty said, suspiciously.

"Nothing." Da Shan couldn't say anything else with everyone watching. He lowered his voice so only Fatty and Ah Jin heard him, and lied to death. "I've been watching all night. Our, er, guest is perfectly quiet."

Fatty and Ah Jin exchanged relieved grins, and bowed to him.

It took a long time to settle everyone's nerves and calm the camp down. He didn't make it back to the grave until the sun was rising on a freezing and watery dawn. The camp was silent by then, with the only sign of life a thin wisp of smoke rising from the kitchen. He snatched up a sack of sticky rice as he glanced into the muddy hole.

The coffin was still empty.

He looked hopelessly around the mullock heaped, shaft riddled landscape. The vampire had far too many hiding places. So many mines, so many piles of earth. It didn't need to return to its grave.

He sat on the cart, and rubbed his eyes, defeated. Then he rallied. He was a Guangdong man. He could do anything! He dragged the coffin lid back into the grave, and covered the hole with its blanket and overturned cart, tucking his sacks of sticky rice inside the cart to keep them dry and out of sight. Then he returned to his tent.

He slept only a few hours before being woken by the bustle of the camp. He tried to keep to his daily routine. He checked last night's take, then supervised rehearsals. His head beat like a drum and his eyes ached. At last he gave in. He went into Ah Jin's tent and found him lying on his camp bed drinking tea.

"Come in, please sit," Ah Jin had several seats for admirers. He graciously gestured Da Shan to his stoutest chair. "I am glad our, ah, guest is peaceful," Ah Jin said. He chuckled. "I let Fatty's stories overcome my common sense." He presented his clasped hands to Da Shan and spoke formally. "Sorry to be such trouble to you."

This was the first time Ah Jin had ever been polite to him, but Da Shan hadn't come here for an apology. He cleared his throat. "Actually," he said, "Fatty was right." Then he told Ah Jin the whole story, including his failed plan to trap the vampire in its coffin.

Ah Jin sat up as the tale went on, drank tea, choked on his tea, and put the cup down. At least he didn't scoff, faint, or run screaming.

"We can't let this thing roam around," Da Shan concluded.

Ah Jin thought a moment. "Your plain is a good one," he said. "But we need to lure it back, somehow."

Da Shan felt immensely relieved. Ah Jin believed him, or was humouring him, but at least he was considering. "That's what I can't think of," he said.

"Chicken blood," Ah Jin reminded him. "They like chicken blood. We'll need Fatty for that. Killing and bleeding chickens is not work for the likes of us." He sat back and admired his delicate, pampered hands.

"That's a great plan," Da Shan gasped, awed. "But how can we tell Fatty without panicking him?"

"You announce a feast," Ah Jin said, calmly. "Tonight, after the performance. Tell everyone you've got some special news. We roast the chickens for the feast. Tell Fatty to set aside the blood to make blood puddings tomorrow."

"What news?"

"I don't know, you work it out," Ah Jin waved his hand airily. "A raise perhaps." This set Da Shan up with no end of extra trouble and expense, but if it worked! If it worked!

†   †   †

The disadvantage of the plan did not dawn on Da Shan until that night, when he and Ah Jin squatted by an open grave, with a pot of chicken blood before them. The clouds were gone. It was a cold clear evening. They huddled beneath the cart. Streaks of light stole from the opera tent. Cymbals clashed, the clapper beat, the pipa bowed, and the chorus sang:

True lovers are immortal
Though the spirit world is far away,
True love can reach it,
Love transcends life and death.

"We are bringing it here. To us," Da Shan hissed, as realisation that this might not be his smartest act finally dawned. It hadn't seemed so bad, in safe, sane daylight.

"To you, actually." Ah Jin was listening to the song. "That's my cue. I need to go get ready for Lady Yang." He picked his way carefully across the slippery mud to the opera tent.

Da Shan left the shelter of the cart as he realised he couldn't see behind him. He revolved to keep a sharp look out in all directions. That made him feel dizzy, so he sat again, staring at the pot of slowly congealing chicken blood.

"Here's your tea, boss."

Da Shan nearly shrieked. He whirled to face Fatty who held a steaming cup in his hands. Fatty saw the pot of blood. His eyes widened. "What's that doing here?" he stuttered. Then he looked over Da Shan's shoulder and dropped the tea. He tried to speak, and failed, then took a deep gasp and clapped both hands over his mouth.

Da Shan turned.

The corpse was moving towards them through the mullock heaps, arms outstretched. Its gait was unmistakable, the strange stiff leaps. The stench of death preceded it, rotting clay, flesh and cloth.

"I lied. It is a vampire. I'm sorry to death. Please help," Da Shan said.

Fatty saw the sacks. "Sticky rice!" he mumbled, behind closed lips.

"Leave the rice alone. We need to bring it here," Da Shan said.

Fatty paid no heed. As the vampire moved towards the pot of blood, Fatty grabbed handfuls of sticky rice and hurled. It pattered over the corpse's face and shirt, making a hissing sound, and leaving black, charred marks.

The vampire stopped, and swayed.

"Hopping corpse!" Fatty howled. Fortunately the music from the opera tent drowned out his shouts.

Da Shan grabbed him. "Keep quiet! Stay here! And stop throwing rice. We want it to get into the grave," he hissed.

But Fatty was too far gone to hear. "Vampire!" he bawled, clawing to break himself free. In the struggle Da Shan took his eyes off the corpse. They broke apart and Fatty started to run then stopped. "Where is it?" he whispered.

The vampire had clearly lost its taste for chicken blood after the sticky rice assault. Now, it had vanished.

Then the orchestra came to a discordant halt. Shrieks rose from the opera tent. The two men's eyes met. Da Shan enunciated carefully. "Fatty we have to follow it, drive it out or lure it back. I carry the sticky rice, you carry the pot. Agree?"

"I don't want to carry the pot. That will attract it to me."

"If it gets near, dump the pot and run. It will stay with the chicken blood," Da Shan said.

A second, louder round of shrieks rose from the opera tent. The audience! He grabbed a sack of rice and ran, trusting that Fatty's loyalty would win over his fear.

Da Shan burst into the opera tent through the stage entrance. The vampire had hopped into the orchestra, scattering the players on both sides, some to the stage and some amid the tables and chairs of the audience. The actors in full rig confronted it: Lord Guan, with his red face and long beard, Monkey with his stripes and coloured cheeks, and Lei the Lute Player, patriot and rebel, clutching his lute. The chorus cowered behind them.

Da Shan's heart sank when he did not see Ah Jin among the actors. He could only pray to Tang Ming Huang that the vampire had not already met him.

The audience wondered for a moment if this was stage illusion. But the stink of the corpse fought the smell of greasepaint, hot lights, tea and steam buns, fought them and won. Then it made a deep hissing sound, a sucking in of breath. The entire front row of the audience rolled their eyes back, and collapsed to their knees before it. Their breath came out of their mouths in frozen clouds. The vampire hopped forward and sank its outstretched hands into the throat of the nearest man. The man screamed, shuddered, and the last of his breath spurted out. His head fell back limp on his neck, then his body slumped. He was dead just like that.

The vampire let the dead man drop, and turned to the next. Da Shan recovered from his shock. "Get the hell out of my theatre!" he screamed at the vampire. He pelted it with sticky rice, burning its exposed face and hands. Its wet clothing steamed. It turned to face him.

It was a horrible sight. It had bloated further with dead man's breath. Its nose had fallen in, and its face turned blue. Black streaks of rot ran like tears from its closed eyes down its cheeks. Crusted blood streaked from the corners from its sealed lips.

With the vampire turned away from them, the audience broke from its spell. Shrieking and tumbling over the furniture, they scrambled to escape. Tables overturned, chairs smashed, scalding tea went flying. They fought each other to escape through the entrance, then tore their way through the damp canvas to freedom. Their screams sounded through the Han camp. Only those weakened by the vampire's first blast remained, dragging themselves backwards as if paralysed, desperately trying to rise to their feet.

Still facing Da Shan and his deadly load of sticky rice, the vampire leaped back, without bending its knees or showing any effort. It landed on the stage, right in the middle of the actors.

The actors fled as one, with orchestra and chorus close behind. Several of the chorus were clutching lanterns. The vampire leaped after them, in impossible, stiff bounds.

"Run to your death!" Da Shan screamed, chasing after all of them. A glance over his shoulder warmed his heart, even in this disastrous instant. Loyalty had won out. Fatty Sam was puffing in his wake, holding the pot of chicken blood.

Da Shan's one consolation was that they rapidly left the Han camp behind, so the rest of his audience was safe. But out in the darkness of the diggings, the chase broke up in the confusion of moonlight and shadows from the mullock heaps and windlasses.

Da Shan stumbled in the mud, skirting lone tents. The last thing he wanted was foreign devils joining the chase. He lost his actors. He lost the vampire. He even lost his faithful Fatty. He cast around and heard fresh screams. The cast must have circled around trying to get back to camp, for they were well to the south. He cut across the circle, bolting with no heed for the numerous unmarked shafts.

He ran into lantern light. His cast and chorus were turned at bay against a mullock heap. The vampire leaped towards them, to a chorus of shrieks.

"Keep your filthy paws off my actors," Da Shan roared. He pelted the vampire with handfuls of sticky rice. It stopped to ward him off. He put on a burst of speed, spilling sticky rice in a circle of safety around his cast. He had a half sack left. It was time to be gone. "Follow me, you no good hopping sack of rotting shit," he roared.

It leaped towards him.

"Save your life!" Fatty came charging in from behind the actors, clutching his pot. He stopped at the circle of lamplight, and dropped his precious load, then grabbed handfuls from the pot and pelted the vampire.

Fatty hadn't wanted to leave the sticky rice, and he hadn't wanted to leave the pot. So he'd poured the rice into the pot and now hurled what could only be described as bloody rice balls. The corpse turned back. Fatty threw a bloody rice ball right in its face. It champed its jaws, confused.

"Stop! I want it to follow me, you idiot," Da Shan yelled.

Seeing their boss in danger galvanised the rest of the cast. They grabbed for the contents of the pot.

"I shall never forget my hatred!" yelled Lei the Lute Player, hurling packed handfuls.

"Look out, Demon! Monkey is going to smash you," yelled Monkey, following suit.

"The three of us swear to live together and die on the same day," roared Lord Guan, getting in an excellent shot straight to the chin.

The corpse staggered in one direction then the other, from Da Shan to the cast, as rice balls pelted it, as piles of bloody rice stacked around its feet and rivulets of blood and rice ran down its cheap Western suit.

"The sticky rice needs to be raw," Da Shan called, but no one was listening. The cast only stopped throwing rice balls when the pot was empty.

The vampire was still moving. Da Shan gathered his wits, dismayed. He had half a sack of rice left, and no chicken blood to lure the corpse back to its coffin. Disaster loomed.

Then the vampire hopped towards him. He started to run, too late. The vampire hissed, a long intake of breath. Utter weakness overcame Da Shan. His knees buckled, and he dropped to his knees. He tried to hold his breath, but he couldn't. He was paralysed. He couldn't even lift his hands. He couldn't stop his breath streaming out, a long, helpless gasp. Through eyes blurred with fear he saw the vampire leap towards him. It fastened its hands around his throat.

It was a cold, slimy, stinking grasp, claws digging in and throttling hard, yet its bloated palms were soft with rot. It was the worst thing he ever felt. Overwhelmed with stink, Da Shan's last breath steamed out.

Over the mullock heap leaped a figure, light as a spirit. She was wearing robes of white silk with a white satin ribbon around her throat, the belt with which she was hanged. She landed, the lithe dancer, rose, then stood, gathering all eyes. She made two delicate, sweeping, pitiful gestures of her hands and sleeves.

The vampire let go its hold of Da Shan and spun to face her. Even the dead knew the ghost of Lady Yang, the doomed and beloved concubine. Stiffly, strangely, it bowed.

Then she sang:

Amid confusion and uproar my life was ended,
And here I drift, a wandering spirit.

Her voice soared to exquisite perfection. The orchestra rose to the occasion beyond belief. Halfway through the song the clapper started up, then kept the time. The cymbals clashed. Last, the erhu and the jinghu gathered their nerve and chimed in. Da Shan gasped for air, and rubbed his bruised and bleeding throat, then crawled to the safety of the circle of sticky rice. Fatty reached out and hauled him in.

My body is no more;
But my love remains unchanged.

Lady Yang finished her lament. She knelt, eyes modestly lowered, waiting for applause.

Such perfection demanded instant appreciation, a signed contract, gold hurled at her feet. The vampire had nothing to give. It stood swaying. Then it opened its sealed lips. A silver cloud rose. It gave her the only thing it had, its last breath.

Then it fell over backwards onto the dirt.

"What the hell is all that caterwauling!" A foreign babble rose from behind the mullock heap. Then the Protector, closely followed by Greasy Wang, scrambled over the top. "Good God!" The Protector took in the scene, the richly robed actors, the mounds of red rice, the man lying on the ground.

Greasy Wang, unlike the Protector, recognised the corpse. He was quick witted enough to realise the significance of the sticky rice and chicken blood.

Da Shan saw him put the corpse and the strange acrobatic murderer together.

Greasy Wang's face blanched, and he backed, casting an eye over his shoulder for escape. Then, magnificently, he pulled himself up. Perhaps it was just the realisation that the Protector was his meal ticket: he had to protect the Protector.

"It's a rehearsal, sir," he gasped. His eyes swept over the company, trying to think of a title that would suit this scene. "Eight Immortals defeat the King of Hell."

The Protector's eyes narrowed. "Isn't that chap dead?"

"No sir, he's an actor."

Fortunately for the Protector, if he couldn't distinguish one Celestial from another, he certainly couldn't distinguish a dead one from a live one at a distance. But he frowned as his gaze brushed over the offending crew. His eye met Da Shan's. If he wasn't a Celestial, he almost would have said he recognised him. He relaxed a little. "It's dangerous out here. Tell them to get back to the Protectorate camp," he ordered.

"Yes sir."

A shaky chorus of "Thank you Excellency," rose from the cast, as Greasy Wang translated their narrow escape. The Protector strode off.

"We are going to cremate him and send his ashes home," Da Shan assured Greasy Wang. "You'll have no more trouble from your mysterious murderer."

Greasy Wang sniffed, curtly, and followed the Protector.

The opera company picked their way back to camp, and reverently returned the corpse to his coffin, which was placed on trestles in its own tent with candles, fruit and incense before it. They started to recover from their fright, but everyone knew they were done with this diggings. No one would come to an opera where vampires were likely to drop in.

Da Shan tried to rally the troupe's nerve. "Come on, let's start packing. There's always another gold field," he encouraged them. But for all his bold face he knew he'd never be so confident and commercial again. The bloody claw marks and purple bruises on his throat were not so raw as the wounds within. He could feel a chill wind on his back, blowing through a thin partition, a paper shell. It was all that separated him from the restless, angry, hungry ghosts of Hell.

Ah Jin washed his wounds and bandaged them, told him to rest, then supervised the respectful burial of the dead man in the opera tent.

Fatty returned from the kitchen with a dismal face. "The feast is ready," he reported, dolefully.

Da Shan clapped hands. "Eat while it's hot!" he ordered.

Everyone remembered the news he was going to tell them, and gathered hopefully at the tables. All but Ah Jin. Da Shan went looking for him. Besides, he still didn't know what news he was going to tell them. After tonight's performance, a raise was out of the question.

He found Ah Jin kneeling before the coffin, incense sticks in his hands. He rose as Da Shan approached.

"For once this isn't your fault," Da Shan sighed. He gazed at the coffin. "We still don't know his name," he said. A nameless ghost, without descendents to pray for him, must wander the earth forever. He had a horrible feeling he hadn't seen the last of this corpse.

"Oh, I fixed that," Ah Jin said, airily. "You know I'm an orphan. I have no ancestors. He has no descendents. So I've told him I'll adopt him, and I and my sons will look after him. He'll never go hungry again."

"I didn't know you were married," Da Shan said, startled.

"I'm not," Ah Jin sighed. "But I'd better get married if I'm going to have sons," he said.

Da Shan gazed from Ah Jin to the coffin. He couldn't believe what he was hearing. Was his feckless star settling down at last? The ghost of his old careless confidence returned to him. He almost wanted to kiss the corpse. "That's very filial of you," he gasped.

Ah Jin shot him his haughtiest look. "He gave up his last breath for me. I must return the favour. Besides, I've worked out the reason for the coffin." With a respectful bow, he started feeling his way around the timber, checking every carving, every knothole. "We know he was murdered. That's enough to make anyone an angry ghost. But he was murdered for a reason, I guess, by one of the societies involved in the rebellions. They needed to get money secretly back to China."

"But how could a corpse help them?" Da Shan asked.

"They didn't need a corpse. They needed a coffin. The corpse just provided the reason." Ah Jin tugged at a notch. "Remember how you and Fatty said the coffin was so heavy? But it was empty." He pulled the notch up. Gold dust poured out. He caught the glittering stream in the palm of his hand and shoved the plug back in again.

"How much gold is in there?" Da Shan asked, awed.

"Enough to set us up with the finest theatre in Guangzhou," Ah Jin said, simply. "You must manage it. I like your style." He laughed at the shock on Da Shan's face. "We have to leave. All of us. Now. The society will be chasing their gold. "Return home with wealth and glory"," he chanted, gleefully. "But we have to do the right thing by him." He bowed to the dead man. "Otherwise he'll be out of his coffin and after us again."

"Now I do have a reason for the feast," Da Shan realized.

Ah Jin swept the dust from his hands. It drifted away glittering into the chill night, returning to the clay and the quartz that gave it birth. "No wonder this poor soul was earthbound, with all that gold weighing him down. Now his spirit can ascend to heaven, where his sins will be forgiven."

"How did you know that your singing would stop him?" Da Shan asked

Ah Jin looked surprised. "All Han love opera," he reminded him. "He was a true Han, even though he was a vampire."

AFTERWORD TO "LADY YANG'S LAMENT"

When I heard about Russell's anthology I decided to bend the rules a little.

A few years ago my husband would present double bills of classic Hong Kong films at Melbourne's Chinatown Cinema, which had the distinction of being the last surviving Chinese cinema in the world (outside of Asian countries).

In the 1980s Hong Kong produced some wonderful Chinese vampire movies, notably Sammo Hung's classic Encounters of the Spooky Kind, and Ricky Lau's Mr Vampire starring the legendary Lam Ching Ying. There was even a Shaw Brothers/Hammer Horror co-production, Legend of the Seven Golden Vampires (1974), which brought Peter Cushing, as Van Helsing, to China.

The movies were horror comedy based on a monster that never existed, a gleeful fusion of Taoist and Christian beliefs. The best gave the Western viewer a glimpse of the bewildering historical cultural beliefs about life and death, and the righteous kick arse Taoist action required to pound the unquiet dead back into their rightful place.

My father, Harold Love, wrote The Golden Age of Australian Opera, about the English opera companies that toured the Goldfields in the 1850s. In the course of his research he found that Chinese opera companies would also tour. There was clearly enough gold being dug out of the ground to support a rich cultural life. Some friends gave me my treasured copy of The Palace of Eternal Youth, and my story elements were complete.

Sadly in 2009, the Chinatown Cinema closed its doors. Both the touring companies on the goldfields and the Chinatown Cinema are gone. Their styles of entertainment no longer held the crowds. But while they existed, they were gold.

All songs taken from The Palace of Eternal Youth by Hung Sheng, translated by Yang Hsien-Yi and Gladys Yang, Foreign Language Press, Peking, China, 1955

ABOUT THE EDITOR

RUSSELL B. FARR was born in Perth, Western Australia in 1973. He founded Ticonderoga Publications in 1996, and has published over twenty titles. In 1999 he established *ticon4*, now Australia's longest running semi-professional science fiction webzine. Previous works as editor include the award-winning anthology *Fantastic Wonder Stories*, award-winning collection *Magic Dirt: the Best of Sean Williams*, *Belong*, an anthology of interstellar migration stories, and Australia's first work-themed anthology *The Workers' Paradise*. Russell lives in the northern suburbs of Perth with his wonderful partner, a sociopathic cat and a neurotic dog.

ABOUT THE CONTRIBUTORS

JOANNE ANDERTON lives in Sydney, Australia, with her husband and too many pets. By day she is a mild-mannered marketing coordinator for an Australian book distributor. By night, weekends and lunchtimes she writes dark fantasy and horror. Her short fiction has recently appeared in *Midnight Echo, Andromeda Spaceways Inflight Magazine* and *Worlds Next Door.* She was shortlisted for the 2009 Aurealis Award for best young adult short story. Her debut novel, *Debris* (Book One the Veiled Worlds Series) will be published by Angry Robot Books in 2011, followed by *Suited* in 2012. website: http://joanneanderton.com twitter: @joanneanderton

ALAN BAXTER is an author living on the south coast of NSW, Australia. He writes dark fantasy, sci fi and horror, rides a motorcycle and loves his dog. He also teaches Kung Fu. His work has appeared in a variety of Australian and international anthologies and journals and his dark fantasy thriller novels, *RealmShift* and *MageSign*, are available now from Gryphonwood Press. Read extracts from his novels, a novella and short stories, and follow his blog, at his website, www.alanbaxteronline. com and feel free to tell him what you think. About anything.

SIMON BROWN has been writing for forty years. He has published novels and short stories in Australia and overseas, and currently lives in Thailand with his wife and two children.

JAY CASELBERG is an Australian author based in Germany with over 100 short story publications to his credit in various venues around the world including *Aurealis, Interzone, Polyphony, Crimewave* and many others. His novels have been published by Roc Books (a division of Penguin) and also at Book View Cafe online and are available through Amazon. His website can be found at jaycaselberg.com

DAMON CAVALCHINI is an amalgamation of suave super-spy, media magnate, insane genius, and all-round delusional nice guy. Not wishing to be restricted by the boundaries of reality, he drifts into the world of literature with astonishing ease and is often found enjoying the fantasy life in his head rather than the mundane normality of everyday life. For past five years he was a member of the Management Committee of the Aurealis Awards and, in 2010, finished a three year term as the President of Fantastic Queensland. His short stories have appeared in various charity anthologies including *Perfect Timing*, *Perfect Timing 2*, *Missing Pieces* and *Shelf Life*. His short story, "The Tenth Life of Sargeant Tom", was included in the 2006 anthology, Journeys of the Mind. He has written and directed plays for local theatre and is currently seeking a home for an original novel.

JODI CLEGHORN is a short story writer, editor, publisher, mother, and connoisseur of collaborative writing and crowd sourced fiction. In 2008 she founded eMergent Publishing with Scottish business partner, Paul Anderson. Together they have published *The Red Book* and *The Yin and Yang Book* under the Chinese Whisperings imprint. She is the co-producer of *100 Stories for Queensland* and the creator of *Literary Mix Tapes*. Once overheard saying "Oh, but I don't write science fiction" she now embraces the spectrum of speculative fiction, revelling in the freedom and challenges. She is inspired by themes of love, loss, inequality, the eternal question "what if?" . . . and the voices in her head! This is her first vampire story and Australian publication. Jodi lives in the leafy southern suburbs of Brisbane with her partner, six year old son, The Fish of Bo, a crazy chook named Madame Houdini and an overflowing mess of books.

Melbourne-based writer FELICITY DOWKER is a Ditmar and Chronos Award winner and an Aurealis and Australian Shadows Award finalist. Felicity's short stories have been published in Australian and international journals and anthologies including *Aurealis*, *Andromeda Spaceways Inflight Magazine*, *Midnight Echo*, Morrigan Books' *Scenes From The Second Storey*, and Ticonderoga Publications' *Scary Kisses*, among others. Felicity's debut short story collection *Bread and Circuses* is forthcoming from Ticonderoga Publications in 2012. Felicity can be found online at http://felicitydowker.livejournal.com.

JACOB EDWARDS was born in 1976 and studied at the University of Queensland, graduating with a BA (English) and an MA (Ancient history). When not arranging deckchairs for *Andromeda Spaceways*— for whom he edited #45 of the much-pulped *Inflight Magazine*— Jacob writes fiction, creative and academic non-fiction, and even a smattering of poetry. His works appear in magazines, anthologies and academic journals in Australia, Europe, Canada and the USA. He lives in Brisbane with his wife and son, playing the odd game of chess in his spare time and lamenting both the declining popularity of beanbags and the demise of the classic 80s DOS text adventure.

JOANNA FAY is a poet, short story writer and budding epic fantasy novelist. She has a professional background in the visual arts, having studied and worked as a tapestry weaver, illustrator and art history researcher, experiences which seep into her writing as a love of saturated sensory images. Her poems have won multiple awards and been published in journals and anthologies in Australia and overseas. Her short story "Swan Wing" shortlisted in the International Aeon Award in 2008, and her fantasy stories "Threadsongs" and "Feather Fall" have been published in the last year. Joanna is currently working on a quartet of fantasy novels set in a storyworld she has been passionate about for as long as she can remember. She blogs as part of a group of aspiring fantasy novelists at http://egoboo-wa.blogspot.com/ . Her first novel is roaming around looking for a publisher, so watch this space!

RAYMOND GATES is an Aboriginal writer based on the Gold Coast, Australia, whose childhood crush on horror evolved into an adult love affair with writing. His stories have featured in *AntipodeanSF*, *Caste Macabre* and the *DFE Quarterly* series from Pill Hill Press. He is fighting to drag the novel that lurks within him into the light. When not writing, he divides his time between plotting to change the world, tormenting his family, and being a dragon with his daughter. Delve into his mind at: www.raymondgates.com

LISA L. HANNETT lives in Adelaide, South Australia—city of churches, bizarre murders, and pie floaters. She has sold stories to venues including *Clarkesworld*, *Fantasy*, *Weird Tales*, *ChiZine*, *Electric Velocipede*, *Shimmer* and *Steampunk II: Steampunk Reloaded*. She is a graduate of the Clarion South Writers Workshop. Her first collection, *Bluegrass Symphony*, is being published by Ticonderoga Publications in August 2011. *Midnight and Moonshine*, a collaborative collection with Angela Slatter, will be published by Ticonderoga in 2012. You can visit her online at http://lisahannett.com.

DONNA MAREE HANSON lives in Queanbeyan, New South Wales, Australia right next door to Canberra. She has been writing speculative fiction for nearly ten years, with publications in: *Redsine Magazine*, *AntiSF*, the CSFG anthologies, *Machinations*, *Elsewhere* and *Masques*. In 2010, she had stories in *Belong* and *Scary Kisses*, both by Ticonderoga publications and two other stories, "Liquid Night" in *Novus Creatura* (Aurore Wolf) and "Warning Buoy" (Static Movement). In 2011, she will also appear in *More Scary Kisses* edited by Liz Grzyb. Donna has also edited an anthology, two single author collections and managed a small press as well as running a couple of science fiction conventions. She is currently writing a new novel length manuscript as well as new short stories.

KATHRYN HORE is a Melbourne-based writer and photographer with a love of speculative fiction in all forms, from horror to sci-fi and everything in between.

Blessed with a lively imagination SHONA HUSK spent most of her childhood making up stories. As an adult she discovered romance novels and hasn't looked back. Dark fairy tales and the paranormal have always fascinated her and it's not uncommon to get to know spirits, vampires, were-creatures and demi-gods through her books. Her paranormal romance trilogy, being published by Sourcebooks, begins with *The Goblin King* in October 2011. For more information visit her website: www.shonahusk.com

GEORGE IVANOFF is an author and stay-at-home Dad residing in Melbourne, Australia. He has written over 40 books for children and teenagers, as well as lots of stories and articles. He has books on both the Victorian Premier's Reading Challenge and NSW Premier's Reading Challenge booklists. His teen, sci-fi, computer gaming novel, *Gamers' Quest*, won a 2010 Chronos Award. The sequel, *Gamers' Challenge*, will be published late 2011 by Ford Street Publishing. Check out the Official *Gamers' Quest* website: http://gamersquestbook.com Also, check out George: website: http://georgeivanoff.com.au

PATTY JANSEN lives in Sydney, where she spends most of her time writing Science Fiction. Her story "This Peaceful State of War" placed first in the second quarter of the Writers of the Future contest. Her hard SF novelette "His Name in Lights" has been published in the January 2011 issue of the *Universe Annex of the Grantville Gazette*.

PETE KEMPSHALL's first experience of vampires was watching Peter Cushing slap two candlesticks together to put paid to Christopher Lee. A Ditmar-nominated writer whose fiction has been published by Big Finish, Morrigan Books, Apex Publications, Twelfth Planet Press, Dark Quest Books and ASIM, Pete also co-edited the anthology *Scenes From the Second Storey*, a collection of tales by some of Australia's most talented writers. Pete lives in Perth, Western Australia—where mining is more important than pretty much anything else—and keeps an occasional blog at www.tyrannyoftheblankpage.blogspot.com.

CHRIS LAWSON is a doctor, teacher, and writer who lives on the Sunshine Coast, Queensland. He likes rainbows, kittens, and existential dread.

Perth-based MARTIN LIVINGS has had more than sixty short stories published in a variety of magazines and anthologies. His work has appeared in *The Year's Best Australian SF & Fantasy*, *Australian Dark Fantasy & Horror*, and the Australian horror omnibus *Macabre*. His first novel, *Carnies*, was published in 2006, and was nominated for both the Aurealis and Ditmar awards. www.martinlivings.com

PENELOPE LOVE lives in Melbourne, Australia. She recently accepted a voluntary redundancy after working in university administration for twelve years, and is using the money to spend some time pretending to be a real writer. Her stories have recently been published in the anthologies, *Belong* and *Cthulhu's Dark Cults*.

TRACIE MCBRIDE is a New Zealander who lives in Melbourne, Australia with her husband and three children. She is a member of the Melbourne-based speculative fiction writers group SuperNOVA. Her work has appeared or is forthcoming in over 50 print and electronic publications, including *Andromeda Spaceways Inflight Magazine*, *Hecate*, *Devil Dolls and Duplicates*, *Abyss and Apex*, and *Electric Velocipede*. She won the Sir Julius Vogel Award for Best New Talent for 2007. She is an associate editor for horror magazine *Dark Moon Digest* and vice president of the writer's co-operative Dark Continents Publishing. Her blog can be found at http://traciemcbridewriter. wordpress.com/

SONIA MARCON began writing creatively since she knew how to put pen on paper. She has experimented with other creative means also since she was young, such as theatre and music, but writing is the one that she feels closest to. Her first publication, "Phantom Limbs", appeared in *Fantastic Wonder Stories* (Ticonderoga). This was followed by "Sentinel" appeared in *Voices* (Morrigan Books). "Sky in the Morning" is her third publication.

ANNE MOK lives in Sydney, where she juggles legal editing by day with fiction writing by night. She is a graduate of Clarion South. Like everyone else, she is working on a novel. Her website is www.annemok.com.

JASON NAHRUNG grew up on a Queensland cattle property and now lives in Melbourne with his wife, the writer Kirstyn McDermott. A journalist and editor, his coverage of Australian speculative fiction has earned him a William Atheling Jnr Award for review and criticism. His fiction is invariably darkly themed, perhaps reflecting his love of classic B-grade horror films and 80s goth rock music. He is the co-author of the novel *The Darkness Within* (Hachette Australia), and continues to beaver away at novel-length manuscripts. A love of travel has resulted in an enduring love of New Orleans and a keen interest in photography. www.jasonnahrung.com

AMANDA PILLAR is a speculative fiction author and editor who lives in Victoria, Australia, with her partner and two children, Saxon and Lilith (Burmese cats). She has had numerous short stories published and is the in-house editor for Morrigan Books. Amanda has co-edited the fiction anthologies *Voices* (2008), *Grants Pass* (2009), *The Phantom Queen Awakes* (2010), and *Scenes from the Second Storey* (2010). She is currently working with Liz Grzyb on the anthology, *Damnation and Dames*, due for publication in 2012. In her free time, she plans on becoming the next Indiana Jones.

JANE ROUTLEY has written five novels for adults, including the Aurealis Award wining *Mage Heart* and *Fire Angels*. She has just completed a young adult science fiction book. Her short stories have been widely anthologised, have appeared in *Meanjin* and been read on the ABC. She enjoys mentoring emerging writers and has had many years experience in doing so.

JEREMY SADLER grew up in country Victoria but didn't let that stop him from becoming a fan of science fiction and fantasy. He now lives in Melbourne with his wife and daughter, where the internet is a constant distraction from writing. He wrote and edited for the ASFMA winning *Frontier: The Australian Science Fiction Media Magazine*, and maintains an online presence at http://www.jeremysadler.net.

ANGELA SLATTER writes speculative fiction. Her short stories have appeared in *Dreaming Again, Steampunk Reloaded, Strange Tales II & III, 2012, Lady Churchill's Rosebud Wristlet* and *Shimmer*. Her work has had Honourable Mentions in the Year's Best Fantasy and Horror anthologies and has three times been shortlisted for an Aurealis Award. She is a graduate of Tin House 2006 and Clarion South 2009, and she blogs at http://www.angelaslatter.com/. She had two short story collections out in 2010: *Sourdough & Other Stories* (Tartarus Press, UK) and *The Girl with No Hands & Other Tales* (Ticonderga Publication, Australia). In 2012, Ticonderoga Publications will publish her collaboration collection *Midnight and Moonshine* with Lisa L. Hannett.

Gold Coast writer HELEN STUBBS loves the beautiful weird, especially fiction about the future and alternate realities. She writes tough heroines doing terrible things. Her unpublished novel, *Black Earth*, is currently a quarter-finalist in the Amazon Breakthrough Award. Helen's short stories appear in *Midnight Echo* and the Aussiecon Four Souvenir Booklet. She is working on a novel called *Verdan's Marsh*. Her interests include chatting to strangers, fretting about the environment, and marvelling over art and innovation. She is a member of Prana Writers and Vision Writers. You can find Helen at twitter.com/superleni and helenstubbs.wordpress.com.

YVONNE EVE WALUS is an award-winning novelist, a mathematician, a wife, a mother and her two cats' slave . . . not necessarily in that order of importance. She's lived on three continents and her work reflects the wealth of her cultural background. Her murder mysteries, featuring amateur detective Dr Christine Chamberlain, are set in the tumultuous and exotic South Africa. In 2004, Yvonne made (local) headlines by winning 1st, 2nd and 3rd places at the international SFSA short story competition. Please visit Yvonne on http://yewalus.kiwiwebhost.net.nz/.

JEN WHITE has had stories published in various anthologies and magazines. Her work appeared recently in the anthology *The Tangled Bank: Love, Wonder and Evolution*, and she has a story in the upcoming anthology *Bewere the Night*. Jen lived for some time in the Northern Territory. Although she has now moved to gentler climes, she still finds inspiration in the vibrancy and mystery of Australia's north.

MARTY YOUNG is a Bram Stoker Award nominated editor and sometimes ghost hunter. He was founding President of the Australian Horror Writers Association (AHWA) from 2005–2010, and one of the creative minds behind the internationally acclaimed *Midnight Echo* magazine. His horror fiction has been reprinted in *Australian Dark Fantasy & Horror*, repeatedly included in Ellen Datlow's year's best recommended reading list, and nominated for both the Australian Shadows and Ditmar awards. Marty's essays on horror literature have been published in journals and university textbooks in Australia and India, and he is also co-editor of *Macabre; a Journey through Australia's Darkest Fears*, a landmark anthology showcasing the best Australian horror stories from 1836 to the 2010.

ACKNOWLEDGEMENTS

"The Tide" copyright © 2011 Alan Baxter, Felicity Dowker, Patty Jansen, Devin Jeyathurai, Martin Livings, Chuck McKenzie, Andrew J. McKiernan, Lezli Robyn, Daniel I. Russell, Carol Ryles & Kaaron Warren

"Mutiny on the Scarborough" copyright © 2011 Shona Husk

"Sun Falls" copyright © 2011 Angela Slatter

"Such is Life" copyright © 2011 Jeremy Sadler

"Apolotoi" copyright © 2011 Chris Lawson

"Punishment of the Sun" copyright © 2011 Alan Baxter

"Red Delicious" copyright © 2011 Felicity Dowker

"Just a Matter of Economics" copyright © 2011 Yvonne Eve Walus

"Quarantine" copyright © 2011 Patty Jansen

"Out of the Grave" copyright © 2011 Amanda Pillar

"Desert Blood" copyright © 2011 Marty Young

"Thin Air" copyright © 2011 Simon Brown

"Kissed by the Sun" copyright © 2011 Jodi Cleghorn

"Bats" copyright © 2011 Jane Routley

"Black Heart" copyright © 2011 Joanna Fay

"Renfield's Wife" copyright © 2011 Damon Cavalchini

"Listening to Tracy" copyright © 2011 Jen White

"Breaking the Drought" copyright © 2011 Jay Caselberg

"Children of the Cane" copyright © 2011 Jason Nahrung

"The Sea at Night" copyright © 2011 Joanne Anderton

"Sky in the Morning" copyright © 2011 Sonia Marcon

"Taking it for the Team" copyright © 2011 Tracie Mcbride

"All that Glisters" copyright © 2011 Pete Kempshall

"The Rider" copyright © 2011 Martin Livings

"Vitality" copyright © 2011 George Ivanoff

"Coming Home" copyright © 2011 Kathryn Hore

"The Little Red Man" copyright © 2011 Raymond Gates

"Deathborn Light" copyright © 2011 Helen Stubbs

"The Life Stealer" copyright © 2011 Donna Maree Hanson

"Behind the Black Mask" copyright © 2011 Jacob Edwards

"Interview with the Jiangshi" copyright © 2011 Anne Mok

"White and Red in the Black" copyright © 2011 Lisa L Hannett

"Lady Yang's Lament" copyright © 2011 Penelope Love

All stories appear here for the very first time. All rights reserved.

THANK YOU

The publisher would sincerely like to thank:

Elizabeth Grzyb, Martin Livings, Shona Husk, Angela Slatter,
Jeremy Sadler, Chris Lawson, Alan Baxter, Felicity Dowker,
Yvonne Eve Walus, Patty Jansen, Amanda Pillar, Marty Young,
Simon Brown, Jodi Cleghorn, Jane Routley, Joanna Fay, Damon
Cavalchini, Jen White, Jay Caselberg, Jason Nahrung, Joanne
Anderton, Sonia Marcon, Tracie McBride, Pete Kempshall,
George Ivanoff, Kathryn Hore, Ray Gates, Helen Stubbs, Donna
Maree Hanson, Jacob Edwards, Anne Mok, Lisa L Hannett,
Penelope Love, Devin Jeyathurai, Chuck McKenzie, Andrew J.
McKiernan, Lezli Robyn, Daniel I. Russell, Carol Ryles, Kaaron
Warren, Jonathan Strahan, Peter McNamara, Ellen Datlow,
Grant Stone, Jeremy G. Byrne, Sean Williams, Garth Nix,
David Cake, Simon Oxwell, Grant Watson, Sue Manning,
Steven Utley, Lew Shiner, Bill Congreve, Jack Dann, Stephen
Dedman, the Mt Lawley Mafia, the Nedlands Yakuza,
Shane Jiraiya Cummings, Angela Challis, Kate Williams, Kathryn
Linge, Andrew Williams, Al Chan, Alisa Krasnostein, everyone I've
missed . . .

. . . and *you*.

www.ingramcontent.com/pod-product-compliance
Lightning Source LLC
Chambersburg PA
CBHW020824030726
47496CB00001B/74